The Riverton Vet

Jennifer Scoullar is a bestselling author of Australian rural fiction, and lives with her family on a small property in West Gippsland. Her house is on a hilltop, overlooking valleys of messmate and mountain ash. She grew up on the books of Elyne Mitchell, and all her life she's ridden and bred horses, in particular Australian stock horses. Jennifer writes page-turning stories set in and around Australia's magnificent wild places. She has twelve published novels, including the best-selling *Brumby's Run* and the historical adventure series The Tasmanian Tales.

JENNIFER SCOULLAR

The Rivertown Vet

MICHAEL JOSEPH
an imprint of
PENGUIN BOOKS

MICHAEL JOSEPH

UK | USA | Canada | Ireland | Australia
India | New Zealand | South Africa | China

Michael Joseph is part of the Penguin Random House group of companies whose
addresses can be found at global.penguinrandomhouse.com

Penguin
Random House
Australia

First published by Michael Joseph in 2024

Cover photography courtesy of Adobe Stock (woman – mimagephotos;
wombat – Susan Flashman; landscape – Veronica)
Cover design by Nikki Townsend Design © Penguin Random House Australia Pty Ltd
Typeset in 12/17 pt Sabon LT Pro by Post Pre-press Group, Australia

Printed and bound in Australia by Griffin Press, an accredited
ISO AS/NZS 14001 Environmental Management Systems printer

A catalogue record for this
book is available from the
NATIONAL
LIBRARY   National Library of Australia
OF AUSTRALIA

ISBN 978 1 76134 245 5

penguin.com.au

MIX
Paper | Supporting
responsible forestry
FSC   FSC® C018684
www.fsc.org

We at Penguin Random House Australia acknowledge that Aboriginal and Torres
Strait Islander peoples are the Traditional Custodians and the first storytellers of the
lands on which we live and work. We honour Aboriginal and Torres Strait Islander
peoples' continuous connection to Country, waters, skies and communities. We
celebrate Aboriginal and Torres Strait Islander stories, traditions and living cultures;
and we pay our respects to Elders past and present.

To Aussie Ark – creating a long-term future
for Australia's threatened wildlife

CHAPTER 1

Jana stood beneath a lonely, old swamp paperbark. It had somehow escaped the axe when this land had been cleared for pasture one hundred and fifty years ago. She loved melaleucas, and this was a particularly fine specimen. Its trunk textured and weathered, its bark like the faded pages of an ancient book. Each layer peeling away to reveal a palette of soft ochres, burnished browns and whispers of pale gold. Its slender leaves fluttered in the slight breeze, reflecting the cold mid-winter sun with a luminous shine.

She gazed across the grassy clearing, then glanced up at the threatening sky. Dark clouds were rolling in from the west. A storm was on its way. In the distance, a row of red gums marked the course of the Murray River. How she'd love to head over there to look for platypuses in her favourite billabong, but no, not today. She had more pressing matters: taking grass samples and retrieving Wall-E one last time.

Jana was part of a statewide research team studying the southern hairy-nosed wombat. She and her sister also ran a sanctuary for orphaned and injured wildlife. These

chunky characters were the marsupial equivalent of exca-
vators. Known as 'bulldozers of the bush', they were South
Australia's faunal emblem. With their charming faces, large
noses and small bright eyes, she considered these wombats to
be Australia's most beautiful and charismatic creatures.

Jana loved their quirky personalities, their determination and their affectionate nature. She loved their work ethic
and stubborn dedication to earthmoving, thus improving
soil health by bringing nutrients to the surface and burying
organic matter. The ground ahead was dotted with dozens
of mounds and burrows, all connected by a complex tunnel
system. These passageways had multiple entrances and
extended nearly ninety metres underground.

Jana should know. She'd spent the past fortnight
exploring the twists and turns of this particular warren with
a Wombot – one of the state-of-the-art exploratory robots
developed by the University of Tasmania to study conditions
within burrows. It was down a warren right now, equipped
with sensors and cameras.

Jana checked the video feed being sent back by the Wombot
and adjusted its course. She'd nicknamed it Wall-E and had
grown quite fond of the intrepid little robot. Unfortunately, it
was only on loan, and she had to send it back to the university
tomorrow. She'd be sad to see it go.

Wall-E reminded her of a scaled down Mars rover, remote-
controlled and able to traverse rough, inaccessible terrain
while sending back a live video feed to the accompanying
tablet screen in Jana's hands. She marvelled at the intricate
tangle of passages and the unexpected residents that Wall-E's
camera had revealed. She now had proof that tawny dragons,

echidnas and snakes often shared the wombat tunnels. Even a burrowing bettong or two. That had made her laugh. Lazy little buggers – couldn't they dig their own homes? But Jana had been heartened that such a rare species had been found here at Odessa, the farm that had been in their family for three generations.

She frowned as two rabbits appeared on the video feed. Of all the threats her precious wombats faced, competition from feral herbivores was near the top of the list, along with mange and introduced weeds invading their grasslands. Potato weed and onion grass were taking over large swathes of the Murraylands, crowding out the native grasses. Their toxins poisoned the wombats' livers, killing many and leaving others sick and emaciated.

For the past few years, Jana and her younger sister, Sash, had worked hard to eradicate rabbits, wild goats and weeds from their land. They'd replanted hectares of degraded pasture with native Mitchell and spear grasses. Thanks to their efforts, the wombat population at Odessa was recovering. And thanks to Wall-E, Jana now had a working map of this sprawling warren, together with humidity and temperature readings. Understanding the secret life of wombats would make it much easier to protect them. For example, knowing the relative humidity inside burrows could help in controlling the parasitic sarcoptic mange mites that caused crusty, bloody skin lesions and even blindness. And access to birth dens could cast new light on the rare marsupial's reproductive biology.

Jana checked her phone. Two o'clock. Reluctantly, she switched to the Wombot's rear-facing camera. She was due for her shift at the Rivertown Vet Clinic at three and had already been late twice in the past week. If Oliver docked her wage again, paying this month's feed bill for the animals would be a problem.

Wall-E reversed and began trundling back through the maze of branching tunnels. But when it was a few metres from the surface, it stopped – caught on a tree root.

'Come on,' urged Jana, jiggling the remote. But Wall-E merely spun on its tracks. The robot was well and truly stuck.

After a few minutes of useless manoeuvring, Jana checked her phone again. It really was time to leave. The clinic was almost an hour's drive away. She pulled impatiently on the ethernet cable connecting Wall-E to the ground station at her feet. Yes – the robot moved a few inches. Encouraged by this progress, she tugged the cable again, harder this time.

Suddenly the cord came free in her hand and Jana lost the video feed. Shit. She'd yanked the cable clear out of the unit, losing all connection with Wall-E. Now the Wombot was not only stranded underground, but it was broken as well.

Jana kicked at the wombat hole that yawned before her. The little robot was only a few metres underground, tantalisingly close. Maybe if she lay down, she'd be able to reach it. Jana dug around in the pack for her head torch, tied back her dark hair, knelt on the ground and shone her torch into the hole. No sign of Wall-E. She got down on her stomach and wiggled into the entrance. What was that? Something glinted in the torchlight. She wriggled in a bit further. It was Wall-E all right, out of reach by less than a metre.

Jana gritted her teeth and crawled in as far as she could, arms extended like those of a diver to make her shape as streamlined as possible. It was a tight squeeze, but soon her groping hand almost had a grip on the little robot. One last squirm, a mouthful of dirt and – success! Her fingers closed on Wall-E. She jiggled it free of the root and let out her breath. Thank goodness. Hopefully Sash, who was a tech whizz, would be able to reattach the ethernet cable tonight.

Now, time to get out of here quick smart and hightail it into Rivertown. She might make her shift after all. But when she tried to back out of the tunnel, she found herself wedged fast. With her arms outstretched as they were, she couldn't use her elbows to push herself backwards. And her knees were jammed fast against the floor of the burrow. No matter how much she wriggled and squirmed, she couldn't move an inch.

After what seemed like hours of futile attempts to free herself, Jana was spent. She lay exhausted, sniffing back tears and spitting dust.

At least her head torch lit up the narrow tunnel ahead. Without its light she'd be suffering a serious case of claustrophobia. Jana could feel her heart racing and soil sticking to her sweaty palms.

Her phone rang in her pocket – probably Oliver ready to berate her for being late. Amazed that it still had reception, she instinctively tried to answer it, then swore as it rang out. How long would it be until someone came looking for her? Jana had no way to call for help, but eventually her sister would wonder where she was. Eventually. Sash had the day off from working at the produce store, which meant she was home, but Jana had left her tinkering in the shed that morning – she was trying to build a solar-powered automatic opener for their front gate. Once Sash got stuck into one of her projects, she could barely drag herself away. It could be five o'clock before she noticed that Jana wasn't back to help feed the orphans.

A rumble of thunder sounded, and a cold, wet feeling began creeping up her jeans from the direction of her feet. Jana groaned. The forecast had been for a substantial downpour, and wombat burrows could flood or even cave in if it rained hard enough. At best, Jana faced a miserable few hours trapped down this damp hole. At worst . . . Well, she didn't want to think about it.

Something touched her ankle, startling her. 'Sash?' she called. 'Is that you? I'm stuck.'

She strained her ears for the sound of her sister's voice, but all she heard was a sharp crack of lightning.

The touch on her leg came again, higher now, nearer to the top of her calf. A shiver of fear ran down Jana's spine. Something was moving along her body towards her face. Jana held her breath as she felt a slight pressure on her neck, soft as silk. It was all she could do not to shout out loud as the head of a large tiger snake emerged from behind her ear. *Stay quiet*, she told herself. *Don't alarm it.*

The snake slid over her head, making her shudder and blink as the tail flicked her eye. It coiled its black-and-tan striped body around the root that Wall-E had been snagged on. The two of them stared at each other by the light of Jana's torch, which seemed to be dimming. Great. Meanwhile the wombat hole was turning into a muddy pit as the rain continued to fall. The snake's tongue flicked in and out, tasting the air. Jana licked her own lips and shut her eyes, hoping that the roof wouldn't cave in and kill them both.

CHAPTER 2

Mark Bell drove slowly along the dirt road while the rain lashed his silver Audi sports car. It was three o'clock in the afternoon, but so dark he could barely see five metres ahead of him. The car jolted alarmingly as he hit another pothole.

'There!' shouted twelve-year-old Karly, who was seated beside him. She pointed out the passenger side window. 'Turn left there. Hurry, Dad.' He could hear the distress in her voice.

Mark slowed to a crawl. A driveway emerged from the gloom, and he spun the wheel. Karly cradled the small bundle on her knees tighter as they passed through an open farm gate. A battered sign read 'Odessa' in a large, faded script. Underneath, in hand-painted writing, were the words 'Wombat Sanctuary'.

Mark parked beside a rambling old farmhouse that looked much the worse for wear. What may once have been a charming wraparound verandah now told a tale of neglect, with rain gushing through gaps in the corrugated-iron roof to flood the splintered wooden decking below. The home's weatherboard facade was bleached and peeling.

He glanced across at Karly, who was hugging her bundle and crying softly.

'Wait here.' Mark sprang from the car and dashed through the deluge to the shelter of the verandah. A knock on the front door drew no response. He knocked again, harder this time. Damn – it seemed like nobody was home. Yet two cars were parked in the driveway. His eyes landed on a shed about fifty metres from the house. Shielding his face from the rain with one hand, he ran across to the ramshackle building and pushed through the door.

A young woman, her fair hair pulled back in a ponytail, was tinkering with a motor that sat on a broad worktable.

'Knock, knock.'

She glanced up, seeming unsurprised by her visitor, then returned her attention to the motor. 'It's this chain that's the problem,' she said. 'I got it from an old garage-door opener, but I think it's the wrong size.'

The woman took no further notice of him.

'My name's Mark Bell.' Still no response. 'I have a baby wombat in the car.'

At that, she finally put down her screwdriver. 'Well, why didn't you say so? My name's Sash, by the way.' She grabbed a broad-brimmed hat from a wall hook and nodded towards the door. 'Come on then.'

Mark led Sash to the car at a run to collect Karly and the baby. Then they all made a dash through the rain for the house, with Mark holding his coat over his daughter's head as best he could.

'Come into the kitchen,' said Sash.

Karly's lip trembled as she handed over the towel-swaddled

bundle. Sash gently unwrapped it, revealing a barely furred wombat joey. 'Not a pinky, then,' she said, sounding relieved. 'A little boy, five to six months old at a guess.' She checked it over briefly. 'I think his leg is broken.'

Karly gave a horrified gasp. 'We found him in his mother's pouch. She'd been killed by a car. Will he die too?'

Sash gave Karly a reassuring smile. 'My sister's a vet. I'll ring her now. But let's get this little fellow warmed up first.'

She filled a hot water bottle with warm tap water, wrapped it in a cloth nappy and placed it along with the joey in a flannelette pillow slip. Then she took the bundle into the next room.

Karly and Mark trailed after her, finding themselves in an eclectic cross between an average lounge or TV room and a makeshift vet clinic. They waited there for Sash, who'd disappeared down the hall with the joey. 'The baby will be fine,' soothed Mark, hugging Karly to him as she buried her face in his chest. 'These people are experts.' He hoped he was right. Karly had already suffered too much heartbreak in her young life. She sure as hell didn't need any more.

A few minutes later Sash came back with a frown on her face. 'I can't reach Jana. Apparently, she didn't show up at work this afternoon, and she's not answering her phone.'

'Jana?'

'My sister. I'm worried about her. We'll have to go looking.'

We? Whatever did she mean? 'Sorry, but Karly and I have to go.' Mark backed towards the front door.

Sash was pulling on her coat, oblivious to his objection. 'Jana might have had an accident. She's been monitoring more than a hectare of burrows. I could use the help.'

Mark took Karly's hand. 'You'll have to find someone else. My daughter and I have an appointment, and we've already detoured an hour out of our way.'

Karly pulled away, glaring at him accusingly.

'I'm sorry love, but it's important. It wasn't easy getting you into Scarborough College midterm like this. I had to pull plenty of strings. You can't afford to miss your enrolment interview with the principal again. First impressions count.'

'Who cares?' cried Karly. 'I never wanted to go to your stupid school anyway.'

'Sorry to interrupt your argument, guys,' said Sash. 'But we really must find Jana. Without a vet, that joey will die.'

'Dad!'

Mark looked from Karly to Sash and back to Karly, seeing the desperation in his daughter's eyes. He ran a hand over his head and heaved a sigh of defeat.

Sash threw Karly a coat. 'We'll go in my Jeep.' She cast a contemptuous glance out the window at Mark's Audi. 'Your car would get bogged, nothing surer.'

Jana didn't know how long she'd been trapped underground, but it seemed like an eternity. She was lying in a pool of slowly rising water, and her body shivered with a combination of cold and fear. Her reptilian companion hadn't moved once. It fixed her with twin amber globes, half hypnotising Jana with its cold, unblinking glare. When Jana closed her eyes to break the spell, she no longer knew where the snake was. So she'd open them again, only to once more be captured by its mesmerising stare.

Her torch's battery was running out. On medium it could last thirty hours, but it was set to high, and she hadn't fully recharged it last night. In her rough estimation she had one, maybe two hours of light left. She tasted mud, spat it out and bit her lip. Her mouth was dry as sawdust. *Please let help arrive soon.* She dreaded the moment the torchlight would flicker out completely, leaving her to share the dark with her deadly companion.

A clod of earth fell from the roof, striking her temple, making her head jerk involuntarily. The snake, who'd been frozen in place for hours, recoiled with a sudden hiss. It flattened its body and raised its head in a classic prestrike pose. Jana stared in horror as the snake's forked tongue darted in and out between thin, glossy lips. *Stay still*, she told herself. *Don't flinch or make a sound.*

'Jana!'

A shout from above – Sash's voice. The snake reared higher at the sound. Jana groaned inwardly. Of all the times for help to arrive.

'Are you all right down there!'

Of course I'm not, Jana wanted to shout. But instead, she held her nerve and her silence. Goodness knows what Sash would think when she didn't answer.

Jana tried to kick her feet, but her legs had gone to sleep. Suddenly, she felt a wrench on her ankles, hard enough to drag her back a few centimetres. The shock made her scream, and the snake vanished deeper into the tunnel.

'She's alive!' came Sash's excited voice from above.

'Ow!' Another hard yank on her ankles. Sash must be stronger than she looked. Jana groped for Wall-E, and her fingers grasped the robot just before Sash dragged her another metre or two towards the surface. Jana closed her mouth tight and turned her head to avoid receiving a face full of mud. Two more tugs and she was out, squirming on her belly like a landed fish, trying to bring back feeling to her cramped, frozen limbs.

Sash took hold of Jana's hand and helped her to her feet as the drenching rain threatened to drown them both.

'Thank Christ you've come,' said Jana through chattering teeth, barely able to stand.

Sash steadied her. 'What on earth were you doing?'

'Wall-E was stuck on a tree root, and I accidentally pulled his cable out.' She offered the robot to her sister. 'You have to fix it, Sash. Wall-E has to go back tomorrow.'

'Never mind that now.' Sash shouldered Jana's soaking backpack, then bent down to retrieve the Wombot's ground station.

'Here, let me,' said another voice – a male voice.

A man stepped forward and picked up Wall-E's heavy base unit.

Sash thanked him, then turned to her sister. 'You should thank this bloke too. I didn't drag you out of that muddy hole. He did.'

The man must have been there all along, but Jana hadn't noticed him through the curtain of rain. Who was he, and why was he here? Nobody apart from herself and Sash ever visited this remote corner of the farm.

A sudden squall of hail had them all running for the Jeep, although Jana's gait was more of a fast hobble. While Sash and the stranger stowed the gear in the boot, Jana climbed into the front passenger side and sat there shivering with Wall-E on her lap. A young girl sat on the back seat, sobbing softly. Jana recognised the school uniform that the child was wearing. It belonged to Scarborough College, where Jana had spent six years as a scholarship student – six long, lonely years.

The man climbed in beside the girl. 'This lady is a vet,' he told her. 'She'll help your wombat.'

The girl's sobs abated.

It was typical of Sash not to provide Jana with introductions, or even any explanation for the presence of the visitors. Sash often ignored such social niceties. She put the Jeep in gear and they were off, zigzagging through the paddock to find the firmest ground.

'Now, what's this about a wombat?' Jana asked, turning in her seat to address the man, facing him properly for the first time. And she found herself staring into a pair of eyes that she'd hoped never to see again.

CHAPTER 3

Mark Bell. He and his posh mates had once been the bane of Jana's existence. But her resentment towards this man went way beyond being bullied at school. She blamed him for something far more serious than that. His actions all those years ago had set in train a disastrous series of events that had resulted in a family tragedy.

Jana had been a happy Year 6 pupil at tiny Tanunda Primary when her mother, Lena, decided that she should sit the Scarborough College scholarship entrance exam. Jana hadn't been keen. She'd expected to attend the local high school along with her friends.

'Scarborough is one of the best schools in South Australia,' Mum had urged. 'Jana, you're a smart girl. You have a real shot at this. Jacob, tell her!'

Jana's father, Jacob, had been less enthusiastic about the idea. 'But it's a boarding school, Lena. Do you really want our daughter living an hour away with strangers?'

'I want her to have chances that I didn't have as a child. My parents could never afford to send me to a school like

Scarborough.' Her face softened. 'I want our girls to experience all the opportunities this country has to offer. They shouldn't be held back by how much money we make. And the chance for a girl like Jana to attend such a fine school free of charge is surely a miracle.'

Jana had rolled her eyes. Her family might have been poor as church mice, but it didn't feel that way to an eleven-year-old who'd been born with a passion for nature and an independent spirit. As far as Jana was concerned, Tanunda held all she needed: a loving family, good friends and the wide, sunlit Murraylands on her doorstep – just begging to be explored.

However, her carefree days of running wild by the river had come to an end. Jana had won her scholarship and was packed off to Scarborough College by a proud but tearful family. And so began six long years of feeling like a complete outsider. At Scarborough everything that Jana thought she knew about the world was turned on its head. The other students were from wealthy families. The few, like Jana, who came from less fortunate backgrounds had quickly learned to keep quiet about their circumstances for fear of ridicule.

But keeping her head down wasn't so easy for a girl like Jana. She was naturally outspoken and forthright, with a rebellious streak – not someone to hide who she was – and making no apologies for her second-hand uniform and textbooks. And one look at her scuffed Big W runners and her unstyled blue-black hair, always pulled back in a practical ponytail, set her apart from the rest. Even her surname, Malinski – courtesy of her Polish grandparents – made her the butt of jokes, though for the life of her, Jana couldn't understand why. She'd never suffered that sort of casual, petty bullying before. One student in particular, Harper Clark, seemed to be set against her. Harper, with her bouncy blonde curls and who always had the latest iPhone, was the quintessential mean girl who never tired of making snide, hurtful remarks.

There were upsides to the new school, however. Firstly, the teachers. They recognised and appreciated Jana's quick intelligence and zest for learning. She excelled at maths and science, becoming particularly fond of her biology teacher, who shared her enthusiasm about the natural world. Mrs Washington privately called Jana her 'rose in a garden of weeds'. Unfair to the rest of the student body, no doubt, but it had made Jana feel special.

Secondly, she loved the two-storey state-of-the-art library, so different from the corner of one room set aside for books at the single-teacher primary school in Tanunda. At Scarborough a world of knowledge lay at Jana's fingertips, and she often had to be pried away from her studies for meals or bedtime. This didn't help her image, of course, as she became known as a nerdy swot as well as a poverty-stricken scholarship kid. She never let on to her parents how unhappy she was, although she sometimes thought that Dad guessed. Mum was so proud of Jana and her stellar academic achievements – the truth would break her mother's heart.

Life at Scarborough became even more intolerable when Jana reached her final senior years. That was when Harper started going out with Mark Bell, who became complicit in her relentless bullying campaign. Until then, Mark hadn't bothered Jana. In fact, he'd completely ignored her, unaware that she'd formed a secret schoolgirl crush on him somewhere around Year 9. Jana knew it wouldn't go anywhere. Mark

Bell was rich as buggery, and handsome in a tall, fair-haired, chisel-jawed sort of way – what Americans would have called a jock. Captain of everything, every year – school captain, sports captain, debating captain, captain of both the football and the cricket team. Jana used to have pleasant daydreams about him, imagining that he suddenly lost interest in spin bowling and became fascinated by wildlife conservation. He'd seek her out, pledging love and swearing that nobody shared his passion for animals the way she did. Then he'd kiss her and ask her to be his girlfriend.

But of course, he asked Harper instead. For eighteen months the pair basked in the status of being the senior school's golden couple. Girls wanted to be Harper, and boys wanted to be Mark. Everyone wanted to be admitted to their select social circle. Then, halfway through Year 12, Harper abruptly left Scarborough College. Jana had taken a relieved breath when she heard the news. Life at Scarborough was bound to improve in the absence of her chief tormentor.

How wrong she'd been.

All this and more flashed through her mind as she gazed into the piercing blue eyes of her saviour, staring at her from the back seat of her sister's Jeep. What would happen when he realised who she was? Would he have the good grace to look ashamed? Would he apologise? Time seemed to stand still. Jana waited, sick to her stomach with apprehension, not knowing what would come next. But what she didn't expect was to see no flash of recognition in his eyes at all. Apparently, Mark Bell had forgotten that she ever existed.

CHAPTER 4

When they arrived back at the house, Jana switched her brain to professional mode. She had an injured joey to assess, and that task required her undivided attention. But bubbling close to the surface was a growing anger. After everything this man had caused her to endure, didn't she deserve a place in his memory?

Karly looked on with wide, worried eyes as Jana examined the joey in the loungeroom. 'You're right,' Jana told her sister. 'His back leg is broken, but apart from that he appears to be uninjured. His gums are nice and pink, so I doubt there's internal bleeding. He's quite dehydrated, though. I'll try to get some fluids into him, then take him into the clinic for an X-ray.'

'Will he be all right?' Karly whispered. Jana turned and took her first proper look at the girl. She was fairer than her father, but the family resemblance was plain.

Jana put the joey into a soft pouch and hung it from a digital scale. 'Four hundred grams.'

Karly sniffed back some tears. 'Four hundred grams. Is that good, then?'

'Quite good, yes, and I think he's warm enough for some milk. His eyes are open, which is also good. Orphaned wombats are always suffering from shock, and that can be deadly, but I think this one stands a good chance. Sash,' she said. 'Can you get a feed ready, then pull the curtains and turn the main light off?'

A few minutes later, her sister emerged from the kitchen with a bottle of milk and handed it over. Jana tested the temperature by letting a few drops trickle onto her wrist, just as one would do for a human infant. She waited for the room to darken, then guided the odd, extended teat into the joey's mouth. 'Come on, now,' she murmured.

After a few anxious moments the baby closed his eyes and began to suck. Jana relaxed and shot an encouraging glance at Karly. The girl smiled back shyly, such genuine relief in her bright blue eyes that Jana couldn't help warming to her. So, Mark had a child. He must have married very young, although he wore no ring. The girl looked to be eleven or twelve years old, the same age Jana had been when she first attended Scarborough College. Although Jana had never had a brand-new uniform and expensive shoes like Karly's.

'Poor thing,' said Karly, peering at the little wombat who'd gone to sleep in Jana's arms. 'I'm going to name him Womble. Do you like that name? You said you'd X-ray him. Do you have an X-ray machine here?'

'I'll take him to the vet clinic in Rivertown,' said Jana, placing Womble back in the pillowcase. 'Just as soon as I make up a new hot water bottle for the trip.'

'Let me do that,' said Sash, taking Womble from her.

'Can I come?' asked Karly.

'No,' said Mark, who was standing behind his daughter and checking his watch. 'We need to go now and let this lady get cleaned up.'

Cleaned up? In between caring for the joey and her astonishment at recognising her rescuer, Jana had forgotten how filthy and bedraggled she was after her extended stay in the muddy wombat burrow.

Mark put a hand on Karly's shoulder, but she shook it off. 'When can I come back to visit Womble?' she asked, eyes on Jana.

Jana stayed silent, taking in Mark's impatient body language and exasperated expression. She didn't want to get in the middle of an argument, and she certainly didn't want him returning to Odessa.

'I don't think that's a good idea,' said Mark. 'This busy lady doesn't want you bothering her.'

Jana bridled at this. Who was he to say what she did or didn't want?

Karly rounded on her father. 'I hate you. I wish you weren't my dad.' Then she dissolved into tears. 'Please,' she sobbed. '*Pleeease*. I'll never ask for anything else ever again.'

Mark looked to Jana with faintly raised brows, as if he hoped that she might support him. She glared back. The nerve of the man!

'You're welcome to come back whenever you like, Karly,' said Jana, partly to piss Mark off, and partly because she could see how much it meant to the girl.

Karly rushed over and wrapped her arms around Jana's waist. Her school dress was now almost as wet and muddy as Jana was.

Mark sighed and scrubbed a hand over his face. 'Can we go now?'

Karly nodded glumly and detached herself from Jana, who offered her a box of tissues. The girl blew her nose with a loud honk, then fixed her gaze on her father. 'Dad, when can we come back? This weekend? On Saturday?'

'Well, I don't know if . . .'

Jana watched Mark squirm and couldn't help herself. 'Saturday's fine. It will be nice to have an extra helper. We have some other joeys apart from Womble to care for. But he's by far the youngest.'

Karly's eyes grew large. 'Wow. Can I see them?'

'Not now,' said Mark, firmly. 'You can see them on Saturday. If it's all right with these people, that is.'

His words surprised her. Jana hadn't really expected that he'd be back on the weekend. She glanced at the girl's tear-stained face and suddenly hoped that Mark meant what he said about visiting. She hated the idea of seeing him again, but if he broke his promise, it would clearly disappoint the young girl.

Mark shuffled his feet and glanced towards the door. 'I'd like to make a donation towards the wombat's—'

'His name's Womble,' corrected Karly.

'Towards Womble's upkeep.'

This was very welcome news. Their expenses had outstripped their income for months now, but Jana still couldn't bring herself to thank Mark for his offer. Instead, she took an information pamphlet from a desk drawer and thrust it at him. 'This has our web address. Odessa Wombat Sanctuary. There's a donation page. Now you need to go, because I have lots to do.'

Jana knew that she was being brusque, almost rude, but she didn't care. She turned her back on Mark and ran her tongue over the dried-up crud around her mouth. She felt suddenly weary. The adrenaline was wearing off, her body ached all over, and she desperately wanted to shower and change her muddy clothes. To have a steaming hot cup of coffee. To have some private time in which to process her feelings about seeing Mark again. He didn't recognise her. Unbelievable. If Karly wasn't there, she would have confronted him, demanded to know why he'd strung her along, broken her heart and humiliated her so publicly. She would have explained about the car accident that had wrecked her family and why she still blamed him for that more than ten years on.

Mark called to Karly from the door. This time the girl reluctantly obeyed, whispering her goodbyes before following her father from the room. Once they left, Sash gave her an odd look.

Jana glared at her sister. 'What?'

Sash grinned. 'Oh, I don't know. You're supposed to be the people person. And yet you didn't thank the man who rescued you from a muddy pit, and then you behaved as if he was somehow on the nose. Even when he offered a donation, it didn't help. Usually, you talk this place up and give that cheesy spiel about how public support is our lifeline, blah, blah, blah. Instead, you threw a pamphlet in his face and told him to leave.'

How should she respond? She wished it was as simple as saying, 'That man is Mark Bell.' But that wouldn't explain anything, because Jana hadn't told anyone about what Mark had done to her at school, not even her sister. Nobody knew why Jana had run away from Scarborough College in the middle of the night just before her final exams. She'd hitch-hiked as far as the tiny town of Overland Corner and then rung her parents.

She recalled that whole nightmare as if it was yesterday. Wandering deserted streets in the early hours. Wanting to ring her parents but at the same time horrified by the idea. Finally finding the courage to call, and her words coming in a muffled rush, muddied by the sobs she fought to keep back. Her mother's voice when she answered the phone, thick with sleep and worry.

Her parents had been on their way from Tanunda to collect her when a truck hit their car, leaving them both with serious injuries. Her mother had recovered, although it had taken months. Dad hadn't been so fortunate. He'd been left with permanent brain damage. The accident had uprooted the whole family. They were forced to move to Adelaide for the intensive medical rehabilitation her father needed. Mum became his full-time carer, leasing out the family farm to a neighbour.

But both sisters had yearned for the Murraylands. When Jana finished her studies, and she and Sash returned to reclaim Odessa, the place was seriously rundown – overgrazed, with weed-infested paddocks and great gutters of erosion extending for hundreds of metres along the riverbank. During the past three years they'd made good progress at destocking, rehabili-tating the land and planting thousands of native seedlings. The problem was that they'd run out of money. They now faced the depressing prospect of abandoning their dream of turning Odessa into a wildlife sanctuary, maybe even having to give up their rescue work completely. And as if that wasn't awful enough, Jana running into Mark Bell again had dredged up a slew of painful memories that she'd hoped to leave in the past.

'I need a shower,' she said and left the room. Thank goodness her sister wasn't too nosy. She'd soon become distracted by her next tech project and forget about Jana's uncharacteristic rudeness. And just as well, because Jana would never explain to anybody what Mark Bell had done and how deeply he'd hurt her. And she'd never allow herself to be that vulnerable again.

CHAPTER 5

'Come on,' Mark called. 'You'll catch your death.'

Karly stood in the pouring rain, leaning over a paddock fence and holding out her hand to a group of eastern grey kangaroos. They were sheltering in a straw-lined shed made out of half a corrugated-iron water tank. The girl took a last, longing look towards the animals before running to the car.

He watched with dismay as Karly dripped all over the front seat. The crisp new uniform that she'd put on that morning was a soggy, muddy mess. She'd pulled the ribbon from her flyaway hair, which had escaped its ponytail and now framed her face in a tangled blonde mop. Her eyes were red from crying.

Mark groaned and picked up his mobile. Even if he could get to Scarborough College in time, which he couldn't, Karly was in no fit state to attend an interview. There was nothing for it but to cancel – again.

The voice on the other end of the phone was curt. 'Mr Bell, we do always try to accommodate the children of our alumni, however, I fear that you're not taking the admission process seriously. The school has made an effort to find a place for Karly, but I'm afraid that I can't hold it for her any longer.'

No, this wouldn't do at all. 'Please, Mrs Hall. Give us one more chance. Schedule another interview for whenever it suits you. I guarantee that we'll be there.'

'You say that, but your availability until now has been rather limited.'

'Yes, I'm sorry about that, but I've been coping with a lot of changes. Moving back to Rivertown with my daughter. Starting a new job. But from now on, Karly's education is my top priority. You've been so very understanding, and I appreciate that more than you know. Just name a time.'

Mrs Hall sounded mollified. 'Well . . . I believe that you've only had custody of your daughter for a short time.'

'That's right. Roughly four months.'

'And you're raising her as a single father?'

'I'm trying to, yes, but it hasn't been easy. My life needed a lot of rearranging.'

'I imagine so. And Karly's mother?'

'Not in the picture at the moment, I'm afraid.'

'Aah . . . Poor child. Parenthood is a full-time job, Mr Bell – the most important job you'll ever have. It sounds like you might finally understand that.'

'Absolutely.' This was more hopeful. Mark didn't say anything further, worried that he might blow it.

After a long pause Mrs Hall finally said, 'I can fit Karly in at nine tomorrow morning. But if you're even five minutes late your daughter's offer of a place will be withdrawn.'

Yes! 'We'll be early, and thank you.'

Mark ended the call before the principal could change her

mind. He was determined that Karly should attend his old school, and he didn't take defeat well. To be honest, it rarely happened. His mother had always said he lived a charmed life, and maybe there was some truth in that. Mark was used to being right and getting what he wanted.

And why was it so important to him that Karly went to Scarborough? The school had been a safe refuge for him during the chaos of his parents' divorce – a genuine home away home, providing him with a surrogate family when his own was in turmoil. He wanted his daughter to have that same kind of security.

Karly was staring out the car window at the rain. *What is she thinking?* he wondered for the umpteenth time, wishing she would open up about her feelings. However difficult this new arrangement was for him, it must be ten times more difficult for Karly.

She'd be missing her mother, of course, but perhaps she'd be missing her grandparents more. She'd lived with Harper's parents on and off for most of her life, until their ill health had made that arrangement impossible. A few months ago, Harper had appeared on his doorstep in Adelaide, demanding that he take Karly.

'It's the least that you can do after knocking me up at seventeen and ruining my life. I'm a flight attendant,' she'd said. 'I'm overseas more often than I'm home. My world isn't set up for a child right now.'

And mine is? Mark had thought. After all, he hardly knew the girl. A few awkward access visits when she was living with her grandparents had been the extent of his contact. He hadn't been welcome there, and he could understand why.

Karly was six when Mark became aware that she'd been born. She'd needed her tonsils out and the hospital had contacted him in order to complete an accurate medical record. It was an understatement to say that he had been shocked. Mark's emotions had veered between joy at discovering he had a daughter and apprehension about how it might change his life. It turned out that he didn't have to worry about that last part. Karly's grandparents seemed to be doing most of her raising, and they were implacably opposed to Mark's involvement with their granddaughter. To be honest, that was almost a relief. Mark himself hadn't felt ready for the responsibility of being a hands-on father. Yet sometimes over the years, he'd drift off to sleep wondering about what toys Karly liked best, or what was her favourite colour. Not knowing had left him feeling strangely empty.

His daughter's existence solved the mystery of Harper's sudden departure from school all those years ago. They'd been foolish kids, playing at adult relationships, too impulsive and irresponsible to be careful. And Harper had paid the price: losing her friends and missing out on graduation. Having to juggle caring for a child while trying to forge a career for herself as a single mother.

Well, it was finally Mark's turn to have his life upended. When Harper had shown up a few months back with a twelve-year-old Karly, his girlfriend had left him, complaining that she wasn't ready to be a mother to some other woman's child. But the truth was that their relationship had already been on the rocks. Mark was a workaholic who had never prioritised his personal life over his career.

That was all about to change. He'd turned down a

promotion because it would have meant that he didn't have time for Karly, then he'd resigned altogether from his position as a senior executive at a leading Adelaide tax accountancy. He'd sold his city apartment and moved back to Rivertown on the Murray where he'd spent most of his childhood. There he'd purchased Paddlewheel, a luxury architect-designed home right on the river with a hectare of garden and its own private pier. He'd bought boys' toys like a sports cruiser and a jet ski, and he'd found a position at Turner & Moore, a large regional accounting firm with its main office five minutes away in town. The reduced salary, reduction in prestige and loss of seniority was a bitter pill for a man as ambitious as Mark Bell. But it was worth it to know that Karly would have a better life in Rivertown than in Adelaide. A slower pace of living would allow both him and his daughter the space and time to connect.

So far, Mark was not enjoying his new job. Howard Turner, the senior partner, seemed to reserve the most difficult accounts for him – clients wanting to minimise their tax situations by pushing boundaries, trying to pass off shady deductions or buy into some sort of 'creative' tax-avoidance scheme. One local developer, Tony Alfonso, was the worst example of this kind of client. Mark had purchased Paddlewheel from Alfonso, and for some reason the man thought that entitled him to preferential treatment. He took up far too much of Mark's time, argued the cost of every bill, and seemed to seek Mark's counsel just so that he could turn around and do the exact opposite. It left Mark having to regularly comb through Alfonso's files to make sure that he wasn't accidentally party to something that could put both the firm and his reputation at risk.

Then there were the 'Wait – I'm supposed to keep track of my expenses?' sort of clients. They kept their documents all higgledy-piggledy in shoe boxes, often mixing up personal and business expenses, which they would then sheepishly empty onto Mark's desk with a hopeful expression.

And finally, there were the clients facing bankruptcy. Some of these could remain solvent with sound financial advice, and Mark tried hard to help them trade their way out of difficulty. But others were lost causes, leaving him feeling sad and a little helpless. The one that had affected him most was a rundown zoo. Wildfell Park displayed exotic animals as well as natives, but the elderly owner was no longer capable of running it and had accumulated substantial debts trying to keep the zoo afloat. She would soon lose her licence to operate the zoo and faced the awful possibility of not only having to let the skeleton staff go, but also having to put down many of the animals.

Having worked in Adelaide for most of his career, Mark was used to dealing exclusively with wealthy corporate accounts, and adjusting to such small-scale clientele in Rivertown took some getting used to. Still, it couldn't be helped. Karly needed stability, and having his father, Don, with his second wife, Gwen, close by at Overland Corner was a major advantage of living in Rivertown. Karly had taken to the pair instantly, and vice versa. Gwen was a retired teacher and had been homeschooling Karly while Mark waited for a position to become available at Scarborough College. If Karly could board at the college during the week, Mark could throw himself into his work, establish himself at his new job, and still have the weekends free for his daughter.

It seemed like a solid plan, but he hadn't banked on Karly hating the idea.

'I don't want to go to boarding school,' she'd screamed, immediately throwing a tantrum. 'I want to live with Grandma and Grandpa.' She'd cried and refused to attend the first interview at all. She'd only agreed to go to the second one when Don had promised her a puppy.

Karly's passion for animals was something that Mark was discovering. He'd bought expensive fishing gear for his boat, thinking that he and Karly might bond during lazy afternoons on the river catching trout and perch. But she wasn't interested. 'Killing innocent fish doesn't sound like fun to me,' she'd said with a frown. Instead, his mystifying daughter would spend whole afternoons in the expansive back yard at Paddlewheel, taking photos of birds or insects. When he did his parental due diligence by checking out Karly's internet search history, he found out that her most visited site was a field guide to South Australian fauna.

She seemed to have a natural affinity with every kind of animal. Brightly coloured king parrots followed her around the garden and took seed from her hand. A bandicoot emerged from under the back steps when she called, accepting offerings of fruit. And they couldn't walk through a park without Karly wanting to stop and pat every dog, their tails wagging excitedly at the sight of her.

Little wonder, then, that she was thrilled at Grandpa Don's offer. 'My neighbour's sheepdog is expecting a litter,' he'd said. 'How does a border collie sound?'

Karly had danced around the room with excitement. 'I've always wanted a pet!' she squealed, then glared at Mark. 'But

I'll never get to see it if I'm going to be at that stupid school all week.'

'Well, yes,' Don had said. 'But your father will bring you here on weekends to visit, right son?'

Mark had agreed to the arrangement. Lesson one of being a father. If all else fails – bribe. And it was a bribe that should still work tomorrow. By hook or by crook, he would get his recalcitrant daughter to Scarborough College in the morning.

His thoughts turned to the series of unfortunate events that had led them to miss this afternoon's interview. They'd left his father's house in Overland Corner with time to spare. Mark had barely noticed the wombat lying beside the road. He'd driven past them plenty of times before. But this time was different.

'Stop,' Karly had said, turning in her seat and craning her neck to keep her eyes on the animal. 'We have to see if it's alive and check its pouch.'

'We do?' asked a bemused Mark as the heavens opened.

'Yes, we do.' Karly was firm, so he turned around and parked nearby.

They got out of the car. The wombat looked dead to him. Thick blood oozed from its mouth. He poked it with a stick. Nothing. Mark glanced at his trembling daughter.

'Come on, honey.' He put his arm around her shoulder. 'There's nothing we can do for it now.'

'Yes, there is,' she said. 'We can check its pouch.'

He made a face. Did she really want him to stick his hand between the bloodied animal's legs and feel around?

'We have to,' she urged. 'What if there's a baby?'

So he did, and there was.

He'd frantically googled wildlife carers, worried that he might not get phone reception on the remote highway. Two bars – thank God. Odessa Wombat Sanctuary was the closest – a forty-five-minute drive in the opposite direction. But what else could he do? Even if his teary daughter hadn't been sitting beside him, he wouldn't have let the little orphan die. And anyway, they had time. They weren't due at Scarborough College for hours. He'd planned to take Karly shopping beforehand in Rivertown for her first iPhone. She desperately wanted one, and he hoped it would put her in a positive frame of mind during the interview. The last thing he wanted was for her to clam up the way she often did when things didn't go her way.

But buying the phone hadn't happened. The entire interview hadn't happened. Because he'd been hijacked into rescuing a woman from a wombat hole in the middle of a storm. What were the odds? And to top it all off, the woman – Jana, the other one had called her – hadn't even thanked him. In fact, she'd seemed hostile from the moment she laid eyes on him. There was no accounting for people. But she had been prompt and professional in caring for Womble, and she'd been kind to Karly, even inviting her back to check on the orphan's progress. And Mark was grateful for it. Heaven knows what would have happened if Womble had died. Karly would have been inconsolable.

He remembered his offer of a donation to Odessa. The wombat sanctuary had a definite air of dilapidation about it. Sagging fences and a potholed drive that desperately needed grading and more gravel. Paint flaked from the home's weatherboards, and inside the carpet was worn right through

33

in patches, exposing the floorboards. Those two sisters were doing it tough, and he intended to be generous. They were providing a wonderful service for the local wildlife, and it gave him a kick to think that he could help. Mark turned their names over in his mind. Sash and Jana. Jana. Now where had he heard that name before?

CHAPTER 6

Jana was putting a sleepy Womble back in the pillowcase after his morning feed when Sash sang out from the spare room cum office. 'Come and look at this.'

When Jana went in and glanced at her sister's laptop, her heart sank. Sash had the sanctuary's online NetBank page open. Jana guessed that they'd finally reached their $4000 overdraft limit. She hadn't been game to check their account lately. It was too depressing. It wasn't as if they had a choice whether to spend or not. In addition to the joeys, they also had some older wombats, some orphaned kangaroos and three aviaries full of birds recovering from various injuries. Some might never be able to be released. Veterinary care, maintenance and feeding costs were high and non-negotiable.

The sisters never mentioned their financial woes to their mother in Adelaide. She had no money to spare. But they did send regular photos and positive updates for her to share with their father. Who knew if they registered with him or not? But Dad had always loved Odessa and its wildlife. He was responsible for fostering a passion for nature in his daughters. The least they could do was send him photographs.

Sash turned to Jana, an amazed look on her face. 'We're in the black.'

'In the black? That doesn't make sense. Don't you mean in the red?'

Sash grinned. 'See for yourself.'

She was right. The account was no longer overdrawn. Instead, it had a credit balance of $1089. But how? Their latest wages had already been eaten up by the electricity bill and a rates instalment. So where had the great mystery deposit of a whopping $5000 come from?

'It's a donation,' said Sash, switching to their website. 'See this comment? "In thanks for helping Womble." My God, not only did that Mark guy drag you out of a wombat hole, but he's dragged us out of a financial hole as well. This is fantastic. We can pay the produce store bill, buy that wire netting for the new aviary, and we'll still be in credit.' Sash's smile suddenly slipped, and she gave her sister a stern look. 'If Mr Moneybags comes back on Saturday like he said, you'd better be a bit more friendly to him. Who knows? We might get another donation.'

Pleased as Jana was for the sanctuary to be solvent again, she couldn't go so far as feeling grateful to Mark. It jarred to think that she was indebted to that man in any way. But Sash was right – they couldn't afford to alienate such a generous supporter. Jana would have to brush her personal feelings aside for the sake of the animals. It would be difficult. She was a naturally honest person, not accustomed to putting on an act. For the first time Jana wondered if maybe Mark had recognised her after all. Was that why he'd been so generous? Was he trying to assuage a guilty conscience?

Jana marched wordlessly from the room, aware of Sash's curious eyes upon her but unwilling to explain. She couldn't help hoping that Mark wouldn't return tomorrow, however much the broken promise might hurt Karly.

Unfortunately, Mark was true to his word. The next morning at 11.00 a.m. his silver sports car bumped its way up Odessa's potholed drive. It was raining again. Jana watched from the porch as he parked by the house, unable to avoid the puddles. The car's gleaming chassis was spattered with mud. It gave her a certain satisfaction to see it.

Karly burst from the car and ran to Jana. 'How's Womble?'

'He's fine. Just fine.'

The radiant smile on her elfin face lit up the grey day. Jana hadn't really paid that much attention to her on their first meeting. She'd been too distracted at finding Mark hauling her from a hole by her ankles. Now she had time to assess the child. Cute, with a button nose and bright blue eyes. But the girl didn't seem to care much about her appearance. She wore an oversized hoody and baggy jeans. Her blonde hair looked like it might have once been cut into a bob, but now it grew wild, with no shape at all. If Jana had guessed Karly's age right, she must have been born soon after her father finished high school. *What about her mother?* Jana wondered briefly, remembering that Mark wore no ring. She shook her head to clear it. No, she wouldn't think of it again. She wanted to know nothing about Mark or his life. That way madness lay.

Mark emerged from the car just as Sash walked up from

the shed. The last time Jana had seen him he'd been wearing a filthy suit and tie, looking almost as wet and bedraggled as she had. This time he appeared casually elegant in a blue patterned shirt, a grey tailored sports coat and sand-coloured chinos. Back at school he'd already had the fresh-faced good looks of a teenage heartthrob, but the intervening years had lent his features an attractive maturity. With his square face and stubbled, dimpled jaw, he might have been a model posing for *Country Style* magazine. Looking at him caused her a stab of pain.

Sash came to stand beside her. 'Great to see you, Mark. We want to thank you for your generous donation, don't we, Jana?' She elbowed her sister gently.

'Yes,' said Jana, frowning. 'Thanks.' Mark tipped his akubra in acknowledgement. 'I need to do a shift at the vet clinic this afternoon. You can pick Karly up at two o'clock.'

The girl's face fell. 'But Dad, you can't go yet. Don't you want to see Womble first?'

He gave his daughter a warm smile. 'As a matter of fact, I thought I'd stay.' He turned to Jana. 'It says on your website that you need volunteers, and by the time I get home to Rivertown it would be almost time to turn round and come back again.'

Karly squealed with delight and hugged her father.

'So,' said Mark with an open-armed gesture. 'My daughter and I are at your disposal. What would you like us to do?'

Jana stared at him, open-mouthed. No. It was bad enough having to thank the bastard. Spending the whole day with him would be unbearable.

Sash glanced at her, rolling her eyes. Jana could imagine

what she was thinking. Here they were with a cashed-up donor who was just begging to help. They should be buttering Mark up, reeling him in. But instead, Jana could barely bring herself to speak to the man.

Sash stepped in to rescue the situation. 'That's great, Mark. Come on, you two. I'll show you Womble. Karly, you can feed him if you like. He's doing really well. In the meantime—' She elbowed her sister again, not so gently this time. 'Jana will decide where you can be most useful, right?'

Jana's nod was barely perceptible. Karly ran after Sash. Mark shot Jana a curious glance, then followed the others into the house. Something sharp lodged in Jana's throat, and tears threatened. She knuckled them away. She longed to go after him, to demand to know why he'd strung her along all those years ago at school, and what he'd got out of humiliating her like that.

Did Mark care about the heartache he'd caused her and her family? Because of him, Jana had left Scarborough College before her final exams, losing her chance to go straight on to study veterinary science at university. It had taken three more years for her to realise her dream and be accepted into the course. She'd repeated Year 12 part-time by enrolling in another school near the Royal Adelaide Hospital, where her parents were being treated, earning a living by waitressing nights and two days during the week.

She'd provided moral and financial support for her mother, who'd been hurt in the car accident, suffering two shattered legs and taking almost a year to regain her mobility. During that terrible time, Jana took on the care of her younger sister, who'd also had to change schools. But her mother's injuries were nothing compared to those of her father. Dad could no longer walk or talk.

Did it matter to Mark that he was responsible, even if indirectly, for her parents' life-changing car accident? She snorted out loud at the thought and felt her fists clench. Of course not. He probably didn't even know about it. He'd had his fun and gone on with his charmed life, unaware of the chaos he'd left behind.

But as outrageous as that might be, the fact remained that Odessa was in trouble financially and needed more donors to survive. The animals depended on her, and she wasn't about to let them down. So Jana racked her brains to think of something that Mark could help with that wouldn't involve spending too much time with him. She drew a blank. The most pressing project – extending the aviaries – would involve close supervision of any newbie. But she had to admit that a helper, especially a tall fit man like Mark, would be handy. They were almost ready to put the roof on, and it would seem strange to Sash if Jana didn't enlist his assistance.

A glance skyward showed patches of blue between the clouds. At least it had stopped raining. With a sigh, she marched down to the aviaries and began sorting and stacking the timber they'd need. She couldn't imagine that Mark would be much use, though. He'd probably never held a hammer in his life.

Half an hour later the others arrived. Karly was in earnest conversation with Sash about, of all things, wombat whiskers.

'That's right,' Sash was saying. 'They do have lots of whiskers, and highly sensitive ones, too. Five sets, actually, to help them navigate tunnels in the dark. A long set on the muzzle, and four smaller sets above the eyes, on the cheeks, under the chin and near the throat.'

Karly was intrigued. 'Did you hear that, Dad? They have five sets of whiskers.' She held up five fingers for emphasis. 'Isn't that amazing! I'm going to be a wombat lady when I grow up, like Jana and Sash.'

Everyone smiled, even Jana. The girl's innocent enthusiasm was infectious. With Sash and Karly to act as buffers, maybe working with Mark wouldn't be so bad after all.

'We'll see you guys later,' said Sash. 'Karly and I are off to check on the kangaroos. Then we'll give the adult wombats fresh hay and clean out all that poo from their enclosures.'

'Yay! Dad, did you know that wombats have cube-shaped poo? How cool is that!' called Karly happily as she trotted after Sash, as if she'd been promised a day at the beach.

Jana's face fell. 'But—' She watched in dismay as her sister and the girl walked off. Jana glanced sideways at Mark and found him looking back at her. His gaze sent prickles down her spine. He stood with an unconscious air of self-confidence as a stiff breeze ruffled his sandy-blond hair. He casually rolled up the sleeves of his shirt, revealing lightly muscled forearms that hinted at a balance between strength and grace.

She took a deep breath and checked her watch. Not even twelve o'clock. How on earth would she get through the next few hours?

CHAPTER 7

Mark couldn't help staring. Jana wasn't his usual type; she wasn't blonde, fair and chocolate-box pretty. And her unconventional beauty hadn't struck him on their first meeting, plastered as she was with mud and filth. But today, as she stood framed in a shaft of sunlight, she looked like a goddess: tall, imperious and unattainable. The sight of her stirred something deep inside him. He couldn't remember ever having such a visceral response to a woman before.

However, his admiration was clearly not reciprocated. Jana's dark eyes flashed with open animosity, although she was speaking to him civilly enough, explaining what they needed to do before fitting the corrugated-iron sheets to the roof struts of the aviary. But body language didn't lie, and he almost ducked when Jana hefted a nail gun.

'Have you used one of these before?' She didn't even try hiding the scornful tone of her voice.

Whatever had he done to deserve such hostility? It was a mystery, and one he intended to solve. Had he met Jana before somewhere, was that it? Had his accountancy firm wronged her or her family in some way perhaps? There was something vaguely familiar about her, but his mind might be playing tricks. Sometimes, when she turned her head at a certain angle, a rush of deja vu hit him. Mark scoured his memory but came up blank. Surely he wouldn't forget meeting someone like Jana, with her striking good looks, shining ebony hair and curves in all the right places. When he got home later, he intended to dig a bit online. See if he could discover exactly who the beautiful Jana was, and why her name and face rang a bell. Until then, he had a whole day to spend with her, and he was looking forward to it, despite her puzzling dislike of him. Maybe he could change her mind.

The sun came out and they set to work roofing the new aviary. To Jana's obvious surprise, Mark quickly proved that he was capable with tools. He'd enjoyed the woodworking elective at school and had spent many happy hours helping his father with his carpentry hobby before his parents had divorced.

Jana stood on the ladder with a tool belt around her waist and half-a-dozen screws held in her mouth. Mark passed her a treated pine two-by-four that he'd already cut to size. He watched with admiration as Jana balanced herself and deftly used a drill to secure the strut to the frame. There was something very sexy about the confidence and skill with which she used her body.

'How long have you lived in Tanunda?' he asked.

No response. Of course not – if she answered, she'd drop her screws. He waited until she came down from the ladder and tried again.

'When did you and Sash open the wombat sanctuary?'

She shot him a poisonous look. 'A few years ago now.'

'Have you always lived here?'

'No.' Jana replenished her store of screws, ending the conversation again.

Two hawks in a nearby aviary screeched, ruffled their feathers and seemed to be giving him death stares. What was it with this place? Jana walked over as the hawks flew to a perch by the wire. They bent their heads and she stroked them as if to say, 'Good birds.'

Mark took his turn up the ladder. Further attempts at small talk were met with monosyllabic responses. Okay, he clearly wasn't going to learn much about Jana that way. He decided to stop fishing for information and just enjoy the smell of fresh, rain-washed air, the distant river views and the welcome feeling of working with his hands again.

They continued in virtual silence, only talking to communicate about the task at hand. They actually made an efficient team, and by one-thirty had completed the corrugated-iron section of roof. Jana offered him the water bottle just as Karly ran up, followed by Sash. A tiny wombat trotted at their heels like a miniature tank.

'This is Care Bear.' Karly beamed and pointed to the joey. 'We're giving him his exercise. When Womble's a bit older, we'll do that with him too, won't we, Sash?' She patted Care Bear who began chewing her sock. Karly laughed with delight. 'Guess what, Dad? Sash milks tiger snakes and death adders, then sends the venom off to make snake-bite antidotes. Isn't that sick?'

Mark glanced at Sash, alarmed at the thought of his young daughter being so close to such deadly reptiles.

'Don't worry,' said Sash, reassuring him. 'Karly only saw the snakes from outside the glass. She's a smart kid, though – quick to learn and full of questions. You must be very proud of her.'

Karly beamed and seemed to stand taller. Mark hadn't observed that sort of vivacity on his daughter's face before. Seeing her happiness made all the challenges and difficulties of the last few months worthwhile.

'The roof looks great,' Sash noted. 'Thanks Mark.'

'You're welcome,' he said, still captivated by Karly's joyful expression. 'Perhaps we can come again.'

Jana gave the slightest shake of her head. It must have been an involuntary reflex, but Karly hadn't missed it. Her smile dissolved and she ran to Jana.

'Please let us come,' she begged. '*Pleease.*'

Jana touched the child's cheek and glanced at Mark's worried face. 'Of course you guys can come again. Well, I have to go now. I'm late for work.' She high-fived Karly. 'See you, kid.'

Mark hurried to comfort his daughter. 'We'll be back next week.' He stroked her tangled blonde hair, picked a leaf from it and kissed the top of her head. 'I promise.'

Jana showered and changed, shaken by the day's events and filled with conflicted feelings. She *was* grateful for Mark's donation and his help with the aviary today, but how could she show it? How was she supposed to simply forget about what he'd done, even though *he* apparently had? She hated that her hesitance about Mark's visit had caused his daughter any pain. She saw so much of herself reflected in Karly – her rebelliousness, her individuality and, most of all, her love of animals. And there was something else, a fragility about the child that said that she'd been hurt before. Well, Jana could identify with that too, thanks to the girl's bastard of a father. She hoped that Karly would never discover what Mark had done all those years ago.

Jana hurried outside to her old Jeep and glanced down towards the aviaries. Good – the others were only halfway up the path, chatting among themselves while Care Bear nipped at Karly's heels. Jana jumped behind the wheel, reversed around and sped off, almost collecting the Holden station wagon turning into the drive. She ignored the driver's friendly wave. Luca Brown worked with Sash at the produce store, and it was no secret that he'd been sweet on her for ages. Everybody else knew before Sash did. She was such a dork. But eventually she'd twigged, and the pair had been 'going steady' for months now. Such an old-fashioned term for it, but that's how Sash herself described it. Luca was only the second serious boyfriend that she'd ever had, but Jana had to admit he was a keeper – gentle, funny and loyal. He was also a great help around the sanctuary – fixing leaking tanks and helping with the animals. Her sister sure had better luck than Jana did when it came to men.

Speaking of men, it looked like Mark intended to be a regular visitor at Odessa for his daughter's sake. She begrudgingly admired him for that. Who'd have thought that the cruel boy she'd known at school would have turned out to be such a caring father? But that didn't change or excuse the past. Nothing would, and she couldn't pretend that she didn't know Mark forever. She refused to live a lie, so she resolved to challenge him on his next visit, whether it jeopardised future donations to the sanctuary or not. He needed to own up to his actions.

Jana hit the brakes and swerved to miss a crow feeding on a road-killed rabbit. Thank goodness the dead animal wasn't a kangaroo or wombat. No need to stop and check a pouch to find another hungry little mouth to feed. She wished for the umpteenth time that she could afford to launch a driver awareness program in the area, maybe along the lines of Tasmania's 'Slow Down Between Dusk and Dawn' campaign. There were so many positive things she could do if she had the money. But Odessa's growing collection of rescued animals swallowed up both Sash's and her own wages each fortnight. There was barely enough left over to feed themselves, and Jana couldn't remember the last time she'd bought herself a small luxury like bubble bath or face cream. Mark's donation had offered them a brief reprieve, but it would be a one-off. Once Jana confronted him, he wouldn't be so generous again.

Jana pulled into the Rivertown Vet Clinic and parked the Jeep. She checked the time and swore – late again. Oliver wouldn't be happy. The car park was full and she felt suddenly weary. She'd been up at six that morning and had already completed a hard day's physical work. She now faced a busy five-hour shift and wouldn't get home until eight o'clock at the earliest. Thankfully Sash was on overnight duty, waking every three hours to feed the youngest orphans. Jana badly needed a good night's sleep. Unfortunately, in the days since Mark had come back into her life, a good night's sleep had been hard to come by. She'd lie awake, tossing and turning, reliving the humiliation he'd caused her all those years ago as if it had happened yesterday. Reliving her panicked flight from Scarborough College, hitchhiking down the highway in the dark, and the sickening realisation that she wouldn't be graduating after all. Reliving the moment she learned that her parents had crashed on their way to fetch her. It wasn't fair – Mark couldn't get clean away with what he'd done. If he returned next weekend, Jana would have it out with him.

CHAPTER 8

Mark watched Jana speed off in her battered old Jeep, its wheels spinning on gravel. She barely missed hitting another car as it turned into Odessa's rutted drive. *Late for work*, she'd said. Maybe so, but he couldn't shake the feeling that she was hurrying to get away from him. Mark ran a hand along the rough wooden fence beside him. He'd tried his best to win Jana over today, working hard and doing a damn fine job, if he did say so himself. Yet she'd still treated him with thinly disguised contempt. This sort of unreasonable attitude was new to Mark; he'd been a charmer all his life and was used to being liked by women. But instead of being turned off by Jana's puzzling rudeness, he was intrigued. And never being one to shirk a challenge, he intended to get to the bottom of it.

Mark turned his attention back to Karly and he laughed as the little wombat dashed about her in wide, joyful circles. Very cute. It occurred to him that this playful baby might have perished of starvation, cold and misery by the side of the road if some compassionate person hadn't rescued it. An unsettling thought, and one that hit a little too close to home. If not for Karly, he'd have driven straight past Womble's poor dead mother, and her little joey would have met that frightening fate. Mark felt a gush of pride for his daughter. How special she was! And he also felt a debt of gratitude to the remarkable sisters who were living on a shoestring themselves so that they could save these remarkable animals. Mark hadn't often come across that sort of self-sacrifice before, and he was deeply impressed.

He called out to his daughter. 'Say goodbye to Care Bear, Karly. We're going to Grandma Gwen and Grandpa Don's. They've asked us to stay the night.'

Karly rolled her eyes. 'You don't have to call them Gwen and Don, Dad. I'm not stupid. Call them Grandma and Grandpa – I'll know who you mean. My other grandparents are Nan and Gramps anyway.'

This was the first time she'd mentioned her other grandparents in months. He didn't know much about her life, but he knew Karly must miss them. They'd raised her. Mark didn't blame Harper for being a mostly absent mother. Heck, she'd been just a kid herself when she gave birth. But whenever Mark tried talking to Karly about Harper and her family, Karly clammed up. It was good that she'd brought up the subject herself this time. It seemed like progress.

It was late afternoon before Mark and Karly arrived at the tiny town of Overland Corner, where Mark's father and his second wife had settled for their retirement. They'd bought a five-hectare hobby farm with a charming two-storey home overlooking the river. Don and Gwen welcomed them with

Karly's favourite dinner of cheesy macaroni and a lively game of Monopoly that lasted until after ten o'clock.

When she'd gone to bed, Mark opened his laptop and googled Odessa Wombat Sanctuary. Mark clicked the first link that came up. He hadn't quite known what to expect, but it wasn't this slick, sophisticated website, worthy of the most professional corporate designer. Uncluttered, with high-quality photos and graphics that helped its conservation message shine through. Simple to navigate and with strong branding. Mark loved the logo – a stylised baby wombat nestled in a helping hand. But the most compelling thing about the site was the content.

On one page a live night vision webcam showed a nest on the ground containing three fluffy chicks. A hawk-like bird stood guard in the grass nearby. The accompanying article told their story: 'These are swamp harriers, raptors that pair for life. The father bird had been shot dead while raiding a chicken run. The female went in search of her mate and became caught in the coop netting, breaking her wing. The farmer's twelve-year-old son had found the bird before his father did and called us. When we arrived, the boy whispered, "I know where their nest is."'

Mark read on. 'We followed him to the river. There on the ground, hidden among dense reeds, lay a straw-and-grass thatched depression containing three eggs. We named the injured bird Binda, a Gundungurra word for deep water. We brought her and the eggs back to Odessa. After splinting Binda's wing, we made a replica nest in an aviary near the dam and sat her back on her eggs. And now here they are for all to see – a healing mother and three healthy chicks.'

It was a moving story, and it seemed that Mark wasn't the only one who thought so. The Harrier Live Webcam, which had only been up and running for a month, had an astonishing sixty thousand views.

There were two other webcams, one set up in an artificial burrow showing an emerging wombat, and another trained on a pond where a large rat-like creature and its young were eating yabbies in the shallows.

According to the text these animals were 'Australia's answer to otters. And like otters, this rakali mother is an intelligent, top-order predator of aquatic environments. She has a broad tail for a rudder, webbed hind feet, and soft waterproof fur that was once in demand for coats and hats. She cares for her young, teaching them how to fish and open mussels. Rakali are useful animals, preying on European carp and rodents. Northern rakali are clever enough to safely eat poisonous cane toads by carefully carving out their edible hearts – a skill they teach their young. Sometimes they're ignorantly mistaken for rats, but comparing a rakali to a rat is like comparing a mangy moggy to a sleek cheetah. What an amazing animal!'

Mark watched the mother rakali tend to her babies with renewed respect. He smiled to himself. Jana had successfully changed his perception of the animal from contempt to admiration. She wasn't only a terrific designer, but she was pretty good at PR as well.

Now his curiosity was even more piqued. He clicked on the About Us tab. A brief biography of the sisters popped up, and Mark immediately focused on their surname. Malinski. Jana Malinski – of course. Now he remembered why she seemed so familiar. They'd gone to school together at Scarborough College. She'd been a shy, nerdy girl, a straight-A student, and a bit of an outsider.

He hadn't had much to do with Jana, although Harper had held a particular grudge against her. As far as he could recall, Harper's hostility had been based on nothing more than jealousy and prejudice. She'd been jealous of Jana's stellar academic record – always dux of their year – and she'd envied her popularity with the teachers. Harper had mocked Jana because of her foreign name and the fact that she was a scholarship girl. Jana had never tried to hide the fact that her uniforms were second-hand, or the fact that her iPhone was so old that the staff couldn't find a replacement for the charger when it broke. She hadn't seemed embarrassed about wearing cheap sports shoes or coming from a farm where she helped with the annual shearing, while the rest of her cohort returned to their luxury city homes for school break or flew to far-off destinations with their families.

Jana had always been unashamedly herself. Mark had liked and admired her for it at school, even though he never stuck up for her against Harper's petulance and bullying. He'd been so besotted with his gorgeous girlfriend that he'd excused all sorts of bad behaviour. He wouldn't believe rumours of her kissing other boys or lying to get others into trouble. In his eyes, back then, Harper could do no wrong.

Was that why Jana despised him now? Because he'd gone along with Harper all those years ago? It seemed an extreme reaction. True, he hadn't called Harper out, but neither had he bullied Jana himself. Mark examined his own behaviour. As far as he remembered, his only possible crime against Jana had been hanging around with the popular kids who'd given her a hard time.

Mark cast his mind back to that final year at Scarborough College. Harper had left halfway through, and he now knew it was because she'd been pregnant. But Jana had also left early – right on the eve of their final exams. Nobody knew why, and to be fair, Mark hadn't thought about it much at the time. Jana hadn't been in his circle of friends. But not sitting her finals would have had major consequences for her future career, and now he couldn't stop wondering why it had happened.

Mark explored a little more on Google. He and Jana must be around the same age, but she'd graduated from university much later than he had. Her wombat conservation work was acknowledged on many websites, including that of the Binburra Devil Park in Tasmania, where she'd conducted post-graduate field research into both wombats and endangered Tasmanian devils. Mark paused at a photo of her smiling at the camera while accepting a Nature Conservancy award. Jana was clearly a talented and widely respected environmentalist. She was also the most intriguing woman he'd ever met.

CHAPTER 9

Mark and Karly stayed at Overland Corner for the rest of the weekend. His father and Gwen wanted to make the most of Karly's last days before she started boarding school. When Monday morning came, Mark cast an approving eye over his daughter. In her brand-new Scarborough College uniform, she looked like a different girl. Face scrubbed clean, her normally untidy halo of fair hair tamed with a blue velvet ribbon, and shoes so shiny you could see your face in them.

'You look lovely,' said a beaming Gwen. She'd helped Karly pack her bag the night before and Mark had put it in the car to prevent his daughter tampering with the contents. The last thing he wanted was for her pet skink lizards to make it to school, along with a shoe box full of grasshoppers.

Don gave his granddaughter a big hug. 'We'll see you next weekend, love. Those pups I was telling you about will have been born by then. We can go next door to visit them.'

But even the promise of puppies couldn't wipe away Karly's scowl. She glared at Mark. 'Why do I have to go to boarding school? Why can't you just pick me up from school every day?'

Karly wasn't the only one looking at him with accusing eyes. Gwen seemed firmly on the girl's side. 'Surely you could manage that, Mark. Scarborough College has day students as well as boarders.'

'Yes, a few, but they're mainly children of staff. And what happens when I'm working late at the office? I'm trying to forge a name for myself at Turner & Moore, and I can't risk leaving Karly to look after herself at Paddlewheel.'

'Then perhaps Karly can live here with us and I can continue to homeschool her?' Gwen glanced at Don for support, but his face remained impassive. All three of his children had attended Scarborough College, and he was an old boy himself. Don wouldn't want it any other way.

Mark could see the rebellion rising on his daughter's face. 'Enough.' He handed Karly her schoolbag and picked up the box of books and stationery that Gwen had painstakingly labelled and covered. 'Say goodbye, Karly. It's time to head into Rivertown.'

An hour later they passed through the high wrought-iron gates of Scarborough College. Karly gazed solemnly out the window at the manicured gardens and green ovals. Broad sprinklers stuttered and hissed among signs announcing 'Bore Water Used Here'.

They parked outside the historic main house – a grand late-Victorian manor with a slate roof and an imposing central tower. Dropping Karly off was more of an emotional wrench than Mark had thought it would be. He'd told himself that she'd be okay. After all, Scarborough was one of the finest schools in South Australia, and he'd thoroughly enjoyed his time there. Their house, Paddlewheel, was only a five-minute drive away and she'd get to go home every weekend – a privilege that most students didn't enjoy.

But as he took Karly's suitcase from the car, she looked so small and forlorn – her schoolbag too big for her slim back – and a powerful flashback hit him. He may well have been confident and happy once he'd adjusted to boarding school life, but his first day had been daunting. Karly was twelve, but he'd only been ten and faced not seeing his family until the end of term. Did Karly feel the same as he'd felt back then – abandoned?

He kicked at the groomed gravel drive, fighting an urge to take his daughter home. No, this was the place for her. If they left now, she'd never get the opportunity to attend Scarborough again, and family tradition demanded that she stay. So Mark shook off his doubts, pasted on a smile that he didn't feel, and guided Karly towards the administration wing.

After a heartfelt hug, he left her with Mrs Stuart, the Head of Girls' Boarding – a plump, motherly-looking person with greying hair and a kind round face. She oozed warmth and even managed to coax a smile from Karly. Mark was grateful that the woman seemed so friendly. If she'd been a grumpy old battle-axe type, he couldn't have gone through with leaving Karly behind.

Mark walked in through the double glass doors of Turner & Moore, one of the few two-storey buildings in Rivertown's new civic centre, and the only one with a lift. He nodded to Stacey, the young receptionist, before going up to his office – a large corner space with a view across the broad Murray. The Rivertown port was a picture postcard: a bustling hub of houseboats, leisure craft and historic paddle-steamers.

Time to get to work. Mark opened his laptop and closed the blinds. The wide windows presented too much of a distraction. It was already hard enough to concentrate knowing that Karly was negotiating her first day at school. Was she making friends? He tried not to think about her packing away her belongings in a strange room and meeting curious classmates. Tried not to think about her battling homesickness and missing him the way he was already missing her.

He browsed his list of current projects: Scott & Son Real Estate, Rivertown Engineering, Alfonso Property Group. No, he'd been putting off dealing with his bankruptcy files, so he flipped through them instead. He preferred working on these first thing on a Monday morning when he was refreshed and energised from the weekend. Less chance of getting depressed by the financial mess so many people had made of their lives. There was a local butcher, a sole trader with a profitable business. He'd lost the family's savings through online gambling and then took out a second mortgage on the house without telling his wife. Now he could no longer afford the crippling repayments. There was a good chance the trustee could be convinced to let that client trade his way out of insolvency. But without the help of Gamblers Anonymous or some similar support, who was to say that the man wouldn't land his family right back in it? Still, that wasn't Mark's problem.

There was a grazier who faced losing the sheep station that

had been in his family for five generations. Hotter summers and five floods in four years had made the farm unviable. And then there was the zoo. That case really tugged at his heart-strings. There'd be no trading out of bankruptcy for Wildfell Park. It would lose its operating licence next month. The four permanent staff would lose their jobs, the elderly widow who owned the place, Hazel Roberts, would have to move into a retirement home, and the animals . . . Well, again, that wasn't his problem, but some quick research had indicated that not all of them could be rehomed.

Mark remembered visiting the zoo as a child with his family, and also on school excursions. Picnics under the shady English elms that dotted the expansive grounds. Feeding bread to the deer and kangaroos. Laughing in front of the monkey house as he watched the playful creatures' antics. And gaping in awe at the magnificent lions and tigers.

Hazel and her late husband, Reg, had owned the zoo for fifty years, and their animal breeding program had been, to put it kindly, haphazard. As far as Mark knew, they'd never kept records, and accidental mating was more common than not. Nobody was sure exactly how many animals lived at the zoo, and of those, how many were inbred. Hazel couldn't remember if the two tigers were related when Mark had asked. The monkeys – he didn't even know what kind they were – had been living together in a group for years without management. And who knew about the three lions? Hazel had been too depressed about the very real prospect of losing the zoo to tell him much, and anyway, her memory wasn't the best.

The whole philosophy of zoos had changed in the past decade or so. In Hazel's day, they were primarily for public entertainment. But now zoos fulfilled a vital new role of conserving and increasing the populations of vulnerable species. They were reluctant to take on inbred animals, which could not be used in captive breeding programs. Mark tried not to think about what that would mean for so many of the animals at Wildfell Park. What would Jana say about the zoo's closure? He was thinking a lot about her and her opinions lately.

Mark stood and opened the blinds. There, to the left of the Rivertown wharf, he could just spot the roof of Wildfell Park's stately home. The house had seemed like a mansion to him as a child, but he imagined it would be in a pretty rundown state today. He didn't intend to visit the place to see for himself. He'd spare himself that sadness.

The phone on his desk rang, startling him from his reverie.

'There's a Frieda Abraham on the line,' said Stacey. 'Shall I put her through? She wants to talk to you about the Rivertown zoo.'

CHAPTER 10

Jana handed the last poodle puppy back to his beaming owner. 'That's it,' she said. 'First vaccinations done. Don't take them out or let them have contact with other dogs yet. They won't be fully protected until after their final needles at sixteen weeks.'

The woman left with her laundry basket of wriggling puppies, and Jana wearily tidied up the examination room, hoping that no last-minute clients showed up. She'd kill for a brew – one of those double-shot espressos from the clinic's new coffee machine. She'd just pulled a double shift, was on joey duty when she got home, and was not looking forward to another night of broken sleep. What she needed was a pick-me-up – a caffeine hit or three.

Jana did a final check of her inpatients: a cat recovering from cancer surgery, a dog who'd been hit by a car, and a pet cockatoo with a broken wing. Then she crept out to the reception area, hoping to see nobody in the waiting room.

Rachael, the vet nurse, saw her and smiled. 'You're safe, Jana. We're officially closed.'

Jana sighed with relief and fetched her mobile from a drawer behind the counter. She hated being at people's beck and call at the best of times, and enjoyed not being available when she was on duty.

'You forgot to turn your phone off and it's been ringing a *lot*,' said Rachael. 'I almost answered it myself.'

Oh dear. Jana hoped that Sash wasn't in some sort of trouble. But the calls were all from the same unknown number. She listened to one of the numerous voicemails. What the—? Jana covered her mouth with the palm of her hand. Mark Bell had been ringing her all day.

'Jana, I have a proposition for you. We need to meet. Please ring me back ASAP.'

Rachael was staring, her brow creased with concern. 'Are you okay?'

Jana barely heard her. What was behind this barrage of calls? She couldn't imagine, and she didn't want to know. Nothing was more unwelcome than any kind of proposition from Mark Bell.

Rachael tried again. 'Is it bad news? Can I make you a coffee?'

A minute ago, all Jana had wanted was that coffee. Now all she wanted was to get out of there and go home. Jana grabbed her bag and hurried outside, fumbling for her keys, annoyed that Mark's calls had her so rattled. She turned the ignition over, stalling twice before exiting the car park without looking, earning angry beeps from a passing car that had to slow down. And despite vowing that she wouldn't think about Mark any more, her mind betrayed her. She couldn't help speculating about the reason for his calls. Had he remembered who she was? Did he want to apologise after all these years? Would it make a difference? A proposition, he'd said. An indecent proposition probably. Mark was a jerk, after all. Jana slammed the steering wheel. Why was she torturing herself? Well, it would stop right now. She turned the radio volume up and let the sad strains of a Taylor Swift song sweep her away.

An hour later Jana arrived home. Shit – Mark's sports car was parked in the drive. He and Sash were leaning against a fence near the house, chatting. They both turned to watch her arrive. Mark looked sharp in grey suit pants with an open-collared shirt, R. M. Williams boots and a charcoal akubra hat – the perfect blend of professional style and country charm. Jana's sister looked like she'd just crawled out of a dust bowl, which she probably had. She was redoing the wiring under the house.

Sash ran up to the car, her face aglow with excitement beneath the grime. 'Mark wants to ask you something.' She yanked the Jeep's door open. 'Come on. I can't wait for you to hear it.'

What on earth? Jana swallowed hard and allowed her enthusiastic sister to drag her over to Mark. His eyes fixed on her like laser beams, almost like a challenge. She wanted to hold his gaze, but to her dismay she looked away. Her skin broke out in goosebumps. Why did this man still have such a physical effect on her?

'Tell her, Mark.' Sash could barely contain her eagerness.

Jana became curious in spite of herself. What could have put her sister in such high spirits? She gulped some air and gestured towards the house. They all trooped in through the back door, took a seat around the 1950s laminate kitchen table, and she and Sash raised expectant faces to Mark.

He cleared his throat before beginning, addressing his remarks to Jana. 'You know the Rivertown zoo, I suppose.'

'Of course she knows it,' said Sash, her voice filled with frustration. 'Get to the point.'

Mark folded his hands on the tabletop before him. 'Wildfell Park has been running at a loss for years. It's facing bankruptcy and will close next month when it loses its operating licence. My firm has been tasked with administering its affairs.'

Jana blinked hard. She'd been bristling for some kind of conflict, but this turn of events took her completely off guard. 'What happens to the animals?'

'If it goes bankrupt? Some will be rehomed. Some won't.'

'I've treated a few of them,' said Jana, shaking her head at the awful news. 'Extracted a rotten tooth from King, their oldest lion. Splinted the arm of a baby macaque. I even pulled a breech-birth bison calf for Hazel. She loves those animals as if they're her children. This will break her.'

'No one doubts that Hazel's heart is in the right place,' said Mark. 'But she's eighty years old and in failing health. Things have been getting on top of her for years now, especially since Reg died.'

'Can't somebody help?'

'Yes,' Sash blurted. 'You!'

Now Jana was more confused than ever.

Mark steepled his fingers. 'Let me explain. A wealthy benefactor has thrown the zoo a lifeline. She's willing to settle its debts and, within reason, underwrite its operation so it can avoid bankruptcy.'

Jana took a relieved breath. 'That's marvellous.'

'On one condition,' said Mark. 'That I find someone suitably qualified to run it, and quickly. This person's ultimate goal will be to restore the zoo's licence to operate. Bring it into the twenty-first century.'

Sash grinned. Jana was astonished at where this conversation was going.

'If I can't fill the job, then many of the animals will be destroyed, the remaining staff will be laid off and the region will lose a wonderful asset.' Mark paused and ran a tongue over his lips. 'Jana, I'm offering you the position of Director and Curator of Wildfell Park Zoo.'

'She accepts,' squealed Sash. 'When does she start?'

'Hang on a minute.' Mark smiled, and a rogue thought crept into Jana's mind – goodness he was handsome. 'Jana, you'll receive a generous salary and have four full-time staff to begin with, and the scope to hire more. You'll have the right to hire contractors, as long as you run your plans past me first. We'll be working closely together on this project. You'll be responsible for organising the animals' care and habitats, maintaining exhibits and supervising staff. I'd also like you to redesign the zoo's website. You have a flair for such things. As the zoo's accountant, I'll be responsible for administration and finance until you're in a position to appoint a chief financial officer.'

'Who is this benefactor?' asked Jana, still in a daze.

'She's asked for discretion about her identity, but I have permission to tell you two. Her name is Frieda

Abraham – currently on the *Forbes* rich list of the fifty wealthiest Australians.' Mark waited for that fascinating snippet of information to sink in.

Frieda Abraham. Jana couldn't help being a little star-struck upon hearing that name. Frieda was friends with David Attenborough and famous for supporting conservation charities all over Australia. She'd donated generously to the Aussie Ark Foundation and sponsored the mass planting of food vines for Queensland's endangered birdwing butterflies. Perhaps the most unusual project Frieda supported was teaching quolls and goannas to steer clear of poisonous cane toads by making sausages from the amphibians' legs and lacing them with nausea-inducing chemicals before tossing them out of helicopters.

Mark continued. 'I've already run your appointment past Frieda, and she's given me the go-ahead. Time is of the essence and frankly, Jana, you're a godsend. A qualified wildlife expert who's also a veterinarian experienced with exotic animals? You're perfect for the job and hopefully' – he held her frozen in his gaze – 'available.'

'Of course she's available,' scoffed Sash. 'Mark, tell her the best bit.'

Jana gaped at her sister. There was a better bit?

'Mrs Abraham also wants to sponsor the wombat sanctuary. She'll provide funds to upgrade the facilities here and pay Sash a full-time salary. In return—'

'Woo hoo,' yelled Sash. 'No more lugging around bales of hay at the produce store.'

Mark tried again. 'In return, you two will make Odessa available as overflow accommodation for the zoo. If there is a surplus of animals to display that are worth keeping, they will come here. In that case, Sash will be given staff to assist her.'

'I'll have staff,' sang Sash, and began boogieing around the kitchen.

Jana stared at Mark blankly, too stunned to make any rational response.

'You'll have to resign your position at the Rivertown Vet Clinic, of course,' said Mark. 'And you'll be expected to move into the manor house at Wildfell Park.'

'What about the animals here at Odessa?' Jana asked. 'Sash can't manage them all on her own.'

'Until I can organise some help, you can move many of them to the zoo,' said Mark. He had an answer for everything. 'Some of the birds, for example, especially those that can't be released. Eventually they can go on display. It will ease Sash's workload and you'll have full-time help with them at Wildfell Park.'

Sash chimed in. 'Anyway, I won't be on my own. I've asked Luca to move in.'

'I need a minute,' Jana shoved her chair back, escaped to the hall and leaned against the wall, breathing hard. There was so much to think about, not least of which was the prospect of working closely with Mark. That was unacceptable in any scenario – except this one. She had the opportunity to not only rescue Wildfell Park, but also renovate and expand the wombat sanctuary – something she and Sash had been working towards for years. They'd tried so hard, and it had always been one step forward, two steps back. But now?

Jana closed her eyes. Their mission was all that mattered. Personal feelings must not get in the way. She'd have to keep

things strictly professional with Mark. No sabotaging resentments or wayward attractions. No trawling over the past. And
her plan to reveal herself to him would have to go on the back
burner, perhaps indefinitely. What if she confronted him and
he refused to work with her? She could lose this dream chance
to save the zoo, and to set Odessa up for a brighter future
than she could ever have imagined. She wouldn't risk that.
A powerful determination rose in Jana like the incoming tide.
She'd bury her emotions for the common good. What use were
they anyway? They'd caused her nothing but pain.

Jana put a hand to her heart. Sash was calling to her from the
kitchen. If she didn't make a move soon, her sister would come
looking. Talk about pressure. And what about Sash already
inviting Luca to move in? Cheeky bugger. She pulled herself
together and returned to the kitchen, back into Mark's orbit.

'You don't have to give me your answer right away,' he
said, as if she'd never left.

Jana's gaze locked onto his, and the resentment that lived
like a coiled snake in her belly stirred restlessly. There Mark
sat, the personification of so much past pain, but the earnest-
ness in his clear blue eyes was disarming. He wasn't just the
boy who'd wronged her; he was also the man now offering
her a golden opportunity. His voice held a note of respect that
was both unexpected and welcome. Jana felt the conflict build
within her like clashing storms.

Mark smiled his encouragement. 'It's a lot to process.
I'll organise a tour of the zoo for you tomorrow, and you'll
have until the end of the week to decide. After that I'll have to
widen my search. But the chance of finding another suitable
candidate within the time frame is slim.'

Sash stared at her in disbelief. 'Jana, you have to do it. It's the opportunity of a lifetime for everybody.'

Yes. Jana heaved a great sigh, sucking as much air as possible into her lungs. The game was afoot, the challenge accepted. There was nothing for it but to shake Mark's hand.

CHAPTER 11

Jana arrived at the zoo bright and early the next morning, before it opened for visitors. Its front gates were crafted from heavy timber and bore intricate carvings of exotic animals that hinted at the marvels inside: lions and tigers and bears, their outlines now blurring into the wood grain. Massive stone pillars framed the entrance, moss creeping up their sides. The name of Wildfell Park arched over the gateway, the sign now peeling and discoloured. Two tarnished brass lamps topped the pillars, their broken glass panels allowing climbing honeysuckle to curl within. Driving through those gates brought back a kaleidoscope of memories. Jana had loved this place as a child.

Nestled on the picturesque banks of the mighty Murray River, Wildfell Park encompassed an impressive twenty hectares. Her eyes were immediately drawn to the historic manor house that stood a few hundred metres in from the entrance. The building's weathered stone and ivy-covered facade whispered of days long gone. Its overgrown gardens were a colourful tapestry of flowering camellias, rhododendrons and azaleas run wild. A broken dragon statue rose from a tangled bed of bush roses and forget-me-nots, while the torso of a centaur flanked the path. Lifting her gaze, Jana noticed the chipped stone gargoyles perched below the roofline. The gothic guardians seemed to be watching her.

Beyond the manor house stretched expansive overgrown lawns, punctuated by majestic elms and oaks. Jana knew that beyond them again lay gullies of fragrant eucalyptus trees and vibrant bottlebrush, painting the landscape in shades of green and red. The air was alive with a chorus of birdsong, their melodies adding to the enchantment of the surroundings. It was a magical place.

Mark's car was already there. Jana parked in front of the manor, grabbed her bag, and when she turned around, he'd opened the car door for her. She hadn't expected that he'd be so eager to get started. After all, this was simply another business arrangement for him.

They met Hazel Roberts on the front verandah. Although the manor was a little the worse for wear, it still seemed grand to Jana. It reminded her rather unpleasantly of the boarding house at Scarborough College. How strange it would be living here after the rundown Odessa farmhouse. She gazed up at the row of first-floor windows, wondering which one would be her room.

Hazel had aged since Jana's last professional visit a year ago. Back then Reg had been alive, and a happier couple she couldn't have imagined. They still held hands after fifty years of marriage. Jana felt a small pang at the memory. How many people experienced that kind of love?

Now Jana saw Hazel as if for the first time: a diminutive

woman with silver hair and a baseball cap, who appeared reasonably fit for her eighty years. Yet something was different. She seemed to have shrunk, her once straight back hunched, her pale blue eyes dull and listless. Hazel was missing a certain spark and seemed to be just going through the motions. Jana's heart went out to her. She couldn't imagine how it must feel to turn your life's work over to virtual strangers.

Mark wanted a tour of the house first, but Hazel quickly shut the front door and led them down a concrete path to the zoo proper. Walking through the grounds transported Jana back to childhood. This had been one of the few outings that her parents could afford, and their family had spent many happy Sundays exploring the place. Her father would encourage Sash and her to carefully read each exhibit's information plaque, and he always asked questions of the keepers when he saw them. Later on, there'd been class visits as a student at Scarborough College. The little zoo was familiar in so many ways, but also completely different. It was like picking apart a poem when studying English. She could no longer simply appreciate the writing – in analysing its structure and form, something was inevitably lost.

Jana's rose-coloured glasses had slipped, forcing her to see Wildfell Park as it truly was. The enclosures were ugly throwbacks to the seventies, surrounded by too much concrete and wire. All the timber structures, from fences to picnic tables, showed varying degrees of rot. The Safari Café hadn't operated for months, but Jana could picture the possibilities. The little building was perfectly situated on a rise with expansive views across both the zoo and the river. Yet it was open to the elements on one side, where it really needed floor-to-ceiling windows to protect diners from inclement weather. The charming thatched roof required urgent repairs. The outdated chrome and Formica tables were laid out in rows reminiscent of a school canteen. And was it Jana's imagination, or did a greasy film coat the furniture and walls?

Then there were the animals themselves. To Jana's relief they all appeared healthy and well fed. But the petting zoo that Jana remembered so well from childhood was overrun with rabbits and guinea pigs. Many grazed on the unmown grass outside the fence and skittered underground as she approached; an untidy warren of dusty diggings and tunnels showed how they got in and out of their original home. Children wouldn't be able to pat these feral descendants of the original placid display animals. A pair of white donkeys painted like zebras had lost half their black stripes, and the baby lambs had grown into adult Merinos with dangerous-looking curly horns. One of them rammed the rusty gate that bore one sign reading 'Welcome Children' and another saying 'Keep Out'.

Two ragged-looking goshawks perched in the otherwise empty mews. One of them flew to Hazel as they passed, and she stopped to scratch its head through the wire. Peacocks strolled the unkempt lawns and ibis foraged in the bins. A small herd of fallow deer took off through a bedraggled rose garden, leaping gracefully as they went, just for the joy of it. A scurry of movement up a tree trunk caught Jana's eye. A small grey animal with a white striped back held its bushy tail aloft. It resembled a numbat, except the stripes went the wrong way.

'I think there's a squirrel in that tree.'

'Probably,' said Hazel with a casual glance. 'The palm squirrels escaped through a hole in their pen and Reg never got around to fixing it. They now live wild in the park. People love them.'

Jana frowned. Zookeepers were tasked with a solemn duty of care to manage their charges responsibly. The wayward squirrels wouldn't be receiving health checks, inbreeding would be rife, and they could easily spread to the surrounding countryside. The guiding principle of animal welfare applied to all creatures, great and small. And people would not be so sanguine if more problematic animals were on the loose. Jana thought of the two-hundred-kilogram lion who'd needed a dentist last year. The zoo would never get its licence back if exotic animals ran wild, even cute little ones that seemed harmless. Some years ago, palm squirrels had escaped from Perth Zoo and formed colonies in nearby parklands. They'd been declared noxious pests, capable of damaging a wide range of fruit, vegetable and nut crops. High on her list of tasks would be recapturing the furry runaways.

This was the zoo's last day before closing, and visitors were beginning to arrive. A school group and a few couples with small children wandered past. They were heading for the big cats, which were always the top drawcard. Jana followed them to Tiger Island, an exhibit where tangles of blackberries and thistles competed with the overgrown grass. A few straggly gum trees, their trunks ravaged by giant claws, cast scant shade. In places, bleached white bones showed through the greenery, giving the place a sinister feel. And above them, on a high paved platform, lay a languid white tiger.

Jana had met Raj before, but her heart still raced. His size and strength inspired awe in all who saw him. She couldn't see Ruby, the second tiger, and felt a brief wave of disappointment. Then Mark bent close, brushing against her as he pointed to a striped tail peeking out from behind a bush, and her heart raced again. Was it because of the tigers, or because of Mark? The more time she spent with him, the harder it was to deny the unwelcome pull she felt in his presence.

Stop it, she told herself. *Put aside your emotions.* She'd need to be doing a lot of that from now on. Jana cast a critical eye over the exhibit. Wildfell Park's Tiger Island was a far cry from Dreamworld's lavish exhibit of the same name. Yet though it was plain and utilitarian, the display had potential. It consisted of a raised islet surrounded by a walled moat and stand-off barrier. Now that Jana was responsible for visitor safety, she couldn't help thinking that both the barrier and the wall looked a little low. The generously sized area was well situated with a southerly aspect, and once they cleared the thickets of weeds and scrub, it would more than double the space available for the tigers.

They moved on to the lions, who were nowhere in sight. A young keeper was cleaning their enclosure, which was way too small. Jana looked around – the adjacent picnic ground could easily be sacrificed in order to extend it. She made a mental note.

As the tour continued, Jana's ambitions for the zoo grew. The monkey house had a concrete floor and grimy loops of rope hanging from the roof. She imagined a treed enclosure with a raised pathway for visitors. The magnificent macaws and other parrots lived in narrow domed cages. She pictured walk-through free-flight aviaries that incorporated the ferny stream that bisected the zoo grounds. And when the friendly dingoes ran up to the fence, tails wagging, she imagined dingo encounters, with keepers taking them for regular walks around the grounds.

A timber shed, grandly labelled the Palace of Snakes, contained several shelves of glass terrariums. The first one contained a beautifully patterned carpet python apparently named Sebastian. His sinuous body coiled elegantly around a branch, and Jana admired his glossy scales, dappled in shades of earthy browns and vibrant yellows.

The next three exhibits contained a tiger snake, then a pair of shingleback lizards, followed by some Murray River turtles. The final and largest tank contained a real find – a juvenile heath goanna. These spotted monitor lizards could grow to 1.5 metres in length and were a threatened species in the Murraylands. Best of all, she had another heath goanna back home at Odessa – one that could never be released. The unfortunate lizard had been caught in an illegal leg-hold trap, and Jana had been forced to amputate his foot. If this juvenile was a female, they could potentially mate.

Her mind's eye transformed the humble wooden building into a state-of-the-art, climate-controlled reptile and amphibian house. Jana imagined it being home to collections of rare South Australian animals like Cunningham's skinks, pygmy blue-tongue lizards and earless dragons. Another tank teemed with giant tadpoles of the endangered growling grass frog, with their beautiful coppery pigments and iridescent green sheen. How Sash would love such a place! The tantalising possibilities sent a shiver of excitement through Jana.

It was almost two hours later when they finished the tour

and arrived back at the manor house. Hazel responded to their questions but offered nothing by way of conversation. She seemed reluctant to let them inside and Jana could tell she was holding herself on a very tight leash.

Mark was growing impatient. 'We must look at the house too, Hazel.' His phone rang, then dropped out when he answered it. 'The reception here is terrible,' he said, shaking his head as if that was somehow Hazel's fault. 'Now, when can we arrange a time to meet with the staff?'

Hazel dissolved into tears, her leash finally snapping. She sank onto the bench beside the front door, sobbing her heart out. Jana sat beside her and took hold of her hand. Mark opened his mouth to speak, but Jana shushed him with a finger held against her lips. She waited for Hazel's tears to dry, then asked gently, 'What's the worst thing about all this for you? Tell me.'

Hazel squeezed Jana's hand and held it tighter. 'It's not that I'm ungrateful, dear. Quite the opposite. I'm thrilled that you want to save the zoo, and I'm sure you'll do a wonderful job.'

'Then what is it?' asked Jana.

'It's the thought of moving to that damn retirement home.' Her voice faltered. 'What will I do with myself? Do you know my garden there will be as small as a postage stamp and somebody else will look after it anyway?' She gazed across the verandah to the colourful flowerbeds, awash with an early flush of dahlias and roses. 'I've lived here with Reg for fifty years. We never had any children, so the animals became our family. I can't imagine leaving them behind.'

'Then why move?' asked Jana.

Hazel furrowed her brows. 'What do you mean?'

'I mean, why don't you stay on here? Nobody knows the staff and animals like you do. You'd be a big help to me.'

Hazel's frown turned into an uncertain smile, as if she didn't quite believe what she was hearing. 'I can't decide who I'll miss more if I leave,' she said. 'Nala or the goshawks. I raised Shadow and Storm from chicks. Someone chopped down the tree their nest was in. We used to do free-flight demonstrations to wow the visitors. Until they got too old. Those birds must be sixteen or seventeen years if they're a day.'

'Why, that's marvellous,' said Jana. 'I have a young peregrine falcon and another goshawk at Odessa. Their injuries mean that they can't be released, but they'd be perfectly fit for some limited free flying. It would do them good. Do you think you could train them?'

'Now hang on,' said Mark. 'Hazel's not part of the deal. I've already booked the movers.'

'Well, unbook them,' said Jana, firmly. 'Hazel's changed her mind. She's staying here.'

'Yes, young man,' said Hazel, her voice growing stronger. 'I've changed my mind.'

Mark looked grim. 'Jana, can I have a word with you in private, please?'

He gestured for her to follow him down the verandah steps. When they were out of earshot, he whispered, 'Hazel can't possibly stay here. By making false promises you're just making the situation harder for her.'

'I don't understand,' said Jana. 'Why can't she stay?'

'Hazel is a frail old woman who needs care. Who's going to look after her here?'

'I will,' said Jana, defiantly. 'And I wasn't just being kind when I said she'll be a help. Imagine the depth of experience she has with these animals. We'd be foolish to let all that knowledge go to waste.'

Mark crossed his arms, and his lips formed a tight line. 'Not a good idea, Jana. You need to focus full-time on the animals.'

'Hazel's no invalid,' argued Jana. 'She was moving because she couldn't look after the zoo, not because she couldn't look after herself.'

But Mark remained stony-faced. 'It's an unnecessary complication, and I don't like complications.'

'Please!' It killed her to beg, especially to him of all people – the man who'd so cruelly betrayed her and who'd then forgotten her entirely – but this was important. She put a hand on his arm. 'Complications are what make life worth living.'

His face softened. She must have hit a chord with that last remark.

'All right, I'll run it past Mrs Abraham,' he said. 'If it's okay with her, it's okay with me.'

Mark's mobile rang. 'Speak of the devil,' he said, glancing at the phone. 'Hello, Frieda . . . Yes, I have those budget projections for you.'

Jana listened wide-eyed as Mark bandied around mind-bogglingly large expense forecasts. Then he brought up the subject of Hazel staying on at Wildfell Park.

'Here.' He offered Jana the phone. 'She wants to talk to you.'

She hesitated before taking it, a little overwhelmed at the prospect of talking to the celebrated conservationist.

She couldn't help a brief fangirl moment, stammering out how much she admired Frieda and thanking her for saving the zoo. They chatted for a few minutes about the project and the importance of Wildfell Park.

Frieda's voice was strong and resonant. It rose and fell with the lilt of someone who'd spent many years speaking for those who had no voice – the flora and fauna she so tirelessly championed. Even over the phone, Jana could sense that Frieda's eyes must sparkle with the kind of spirited light that comes from a life of passionate dedication.

'Of course Hazel Roberts must stay,' said Frieda when Jana explained the situation. 'That wonderful woman has gifted us her zoo in a living trust. Such a grand and generous gesture. The least we can do is honour her wish to live out her life there.'

Jana didn't think she could have admired Frieda Abraham any more than she already did. She was wrong. And she couldn't wait to tell Hazel the good news.

CHAPTER 12

Mark brought Karly to visit Wildfell Park the following weekend. From the moment she arrived she was in a constant state of wide-eyed excitement. After all, what child wouldn't enjoy spending a sunny Saturday at the zoo? And with a behind-the-scenes pass at that. But Jana knew that for an animal lover like Karly, it was pure joy.

Her favourite animals were the big cats, closely followed by the monkeys and water buffalo. Jana took Karly and Mark for a Jeep ride into one of the paddocks. Past the deer and donkeys, they stopped near the gum-tree gully where the buffalo were resting in the shade.

'I've seen that show *Outback Ringer*,' Mark said, glancing at Jana. 'Were these guys taken wild from the Northern Territory?'

'Nothing so exciting, I'm afraid. They're from a local buffalo farm.'

Karly was particularly enamoured of a curious month-old calf who trotted right up to the vehicle.

'Meet Genghis,' said Jana. 'Maru's baby.'

Mark had to stop his daughter from jumping out of the Jeep to pat him.

'Buffalo are generally peaceful animals,' explained Jana. 'But Maru will protect her calf if she thinks it's being threatened. And that young bull over there? Jango's feeling his oats a bit too much lately. I'm castrating him soon.'

Mark flinched a little at this matter-of-fact statement.

After the tour they ate lunch at one of the picnic tables and drank glasses of lemonade bobbing with ice cubes. Jana had made salad rolls and bought pastries from a bakery in town. Karly chatted non-stop and fed most of her lunch to the peacocks. She was so full of questions that she didn't have time to eat. 'How old is the sun bear? Isn't he lonely by himself? Can you pat the lions once they get to know you? Do the tigers drink milk? Can I name the new fawn Bambi? Can I come and live here? When will you get elephants?' Jana answered this interrogation as best she could, relieved that Karly's endless questions prevented her from having to make awkward conversation with Mark.

When lunch was done and they began to pack up, Karly was still talking. 'Will Womble be coming to live here?'

'He will,' said Jana. 'But not until we have a lovely new wombat home built for him. Then, when he's old enough, he'll go back to Odessa for a soft release. That means we'll open his pen and let him come and go as he wants. One day, when he's ready, he simply won't come back.'

Karly cocked her head to one side in that thoughtful way she had. 'That will be sad for me, but good for Womble.'

She may be a chatterbox, thought Jana, *but she's wise beyond her years.* However, when Jana asked about school as they walked back to the manor house, Karly suddenly clammed up. Jana couldn't coax a single word from her. It was only when Mark took the plates to the kitchen that Karly responded.

'I hate that school,' she hissed beneath her breath. 'Everyone's mean to me, especially Tegan, the girl who shares my room. She calls me stupid and ugly. She makes a mess in the bathroom, won't clean it up, and then blames me for it.' Karly wiped her eyes. 'And she says things behind my back.'

The girl's words hit Jana like a punch in the guts. She'd suffered the same sort of bullying for years at Scarborough. 'You're the smartest, kindest, most beautiful girl I know,' Jana said firmly, giving Karly her business card. 'Here's my number. Ring me anytime if you want to talk – day or night.'

Jana didn't have time that week to worry too much about Karly. She was conducting an audit of every animal at the zoo, down to the last feral guinea pig and errant squirrel. It was a huge job, requiring all hands on deck, and Jana was grateful not only for the four dedicated staff that had remained at the zoo, but also for Hazel Roberts.

Mark, though, only tolerated the old woman's continued presence at Wildfell Park. He took a hard-headed accountant's approach to the matter. Since Hazel held no practical or formal role, he saw her as superfluous to their business plan. He was the zoo's official bean counter after all. But his attitude verged on the condescending, almost as if Hazel remained as an indulgence to Jana, nothing more.

This irritated Jana no end. She quickly came to see Hazel as a valuable part of the zoo team. At times she didn't know how she'd manage without her. What a waste it would have been to have Hazel, with all her knowledge and experience, languishing in a retirement home. Not only did Hazel know the animals as individuals, even the camels and bison, but she also knew the keepers.

'Bruce is a skilled craftsman and builder,' she told Jana. 'The salt of the earth and indispensable to the zoo.' Standing at a towering one hundred and ninety-five centimetres, the man's muscled shoulders and weathered skin told the story of years spent toiling under the sun. His neatly cropped grey hair framed a kind but craggy face that always lit up when he talked of his young daughter, Lisa. 'He wears his love for family and his passion for work on his sleeve,' said Hazel. 'The true embodiment of a gentle giant.'

'And Johnno?' asked Jana. The second keeper sported a long, untamed mane of red hair cascading down to his shoulders. His equally fiery beard added to his wild appearance. It concealed most of his face save for a jagged scar running from his left eyebrow down to his cheek.

'He claims that scar was caused by a lion's claw,' laughed Hazel. 'But I know better. It's the result of an unfortunate drunken encounter with a tree branch. Johnno likes to whistle tunes and recite bush poetry as he goes about his work. You'll get used to it. He's annoying and entertaining in equal measure.'

The third keeper, Lexie, was a serious young woman who wore her sleek, chestnut hair pulled back in a no-nonsense ponytail. 'Lexie rarely smiles,' said Hazel, 'but her passion for the animals under her care radiates from her every action. She stayed on at reduced pay, you know, in order to help keep the zoo afloat. They all did, except for Maggie, our youngest keeper. She gave up her salary altogether and became a volunteer.'

Twenty-one-year-old Maggie, a slender, athletic girl with short, spiky brown hair, had a quick wit and a contagious laugh. And despite her tomboyish appearance, she was quite a looker. 'Maggie is a fully qualified vet nurse who's always dreamed of working with more exotic animals than cats and dogs,' said Hazel. 'She's worth her weight in gold.'

When Jana and Mark first met Maggie, she'd explained how she could afford to work for no pay. 'I moved home with my mother, Jean. It's pretty convenient. Mum only lives a few doors down from the zoo.'

'Well, your loyalty will be rewarded.' Mark had called a staff meeting, reinstating full salaries with generous top-up bonuses. 'We're doubling our workforce over the next few months,' he told them. 'Each of you will be responsible for training a new keeper. And there will be more in the future.'

Group morale, which had understandably been down in the dumps, now soared, and efficiency improved along with it. Simple jobs like preparing food and cleaning enclosures had once seemed to take people all day, leaving them little time for helping Jana with important tasks such as health checks and animal counts.

Now, suddenly, the routine jobs were completed by lunchtime. But although the staff were willing enough, just like the animals, they had their eccentricities. And understanding eccentricities, whether human or animal, was where Hazel really came into her own.

'Take the radio out of the workshop on Wednesday afternoons,' she warned Jana. 'The local station does a race day broadcast after lunch and Johnno's a sucker for a bet. He'll stop to listen to every race and never get any work done.'

And, 'Maggie's iPod is broken and she can't afford to replace it. If you buy her a new one, she'll do her rounds in half the time. Loves listening to music, that girl. She'll fairly dance her way around the zoo.'

And, 'Be extra nice to Lexie, won't you? She's left her husband and is feeling pretty low. It's her birthday next Thursday, so remember to wish her the best. She'll be thirty-three and I'm baking her favourite cake – red velvet.'

'That's very thoughtful Hazel,' said Jana.

'Nonsense, dear. I do it for all of them. It's my way of saying thank you from the animals.'

'You'll be busy when we take on new staff then.'

'The busier the better. You have no idea how good it feels to be needed again.' Hazel was positively glowing. 'Now, when's your birthday, dear?'

Jana smiled. No wonder the keepers were so loyal. You couldn't buy that sort of employer–employee goodwill, and she didn't understand why Mark couldn't see Hazel's value. His wilful ignorance on the subject made it even harder to work with him.

Jana turned away from Hazel, struggling with her feelings about Mark. She loathed the man, yet she needed his help to save the zoo. What an impossible situation! Yet somehow, for the sake of the animals, she'd have to rise to the challenge.

The first few weeks at the zoo passed in a busy blur. Mark devoted a lot of time to the project, encouraging Jana to draw up plans for new exhibits with the help of a professional drafter. He engaged surveyors, sourced building materials and liaised with the local council. He also hired someone to assist Sash at the wombat sanctuary until the new zoo enclosures were ready to house a portion of Odessa's animals.

Hazel had finally dropped her defences and welcomed them into the manor. She'd long ago lost the key to the home's grand front entrance, so everyone used the back door, which led straight into a huge farmhouse kitchen.

Jana's upstairs bedroom was the epitome of faded glory. Peeling gilded wallpaper. High corniced ceilings and dusty, cobwebbed chandeliers. It boasted its own fireplace and dressing room. The graceful casement windows had sills riddled with woodworm, but Jana still loved them. They overlooked the rear garden, with spectacular views of the river.

The lower floor of the labyrinthine eight-bedroom house was crammed with stuff. Teetering shelves of zoology books and journals in the dusty library. Cages and nets, medicines and piles of musty blankets and towels. An entire fallow deer, preserved via taxidermy, lived in the old ballroom.

When time permitted, there'd need to be a serious clean-out, but for now that could wait. The zoo's operating licence had officially expired, and they'd only been granted a temporary permit to house the animals. That period ended on the first of December, less than four months away. Then they'd have to successfully reapply or disband the collection. It was a tight deadline, so suppressing her animosity towards Mark had become a daily necessity.

The truth was that he seemed genuinely committed to the zoo, and he was being so helpful that being around him was getting easier. But it was becoming harder to repress another powerful feeling – her growing physical attraction to the man. Handling these conflicted emotions was taking its toll.

Mark had taken to popping around most mornings before work so Jana could show him how the building program was progressing and to fill him in on the latest news. A knot formed in her chest whenever he strolled in the back door – dread or anticipation, she couldn't be sure.

That morning she'd proudly revealed the extended herbivore paddock – securely fenced and almost three times its original size. 'We can graze the bison, buffalo, deer and Barbary sheep together now. Oh, and the camels and emus. Maybe give visitors rides through on a buggy. Once we get our licence, I'd love to get some zebras too. Real ones, not donkeys painted with stripes.'

Mark grinned at that, and his smile lent his gorgeous blue eyes a disarming warmth. Jana almost matched it with a smile of her own. She caught herself in time, turning away to take a sudden interest in the gatepost.

'Those donkeys fooled plenty of people back in the day,' said Mark. 'And not just children.'

Yes, they did, Jana wanted to say. *Remember when the local paper did an article on the zoo? They featured the 'zebras' and even had a paragraph about them losing their habitat back home in Africa. Everyone at Scarborough was in hysterics.*

But she couldn't say that, could she? She was still pretending not to know him, and he still hadn't remembered. The old resentment welled up. When Jana turned around and looked at Mark, all she could see was the person who'd caused her so much pain.

When they arrived back at the house, Mark changed into his business suit in the corner alcove of the kitchen. Not that she was looking, but she did catch a glimpse of nicely toned abs and muscular thighs. There was no denying that Mark was seriously sexy. But Jana didn't want to feel that old, familiar tug. She wasn't a naive teenager any more, crushing on the school football captain. She knew what he was capable of.

'I'll make us both a coffee,' said Mark once he'd changed.

Jana shook her head. 'I don't have time.' Would he never go?

Mark's face fell. He opened his mouth as if to speak, then closed it again. 'Fair enough.' He packed his bag and headed for the door.

'Wait,' she said as Mark was leaving. 'I was wondering . . . Is Karly fitting in any better at school?'

Mark turned, frowning. 'My daughter's a stubborn one. She won't give Scarborough a fair go.'

So, the answer was no. Jana had suspected as much.

CHAPTER 13

Mark checked the clock for the umpteenth time then snapped shut his box file. Finally! He had a lunchtime meeting with Jana at Wildfell Park to discuss the zoo's new website, and the truth was, he couldn't wait.

Life in peaceful little Rivertown was proving far more complicated than he'd imagined. The decision to return had seemed straightforward enough. He'd be close to his father, who would help give Karly some stability. The best school in South Australia, his own alma mater, would be on his door-step. And he could downscale from his high-powered city job to allow himself more time to spend with his daughter. Single fatherhood and a top-flight career did not make for a good match. Back in Adelaide he'd worked six days a week and frequently travelled interstate and overseas. In Rivertown he'd be able to relax and keep his weekends free for Karly.

However, things hadn't turned out that way. For one thing, Karly was more of a handful than he'd expected. She might be at boarding school throughout the week, but she still managed to cause him headaches. He received daily phone calls from the college about his daughter's antisocial behaviour. She talked back to teachers. She wouldn't do her homework. She'd pulled her roommate's hair. She'd let the sports teacher's pet cockatoo go. The list of infractions seemed endless.

'I believe your daughter is acting out because she misses her mother,' Mrs Hall had told him. 'I'm sure that you're trying your best, but a child's primary role model is the same-sex parent. Quite frankly, Mark, Karly needs her mum.'

Mark had rolled his eyes. Of course she did. Nobody needed to tell him that. But the problem was, he couldn't reach Harper. He'd tried often enough, but even her parents weren't sure of her whereabouts. When she was rostered on international routes, Harper rarely checked in with family. So the school had organised counselling for Karly to help address her behavioural issues. She refused to go.

Mark had tried everything to get through to his daughter: kindness, anger, reason, bribes and even threats. Last weekend when he'd collected her from school, Karly had demanded that he withdraw her from Scarborough College. He'd barely started the car when she began to argue.

'You say I have to board during the week because you often have to work late and can't pick me up. But there's a high school just down the road and it would take me five minutes to walk home to Paddlewheel. Why can't I go there?'

'I don't want you home alone.'

'Dad, I'm not a baby. What do you think is going to happen to me? Or do you not trust me to be sensible, is that it?'

Mark hadn't responded. The truth was that he *didn't* trust her, not after the way she'd been behaving at school.

Karly glared at him. 'Okay, I'll ask Grandma and Grandpa

if I can live with them. They can keep homeschooling me. That way I won't have to put up with you.'

Put up with me? thought Mark. That was a good one. Karly was causing all the trouble – not him. But he had to remind himself that her life had undergone some massive upheavals recently.

'Enough,' he said, trying to keep his temper. 'You'll stay at Scarborough and you'll stop misbehaving. I'm sick of fielding phone calls from Mrs Hall about your latest antics when I'm trying to work. If you don't stop acting up, you won't get that puppy.'

This last remark had resulted in a flurry of tears and a girl who wouldn't speak to him at all. Parenting was much harder than he'd imagined. Perhaps Don and Gwen could help. He'd take Karly to visit them on the coming weekend and see if she'd open up to them.

The other complication in Rivertown was Jana. Mark was falling hard. Working so closely with her and not being able to express his feelings was driving him crazy. It would have been unprofessional, and anyway she didn't even know that he remembered her. He'd changed his mind about fessing up for the time being. She'd been so unfriendly when they first met, and the only reason he could think of was that she'd recognised him from school and held some sort of grudge. Probably because of Harper's bullying. There was a good chance that Jana had tarred him with the same brush. Thinking back, Harper had been seriously mean, and not just to Jana. Mark was ashamed to think that he'd done nothing to stop her.

But since the two of them had entered into the zoo project together, Jana had become somewhat less hostile. This small change gave Mark hope. The last thing he wanted to do was spoil it by reminding her of their time at school together. Remind her of how he'd been Harper's lapdog, so besotted by her beauty and popularity that he'd turned a blind eye to her faults. Her craving for attention. Her selfishness and spite. How shallow he'd been back then.

But he wasn't a foolish, lovesick kid any more. He knew Harper for who she was. And although he regretted the impact that the unplanned pregnancy had had on her life, he couldn't forgive her for abandoning Karly. What sort of a person would do that?

Not Jana. He'd never met anyone kinder and more caring than the vet. The contrast to Harper was striking. At one time such qualities might not have seemed important, but having Karly had made him appreciate them above all others. And it didn't hurt that Jana was drop-dead gorgeous and all class. Tall and slim, she carried herself with style and poise. Raven hair framed her lovely face, and high cheekbones added a sculptural elegance to her features. Dark lashes framed her large brown eyes, giving them a sultry allure. An irresistible blend of inner grace and outer charm made Jana utterly captivating.

Mark thought about her constantly. He'd look out the window of his office, his eyes skimming over the picturesque Murray view before settling on the distant roof of Wildfell Manor – only a stone's throw from his own riverfront home. He'd wonder if she was in the house, picture her doing something simple like making a cup of coffee or brushing her hair. Taking a shower . . . Now that was a pretty picture. At times she took up so much space in his brain that he found it difficult to work. He'd open a file on his computer, staring blankly at the screen, seeing the soft curve of her face instead of a stack of numbers.

Mark had always been a stylish dresser, but now he took extra care to appear more casual. A sharp outfit wouldn't impress Jana the way it would the women he normally dated. He could tell she disliked pretension. He was so far gone that he even planned their conversations, practising a joke, an interesting story or a clever phrase in his head.

Working together on the zoo project offered the perfect opportunity to spend more time with Jana and try to win her over. He sometimes noticed her looking at him sideways, with an odd expression on her face – one he couldn't read. He'd have to come clean soon about recognising her from school, even if it did cause an issue between them. How much worse would it be for Jana to believe she was entirely forgettable?

Shutting the blinds, he pulled on boots and changed from his suit into jeans and a T-shirt. Mark had told himself earlier that he wasn't a foolish, lovesick kid any more, but maybe he was wrong. He had butterflies at the prospect of seeing Jana again.

The phone on his desk rang just as he was leaving for the zoo. Dammit. Impatience to depart almost made him ignore it – but what if it was the school? What if Karly needed him? Arrgh! Reluctantly, he turned on his heel and took the call. Not the school after all; it was Jana. A flush of pleasure spread through him at the sound of her voice.

'I've lost the buffalo.'

'What? Which one?'

'You don't understand,' she said, her voice low. 'The word "buffalo" is plural as well as singular.'

'You mean—'

'I mean I've lost the lot. All five of them.'

'Are you sure you've checked the paddock properly? What about behind the trees?'

'Mark, just get over here, will you?'

'On my way.' Despite the emergency, he still got a buzz hearing her ask for him.

Mark dashed to his car, wondering how serious the situation at the zoo really was. He'd never taken much notice of the buffalo before, but he remembered they'd been rehomed from a farm, so he guessed that meant they were fairly tame. He pictured the big grey beasts grazing in the sunshine or dozing among the trees in their paddock at Wildfell Park. They'd seemed lazy and quiet. Surely they wouldn't have gone far. He was almost happy about their escape – maybe he'd get a chance to be a hero and impress Jana.

When Mark arrived at the zoo, the first thing he noticed was the strengthening wind, whipping through the treetops and nearly stealing his hat. Blue sky was turning to grey. Dark clouds boiled in from the west, and he felt the first fat plops of rain on his skin. It made him think of his old life in Adelaide, before Karly and Jana and the zoo had become his main priorities. Back then the weather didn't matter. Working in a tenth-floor office and living in a high-rise apartment, there had been days – weeks, even – when he'd barely touched the earth. When he travelled on business, it was to Hong Kong or Singapore, places even further divorced from the natural world than Adelaide was. But now? A squall brought Mark the fragrance of river mint as he trailed his boot in the dirt. Funny how a scent could evoke powerful memories – memories of a childhood on his family's vast Murray River farm. Here in Rivertown he was becoming grounded again.

Faint shouts came from the rear of the zoo, and Mark hurried towards the sound, past the house, past the parrot aviaries and out to the large herbivore paddock. It was immediately obvious how the animals had escaped. A red gum had shed an enormous branch directly over the newly completed boundary fence beside the river. The buffalo had simply stepped over it.

To his left, three people were herding the remaining animals in the exhibit into the holding yards, hooting and shooing to drive in the last recalcitrant bison. With such a major break in the fence, it was amazing that they hadn't lost the lot.

Jana appeared from beyond the breach. She waved a pair of wire cutters in the air and shouted, 'I've found them!'

Mark jumped the fence and raced over to her. They were quickly joined by the rest of the staff, all wearing worried frowns.

For a moment Jana was too puffed to speak. She bent over, hands on knees, trying to catch her breath. Mark resisted the urge to rub her shapely back.

'They're in the river shallows,' she managed at last. 'Wallowing.'

Despite the seriousness of the situation, nobody could resist a smile. They were water buffalo after all.

'Right,' said Jana. 'All hands on deck. Lexie – go and bring back as many brooms and rakes as you can find. Pots and pans as well – anything that can make a noise. And throw in ropes and gloves too. Bruce, bring us some bales of lucerne hay. And Johnno, go get the chainsaw to clear that fallen branch.'

Johnno looked grim, the scar stretching across his face as he frowned. 'And the rifle?'

Jana's lips formed a tight line as she gave him the nod.

CHAPTER 14

Jana watched the quad bike zoom off, and then she handed Maggie the wire cutters. 'Make the gap as wide and safe as you can. Mark and I will keep an eye on the escapees.' She had to admit she was surprised that Mark had responded so promptly to her call for help – surprised and, yes, impressed. An extra person could make all the difference, although being grateful to Mark still made her feel uncomfortable.

She checked her watch. 'Shit. The *Murray Duchess* will be passing by in exactly one hour. We have to retrieve the buffalo before then. If a whole paddle-steamer full of people sees our herd running wild, we'll never get our licence back.'

Mark followed her over the fence breach and they half-ran, half-slid down the bank. On the other side of the river rose spectacular limestone cliffs, the tallest along the entire Murray River. Jana had always marvelled at the sheer yellow rockfaces that contained millions of ancient ocean fossils and whose nooks and crannies provided nesting sites for thousands of birds. But today the cliffs served another purpose; the buffalo wouldn't be able to escape across the river.

Mark looked around. 'I can't see them.'

What was wrong with him? 'Right there.' She pointed to where Bessie, the quietest cow, was browsing on weeds by the water. To be fair, she was well camouflaged among the reeds, her dark coat blending seamlessly with the dark undergrowth.

Once Mark had spotted Bessie, he could make out the other buffalo grazing nearby.

Jana picked up a solid stick almost two metres long. 'Find yourself something like this. I'll make my way upstream and try to herd them this way. Stay here and make sure they don't get past you. There's a deep, marshy place behind you. It will be much harder to get them out of there.'

'Right.' Mark hefted a fallen branch and stripped the twigs from it. Then he positioned himself in the middle of the path and planted his feet wide. 'You shall not pass!' he boomed and thumped his stick on the ground.

'Stop mucking around, will you?' But Jana smiled in spite of herself.

She headed upriver, positioning herself a little west of the buffalo, and waited for the others to arrive. Why were they taking so long?

As if the thought had summoned him, Johnno rang. 'I'll be there in five. Do you still have eyes on them?'

'I do.' She checked the time. Only fifty minutes now before the paddle-steamer sailed past. 'I'll try to push them downstream to save time.'

'No, wait for backup.'

But Jana was already shouting and waving her hat at the animals. Bessie looked up, chewing her cud, pondering her next move. Then she lumbered off towards Mark. A few more shouts and the four others followed, led by Maru and her calf. The young bull brought up the rear.

As they neared the break in the fence, a gunshot sounded from over the river somewhere. Water buffalo were sensitive to noise and frightened easily. They broke into a surprisingly fast gallop, heading straight for Mark.

Hold your nerve, Jana thought, as she hurried after them. To Mark's credit, he stood his ground, but the animals were thoroughly spooked and kept on coming. To add to Mark's difficulties, the calf had dashed ahead of its mother. Maru tossed her horns protectively, and Mark leaped aside just in time. The herd charged off into the marshy part of the river. Dammit. How would they ever retrieve them now?

The quad bikes arrived, their noise startling the buffalo again. They retreated further into the river. Great. The herd was more exposed than ever – prime viewing for anyone in a boat rounding the bend.

Deep down, Jana knew this was her fault. She'd acted prematurely, against Johnno's advice, desperate to recover the buffalo as quickly as possible. Now her impatience had cost them precious time.

Mark was extracting himself from the prickle bush he'd dived into. Before he had a chance to speak, Jana unleashed the full force of her fear and frustration on him.

'Why didn't you turn them?' she shouted. 'Now we'll never get them back in time.'

Mark stood open-mouthed, clearly taken aback by the unfairness of her complaint.

Johnno followed Jana's gaze to the buffalo, then shot her an accusing look. 'Goddammit. I told you to wait.'

Jana had the good grace to feel ashamed, both for her impetuousness and for blaming Mark. But there was no point dwelling on those mistakes. According to her watch, they had less than half an hour before the paddle-steamer came chugging down the river.

There was nothing else for it but to go in after the buffalo. They did just that, wading into the muddy water until it swamped their boots and soaked their trousers. The animals eyed the humans warily as they fanned out, trying to get behind the massive creatures. But when they began shouting and banging the pots and pans Lexie had brought, the commotion only served to drive the buffalo deeper into the water.

Mark moved nearer and nearer to Bessie, making a lot of noise until he was close enough to poke her dark grey flank with a stick. *Good work*, thought Jana, impressed. As herd matriarch and leader, if Bessie moved, so would the rest of them. With one final prod of Mark's stick, she plodded off towards the bank. The rest of the buffalo followed her, all except Jango, the young bull. He was enjoying his day on the river way too much to go home.

The two-year-old was nearing his prime, and challenge showed in his proud, square stance. Jango's massive head was crowned with a pair of formidable, crescent-shaped horns that curved outwards. He defiantly turned his back on the herd, which left his pointy end facing the keepers.

Jango snorted and mock-charged at Lexie, who backed away. As he moved, cords of muscle rippled beneath his sleek skin. The young bull exuded raw power, causing Jana to hold her breath and look towards the shoreline where Johnno had his rifle ready. Jango charged again, and this time Lexie turned

and ran – as well as a person could run when in thigh-deep
water – slipping and stumbling in the muddy riverbed. They
all hurried towards her, yelling and making a din to distract
the bull. At any moment Jana expected to hear the crack of
a bullet. But Jango pulled up short, shaking his horns. Lexie
grimaced in pain as Bruce helped her to her feet.

'She's cut her leg,' he called. 'I'm taking her back to the
house.'

Jana was close to tears. With Lexie and Bruce out of
commission, and Johnno spotting the buffalo with the rifle,
it left only three people to herd them back to their paddock.
They hadn't managed it with five. How could it work with
three? She gazed around and frowned. Make that two. Mark
was nowhere in sight.

Maggie shrugged, guessing who Jana was looking for. 'He
ran off a few minutes ago. No explanation at all.'

Coward, thought Jana. Jango's last charge must have broken
his nerve. Well, they could manage without him. She checked
her watch for the umpteenth time. Fifteen minutes left to clear
the buffalo from the Murray. Otherwise, the paddle-steamer's
passengers would have some unique holiday snaps.

Jango stamped his feet, standing his ground. Jana groaned
as the rest of the herd began drifting back towards him. The
young bull's defiance seemed to be inspiring rebellion in
the others. Suddenly, Bessie dashed past Jana and Maggie,
ignoring their shouts and waving brooms. Johnno dropped
the rifle and rushed to help, but it was no use. The whole herd
was back in the river.

Jana hung her head, defeated. They needed three or
maybe four times the number of helpers. She'd better inform

the council ranger before public reports of wild buffalo in the Murray came flooding in. They'd been lucky so far – no witnesses – but that was about to change. An approaching engine sounded from upstream. A motorboat? Someone was about to cop an eyeful. Jesus, it was loud.

A jet ski roared into sight. God, Jana hated those things. Most people came to the Murray to find some peace and get away from it all, away from the traffic and crowds and noise. Most people wanted to reconnect with nature. Jet ski hoons were the opposite, ruining it for everybody. Tearing through the quiet, polluting the water and wrecking the whole river-side atmosphere in general. They always came buzzing within metres of the bank, regardless of swimmers and fishermen. Why they weren't banned was beyond her.

A four-knot speed limit applied to personal watercraft all along the length of the Murray. This clown clearly didn't know that. He came careening towards the water buffalo, not even wearing a life jacket. Any moment now he'd see them and get the shock of his life. It would serve him right if he fell off.

But it was Jana who wound up being shocked. The herd apparently hated jet skis as much as she did, and she watched in amazement as they stampeded from the water and galloped back to their paddock. Simple as that. And a few minutes later, as the *Murray Duchess* rounded the riverbend, proudly tooting her steam whistle, the buffalo were camped calmly in their favourite shady spot among the trees.

Jana collapsed in the shallows, heart pounding. It couldn't have been a closer call. The jetskier beached his craft further down the bank, crossed his arms over the handlebars and laid his head down. Was he all right?

Jana heaved herself from the water, covered with algae and mud, dripping wet and weak with emotion. Her legs could barely drag her up the bank, but still she began plodding wearily upstream. The man might be a fool, but he'd inadvertently saved the zoo. She should at least check on his welfare. But as Jana approached, he raised his head and the truth dawned on her. The clown on the jet ski was Mark.

Jana's fatigue vanished and she hurried to him, smiling. 'That was brilliant! Why didn't you tell me what you were planning? I thought you'd ducked out on us.'

Mark grinned back and climbed off the jet ski. 'Oh, ye of little faith. But seriously, the idea just popped into my head at the last minute. There wasn't time to run it past you. My place is only a few hundred metres upriver, but even so I barely made it back before the *Duchess* arrived.'

Passengers on the paddleboat deck waved to them, blissfully unaware of the tense drama they'd missed. Jana waved back, more cheerful than she'd been in ages. Following her lead, Mark waved as well. A gush of gratitude overcame her. She gave Mark an impulsive hug before remembering herself and pulling away. Mark's eyes lingered on her lips and a sudden thrill of desire ran through her. She hadn't thought she could ever feel anything but loathing for Mark, but at that moment she wanted him. She wanted this man, whose callous actions had set in motion a tragic train of events – one that still reverberated through her family.

What on earth was wrong with her?

CHAPTER 15

Jana had hugged him. She'd actually hugged him! Mark felt like singing. How good it had felt to have her slim arms around him, and to know he'd put that look of joy on her face. And although she'd quickly pulled away, in the split second after she'd released him, he'd seen a certain conflict in her expression that gave him hope.

Mark didn't know how she could blush – not with her perfect tan and polished olive skin – but somehow she managed it. Heat rose in a fascinating way from the cleavage peeping through her open-necked shirt until it reached her cheeks. Good God, she was lovely.

His eyes focused on her beautiful brown ones. This was the time for him to come clean about knowing who she was. It might help to allay the misgivings she clearly had. His gaze held hers, unwavering. Now if she would just stay put long enough for him to choose the right words.

Maggie's scream broke the spell. The two of them ran back to where she was leaping about wildly and slapping herself.

'I stepped on a bull-ant nest,' she gasped between anguished breaths.

Maggie wore only shorts. The furious insects swarmed over her bare legs, inflicting agonising stings. Mark picked her up and ran to the river with her cradled in his arms. Together they collapsed in the shallows, where Maggie's cries abated to whimpers. She clung to Mark, her fingers laced behind his neck. He'd been bitten by bull ants a few times. Their poison combined formic acid with a venom similar to that of wasps, and he remembered all too well the overwhelming pain of a single sting. How much worse must it be for Maggie, whose legs bore more than a dozen angry red welts?

'Johnno went back for fencing gear and left me here to keep an eye on the buffalo,' she hissed through gritted teeth. 'I was watching them so closely that I forgot to look where I was going.'

Jana waded into the river too, brow furrowed in concern. 'That's a lot of stings,' she said as Maggie showed them her legs. 'Have you had a bad reaction to ant stings before?'

Maggie nodded glumly and itched her elbows. Her arms were erupting in a rash of red hives.

'Can you get her to the quad bike?' Jana asked Mark. 'She needs a doctor asap.'

'Come on.' He scooped Maggie up. 'Don't worry. I've got you.'

Jana led the way. Mark navigated through the sucking mud until he reached solid ground, only lightly burdened by Maggie's slender form. He carried her to the bike, gently placed her on the seat, and made sure she was comfortable before climbing aboard himself. 'Can you hang on to me?'

Maggie hugged him round his waist, but her grip seemed weak. Mark changed positions, so that she sat in front of him, held securely between his arms. Jana gave him the nod and mounted her own bike, ready to follow.

'Here we go.' He started the engine, the roar of the quad bike filling the air.

Despite the rough terrain, Mark managed to keep the bike steady. He could feel Maggie's shallow breathing against his chest, and he urged the bike to go faster. It seemed to take forever to reach the manor house.

Jana helped Maggie off the bike and Mark lifted her into his car. By now her face was swelling and her speech sounded slurred. 'The hospital is just a few minutes away,' said Jana in a calm, reassuring voice. 'I've phoned ahead to tell them we're coming. It's going to be okay.'

When they arrived at the emergency room, the staff quickly recognised the severity of Maggie's condition and whisked her away to be treated. Once Mark and Jana knew she was in safe hands, tension slowly drained from them like air from a pricked balloon. They sat side by side in the busy waiting room, attracting more than a few odd glances.

'I must look a sight,' he said.

Jana studied him, taking in his dripping wet clothes covered with mud and water weed. 'The *Creature from the Black Lagoon* springs to mind,' she said with a wry smile.

'So, you like old B-grade horror flicks?' Mark shuffled his feet and fished a slimy stick from his sodden boot while he gathered courage. 'How about we have a movie night sometime?'

He didn't know quite what to expect, but it wasn't such a ready acceptance of his invitation. 'Pick a night and I'll make dinner first,' she said. 'It's only fair that I should thank you for saving the day – twice. You're quite the hero.'

Mark's heart swelled with pride. He'd never heard her sound so animated – or so complimentary.

'Can you imagine what would have happened if you hadn't turned up on that stupid jet ski?' she asked. 'I hate those things, by the way.'

'So do I,' he said, resolving to advertise the jet ski for sale the very next day. 'Stupid, noisy things.'

Jana regarded him quizzically. 'If you think that, then why do you have one?'

'Ah . . . it came with the house,' he lied. 'I'll get rid of it.'

She looked sceptical. 'No, don't do that. What if the buffalo escape again?' Her smile was gently mocking.

'I'll moor the jet ski at the zoo then,' he said. 'It can be our official water-buffalo-retrieval device.'

Jana laughed. Her tongue ran over lips parched from too much sun. He wanted to take the lip balm from his pocket and use it to soothe them. Seeing her so happy and relaxed after the strain of the afternoon brought him a flush of pleasure.

Mark reached for his phone to check the time, but it wasn't in his pocket. Where was it? Dammit – he'd left it in the car. He wondered how many messages he'd received from the office. It must be well after two o'clock, which meant that at the very least he'd missed his appointment with the council's chief financial officer. That was unfortunate. Landing the local government account had been seen as quite a coup by the other partners. He hoped he could square away his failure to show up without too much trouble.

Mark knew he should get back to the office, but he was reluctant to leave Jana. After such an eventful afternoon, the prospect of working on profit-and-loss statements held no appeal. And with an intimate movie night with her in the offing? Well, he might never be able to concentrate again.

A nurse came over. 'Your friend is fine, and she'll be ready to go in half an hour or so. Doctor will send her home with an EpiPen. You know what that is? Maggie should carry it with her whenever she works outside.'

'Of course. This is a huge lesson for us.' Jana thanked the nurse and breathed a great, relieved sigh.

She turned to Mark. 'We need allergy kits on hand at the zoo: EpiPens, antihistamines, all of it. At the moment there's nothing. When I asked Johnno where the first aid kits were the other day, he just shrugged. So I asked Hazel. She dug around in the back of a cupboard in the house and produced a dusty zippered bag with half the contents missing.'

Mark almost said that he'd get onto it right away, which would have sounded faintly ridiculous. The day-to-day organisation of the zoo had nothing to do with him, not officially anyway. He was far too ready to help – too darned eager to impress Jana. His work colleagues had noticed, and they were starting to remark on his particular dedication to the Wildfell Park account. *You're devoting a hell of a lot of time to that menagerie by the river. I've never seen a man so keen for overtime and lunchtime meetings. Wouldn't have anything to do with a certain pretty vet, would it?*

Up until now, the ribbing had been lighthearted and

nobody had seriously complained. After all, Frieda Abraham
was underwriting the zoo's attempt to win back its licence,
and she was by far the firm's wealthiest client. However, now
he'd missed an important meeting and questions would inevitably be asked. In between dealing with Karly's school and
being at Jana's beck and call, his regular duties were sitting in
a poor third place. He intended to change that. But for now,
he'd simply bask in the pleasure of being Jana's hero.

'I can wait and drive you both home,' he offered.

'No need,' said Jana. 'Johnno's already on his way.'

Mark pushed aside the ripple of disappointment. Just as
well. He really needed to get back to work, but all he could
think about was the upcoming movie night. 'Don't forget our
date, will you?' he said as he stood up.

Jana's expression changed subtly at his use of the word
'date'. Her smile faded and her brows furrowed for a fleeting
moment. Her response was measured, her voice laced with a
hint of uncertainty that hadn't been there before. 'Does Friday
or Saturday suit you best?'

His heart fell a little. It was only Monday. Why wait so
long? But as he was about to suggest an earlier day, Jana
continued.

'I'll go online tonight and check out which flicks will be
okay for Karly. Not that those movies are actually scary – more
funny than anything else. But it's different for a child, isn't it?
I remember being terrified by an old movie about giant mutant
ants when I was a kid . . .'

But Mark was barely listening. He hadn't figured on Karly
joining them, and it took him a second to adjust his expectations. Was it really such a problem? He'd still get to spend

time with Jana – that was the main thing. And Karly would be stoked at the idea of a movie night at Wildfell Manor.

Mark gave a cheery wave that he didn't feel, and reluctantly left the waiting room. He missed Jana already. He'd impressed her today, but something was still holding her back. He recalled her early, unremitting hostility. Would the shine of his good deeds wear off in the next few days? He'd just have to wait and see. The weekend couldn't come soon enough.

CHAPTER 16

Jana tidied the small sitting room off the kitchen that she was using to interview new staff for the zoo. It was a more casual, welcoming setting than the upstairs office. Another applicant was coming this morning, but Jana wasn't hopeful. So far, the standard of candidates had been disappointing. Of the dozens who'd applied, only a handful had made it to the interview stage. The rest were either inexperienced with animals, lacked references, or else some gut instinct told her that they wouldn't work out. She had to be able to trust her keepers completely. So much for doubling the workforce. Having the funds to employ more people didn't mean the right people were available. And none of the suitable candidates would commit to leaving their current jobs until Wildfell Park was closer to completion.

Jana swept a few crumbs off the table and tied back the open curtains to let in more light. Chintz chairs faced the narrow fireplace, which was covered with a fine layer of dust. A spider had woven its web over the rusty set of tongs that lay beside the hearth.

'Knock, knock.'

Jana turned to see a twenty-something woman in the doorway. She wore jeans fitted tightly over plump hips. Her dark hair fell in a windswept tangle over intelligent grey eyes.

'Hello there,' said Jana with a smile as she introduced herself. She took a manila folder from a shelf and flipped through it. 'Please have a seat. Good. Now . . .' Jana consulted her notes. 'Amber Brown . . . Your references are excellent. What experience do you have in animal care?'

'Well, I've been volunteering at the local animal shelter for the past two years. I've also worked part-time at a stable where I took care of horses.'

Jana nodded. 'Why do you want to work at Wildfell Park?'

Amber's face lit up. 'I've been following the news about the zoo reopening, and I think it's an incredible opportunity to make a difference. I want to be part of a team that's dedicated to conservation and animal welfare.'

Amber's eagerness impressed Jana. 'That's exactly the kind of attitude we're looking for. Tell me, Amber, have you ever worked with any exotic animals before?'

She hesitated. 'No, I haven't. But I'm a fast learner, and I'm not afraid of a challenge.'

Jana smiled again. She was liking this girl more and more. 'That's great to hear. We'll provide you with all the necessary training, of course. And you'll be starting out as an apprentice to one of our current zookeepers, so you'll be learning along-side an experienced staff member.

Amber looked like she might burst with happiness. 'That sounds perfect. I'm ready to put in the hard work.'

Jana leaned forward. 'One thing to keep in mind is that working with our animals is not just about feeding and cleaning. It's about building relationships with them, understanding their behaviour and providing enrichment.'

'Enrichment?'

'Yes. Enrichment is anything that promotes mental and physical stimulation. It's as essential to animal welfare as nutrition and veterinary care. Some examples might be puzzle feeders that encourage animals to forage for food, or climbing structures that enhance habitats, and training sessions where animals can interact with keepers. It's all part of giving our charges the best possible care. Can you handle that kind of responsibility?'

Amber thought for a moment. 'My younger sister has been sick a lot. Helping my mum and dad look after her has taught me plenty about empathy and patience. If you take a chance on me, I promise to dedicate myself fully to the job.'

Jana nodded. 'I believe you, Amber, and it sounds like your family is lucky to have you. Welcome to the team at Wildfell Park. Can you start in the morning?'

Amber's smile broadened as she stood up. 'Thank you so much. I won't let you down.'

Well, that went well, thought Jana as Amber left. If she could find a couple more candidates like Amber, they'd almost have a full complement of keepers. In the meantime, she'd better ring Mark and ask about hiring some maintenance contractors. They should be a lot easier to find than animal-care staff, and it was a waste having Bruce and Johnno spend so much time in the workshop. They might not have university qualifications, but years of zoo experience made them worth their weight in gold.

Mark. His handsome face swam before her. That chiselled

jawline. Those ocean-blue eyes holding a hint of mystery. The faint stubble on his cheeks that gave him a rugged charm. And his warm, boyish smile. She'd much rather talk to him in person than on the phone. Her impatience to see him surprised her – and it wasn't driven purely by gratitude.

She could no longer deny the slow-burning tug of physical attraction between them. Yet she still blamed him for what had happened at school and for her parents' accident. Jana pictured her father sitting in his wheelchair, smiling but unable to speak as Jana updated her parents over FaceTime about the animals at Odessa and the zoo. A wave of guilt washed over her. Why was she even contemplating a thing with Mark? Thank goodness she'd invited Karly to the movie night so it couldn't be considered a real date – the young girl would be a great buffer.

She'd been too long without a man, that was her problem. If Harrison even qualified as a man. After his base betrayal of her – and of himself – he didn't deserve the title. Jana had met Harrison at Adelaide University – her first proper boyfriend. A fellow vet student, he'd borne a passing resemblance to Mark, with his tall physique, sandy-blond hair and dimpled chin. That likeness should have warned Jana off, but instead it had proved to be perversely alluring.

Their intense affair had opened up a whole world of sensual experience. She'd been so caught up in the thrill and pleasure of great sex that she'd missed something important. They lacked a true emotional connection. It was partly her fault. After what had happened at Scarborough College, she held her heart too tight. Harrison probably couldn't have reached it if he'd tried. But the problem was, he didn't try. Their two-year romance was more like a succession of lust-fuelled hook-ups than a real relationship, and she was too young and inexperienced to realise that.

As a realist and not a romantic, Jana had never expected to find the kind of lifelong soulmate that some of her starry-eyed friends at uni had dreamed of. But she had at least expected loyalty. So she couldn't believe it when, in their final year of study, Harrison plagiarised her research findings and passed them off as his own. In that same week she found him in bed with another girl, and the last vestige of her faith in men withered and died.

After graduation, Jana had fled Adelaide, moving back to Odessa with Sash. She found a job at the local veterinary clinic, and a wonderful new passion for wildlife rehabilitation and research. She'd always known about the wombats that lived at the family farm. They often destroyed fences, and although they were protected, some farmers still shot them, considering them no more than pests.

Not her father, though. He'd taught his children to respect the wildlife that shared their home. 'The wombats were here first,' he used to say. 'We're simply squatters on their land.' Jana had taken his advice to heart, even if it did make her laugh when the marsupials dug cavernous holes right next to his carefully installed wombat gates.

But as a kid she hadn't realised how special Odessa's wombat colonies truly were. Southern hairy-nosed wombats were endangered in the Murraylands, many suffering from starvation, mange and liver disease as a result of eating toxic weeds. After her return to Odessa, she and Sash had become dedicated to their protection.

Caught up in this new passion, Jana discovered that she didn't miss Harrison as much as she'd thought she would. But she did miss the sex, and there hadn't been another man since – not for three long years. Now, here was Mark. She was a young woman in the prime of life, with natural desires, and she knew he was interested. Breaking the drought with him was an undeniably tempting prospect, and during her time working alongside him at the zoo, she'd learned to push her old resentments to the background. For the most part, anyway. Perhaps, if she buried them even deeper, she could allow him into the physical side of her life. But she wouldn't forgive him for what had happened all those years ago – not ever.

Jana had thought Mark might drop by before Friday. After all, they never ended up having that lunchtime meeting about the zoo's website – the wayward buffalo had seen to that. But when she'd rung on Tuesday to suggest they reschedule, he'd sounded crazy busy.

'It'll need to be next week, now,' he'd said. 'Howard thinks I'm spending too much time on the Wildfell Park account. We're still on for the movie night Friday though, right? Karly is so excited.'

Jana had hung up, more disappointed than she'd expected to be. It was probably just as well. Mark was a distraction from the more important things that she should be concentrating on. Such as the problems thrown up by the recently completed animal audit.

They had way too many of some animals and not enough of others. Monkeys, for example. Their small enclosure was overcrowded. Four monkeys – crab-eating macaques, to be specific – had been ostracised from the main group, including an elderly female with an infant. The outcasts huddled miserably in a cramped corner, unable to avoid being harassed. They urgently needed rehousing.

Fallow and hog deer overran the place too. Many had escaped into the surrounding bushland, along with some emus and Barbary sheep. They'd be a nightmare to round up. A neighbouring farmer had already complained to the council. And although the dozens of cheeky squirrels living wild on the zoo grounds had once been a hit with visitors, their escapades couldn't continue. They needed to be trapped and contained, along with many of the peafowl, guineafowl and chooks that roamed the park.

Then there was the other problem: the zoo was short of the most popular, exotic animals. True, they had three lions, but King was almost twenty years old, and the two lionesses were his granddaughters. Hazel had imagined that he was far too old and infirm to father offspring, but she'd been wrong. A few months ago, Nala had given birth to a single cub, who'd survived for less than a day.

A simple solution would have been to castrate King. But that wasn't an option for several reasons. Modern zoo theory discouraged the desexing of captive animals. Anti-zoo campaigners also frowned upon it, and the last thing Jana wanted was to draw the attention of the Animal Defenders, a local animal rights group. They'd made trouble for Hazel in the past, picketing Wildfell Park and protesting about cage sizes and overcrowding. To be fair, they'd had a point back then, but Jana planned to address their concerns and try to win them over.

It wouldn't be easy. Their leader, a charismatic redhead named Annie West, had a regular spot on regional radio. She also hosted a popular podcast where she courted all sorts of controversy. Jana herself was a regular listener. Annie often invoked outrage from the conservative rural community by criticising common agriculture practices, such as the use of feed lots, or pesticides on crops, or live exports. In one infamous episode, she'd stated that the meat industry should be banned, and that farmers should swap beef-growing for tree-growing and make their living from selling carbon credits.

Annie was a polarising figure, sometimes accused of using extreme tactics to get her message across. But on more and more issues, the tide of public opinion was turning in her favour. Many people in the community no longer supported battery farming or animals in circuses, for example. A growing number of European companies were boycotting Australian wool because of the widespread practice of mulesing, where skin was removed from a sheep's backside without pain relief to prevent flystrike. A recent national poll found that three out of four citizens disapproved of live sheep exports.

Annie West encouraged people to recognise the rights of animals to live without fear, discomfort, stress and cruelty. She had a lot of supporters, mainly in Adelaide, but increasingly in regional South Australia as well. Locking up animals purely for the sake of entertainment was becoming more and more frowned upon. Wildfell Park was just such an old-fashioned zoo. Jana planned to drag it into the twenty-first century, putting it at the forefront of modern conservation efforts. Not only was such a plan a dream come true for Jana, but it might also neutralise the threat posed by Annie

West and her group. If Annie could be persuaded of the value of captive breeding programs for threatened species, her tick of approval would go a long way towards securing the zoo's future.

Jana wanted to not only house and rehabilitate southern hairy-nosed wombats at Wildfell Park, but also Tasmanian devils. Her idea was to house a healthy insurance population, far from the facial tumour disease that was ravaging wild populations. Soon she would visit Tasmania's Binburra Devil Park, where she'd done post-graduate work. It was the world's foremost research and breeding facility for these endangered marsupial carnivores. She dreamed of being part of the national network of parks dedicated to protecting them.

But first Jana had to deal with the animals she already had, and the lions were top of her list. After the tragic death of Nala's inbred cub, she'd given the lionesses contraceptive injections. She couldn't have predicted that the altered hormones would cause such a radical change in their behaviour. The five-year-old sisters, who'd lived peacefully together since birth, suddenly hated each other.

Nothing could have prepared Jana for the sheer ferocity and terror of watching Nala and Cleo fight that first time. Thank God Bruce and Lexie had been with her. Their quick thinking – turning a fire hose on the snarling combatants – had undoubtedly saved the lives of one, if not both, of the sisters.

Since then, the two lionesses couldn't be left together, which meant they had to alternate time out in the exhibit. It was an impossible situation – cruel to both animals. Even now, as Jana wandered down the river walk, she could hear Cleo roaring in protest at her confinement and bashing against the walls of her den. She still had four more hours before it would be her turn outside. Jana urgently needed to rehome one of the sisters, but so far she'd had no luck.

Another concern was Sol, the sun bear, who'd been wild born in the dense forests of Cambodia ten years ago. He'd been taken from his mother, who was killed by poachers and sold to the restaurant trade. As a very young cub, confined to a small wooden crate, he too had awaited his future of ending up on a menu. A lucky twist of fate had seen Sol and another bear cub rescued by an expatriate businessman, who also happened to be Hazel's brother. He'd purchased them and taken them to a bear sanctuary in Phnom Penh. The cubs were deemed too humanised to be returned to the wild, so one went to Taronga Zoo and Sol came to Wildfell Park. Sun bears were not only the world's smallest species of bear, but also one of the rarest. Jana hoped she might someday find Sol a mate. *Don't get ahead of yourself,* she thought. They needed to replace the sagging wire fence surrounding his exhibit and upgrade his den if they were to reclaim their licence.

Then there were the two tigers. She'd also given the female, Ruby, a contraceptive injection to allow time to carry out genetic testing on the pair. Thankfully, it hadn't altered Ruby's relationship with Raj, her mate, and the two were still friendly. Jana hoped that if the testing was favourable, they might breed. She imagined a litter of tiny tiger cubs and could already picture the delight on Karly's face.

What had made her think of Karly? With so much to do, it was a miracle that Jana had time to think of anything but the mammoth task ahead. But Mark and his daughter still managed to occupy a fair portion of her thoughts. She could use some downtime, and what fun it would be to introduce the girl to *The Killer Shrews* or *Attack of the Crab Monsters*. She could see them all sitting on the huge old Chesterfield couch, screaming and laughing and eating popcorn, her leg pressed against Mark's. The thought sent a small shiver of desire through her. She quickly shook off the feeling and tried to pretend she wasn't counting down the days until Friday.

CHAPTER 17

Mark turned onto the groomed gravel drive of Scarborough College. As he passed through the imposing gates, a child ran onto the drive.

'Shit!' He slammed on the brakes. Thank goodness he'd been abiding by the twenty-kilometre speed limit. He hated to think what might have happened had he been going any faster. Even so, he couldn't completely avoid the girl. She bounced off his bonnet and slid to the ground, the scene seemingly playing out in slow motion.

Mark dashed from the car to find his daughter slumped on the gravel. 'Oh no, Karly! Are you okay?'

She turned her dust-streaked face to him and managed a wan smile. She looked more shaken than hurt. 'I wanted to surprise you.'

'Well, you succeeded.' Mark's heart pounded like a drum in his chest. His breath came in ragged gasps as he fought to calm himself.

A teacher rushed over as Karly tried to stand. 'No, don't

get up until the school nurse has checked you over.' She was already on the phone.

Mark sat down beside his daughter, arms clasped around his knees. 'I seem to remember us being told the rules about school pick-ups on that first day. "Students are to wait in the quadrangle near the car park until their parents arrive. On no account must they leave the grounds by themselves." Is that how it went?'

'Something like that,' Karly whispered sheepishly as he hugged her to his chest. 'I was just in such a hurry to leave. You know how much I hate this school. I thought I'd make a quicker getaway by meeting you at the gate.'

'Well, that plan sure backfired.' He drew a line in the gravel with his finger. 'Who knows how much longer we'll have to hang around now?'

'But Jana's waiting for us,' she wailed. 'What are we going to do?'

Mark drew some more lines in the gravel. 'Play noughts and crosses?'

'Dad!' She punched his arm but couldn't hide a playful smile. 'Let's just go. Who cares about their stupid old nurse, anyway?'

Mark coughed loudly and poked her gently in the ribs as a female voice sounded from behind them.

'Hello.' They looked up to see a pretty red-haired woman wearing navy scrubs. 'So, Karly . . . that stupid old nurse would be me. You really shouldn't refer to a member of staff like that. What would Mrs Hall say?' The warmth of her smile belied her stern words. 'Right, let's take a look at you.' A few minutes later the nurse gave Karly a clean bill of health.

'Nothing but a few scratches and bruises. Now, Karly, I hope you've learned why students aren't permitted to wander onto the driveway.'

'Oh, I'm sure she has,' said Mark quickly. He glared at Karly, who picked a leaf from her hair and gave a half-hearted nod. Mark thanked the nurse and opened the car door for his daughter. 'We'd better skedaddle,' he whispered. 'In case you get kept back for detention, or something.'

Karly leaped in and they were off before anything else could go wrong. Why, oh why, did he have such a wild child? Mark couldn't understand her aversion to school. As a child he'd loved Scarborough College. With his actress mother overseas a lot and his politician father in Canberra more often than at the family farm, Mark could never wait for his lonely holidays to end. And after his parents divorced, well – boarding school had become a true home away from home. His friends were there, his sporting life, his teachers and mentors.

Scarborough had been the centre of his world. Mark's sense of identity had been inextricably linked to the school, and he wanted Karly to experience that same satisfying camaraderie. But to hear her talk, Scarborough was more like a prison than a refuge. He glanced across at his daughter, her face shining at the prospect of a night at the zoo. *Give her time*, he thought. *Give her time.*

'I love Nala.' Karly snuggled closer to the den. The lioness made a soft chuffing sound, bumped the wall with her head, and stretched out beside the girl on the other side of the wire.

Mark knew that his daughter was safe. Not even a child's finger could fit through the tightly woven steel mesh separating her from the big cat. But he still felt an instinctive, creeping fear – an evolutionary response. Humans weren't supposed to meet such powerful predators and live.

'Why is the lion making that noise?' he asked Jana, not knowing why he whispered. Nala turned a baleful eye on him.

'It's kind of like a big cat version of purring,' said Jana. 'Karly's lucky. I've never heard Nala make that sound for any human except for Hazel. It's a friendly vocalisation used between a mother and her cubs, or towards a mate. And sometimes a favoured keeper.'

'Well, it's giving me the creeps,' he said. 'Come on, Karly, it's almost dark. Let's go collect dinner.'

'It gets dark so early,' complained Karly. 'I haven't even said hello to the bear yet.' She turned to Jana. 'It's Dad's fault we got here so late. He ran me over in his car.'

Jana turned wide, shocked eyes on Mark, who sputtered in outrage.

'I didn't run her over. I just hit her with the bonnet – quite gently, really – and the car was barely crawling . . .' Jana's eyes widened further. 'And anyway, it was Karly's fault. She ran onto the road.'

Mark groaned inwardly. By trying to salvage the situation, he'd only dug himself into a deeper hole. Who blamed a child for being hit by a car?

'Is that how you got those cuts and bumps?' Jana asked Karly.

She nodded and turned solemn eyes on her father. 'Don't worry, Dad. I forgive you.'

'Right.' Mark marched over to Karly and grabbed her hand. Nala's chuffing became a growl, but he held his nerve 'We're going to the pizza shop before Jana calls child protection services on me.'

When they returned with the food, Mark was delighted to find Jana relaxing into the evening. As she fetched plates and glasses from the kitchen, she talked eagerly of her forthcoming trip to Binburra Devil Park in Tasmania.

'When do you leave?' he asked. Her enthusiasm was infectious.

'On Monday. I met Penny Abbott, the park director, during my research stint at the University of Tasmania. We hit it off.' She shot him a wry glance. 'I don't usually do that with people. Anyway, we talk all the time now, and she's promised me some devils once we have our operating licence. Wildfell Park and Odessa will be part of the Aussie Ark program, providing insurance populations of healthy devils. There are even plans to return them to the wild in mainland Australia for the first time in thousands of years. Maybe Odessa could be a release site. It already has a licence, and Sash says she'd be happy to manage devils there. Isn't it amazing?'

You're amazing, he wanted to say. Jana was a beautiful woman, but passion and excitement now lent her a special loveliness. Some unexpected magic transformed her from beautiful to radiant when she smiled. Mark couldn't hide his lovesick grin, although Jana didn't seem to notice.

They all sat on the old leather couch in front of the television, eating and drinking and watching terrible movies. Karly alternated between screaming with laughter and screaming in fright. Watching her was way more entertaining than watching the screen. Mark and Jana exchanged frequent, amused looks, ate way too much pizza and sat close enough together for their thighs to touch.

Jana laughed and talked and flicked her dark, shining hair. She'd never seemed as well-disposed towards him. So much so that Mark wondered if he'd imagined her former hostility. Jana's buoyant mood got him thinking – was tonight the night to confess that he knew who she was? That he remembered her from school? The crowd he'd hung around with back then, mainly Harper's friends, had treated Jana badly, and he'd done nothing to stop their bullying. Jana deserved an apology, however belated.

But he couldn't have that little heart to heart with Karly listening in. He checked the time – almost ten o'clock. The opportunity was fast slipping away.

Just then Hazel came in. 'What's all this noise?' She wore mismatched pyjamas that clashed in the most endearing way. Her top sported Beatrix Potter cartoon characters, while her pants were printed with tiny silver pocket watches hanging from golden chains. Hazel wore curlers in her silver hair, the small vanity at odds with her practical disposition. The curlers were a mix of pastel hues – soft pink, baby blue and pale yellow – all neatly arranged in rows across her head like a colourful crown. Karly gawked at the unfamiliar sight, but she was too polite to say anything.

'Sounds like you lot are having a party,' said Hazel. 'Why wasn't I invited?'

'You were, Hazel,' said Jana, pausing the film. 'I told you

we were having a movie night, but you said that you didn't like horror flicks. Remember?'

Hazel glanced at the screen. 'What are you watching?'

'*Attack of the Giant Leeches*,' said Karly, enthusiastically. 'It's great. People are disappearing into this swamp where monster leeches suck out all their blood. Do you want to watch it too?'

Mark expected some sort of criticism from Hazel for exposing his twelve-year-old to such a film, but instead the old woman's eyes twinkled with delight.

'When I said I didn't like horror flicks, I meant the modern ones filled with chainsaws and blood,' she said. 'But I like the old ones. In fact, I remember this particular film. It's surprisingly good.'

'Then come and watch it with us,' said Karly, sitting on the floor rug to make room on the couch. 'Here, have some pizza. And there's lemonade.'

Hazel sat down and took the plate Karly offered her. Jana restarted the movie.

This could be his chance. Mark waited a few minutes until Hazel and Karly became engrossed in the film. Then he tapped Jana's knee, pointed to the kitchen and whispered, 'Can I have a word?'

CHAPTER 18

Jana followed Mark into the dimly lit kitchen, their footsteps echoing in the old house. Her heart quickened, all senses on high alert. Was this it? Would he finally admit his monstrous deceit? And if so, could she forgive him? Perhaps, if his apology was sincere enough. He'd only been a kid, after all – seventeen years old. No, she was getting ahead of herself. She'd have to wait and see.

Mark gestured for her to take a seat at the massive kitchen table. The worn wood felt cool against her palms when she gripped its edge, as if holding on for safety. Jana watched him carefully, her eyes searching his face for any hint of what was to come.

And then it happened. 'I've known who you are for some time now, Jana,' he said. 'Not when we first met, but after doing some online sleuthing, your surname triggered my memory. We went to school together, right?'

He looked at her expectantly. Unbelievable. Did he expect her to help him?

After a long pause he continued. 'Did you recognise me straight away?'

She nodded, too stunned to speak. How on earth would he handle this? How would she? Would Mark try to justify his appalling behaviour? No, that wasn't possible. There was no justification for such a malicious act, and the shine had well and truly come off the evening. This conversation was unearthing all the bitterness and blame that she'd tried so hard to bury. Jana suddenly wished that he wasn't coming clean – wished that they could go back to the way they were before he'd led her to the kitchen.

Mark nervously cleared his throat. 'I just want you to know that I remember how mean Harper and her friends were to you back then. They treated you like crap. I should have called them out at the time, but I didn't. It was wrong and shameful and I'm truly sorry.'

Finally, an admission of guilt. But what exactly was he sorry for? Jana's eyes remained fixed on him, waiting, keeping her expression blank. Harper had been a bitch, but she wasn't the main issue here. Mark's attempt to shift the blame was only making things worse.

He ran a hand through his sandy-blond hair. 'That's why you've taken so long to warm to me, isn't it?' Mark finally asked, his eyes searching hers. 'Because of what Harper did to you back at school?'

Jana nearly laughed, a bitter edge to her amusement. Was he serious? A retort hovered on the tip of her tongue, but she swallowed it down. What did he want her to say? His half-hearted apology fell so far short of what she'd needed to hear.

Did he truly not remember what he'd done? Or did he just not want to admit it to her – or maybe even to himself?

An awkward silence yawned between them. Jana couldn't bring herself to look at him. The hurt she'd carried for so long, for so many years, felt overwhelming. She pushed her chair back abruptly and stood up, the loud scrape against the wooden floor breaking the quiet of the room.

'If that's all,' she said coldly. 'I don't want to miss the end of the movie.'

Afternoon shadows lengthened as Jana gazed at the view from the verandah of Dr Penny Abbott's modest weatherboard home. Situated on the rim of Tasmania's vast Tuggerah Valley, the house was perched halfway up the hill above Binburra's home compound. The park stretched out before her under a cloudless sky. The buildings and enclosures were designed to blend seamlessly with the native trees and gardens, providing as natural an environment as possible for their residents. In the distance loomed a series of rugged peaks, rising like battlements into the blue. A shiver ran up her spine knowing that thirty thousand hectares of pristine World Heritage–listed wilderness surrounded her.

Penny joined her at the railing. She was an attractive woman with a full figure, copper-coloured hair, freckled dimples and clear blue eyes.

'You have the best view in the world,' sighed Jana.

Penny grinned. 'True. Although your riverlands are lovely too. Matt and I took a houseboat up the Murray once. The waterbirds, the red gums, the play of light on water. So peaceful.'

'A subtler beauty,' agreed Jana, sweeping her arm to indicate the grandeur all around. 'Nothing as dramatic as this. Although if you ever saw the Murray in flood, you wouldn't call it subtle.'

'I guess so. Come on,' said Penny. 'You can give us a hand feeding the orphans. We always have too many.'

Jana's pulse quickened. 'Do you have devil joeys?'

'We do. Devil, wallaby and wombat joeys. Take your pick.'

'Wombats?' laughed Jana. 'Well, I'll feel right at home.'

Jana had spent the day touring the park, paying particular attention to the devil enclosures and breeding facilities. Penny had been generous with her time, providing all sorts of practical information and scientific notes to help Jana prepare Wildfell Park and Odessa for the future arrival of devils.

As evening fell, the two friends finished their work and headed to the Hills End pub for a well-earned feed. Penny's husband was away with their five-year-old twins and wouldn't be back until tomorrow. 'Matt's taken the kids to visit their grandfather in Hobart. Fraser is in a hospice.'

'I'm sorry to hear that.'

'The doctors say that he hasn't got long to live, but frankly they've been saying that for years. The stubborn old bugger is determined to prove them wrong. Why don't you stay tonight?' said Penny. 'That's if you don't mind sleeping in the twins' room. We'll have to sweep the Lego off the floor first. That stuff is deadly for bare feet. And you have the choice of a steam-train themed bed or one decorated with lion cubs.'

Jana jumped at the offer. 'Lion cubs will be perfect.' Who knew when she'd get a chance to visit Tasmania again, and she was determined to make the most of it. She sipped her wine. Delicious. What was it about Tasmania that made everything taste better? Maybe it was the air – the cleanest in the world. Or maybe it was the remoteness. Or the primeval wilderness and wild oceans. Whatever it was, her senses seemed heightened, more attuned to her surroundings. She hadn't felt this relaxed and connected to nature since before Mark had pulled her out of that wombat hole.

When they arrived home from the pub, Penny opened another bottle of wine. They took it out to the verandah, sat on a pair of comfy old armchairs, and talked long into the night about all and sundry.

'How did you meet Matt?' asked Jana. Penny's husband was head ranger at Binburra National Park. To Jana it seemed like a match made in heaven.

'We met at the Hills End show, at the woodchop,' said Penny. 'My boyfriend back then was state champion. Anyway, Matt came over to me and asked if I would go on a date with him if he won the woodchop. I was that flattered. He was the best-looking bloke I'd ever seen, so I said yes.' She smiled, a little ruefully. 'Does that sound shallow to you?'

'Yes,' laughed Jana. 'But I would have done the same thing.'

'Well, there's not much more to say. Matt entered the comp at the last minute and won.'

'And what about the boyfriend?'

'He was furious. My uncle had to break up the fight. I kept

my word, though, went on the date, and the rest is history. We were married six months later.'

'How old were you?'

'Eighteen.'

Jana felt bewildered. 'That's very romantic, but you were both so young. How did you know it would last?'

Penny shrugged. 'Beats me. We just did.' She poured Jana another shiraz. 'Your turn. You've told me all about the zoo and Odessa. How's your love life?'

'I haven't been so lucky.' Jana took a big swig of her wine. The temptation to unburden herself was strong. She could share her impossible romantic dilemma with Penny in a way that she couldn't with her mother or sister. Distance made her feel safe.

So Jana poured out her heart. She told Penny of her long, lonely years at Scarborough. Of the awful treatment she'd received at the hands of the popular kids and mean girls. She told her of the humiliations heaped on her by Harper Clark. 'She'd sit behind me in class, passing notes to her friends with snide comments about my looks. Sometimes she'd scrunch them up and throw them at the back of my head, making the entire class erupt in laughter. And once, during gym class, I opened my locker to find it filled with crumpled paper and smelly, stale food. Harper had scrawled "Trash for the trash" on the inside of the door. It mightn't sound so bad, but . . .'

'Mightn't sound so bad?' echoed Penny. 'Are you kidding? It sounds absolutely appalling, especially considering you were a vulnerable teenager. And to think you were stuck there twenty-four seven with those dropkicks. Way to ruin your self-esteem.'

Jana looked gratefully at her friend. How wonderfully validating to have a sympathetic ear. It tempted her to go further.

'I had a crush on a boy right through high school. Mark Bell. Captain of everything. Rich family. Movie-star good looks.' Jana smiled to herself at the sheer absurdity of her feelings back then. 'You think *you* were shallow going for Matt because he was handsome? Well, you should have seen *me*! Mark only had to point his dimpled chin in my direction and I went weak at the knees.'

Penny nodded, her expression wistful. 'Nothing moves you quite like first love, does it? It's a powerful thing.'

Jana forged on, convinced now that if anyone could understand, Penny could. 'Of course, I never acted on it. The nerdy scholarship kid and the football captain? And besides, he was sweet on Harper. No, a secret infatuation was enough for me.' Jana faltered. She was about to tell Penny something that she'd never told a single soul.

'Then in the final term of Year Twelve, Mark sent the first text message.' A weighty pause. 'Harper had left the school by then. He said that he'd always liked me and wanted to go out with me.'

'You must have been thrilled.'

Jana flinched at the memory. 'Thrilled is an understatement. For three weeks I lived in a state of euphoric bliss, unable to sleep, to eat. Unable to concentrate on studying. I really opened up to him about my life – but it was all via text. That should have rung alarm bells, but I was so stupidly head over heels . . .'

For a moment she couldn't continue. Penny smiled in encouragement.

'I confessed how lonely I'd always been at Scarborough and my dream of being a vet. I told him how much I missed my parents and what it meant to have finally found a friend. He said that he missed his parents too and understood how I felt. Mark was a terrific listener and really seemed to care. But he explained – again by text – that he didn't want us to go public until after the exams so it wouldn't become a big distraction. When we saw each other in class, Mark was friendly, maybe a little flirtatious, but he kept his distance – even though I was dying to kiss him.'

'I suppose that makes sense,' said Penny, but she looked doubtful.

'I was so head over heels that Mark could have told me that black was white and I would have believed him. Then he started saying that he loved me. Well, I fell right into the trap, writing soppy love poems about him being my whole world – you know the sort of thing.'

Penny frowned and shifted in her chair. 'I don't like where this is going.'

Jana took a bottomless breath. She couldn't stop now. 'On the day before my first exam, Mark dropped his bombshell. It had all been a joke. His mates had made a bet that he couldn't make the geeky scholarship girl fall in love with him. To win the bet and prove that I'd fallen for him, he had to publicly post everything I'd sent him to the Year Twelve Instagram account.'

'Shit, Jana. Everything?'

Jana was grateful for the darkness as she felt her face flush scarlet. 'Everything. Every idiotic, lovesick message that I'd sent him. He said it was my own fault for being gullible enough to believe that he liked me. He said I should try to see the funny side. Then he blocked me.'

For a long time, nobody spoke. Jana allowed the awful revelation to sink in before continuing. 'I couldn't stick around to watch the fallout. I ran away that night and tried to hitch-hike home. When I got halfway, I rang my parents to come get me.' She was rushing her words, hurrying to reach the end of the terrible story. 'A truck hit their car. My dad has permanent brain damage, and my mum is his full-time carer.'

'Fuck, Jana. That's some story. Do you know what happened to the prick?'

'I do,' she wailed. 'He's the accountant for Wildfell Park. And despite everything he did to me, I think I'm falling for him all over again.'

CHAPTER 19

Wednesday morning, and Mark didn't recognise the female voice on the end of the phone.

'I'm coming to Rivertown this weekend,' the woman said. 'And I'm planning to stay with you.'

It took him a few moments to make sense of what he'd heard. 'Harper? Is that you?'

'Well, of course it's me. Surely you know my voice?'

He thought he did, but she sounded different somehow, like she was putting on an even posher than usual accent. And why on earth would she want to stay with him? In the last conversation he'd had with Harper Clark, she'd accused him of ruining her life.

'How are you, Mark? How is our daughter?'

How was Karly? She was wonderful on weekends – sunny and enthusiastic about the time they spent together. Loving their visits to Grandpa and Grandma, and Jana. But during the week at boarding school, she was a different child. Surly and troublesome. A rude and rebellious loner with dismal grades, according to her teachers. Mark had been so sure that

Scarborough was the right place for her. He knew from experience that it was a wonderful school. Surely things would turn around soon.

'Mark, I asked you about Karly. Is she enjoying school? Your father sent Mum a photo of her in her uniform. So cute! That picture really took me back. It could have been me.'

No, it couldn't have, he wanted to say. Karly was nothing like Harper.

'I hope she's keeping up academically. She was an A student when she lived with my parents.'

Well now she lived with Mark and was a D student – when she passed at all. Mark struggled to find a way to answer Harper's question. How was Karly?

'Karly's fine,' he said at last. 'Just fine.'

'I can't wait to see her,' said Harper. 'I've missed her much more than I thought I would.'

Really? thought Mark, though Harper sounded sincere. In the past few months, she'd only rung her daughter once – the day after Karly's birthday. 'I meant to ring you yesterday,' she'd apparently said. 'But I was in Dubai and the phone reception was dreadful. Did you get my present? I sent it ages ago.'

A birthday gift with a card from Harper had arrived the next day. Sender? Harper's mother.

'Mark? Has the cat got your tongue? You've hardly said a word. Anyway, I thought Karly and I could do something special this Saturday. I've booked us a mother–daughter pamper day at the Riverside Spa to make up for missing her birthday. I didn't know that Rivertown even had a spa. It must have come a long way since when we were at school.'

Oh no. Jana had promised Karly that she could help round

up squirrels at Wildfell Park on Saturday. Unlike Australia's possums, squirrels were diurnal – active during the day. The staff had spent weeks accustoming them to entering spring-loaded cages baited with fruit and nuts, hung from trees throughout the zoo. They planned a trapping blitz this weekend, and it was going to be all hands on deck. Even Mark had been roped in to assist with health checks and record keeping. Not that he minded. Mark welcomed any excuse to see Jana. He could just imagine Karly's disappointment at missing out. She wasn't a day-spa kind of girl.

'I wish you'd given us more notice. Karly and I already have plans for Saturday.'

'Then change your plans. I've gone to a great deal of trouble to organise this weekend, and I'm entitled to see my daughter.'

There was an edge, now, to Harper's voice. Mark thought furiously about how to handle her request. Quite a nerve, to simply invite herself to stay with them. But then again, that was Harper. There was a time when he'd been impressed by her brash confidence. But not any more. He might have only been a full-time father for a few months, but it had been long enough for him to resent Harper barging in and making arrangements for their daughter without consulting him.

And then there was Jana. While she'd been in Tasmania, he'd missed her more than he could have imagined. The view from his office window had seemed diminished. His gaze had automatically travelled to the distant roofline of Wildfell Manor where it showed above the trees, but knowing that Jana wasn't there had left him feeling empty, and he couldn't wait for her to come home. Before she left, he thought they'd been making a connection – that was until he'd confessed to remembering her from school. After that she'd seemed to shut down again, freezing him out. So how would she react to her schoolyard nemesis moving into his home? The timing couldn't be worse.

It occurred to him that before Karly and Jana had come into his life, he'd been adrift. He hadn't really cared about anybody but himself – not properly. Now he was caught in an avalanche of caring. It took some getting used to.

'Mark?' Harper imbued the one word of his name with a frightening frostiness. 'Are you still there?'

What on earth was he going to do? He needed time to think. He squeezed his eyes shut and cursed himself for being a coward. 'Sorry, Harper. I'll need ring you back.' Then he hung up. Pressing the button for reception, he said, 'Stacey? Hold my calls.'

Mark finally got through to Mr Brand, head of the junior school. 'I need to see my daughter today. How does 12.30 work?'

'You must understand, Mr Bell, that it's very disruptive for students to have the structure of their day interrupted. Is this an emergency?'

Was it? 'Yes.'

'In that case, can I inquire what kind of emergency? Has a family member been hurt? Should we arrange for Karly to have counselling around the news?'

'No, it's nothing like that. But it's still important that I see her. It's about her mother.'

Mark endured the long, disapproving silence.

'Very well,' said Mr Brand at last. 'I'll arrange for Karly to be available for you at lunchtime. But please don't make a habit of this.'

'Dad!' Karly ran across the boarding house's formal sitting room and nearly leaped into his arms. She reminded him of an excited labrador puppy. 'I'm so glad to see you. Are we going home?'

Mark led her to a settee by the wide casement window overlooking the grounds. 'Let's have a talk.' He hated letting Karly down. He knew how much she was looking forward to squirrel-catching day. But she needed to know that her mother wanted to see her on Saturday.

Karly grew quiet as he talked, tilting her head to the side and watching him with intense blue eyes. Mark finished speaking and licked his lips, his mouth dry, his heart heavy for his daughter. Yet to his surprise, she brightened.

'Don't look so sad, Dad. I can chase squirrels some other time. I'm sure you won't be able to catch them all in one day.'

At first Mark was relieved that she was taking it so well, but then he became curious. 'Don't you mind?'

'Yes, a bit. But I do want to see Mum.' As she became accustomed to the idea, her rising excitement showed. Her eyes shone and she bounced from foot to foot. 'I can't believe she's actually coming to Rivertown. Is she staying with us? I didn't think she'd ever come here. She took me to a spa once before when I was ten, and then a lady did her make-up. You wouldn't believe how beautiful she looked. I think Mum is the most beautiful mother on earth, don't you?'

Mark pressed his lips together and forced a smile. 'She's very pretty, just like you.'

Karly shook her head. 'Oh no, she's *much* prettier than me. Is she really coming? Can she stay with us?'

A teacher came in and introduced herself. She looked pointedly at her watch and caught Mark's eye. 'Time's up, Mr Bell. Karly will be late for music.'

Mark half-expected his daughter to argue. From the expression on the teacher's face, so did she. However, Karly simply smiled and said, 'Yes, Miss Carver.' She gave him a quick hug and demurely left the room.

'I'll see myself out,' said Mark, swallowing hard. He escaped into the hallway and strode out through the heavy double doors with their intricate stained-glass panels. He paused on the wide bluestone verandah, confused. The meeting with Karly hadn't gone at all as he'd expected. What a fool he'd been. It made perfect sense that she'd rather see her mother than spend another Saturday with him. He'd only had Karly for a few months. She'd lived with Harper and her parents all her life – of course she'd miss them.

A ripple of jealousy travelled through him. Now that he knew his daughter, he wished that he'd made more of an effort to see her in the previous years. A few half-hearted visits to Harper's parents' house. A few awkward outings to parks and cinemas. He'd had no idea what Karly liked. Instead of Barbie movies, he should have taken her to zoos and aquariums. Instead of buying her dolls and jewellery, he should have bought her chemistry sets and books about nature. Karly had confided in him that she'd always wanted a microscope. When she'd told her mother, Harper had laughed and said she needed to be more girly. His daughter could have used an ally, and if he was honest with himself, he could have used the responsibility.

He'd done as he pleased for most of his life, going from one girlfriend to another, never sticking with anybody, his attention always captured by the next shiny thing. Always putting his career first. Women liked him – wealth and good looks meant there was always another pretty girl around the corner. So it had come as a rude shock when Karly came to live with him, demanding by her very existence that he prioritise her above all else. But he'd found a deep and unexpected satisfaction in fatherhood, and a pride too. He wasn't only proud of his baffling daughter, he was proud of himself, as if he'd finally grown up. He liked the life he was building with Karly.

And now Harper threatened to swoop in and change things again. Considering his years of neglectful behaviour, he had no right to feel possessive, but he couldn't help it. What if Harper wanted Karly back? That awful possibility didn't bear thinking about. Perhaps he would let Harper stay with him; it would give him the opportunity to sound her out about her future plans. And it would please Karly.

What about Jana? She'd be back from Tasmania in the morning. They had a long overdue lunchtime meeting to discuss the zoo's website, among other matters. Jana didn't even know who Karly's mother was yet. He'd have to tell her about Harper – about her coming to stay for the weekend. He should have mentioned it earlier, but he'd been too much of a wimp. Mark had a terrible feeling that his cowardice was about to come back and bite him.

Mark looked around, as if he might find the answer

somewhere in Scarborough's manicured grounds. Losing Jana's friendship would be unbearable; she meant that much to him. He kicked the verandah post. Damn Harper! Then an even scarier thought struck him. Perhaps he was fooling himself. Perhaps Jana wouldn't care at all.

CHAPTER 20

Jana pulled her Jeep into the sweeping driveway of Wildfell Manor. She'd made some important decisions while she was in Tasmania – and they weren't just about devil enclosures and conservation plans. Jana had made a decision about Mark too. She'd been right – it had helped talking to Penny. Someone who was totally removed from the situation. It had put things in perspective.

'Mark behaved appallingly,' Penny had said, visibly shocked by Jana's tale.

The scarring memories, Mark's base betrayal – none of it seemed quite so painful once she'd voiced it. Sharing her story had somehow diminished its power to hurt her.

'So how on earth could I have feelings for the man again?' she'd asked her friend. 'I must be a fool.'

Penny had looked thoughtful. 'Don't be so hard on yourself. However callous and shallow Mark's behaviour was, it happened twelve years ago when you were both kids. And you said yourself that he's a good dad to Karly. Becoming a father might have changed him.'

'Maybe. I can't imagine the Mark I know today being so cruel. The whole situation is weird. He finally confessed to knowing me at school, and he apologised for hanging out with my bullies and not standing up for me. But he didn't apologise for stringing me along with texts and then publicly humiliating me online. He's either in denial or he actually doesn't remember.'

'That is weird. Call him out when you're ready. But it's not as though you're contemplating some deep and meaningful love affair with this bloke. You said you've got the hots for him and there's nothing wrong with that. Maybe you should just go for it – get him out of your system.' Penny pinned her with serious eyes. 'Only if you can keep hold of your emotions, though. Try to think like a male. Don't complicate things.'

So that's what Jana intended to do – have a fling with Mark and get him out of her system. Then she could stop mooning over the man. With so much to do at Wildfell Park, she didn't need the distraction. And at the moment Mark was distracting her in a major way. The mere thought of their lunch meeting later that day gave her goosebumps.

Jana spent the rest of the morning catching up individually with the zookeepers. 'How's Amber doing?' she asked Lexie, who'd been tasked with taking the new girl under her wing.

'Really well. She's a hard worker, a quick learner and seems genuinely interested in the animals and their routines. I think we're lucky to have her.'

Jana smiled to hear it. She'd had a feeling that Amber would work out. 'I'm going to quickly look in on the big cats.'

She checked the time on her phone. 'Can you get everyone to meet me at the café in half an hour?'

Thirty minutes later, Jana waited inside the partially renovated café. Eleven o'clock and not a tradie in sight. She made a mental note to call the builders. With such a tight deadline, they couldn't afford to waste entire mornings without progress.

When everyone had arrived, Jana began. 'I'm pleased to announce our plans for the new devil enclosures. Two display dens will go beside the main wombat exhibit,' she explained. 'Their low concrete walls will be in keeping with the rest of the area. And we'll have multiple breeding pens behind the veterinary centre that will be off limits to visitors.'

'So we're definitely getting devils?' asked Amber.

'Definitely. Dr Penny Abbott, the director at Binburra Devil Park, has guaranteed it, along with our place in the Aussie Ark program.'

A murmur of excitement rippled through the assembled staff. Jana continued. 'But it all depends on us getting our operating licence back, so let's get cracking. Johnno, we need the sun bear's fence completed by Saturday to keep our renovation schedule on track. Bruce, go ahead and order that extra timber for the new monkey house.'

'I have bad news,' said Johnno. 'The builders found asbestos in the café's roof and have stopped construction. They're waiting on a removal company to start work. It could be a long wait.'

'How long?'

'At least eight weeks.'

Jana frowned. 'Can't we hurry them up somehow?'

Bruce shrugged. 'We could order a rush priority job, but that will cost almost double.'

'Do it.' She was supposed to run any major new expenses past Mark, but they couldn't afford an eight-week hold-up to their restaurant build. It had to be finished by the first of December, along with everything else, and they'd be cutting it fine as it was. Thank goodness for Frieda Abraham's generosity and deep pockets. Frieda had been thrilled to hear of Jana's plans for the devil conservation program and had happily funded the new compound. Jana didn't doubt that she'd understand how urgent the café development was.

Returning to the matter at hand, Jana asked, 'And Lexie, are the squirrel cages ready? We'll need a lot of them. Karly can help you set them up on the day with fresh hay, food and water.'

Lexie smiled and saluted. 'Yes, sir.' Then she added, 'That girl's going to have a ball.'

At noon Jana rushed back to the manor house to shower and change. Not that she intended to dress up for the meeting with Mark. During the week, she and the staff wore khaki keepers' uniforms, à la Steve Irwin. But she'd at least put on a clean shirt.

Jana sat upstairs in the office with a strong mug of coffee. She scrolled through the zoo's updated online presence, all the while keeping an eye out the window for Mark's car. The new website and social media accounts wouldn't go live until he gave them the thumbs up, but she was proud of her efforts. Jana had worked past midnight most evenings to create the website. The old one had been invisible to search engines and was barely navigable. What a wasted opportunity. There was no point in having a world-class attraction if nobody could find it.

Jana had always been interested in web design and had enthusiastically applied the most up-to-date techniques to the Wildfell Park site. But she also had to give credit to Karly, whose suggestions had given the content a special edge. The girl had spent so many hours with Hazel, learning about the zoo animals. Sol's heart-wrenching rescue from the Cambodian restaurant, hours before he was to be cooked. The blue-and-gold macaw who'd been rescued from a budgie cage so small he couldn't even stand upright. The macaques' endless soap opera. Their social manoeuvrings read like a monkey *Game of Thrones*. Who would come out on top? The endless plots and pranks, alliances and rivalries provided a wealth of engaging material.

These personal stories gave website visitors a special insight into the zoo. They could feel connected to the animals before they even met them. A gallery featured every species held at Wildfell Park, and clicking on a photo took you to an information page that included individual bios of the zoo residents. Combined with live webcams showcasing the big cats, parrots and monkey house, the new site offered plenty of interest.

Jana had added one more feature – a fundraising page with a countdown clock to the last day the zoo could legally hold animals without a renewed licence, barely three months away now. Not that the park was short of money, not with

Frieda Abraham behind it, but extra funds never went astray. Jana planned to keep any donations in a separate emergency account. But she had another motive for including the page: the psychology of it. By donating, site visitors would feel personally invested in the project. It was the same reason why people were advised not to offer dogs free to a good home. A person would value something far more if they'd paid for it.

Jana read over the page, with its call to action, one more time.

'I hope you've enjoyed meeting the animals and birds of Wildfell Park. You may have read that the zoo is currently closed. We are working hard to regain our operating licence by improving the facilities, modernising the animal enclosures, building an education centre and preparing a conservation plan. However, the clock is ticking. If we don't succeed in our efforts by 1 December, the zoo's collection of animals will be dispersed. Some of them will find new homes. Some won't. That will break all our hearts.

'On this page you can donate to our renovation fund or sponsor an animal. But you can also help us in other ways. Volunteer. Get the word out about what we're trying to do. Talk to coworkers in your lunchroom. Write a letter to the editor of your local paper. Put up a link to this site on your Instagram or Facebook page. Come December, a groundswell of public support behind us will be worth more than money.

'Please help save our zoo – your zoo – and turn it into the world-class conservation park that we know it can be.'

Right, that should do. Jana snapped the laptop shut just as Mark's car pulled up. Something caught in her throat as she watched him get out, looking so casually handsome. He stood tall and confident in fitted moleskin trousers, sunshine catching the natural highlights in his sandy-blond hair. She'd been thinking about him all day, looking forward to seeing him. Now she almost wished that he'd turn around and go away. Jana replayed the discussion with Penny in her head. *Get him out of your system*, she'd said. Well, that's what Jana would do – but what would that look like? She knew that Mark was keen on her and that she was overthinking it. She ran her fingers through her hair, undid the top button of her shirt and then did it up again. What was she going to do – seduce him on the desk in the study, with Hazel next door? *Relax*, she told herself, taking a gulp of coffee that by now was lukewarm. *Just go with the flow.*

'Knock, knock?'

Mark appeared in the doorway. Jana's stomach flipped to see him, and she spilled coffee down the front of her shirt.

'Are you okay?' He bounded over, plucking a wad of tissues from a nearby box and firmly wiping the spill.

'I'm such a klutz,' she said, more flustered than ever by his touch. He leaned close, his smile warm. She wanted to capture that smile with a kiss, but the moment passed. 'Well,' she said, regaining her composure and opening her laptop. 'Are you ready to see our new website?'

'In a moment. First, I'd like to talk to you.' He pulled up a chair on the other side of the desk. 'It's about squirrel-catching on Saturday. Karly won't be coming.'

'Why ever not? She was so excited about it, and we could really use her help.'

'Something's come up.' He looked down, then away. 'Can I get you a fresh coffee?'

'No, you can't,' said Jana, mystified. 'You can tell me why Karly can't come.'

Mark swallowed hard, furrowing his brows. He ran his forefinger along the edge of the desk. He still wasn't meeting her eyes. For whatever reason, he was finding this difficult.

'It's Karly's mother,' he said at last. 'She's coming to Rivertown on Saturday. We had no idea – she just rang out of the blue. I'll still help out with the squirrels, if you want me to, but you can understand that my daughter hasn't seen her mother for months, so . . .'

'Of course. Karly must be thrilled.'

'Her mother was away a lot while she was growing up – travelling for work for months at a time. Karly's maternal grandparents pretty much raised her by themselves before she came to live with me. I'm surprised she's willing to miss squirrel-catching day.'

Jana gave him an odd look. 'Well, to be fair, *you* were away for years at a time, and Karly still loves you to bits. And anyway, maybe her mum's had a change of heart. Karly's only twelve. She still needs a lot of raising.'

Mark rubbed the back of his neck and took a deep breath. 'Look, there's something about Karly's mum that I haven't told you. You actually know her – or used to know her, years ago. We both did.'

Jana frowned as confusion washed over her. 'But how? I haven't seen you since—' Then comprehension dawned, and her expression hardened. 'Are you telling me that Karly's mother is Harper Clark?'

CHAPTER 21

Of course. In hindsight, she should have been able to guess just by looking at Karly. The fair curls, the peaches-and-cream skin, turned-up nose and baby-blue eyes. She looked exactly like her mother.

But she didn't behave like her mother. Karly displayed no hint of vanity. Not with her baggy clothes, messy hair and junior Blundstones. Jana was sure that, even at twelve, Harper would have dressed like a fashion plate. Even when wearing the standard Scarborough uniform, she'd managed to look stylish. But their differences ran far deeper than that. Kindness defined Karly, along with scientific curiosity, a lively mind and a deep love of animals. As Jana remembered it, Harper had only been interested in herself.

Jana wasn't petty enough to blame a child for the sins of her parents. If anything, she felt sorry for Karly. Imagine having that spiteful, selfish bitch as a mother. But the knowledge was nonetheless confronting. More than that, it triggered feelings that she was currently trying hard to forget.

Harper had zeroed in on Jana from her very first day

at Scarborough College. Taunting her, ridiculing her, sabotaging her friendships. Making life at boarding school a misery. Sometimes Jana still had nightmares about classmates teasing her and their mocking laughter. But these bitter recollections were inextricably linked to memories of Mark, who'd been Harper's boyfriend during those last two years at school. Despite Harper's venom, she'd never caused the kind of all-consuming, white-hot humiliation that Mark had. Jana blinked hard. Only minutes ago, she'd been fantasising about kissing the man. What was wrong with her? Had she forgotten the awful ramifications of what he'd done?

She met his concerned blue eyes. But instead of butterflies, all she felt was distaste. She'd wanted to get him out of her system. Well, she didn't need to sleep with him to make it happen. His news about Harper had accomplished that goal far more simply.

Mark was talking, trying to explain why he hadn't told her earlier, apologising. She let him finish, not really listening. 'Where is Harper staying?'

He opened his mouth to speak, then closed it again, bowing his head.

'Ah . . . with you.'

'Karly wants her to, and it will give me a chance to suss Harper out.' He scrubbed a hand over his eyes. 'To be honest, Jana, I'm pretty thrown by this. Barely a phone call for months, and now Harper suddenly wants to spend the whole weekend with Karly. It seems odd.'

'There's nothing odd about a mother wanting to see her child,' snapped Jana. She didn't want to talk about it any more. She opened her laptop. 'Now, do you want me to take you through the new website or not?'

Mark nodded, then reached for her hand. She recoiled, like his touch might burn. The corners of his mouth turned down and he looked . . . well, he looked lost. But she wasn't falling for those sad, puppy dog eyes. The thought of Mark spending the weekend with Harper made her feel sick. From now on, their relationship would stay strictly professional, as it should have all along.

'Well, what do you think?' asked Jana when Mark had finished exploring the social media content she'd created for the zoo, including Wildfell Park's brand-new Facebook, Instagram and TikTok accounts. 'I've kept the website streamlined and easy to navigate. I can add some more jazzy features if you like, but I think simple is best.'

Mark widened his eyes and smiled. 'You call this simple? Live webcams and a countdown page? Project material for schools? Dozens of individual stories that personalise the animals? It's fabulous.'

His praise pleased Jana more than she wanted it to. 'The animals' stories are thanks to Karly.'

'Karly? How would she know so much about the animals?'

'By listening to Hazel. Those two have spent hours together. Hazel's a font of knowledge when it comes to the zoo, and Karly's so quick to learn and remember. I had my doubts when she told me that the lions liked to sit in boxes, just like your average domestic cat. So I crosschecked the story with Hazel. She showed me photos of the three lions, each squashed into a cardboard carton and looking immensely pleased with themselves. Did you see it?' She navigated to the lions' page, which featured the photo. 'Apparently Hazel has an arrangement with a local white-goods store. They save their biggest boxes and deliver them to the zoo on the big cats' birthdays. The tigers love them too.'

'That photo's charming,' said Mark. 'People will love it. But why didn't you just go directly to Hazel for these stories?'

'She's not as forthcoming with me as she is with Karly. I think Hazel feels on the outer. This zoo's been her life, but now so much is changing, and so rapidly. We're under so much pressure to meet our deadline that even I forget to consult her sometimes.'

'Well, frankly, why should you? It's not like we'll change a project if she disagrees – which she often does. She took me to task over the new macaque house last week, saying there was too much private space for the monkeys to hide from visitors. She seemed to want them on display every minute of every day. "You'll disappoint the children,"' he mimicked in a high voice.

'Well, that's how things used to be done. Do you know that the last Tasmanian tiger died of exposure in Hobart Zoo because they locked her out of her den in the dead of winter? They didn't even bother to let her back in at night. Visitors had complained that they couldn't see her.'

'That's what I mean. Hazel's idea of a zoo is rooted in last century. You're the director now, Jana. You're the expert.'

'I know. I just wish she felt more valued. That's why I had Sash send us the falcon and goshawk from Odessa: Spirit and Captain. They can't be released, but you should see Hazel with those birds! She's teaching them to free fly and they're loving it. She might not be up to date with modern zoo philosophy or design, but she's an expert with individual animals.'

'Maybe so, but that doesn't justify her interfering. And she takes up your time. I hear that you drive her to the doctor – even take her shopping. It's not fair on you. I still think she'd be better off in a retirement home.'

Jana's jaw stiffened. 'Once – I took her to the doctor once. And I take her shopping after six o'clock, which is technically my own time. Not that anything feels like my own time any more. I seem to work around the clock. I'm not complaining – I want to. But it's a bit rich for you to grumble about what I do after hours. I don't appreciate you checking up on me.'

She glared at him, challenging him to disagree, but he made no response. She suddenly realised that this was the first argument they'd had. It made her miserable. And this whole rotten episode with Harper's forthcoming visit made her even more miserable. Perhaps it was for the best. Karly would have her mother and Jana would have a less complicated life.

'So,' Jana said when the silence grew too awkward. 'Do we go live with the new website or not? I can capitalise on the support that the Odessa Wombat Sanctuary site already has online. We should be able to quickly build an audience.'

'Yes, go live.' Mark looked as wretched as she felt. 'Have you set up a separate account for the donation page?'

She nodded. 'If we fail to save the zoo, we'll return all the money.' Jana stood and glanced towards the door. 'Well, if there's nothing more . . .' But against her better judgement, she wanted to hear more – more about Harper. When was she arriving? How long was she staying? Was she interested in getting back with Mark? These unspoken questions flashed through her mind, seemingly against her will.

'I was wondering about Saturday,' said Mark, his voice halting. It was strange to hear this ever-confident man sound so unsure. 'Do you still want me to join the squirrel catch?'

'No, we'll manage,' Jana replied, curtly. 'You'll be busy with Harper.' Her words clearly stung him, but she didn't care. 'Say hello to Karly for me.'

And with that, she swept from the room.

CHAPTER 22

It was almost school pick-up time on Friday afternoon. Howard and the others were working from the Renmark office, so Mark was alone at work, except for the receptionist. Just as well. He couldn't hide the anxiety he felt about Harper's arrival. He was watching the clock, eager to collect Karly and see how she was coping. Better than he was, he suspected, remembering how excited she'd been at the prospect of seeing her mother.

Mark had barely made it through the last couple of days. He felt like an automaton, coping by keeping busy and working overtime each evening. Taking it hour by hour, day by day, trying not to think too far ahead. Trying to cram his emotions back into the Pandora's box that he'd somehow opened.

He and Jana had seemed to be connecting, getting closer, moving past their troubled history. It had meant the world to him, and now she'd cut him off. The minute he'd mentioned Harper, everything had changed between them. Mark missed her with a vengeance. He dared not close his eyes, for fear of seeing Jana's beautiful face in exquisite detail. Her determined chin, straight, narrow nose and high cheek bones. Her wide-set brown eyes, arching brows and shining raven-black hair.

He'd been with lots of attractive women, but he'd never been *in* love before. Sometimes he'd wondered if it wasn't in him to fall in love. Wondered if some defect in his character made it impossible to care romantically for a woman the way that other men did. Until he met Jana. He was in love with her; he knew it now. He fervently wished that he wasn't, but the anguish he felt at their rift brought the truth home with unbearable certainty. Who knew love could be so painful? All those songs of heartbreak and loss made sense to him now.

It wasn't just her beauty that had entranced him – it was her unique character. Her sincerity, integrity and compassion. Her prodigious intelligence. The fact that she knew her own mind and would not toe the line or bow to convention, even when she'd been a friendless, bullied schoolgirl. She was brave. In Jana he'd found a true free spirit and she fascinated him as no other woman ever had.

To top off all those wonderful qualities, she was a natural role model for Karly. The pair shared so much. Their passion for animals. Their courage and independent spirits. And both were honest to a fault. He'd been pleased to see Karly looking up to Jana, seeking the sort of guidance that a father might not be able to give his young daughter. But now, with her mother back in the picture, Karly might look to Harper instead. That possibility filled him with deep unease.

He'd tidied his desk and stood to leave when Stacey put through a call from Jana. Yes! Perhaps she'd changed her mind and was inviting him to the squirrel catch. He couldn't think of anything worse than moping around at home alone tomorrow, feeling sorry for himself.

'Mark,' said Jana as soon as he picked up the phone. 'We have a problem.'

He'd welcome a problem if it meant that Jana might need him. Mark thrilled at the use of the word 'we'. They hadn't felt like a 'we' this week. 'Can I call you in half-an-hour?' he asked, grabbing his hat. 'I'm about to pick up Karly.'

She seemed not to hear him. 'The zoo's social media accounts have been hacked by trolls. I've had to shut them down. And we've received anonymous threats via the website.'

Mark sat back down. 'What sort of threats?'

'Veiled ones so far. Things like, "If you don't halt work on the zoo you'll be sorry" and "We can arrange for you to feel as desperate as your poor animals." Here's another one. "Zoo curators don't deserve to breathe the air." They even threatened Hazel by snail mail. She received a note that read, "We advise you to withdraw the zoo application immediately. Wildfell Manor is such a lovely old home. It would be a shame if something happened to it."'

'Jesus, Jana. Have you called the police?'

'Apparently, they can't do anything. Even if they knew who was behind it, there's no legally actionable promise of harm. The threats are too ambiguous.'

'I bloody well know who's behind it,' said Mark. 'Annie West and her pack of misfits. What do they call themselves?'

'The Animal Defenders,' Jana replied. 'They have a lot of supporters, even out here in the regions. But we can't be sure it's them. Hazel said there'd been one or two developers sniffing around before we got involved.'

'My money's still on Annie's group,' said Mark.

'Do you think it was too soon to revamp the website?' Her voice faltered. 'Perhaps we should have flown under the radar for longer. Should I take it down?'

'No way.' Mark boiled with protective outrage. 'You've done a spectacular job and we need to get the community behind us. Don't be intimidated by a bunch of nutters.'

'Their leader's no nutter,' said Jana. 'Annie's a qualified environmental scientist. She's actually done some great things. If it wasn't for her, the Walkabout Marshes would have been drained for dairy farming. Now they're an internationally recognised Ramsar wetland.'

'Well, good for Annie. But shutting down Wildfell Park isn't a great thing, is it?' Mark checked the wall clock. 'Look, I have to go. I'll call you tonight.'

'Won't you be busy with Harper and Karly?'

'Jana,' he said, as earnestly as possible, hoping she'd hear the wanting behind his words. 'I'll never be too busy for you, okay?'

A hesitation, then, 'Okay.'

Mark hurried to the car with a renewed spring in his step. He and Jana would deal with Annie's opposition together. It might even bring them closer – if not for Harper's visit, of course. That had really thrown a spanner in the works. It was the only reason he could think of to explain why Jana had gone so cold on him again. He should have come clean with Jana from the beginning about who Karly's mother was – he knew that now. Then it wouldn't have come as such a shock.

But he'd be damned if he'd let Harper's arrival ruin his chances with Jana. Somehow, he'd make Jana understand how much she meant to him.

Mark tried to pull himself together during the short drive to Scarborough College. It was time to stop thinking about himself and start thinking about Karly. She'd need all the support he could give her this weekend.

He picked up a daughter alternately jumping for joy and quaking with nerves, talking nineteen to the dozen one minute and lapsing into apprehensive silence the next. When they arrived home, she rushed around the house, deciding whether each room passed muster. She was a demanding critic.

'I wish you'd bought different toilet paper. Mum likes the sort with flowers.'

And, 'You should have put roses beside her bed. These daisies look lame, and they're all droopy. I'm throwing them out.'

And, 'Dad, you haven't unpacked the dishwasher. Mum's due any minute. Where will I put dirty plates after we have the welcome cake? I can't just pile them in the sink. Mum hates that.'

Mark frowned. Damn, he knew he'd forgotten something.

Karly stared at him, open-mouthed. 'You didn't forget the welcome cake, did you?'

'I'm sorry, love. Get in the car and we'll run down to the IGA. We can buy some fresh flowers as well.' *But not roses*, he thought. There was no way he'd be giving Harper roses.

Karly glared at him. 'Mum won't eat supermarket cake. Will the bakery still be open?'

'I'm afraid not.' Mark rummaged around in the walk-in pantry and emerged with a packet-cake mix. 'How about homemade?'

'What sort is it?'

'Banana.'

Karly shook her head. 'No good. Mum doesn't like banana.'

Mark almost quipped that Harper didn't seem to like much of anything, but he bit his tongue.

'Anyway, there's no time. She'll be here in half an hour.' Karly opened a bottom drawer in the kitchen and took out a pack of Tim Tams. 'These will have to do.'

'Hey,' complained Mark. 'That was my secret hiding spot.'

Karly rolled her eyes at him. 'I'll go and change. Can you pick some flowers from the garden and put them in a vase by Mum's bed?'

'What flowers? I haven't noticed any.'

'That's because you never spend time in our garden. The daphne by the trellis is flowering, and so is the lavender. And there are jonquils and snowdrops along the river path. None of those flowers are very big, but they smell nice. And anyway, they'll be better than nothing. Oh, and put a jug of lemonade and some glasses on the table in case Mum's thirsty. Don't forget to add ice. And lemon slices. Mum likes lemon slices.'

She rushed upstairs, leaving Mark scratching his head. It seemed Karly's nerves were catching. He hadn't spent any time with Harper since Scarborough, at least not without her lawyers or disapproving parents hovering close by. As a schoolboy he'd been naive and – yes – superficial enough to be impressed by appearances. But beauty was indeed only skin deep. He knew that now, and he wasn't looking forward to making stiff conversation with a virtual stranger.

Mark finished putting out the lemonade and glasses. Karly came downstairs, clumsy in high-heeled sandals, and he did a double take. Her hair hung loose, floating like a golden cloud around her slim shoulders. She wore a white halter-neck top and slinky pink miniskirt that made her look like she was sixteen, not twelve. And why were her lips so red?

Karly did an awkward twirl and pinned him with anxious eyes. 'Well, what do you think?'

What did he think? He thought she looked ridiculous. There was nothing recognisably Karly about the girl standing before him. Was this how Harper expected her daughter to dress?

'Dad – how do I look?'

'Very pretty.'

Karly heaved a great, relieved sigh.

'But don't you think you're too young for lipstick?'

'Mum says nobody's ever too young for lipstick.'

'Fair enough.' The last thing he wanted was to make this meeting more difficult for Karly.

'I made this for Mum. Do you think she'll like it?' She showed him an elaborately decorated card, covered with pressed flowers and flowing script. The card read, 'I love you, Mum, and I've missed you like crazy. Thank you for coming to see me.'

'It's beautiful, honey. She'll absolutely love it.'

'Is it six o'clock yet? She said she'd be here at six.'

He glanced at his phone – 6.15 p.m. 'I'll order dinner, shall I?'

'Not pizza,' said Karly. 'Mum—'

'Let me guess – your mum doesn't like pizza.'

Karly nodded.

'What then? Rivertown doesn't offer a great choice of take-aways. There's fish and chips, kebabs or Chinese.'

Karly furrowed her pale brows, as if pondering the meaning of life. She poured herself a glass of lemonade and took small sips until it was almost finished. 'I don't know,' she said at last, wiping her mouth and smearing her lipstick. 'You choose.'

'Chinese it is, then,' he said. It would be the easiest food to heat up if Harper was late.

'Dad?'

'Yes?'

'I think I'm going to be sick.' Karly brought up the lemonade all over the couch and her pink skirt. She stared at him in horror, looking like she was about to cry.

'Never mind,' he soothed. 'You go and change. I'll clean this up.'

Mark watched her rush to the stairs, tripping in her high heels as she went. This could be a very long night.

CHAPTER 23

Almost spring, and the clear blue sky promised a sunny Saturday. A perfect day for the squirrel catch. The zoo staff had arrived early to get a jump on the morning chores, and Jana joined Maggie to help prepare fruit for the macaques' breakfast.

But as they approached the monkey house with baskets of apples, oranges and bananas, Jana sensed that something was wrong. The macaques' usual lively chatter and excited screeches were conspicuously absent. Instead, an eerie quiet greeted the pair. A knot of tension formed in her stomach as she ventured closer, and the reason for the silence became apparent: the gate to the monkey house stood wide open. There wasn't a macaque in sight.

'Shit,' said Jana, as she hurriedly rang Bruce. He was the one responsible for securing the enclosures each night.

'What do we do now?' asked Maggie in a shaky voice.

How am I supposed to know? Jana wanted to say. But instead, she responded calmly with, 'We wait for Bruce and then try to work out what happened.'

In a few minutes Bruce and the others came trooping down the path.

'But I shut it,' he insisted, staring at the empty enclosure in disbelief. 'I know I did. I always double-check, even triple-check the doors.'

This was true. Jana had witnessed his thorough evening routine many times. Bruce was a reliable keeper who'd never once been negligent before. On top of that, he loved those monkeys and would hate to see them come to harm. Jana gazed around the grounds uneasily. She had an awful feeling that this had something to do with the online threats. By tonight she intended to have sturdy new locks on all the enclosures.

'It's not the end of the world,' said Lexie, tightening her ponytail. 'If the monkeys haven't had their breakfast, they'll be hungry and easier to catch.'

'That's great,' said Bruce, his voice heavy with sarcasm. 'Now all we have to do is find them.'

'What about the squirrel catch?' asked Maggie. 'I set all the traps last night. Do we still go ahead?'

'We don't have much choice,' said Jana. 'Two volunteers have already arrived at the house, and half-a-dozen more have promised to turn up later. The truth is that we can probably use the extra hands.'

Distinctly monkey-like screams came from the trees to their left. They all glanced at each other and then sprinted towards the sound. As they rounded a pair of old elms, they discovered a macaque and her half-grown baby caught in a squirrel trap. Apparently, the bait of bananas and watermelon had proved irresistible.

'That's Cheeta and Bubbles,' said an excited Maggie as Bruce ran off to fetch a pet carrier. 'Who'd have thought they'd fit in that little crate?'

Jana scratched her head and smiled. 'Two monkeys down, ten to go.'

'And about a hundred squirrels,' said Lexie. Another protesting screech rose from the bush ahead of them. 'Bingo. I'll get another basket.'

'What do you want me to do?' asked Amber, a quiver in her voice betraying how upset she was by the animals' escape.

'You go with Maggie and Bruce to check the other baited crates. Text me the updated monkey catch count as you go.'

Jana watched them leave, feeling a little better. Thank goodness Maggie had set the traps last night. Catching the truants might not be as difficult as she first thought. But the disturbing reality of one or more intruders entering the zoo remained. Padlocks wouldn't deter determined activists with bolt cutters. Time to hire security. Cost shouldn't be an issue, but she'd have to run the idea past Mark as soon as possible. They needed to formulate a plan for tackling this new challenge. But he was busy playing happy families with Karly and her mother. Harper certainly had terrible timing.

A deep voice sang out, startling her. 'Jana, are you there?'

She spun around to see Karly and Mark emerge from behind the elm trees. Jana checked her watch. Nine o'clock in the morning. Whatever happened to spending the day with Harper?

As the pair drew closer, Jana realised something was wrong. Instead of her usual bright smile, Karly's mouth turned down and her chin trembled. Puffy red eyes contrasted with her deathly pale face. She'd clearly been crying, and even now seemed to be sniffing back tears. Jana's heart went out to the girl. What had happened? And where was Harper?

Jana shot a questioning glance at Mark, who stared back, tight-lipped and grim-faced.

'We were wondering,' he said, hands on his daughter's slumped shoulders, 'if you still need help with the squirrel catch? I know we're a bit late.'

'Well, yes,' said Jana, her anger at Mark forgotten. 'But I thought—'

Mark shook his head firmly, the gesture unseen by Karly, who stood in front of him. A clear warning not to explore the thought further. Jana was dying to know what had happened to Harper's visit, but she'd need to get Mark alone for that explanation. For a moment she chided herself for being so interested, given her decision to keep things strictly professional between them.

But hang on – she was entitled to some good, old-fashioned curiosity after everything that woman had put her through. And though she wasn't normally one for gossip, she'd make an exception when it came to Harper. She'd happily hear something bad about her. But then she looked at Karly's downcast eyes and immediately regretted her harshness. This was Karly's mother that she was thinking about. And the extraordinary girl standing before her only existed because of Harper's sacrifice. She'd put aside her own needs to have her daughter when she was still a teenager herself. Harper deserved respect for that, if nothing else. Jana resolved to curb any vengeful thoughts.

A shriek rose from the trees to their left, startling them.

'Come on, Karly,' said Jana, holding out an encouraging hand. 'Let's go and see. Sounds like we've caught another monkey.'

Karly wiped her eyes. 'A monkey?' Despite her misery, the girl's inquisitive nature was clearly piqued.

'I'm afraid so. Someone opened the monkey house last night and let them out.' Mark shot her a sharp glance, but Jana continued. 'So it turns out that today is a squirrel- *and* monkey-catching day. Double trouble.' She gave Karly a hopeful look. 'We could sure use some help.'

Mark flashed her a thankful smile. 'Of course we'll help,' he said. 'What do you want us to do?'

Amber arrived, cradling a macaque. 'Benny found me! He ran over and jumped into my arms. And Lexie has Koko and Kiki. That means seven monkeys left to catch.'

More cries from the trees caused Karly's eyes to widen with concern. 'It sounds like it might be hurt.'

'Well, we'd better go check then,' said Jana. 'Are you coming, Mark?'

They all headed towards the sound, joined along the way by Bruce, and found yet another macaque caught in a squirrel trap.

'That's Chester,' said Karly, running over to the monkey. 'You poor thing.' Chester stopped shrieking and chattered a welcome. 'He's frightened. Can I give him a banana?' Jana gave the girl one from her shoulder bag. Chester accepted the offering with solemn eyes, then held out his hand for Karly to hold. 'Look,' she cried. 'He wants me to go with him.'

'Good idea,' said Jana, relieved to see Karly smiling. 'Why don't you go back to the monkey house with Bruce? I think Chester would like that.'

Bruce unhooked the trap from the tree. He started for the house with his long stride, as Karly trotted beside him.

Mark watched her go then turned to Jana. 'Thank God for you and the zoo. Nothing else would have taken Karly out of herself. She was completely devastated when Harper didn't turn up.'

'What happened?'

'Harper was supposed to be there at six o'clock last night. Karly tidied the house within an inch of its life. The place has never been so clean. She made a special card and got all dressed up and put flowers in the spare room. Six o'clock came and went. Karly was a nervous wreck – so was I, to be honest.' His voice wavered and his shoulders slumped slightly as he spoke. 'I can tell you, the tension in that house was contagious.' He flexed his fingers, and she heard the bridled anger in his voice. 'At eight o'clock she rang to say she wasn't coming until the morning. Karly wanted to talk to her, but Harper said she had to go.' Mark sighed heavily, pain evident on his face. 'I passed Karly the phone anyway, but her mother had already hung up.' His gaze became distant, as if lost in the recollection. Jana had never seen him look so miserable. 'Well, Karly tried to put on a brave face; she tried to pretend that she wasn't disappointed. But she wouldn't eat any dinner, even though I'd ordered her favourite Chinese food. She went straight to bed.'

Jana felt a sharp pang of sympathy for Mark, touched by his distress over how hurt Karly was. 'I'm so sorry.' She reached out, placing a consoling hand on his arm. 'And this morning?'

'Harper messaged me at half-nine to say she couldn't come after all. No explanations. I've tried calling and texting her, but no response. Karly shut herself in her bedroom. I could hear her crying, but she wouldn't let me in,' he said, sadly. 'She'd pushed the dresser in front of the door. In the end I had to take the hinges off. She completely shut down. It was only when I mentioned the zoo that I finally got through to her.'

'Oh no! How awful!'

'What the hell is wrong with that woman?' Mark's face reddened. 'How could she let her own daughter down like that?'

His questions were rhetorical, and just as well, because there were no answers that Jana cared to give him. It wouldn't help matters to say that Harper had always been a self-centred narcissist, and that she clearly hadn't changed. It wouldn't help to say that Harper couldn't have put herself in Karly's shoes if she'd tried. No more giving Harper the benefit of the doubt; the woman just didn't do empathy.

Instead, Jana simply listened as Mark vented, waiting until he calmed down.

'Thanks for confiding in me,' she said. 'It means a lot.'

And it did. The bitterness she'd felt about Harper's proposed visit had slipped away, replaced with sympathy and concern.

'It would be good if Karly could talk this through with someone,' said Mark, his angry expression replaced with one of hope.

'She probably needs some space from—'

'Oh, I don't mean me,' he said, jumping in before Jana could finish. 'At least not yet. I'm too close and her hurt is too raw. But . . . I thought . . . maybe she'd open up to you?'

Bad idea, Jana wanted to say, barely able to hide a grimace.

Here she was, wanting to pull away from Mark, and he was trying to put her smack bang in the middle of his life. She might feel for him and Karly, but the time had come for some straight talking.

'Look, Mark. I'm the last person who should be talking to Karly about her mother. To be honest, I'd find it hard to be objective. Harper isn't exactly my favourite person.'

'Of course,' he said, holding up his hands in an open-palmed gesture of understanding, but his expression belied his words. His face fell in a way that seemed to convey equal parts disappointment and heartache. She almost wished she could take back her refusal. Almost. Mark had got himself into this mess with Harper, and he'd have to get himself out of it. Providing a sounding board for his daughter wasn't her job.

'Hazel might be able to help,' said Jana, relenting a little. 'Those two have quite a bond.'

'Maybe,' he said, but she could tell that he wasn't convinced. Karly returned just as Johnno and a volunteer arrived carrying two more trapped monkeys. Jana studied the girl. She had more of a spring in her step and looked a lot happier.

'That's all the traps checked,' said Johnno. A monkey's arm snaked out through the wire to pickpocket his phone. 'Hey, stop that!' he said, laughing and retrieving his mobile. 'The last few old-timers won't be so easy to catch. Rafiki and his favourite ladies are holed up at the top of an oak tree. The buggers are having a ball, screeching and pelting me with sticks and leaves. They're not coming down any time soon.'

'Somebody should get Hazel,' said Karly. 'Those older monkeys are her pets. They might come to her.'

'That's a great idea,' said Jana. 'Karly, can you go back with Johnno and help him settle these two monkeys in? Then go get Hazel and see if she has some Pop-Tarts while you're at it.'

'Pop-Tarts?' Mark looked at Jana like she was crazy.

'Hazel knows she's not to feed them Pop-Tarts any more, but Rafiki loves them, especially the chocolate ones.'

Karly giggled as she ran off chanting, 'Softly, softly, catchee monkey.' Jana and Mark shared a smile. The sweet sound of the girl's laughter had gladdened both their hearts.

'We haven't talked about who tampered with the monkey house and why,' said Mark. 'Or what we're going to do about it.'

'Well, to be fair,' said Jana, beckoning him towards the grove of oaks, 'we haven't had a chance. You did distract me with some pretty heavy stuff when you arrived.'

He had the good grace to look embarrassed. She jogged off towards the oak trees.

'Let me make it up to you,' he called, hurrying after her. 'I'll shout pizzas and drinks tonight for everyone who's helping.'

Jana stopped abruptly, causing Mark to cannon into her. 'There's no need – really.'

'But I want to.'

Had he missed the stern tone of her voice, or was he deliberately ignoring it? Mark touched her arm in a familiar way, and she flinched.

'Frankly, you'd be doing me a favour.'

A favour? She didn't quite see how, and anyway, she didn't

much feel like doing him any favours. She was about to turn his offer down flat when he interrupted her.

'I can't take Karly home to an empty house this evening. The distraction of being here and seeing you has perked her up, but I'm frightened that as soon as we're home, she'll sink back down.'

'Take her to your parents, then.'

'I can't. They're away this weekend.'

Jana gazed at his expectant face and a whirlwind of emotions churned inside her. Her lips quivered and the muscles of her face tensed. How could she balance the desire to help with the hesitation born from a deep, unresolved conflict?

'Oh, all right,' she said, at last. 'For Karly's sake.'

'For Karly's sake,' he echoed, and followed her down the grassy path.

CHAPTER 24

Ten very welcome volunteers had shown up that morning to help, and Jana's ragtag team of squirrel and monkey catchers had a successful day. It took until lunchtime, but eventually Hazel managed to lure Rafiki and his gang down from the trees. She'd been all out of Pop-Tarts, but Nutella sandwiches proved to be an enticing substitute.

'Thank goodness they were hungry,' said Maggie as she returned the last monkey to its enclosure. It took a long drink then promptly retired to a hammock bed and fell asleep. 'They seem quite glad to be home.'

'The little mongrels are all tuckered out.' Bruce rubbed his head where Rafiki had scored a direct hit with a stone. 'Running rings around us all bloody morning is tiring work.'

They'd had plenty of luck with the squirrels as well. At the end of the day, twenty-seven of the creatures leaped and chittered in the bank of cages that had been prepared for them.

'They're so sweet.' Karly fed one of the little striped creatures a peanut. 'What are we going to do with them?'

'Good question,' said Jana, as Amber arrived with a pet carrier.

'Caught another one,' said Lexie, a step behind Amber. 'I think there are only about a dozen left in the park. If we keep the traps set, we'll catch the others eventually.' She added the new squirrel to the last cage. 'So, what are we going to do with them?'

'Yes,' said Mark. 'What are we going—'

'Not you too?' complained Jana, all eyes upon her. 'Well, we can certainly place some of them with other zoos and wildlife parks. I suppose I'll have to desex the rest and they'll stay here.' She didn't mention that if Wildfell Park failed to regain its operating licence, the remaining squirrels would be destroyed.

'Can I keep one?' asked Karly.

'Absolutely not,' said Jana. 'For one thing, it's illegal. And for another, they're wild animals, not pets. Now, I want all hands on deck for the evening chores. Maggie, take the volunteers with you. They can help prepare the feeds.'

'I want to give the lions their supper,' said Karly.

'All right. You can go with Lexie and Bruce to lock up the big cats.'

Mark frowned. 'Are you sure that's safe?'

'Dad!'

'She'll be fine,' said Jana, trying to put his mind at rest. The nighttime lock-up followed fail-safe security protocols. There was no danger to Karly. Jana was more concerned about the big cats' safety, considering there may well have been trespassers in the park.

'I'll keep her well out of the way,' confirmed Bruce, putting a protective hand on Karly's shoulder.

'She'll just watch,' said Lexie. 'I guarantee it.'

Hazel echoed the reassurance. 'Those two won't let any harm come to her. I doubt the lions would hurt her anyway. I swear Nala thinks Karly is her cub.'

'Go on then,' said Mark, won over by his daughter's pleading eyes. 'But you must do as you're told. Deal?'

'Deal.' Karly ran to give her father a hug, and his face lit up with love. Jana felt an unwelcome twinge of attraction.

'In appreciation for all your help today' – Mark's voice carried across the group – 'everyone's welcome to stay for a pizza-night celebration at the manor house. Free booze included.'

Jana stared at Mark, and another shiver of desire passed through her. Its power took her by surprise. A crowd of people gathered around, and he addressed them with a blend of authority and warmth. The underlying sense of care and community he demonstrated revealed a depth of character she hadn't expected.

'We're almost at the halfway mark of the zoo's temporary licence extension, and our renovation program is roaring ahead,' said Mark. 'We've all worked very hard for this, and with your continued support, we're on track for a grand reopening of Wildfell Park in three months' time.'

A cheer went up, and Jana joined in. His words were so stirring, she couldn't help herself. With his chiselled features and warm blue eyes, Mark looked very handsome – charismatic, even. A denim jacket accentuated his broad shoulders, and he made his announcement with arms outstretched like a magnanimous king.

Oh, how she wished she hadn't agreed to him staying

today. But Karly's smiling face reminded her of why she had. At least she wouldn't be alone with Mark. Jana counted how many others would be at the gathering, as if every extra person might help save her from herself.

There was Bruce and his young daughter, Lisa, who was close to Karly's age. Lexie, Amber, Maggie and her mum, Jean. Johnno had brought his wife along. Four volunteers had stayed on, and there was Hazel and Karly. Plenty of people to ensure she didn't succumb to a moment of weakness with Mark.

She startled to find him standing close beside her. 'I'm going after Karly to make sure she behaves herself around those big cats. Could you come, maybe?'

He looked so vulnerable, his sea-blue eyes pleading. Jana felt something shift inside of her. 'Sure,' she said softly. 'Let's go find your daughter.'

Jana and Mark listened to Karly chatter away to the lions as Bruce secured them in their individual overnight dens.

'I wish I could be here when you wake up in the morning,' Karly told them. 'I could help give you breakfast. Maybe Jana will let me stay over one night. You're all so beautiful, even more beautiful than Simba the Lion King, or Aslan from Narnia.'

King and Cleo didn't take much notice, merely giving Karly an occasional sideways glance. Nala, on the other hand, seemed entranced. She fixed the child with an unwavering gaze, ears flicking back and forth at the sound of her voice. She moved whenever Karly moved, making the girl laugh with delight. Nala's massive head rubbed affectionately against the wire fence that separated them. Karly pressed the palm of her hand against the mesh and started to sing a lullaby.

Nala's purring throbbed in the evening air, a deep, resonant sound that seemed to vibrate in harmony with Karly's song.

Jana glanced at Mark. His eyes glistened in the dim light, and he seemed visibly moved by the undeniable connection between his daughter and the majestic lioness. Jana felt a tightness in her throat, marvelling at how much he seemed to have changed since high school.

Wind rustled the treetops as the sun set in a pink and amber sky. From the verandah Jana could sense the sway of river reeds in the cool air and hear the soft lapping of water. The frogs began their nightly chorus, and somewhere far off a barge creaked.

A pleasant murmur of voices and laughter filled the graceful old manor house, along with the sweet tang of wood smoke from the open fire. Fridges were crammed with wine and lemonade, while the twin laundry sinks held beer and soft drink buried in bags of crushed ice. People spilled from the dining room onto the wide sandstone verandah, where chairs had been set up and trestle tables groaned under pizzas and plates of cookies. The cobweb-strewn globes of the outside lights had long since blown, so Hazel had placed candles along the tabletops. They flickered in the light breeze, creating a soft, romantic glow.

Jana sat with Karly and Lisa, listening to the dingoes'

howls and King's occasional roars from his den. Earlier in the week they'd settled two young wombats in their new, purpose-built exhibit, although Karly was disappointed that Womble couldn't be there.

'Womble's too young,' Jana had told her. 'And I have enough on my plate without getting up for nighttime feeds. He's safe at Odessa with my sister. But when the zoo gets more staff, I'll bring him here, along with Care Bear, okay?'

This had seemed to satisfy Karly. Jana poured herself yet another glass of wine – a top-of-the-range sparkling burgundy that she'd never normally be able to afford. Mark certainly had good taste. Mentioning the zoo's future always made her feel uneasy, especially now. She still hadn't had a chance to talk to Mark about last night's intruders. For that's what they were – she was sure of it.

Bruce had taken her aside earlier to explain what he'd found outside the monkey house. 'Overnight rain made the ground soft.' He showed her a photo on his phone. 'Fresh footprints near the gate, coming and going from the river path. I'm the only person who should have been there last night, but these prints were made by a woman's boot, or maybe a man with a small shoe size. In any case, they definitely weren't mine.'

Yes, Jana really did need to talk to Mark. Happily, though, the delicious wine was taking the edge off her worry.

Jana heard raised voices from inside the house. Mark and Hazel must be going at it again. Whenever those two were together, they seemed to lock horns.

Karly glanced towards the kitchen and let out a sigh that sounded very grown up. 'I'll go break them up. I wish

Dad and Hazel wouldn't fight. They're two of my favourite people.'

Jana smiled at the long-suffering expression on the girl's face. 'Karly, why don't you take Lisa with you to say hello to Hazel? And send Mark out while you're at it, please. There's something I need to discuss with him.'

A few minutes later, Mark arrived. Shadows flickered and danced across his face in the candlelight, lending him a mysterious charm.

'You wanted to see me?' His voice sounded rich and velvety, like it had been dipped in warm honey. *The wine effect*, she thought, taking another big sip. The bubbly burgundy slid down her throat in a most delightful way.

'Come on.' Jana stood up, leading him away from the crowded verandah. 'This needs to be a private conversation.'

They strolled through the starry gardens by torchlight until they reached the new wombat exhibit. 'Electricity won't be connected until Monday,' Jana said, unlocking the building that housed the dens. 'Let me present to you, the Wombatarium.' They went down some steps. 'Look,' Jana said, shining her torch into the artificial underground warren, separated from them only by a glass wall. 'It's empty. The wombats must be exploring their outside area. That's a good sign. It means they feel confident.' She turned to Mark, not realising in the dark how near he was. She breathed him in – wine, musk and leather. They were almost touching.

Jana backed off. He was too close for comfort – too close for her to think straight. She guided Mark to a corner bench where she told him about the footprints and her certainty that an intruder, or maybe intruders, had released the monkeys. 'We'll have to strengthen the perimeter fence.'

'We'll have to do more than that,' said Mark. 'We need an alarm system and motion-detector cameras. And I'll organise a security patrol first thing next week. Have them come by randomly a couple of times a night.'

'Won't that be expensive?'

'I'll talk to Frieda about the cost. She's been requesting an update. Just be grateful that we found out about the trespassers before they caused any real harm. We won't let anybody stop this zoo becoming a success, I promise.' His voice rang with confidence. 'I'm proud of the way our plans are coming together.' In the faint torchlight, his eyes bored into her own. 'And Jana – I'm proud of you.'

All Jana's anxiety drained away. His words made her feel protected and safe and optimistic about the future. She was suddenly glad that Harper hadn't turned up, despite Karly's disappointment. Glad that Mark was with *her* tonight instead. If that made her a bad person, then so be it.

His arm brushed against hers in the dark. An accident? Then he touched her leg. Heat radiated from his body. The air between them grew electric, thick with anticipation. Jana couldn't recall ever experiencing such a charged moment. Her heart raced and her throat grew dry. It felt like an invisible hand was pulling her to him.

She didn't know who moved first. They seemed to shift in perfect sync. She only knew that as their bodies came together, his lips sought hers. Jana almost abandoned herself to the moment – almost allowed herself to be swept away. But she couldn't quite bring herself to go through with it.

It took all of Jana's resolve to pull away, and she didn't know exactly why she did. Was it too soon? The wrong time? The wrong place? Frustration and confusion made her dizzy as she headed for the Wombatarium's door.

Poor Mark. Poor her.

CHAPTER 25

Mark followed Jana out of the Wombatarium, shaking his head. Disappointment punched him in the gut. Now he was more confused than ever. For a few moments Jana had seemed as eager and passionate as he was. She'd wanted him; he was sure of it. And yet, once again, she'd rejected him. Why was she running hot and cold? He wished he could understand.

When they arrived back at the house, Hazel drew him aside. 'A word with you.'

Mark groaned. The evening was going from bad to worse. What fresh bone did the old biddy want to pick with him now?

'I'll find you in a bit,' he called to Jana, who was hurrying from the room.

Hazel directed him to a private corner of the kitchen.

'It's Karly,' she said, sternly. 'You must remove her from that dreadful college immediately. Rivertown has a perfectly good high school not five minutes' walk from your house.'

Mark saw red. It was bad enough when Hazel interfered in the running of the zoo, without her meddling in his private life too.

'Where Karly goes to school is none of your business,' he snapped. 'So you can keep your opinions to yourself.'

Hazel stared back at him, unflinching. 'Have you spoken to your daughter? She hates it there. No friends, a target for bullies. Living only for the weekend when she's safe at home with you.'

'Leave it, Hazel.' His nostrils flared.

'Not on your life. Someone needs to talk some sense into you. How are her grades?' She didn't miss his flinch. 'I thought so. No child can learn when they're so stressed. And this debacle with her mother will only make things worse. Apparently, Karly told some students about Harper's visit and their day at the spa – bragged about it even. This is a small town. What happens when the kids find out that her mother didn't even bother to show?'

'How do you know all this?' asked Mark, trying to hide his surprise.

'Karly told me, of course. She needs someone to talk to – someone who'll hear her. Believe me when I say that keeping her at that school is a recipe for disaster. You're paying a fortune in fees just to make her unhappy.'

'That's enough,' said Mark through gritted teeth. He hadn't meant to raise his voice, but people turned to stare. Mark softened his tone. 'Listen, Hazel. I appreciate you looking out for my daughter, but I've got this.'

He turned his back on her, painfully aware that his anger might be because she was right. He'd been struggling with what to do about Karly for some time now and he'd even considered taking her out of Scarborough. But that seemed like admitting defeat, and he hated being wrong. He'd loved the school, so why couldn't she? It had the finest reputation in the state. No, Karly's problems were temporary. With time and patience and plenty of love, she'd get through this.

The magic of the evening had slipped away, and things only went downhill from there. When Mark looked for Jana, he spotted her going upstairs with Hazel and Karly. He sighed as they disappeared from sight, missing her already. What were the odds they'd be talking about him? And if Hazel had anything to do with it, it would not be a flattering conversation. Jana had said that Karly and Hazel had grown close, but he'd rejected the idea. What on earth could a twelve-year-old girl have in common with a frail old woman?

He wanted to fetch a beer from the laundry, but when he checked the time on the longcase clock, he saw it was getting late, and he'd have to drive home soon. He couldn't even have a drink to ease his disappointment.

For the first time since he'd become a full-time father, he resented the limitations that Karly put on his life. If not for her, he might have stayed and talked things through with Jana. Tried to understand her sudden change of heart. Would she have opened up to him? Maybe, maybe not – but now he'd never know.

It was almost eleven o'clock and the party was winding down. People were already saying goodbye and drifting off before Hazel, Jana and Karly came downstairs. His daughter looked happy, which was a good sign, but he still felt uneasy. Lord, he wished he could have been a fly on the wall upstairs.

'We'd better go,' he said as Karly yawned.

Mark hoped to see a reaction on Jana's face. Disappointment, maybe? But instead, she gave him a tight smile he couldn't read and said, 'I believe you two are going to meet somebody very special tomorrow.'

'I told them how we're going to visit Grandma and Grandpa, and how they've brought my new puppy home,' said Karly.

Oh God, he'd forgotten. He'd promised the visit in an attempt to console his daughter when Harper failed to show. Karly hadn't even seemed to hear him through her tears. Now he was stuck with it, when all he really wanted to do was spend Sunday at Wildfell Park.

'There's nothing as exciting as a new puppy,' Jana said to Karly. 'What will you call him?'

'I don't know yet. I'll have to meet him and find out about his personality first.'

'Very wise. Now, why don't you go with Hazel to the kitchen? She's saved some cookies for you to take home.'

Jana watched the girl go with a fond smile. 'I think a visit to her grandparents might be just what Karly needs,' she said. 'A puppy, a change of scenery, a break from the pressures of school and the troubles with her mother.'

Jana was right, of course, and Mark felt a little ashamed. He made a mental note to make the drive to Don and Gwen's place as fun and enjoyable as possible for Karly.

As they said their goodbyes, he felt Jana's hand brush against his. It was a small gesture but enough to ignite a flame in his heart. Mark didn't want to leave and go back to his lonely bed, but he'd see Jana again soon. He'd just have to be patient.

*

The drive home was silent. Karly had fallen asleep in the back seat. Mark's mind raced with thoughts he couldn't shake. He'd always believed that by devoting himself to his daughter, he was doing the right thing. But what if he'd been wrong all along? What if school wasn't the real problem? Maybe Karly was unhappy because she was stuck living with him instead of her mother.

When they pulled into the driveway, Mark sat for a moment in the car, staring blankly ahead. He'd promised himself that he'd be the best father he could be, but now he was questioning what that really meant, second-guessing himself. This parenting business was a thousand times more difficult than he'd imagined.

Karly stirred. 'Are we home yet?' she said in a sleepy voice.

'Yes, honey, we're home.' He got out and opened the front door of the house. Then Mark went back to the car and lifted his drowsy daughter into his arms. She clasped her arms round his neck, burying her head in his shoulder. 'What a day you've had,' he whispered. Carrying Karly to her room, he tucked her into bed. She was in dreamland before her head hit the pillow.

Mark stood back, watching his sleeping child, marvelling that someone so perfect and beautiful had come from him. And as he watched her, all the evening's doubts and misgivings faded away. How could it be wrong to dedicate himself to Karly? Yes, he was bound to make mistakes. He'd undoubtedly made plenty already. But as long as he tried his best and put her first, they'd be fine.

He crept from the room, thinking what a selfish fool he'd been. Karly was no hindrance to a romance with Jana. Quite the opposite. If not for Karly, he'd never have met the gorgeous vet in the first place, and one of the reasons he'd fallen for Jana was because of her kindness towards his daughter. The two of them were inextricably connected – both essential to his life. And he vowed to never wish Karly away again.

CHAPTER 26

True to his word, Mark soon arranged a new alarm system and hired security guards to patrol the grounds around Wildfell Park. Jana remained on edge, expecting the intruders to return, but all remained peaceful.

For the past few days, she'd been busy desexing squirrels and macaques. Whether she liked it or not, it was necessary to prevent a population explosion. Jana had managed to find some of them new homes in other zoos, but they still had too many animals at Wildfell Park. To help with overcrowding, they'd constructed another monkey house beside the café. She hoped its strategic position would serve a double purpose; the diners would amuse the monkeys, and the monkeys would amuse the diners.

The building was nearly complete, with only a few finishing touches needed. As Jana stepped into the new monkey house, she was struck by its beauty. The high ceilings and large windows allowed natural light to pour into the spacious enclosure. Walls were lined with branches and ropes for the primates to swing on, and there were plenty of toys and puzzles to keep them entertained. Existing trees, perfect for climbing, were incorporated into a large, grassy outdoor space. Jana had designed it herself with the welfare of the animals in mind, and she couldn't wait to see them in their new surroundings.

Next Jana stopped in at the surgery to check on the progress of the macaques that she'd desexed yesterday. She stood in front of a cage that held Monty – a young male that she'd managed to place with a wildlife park north of Adelaide. He looked up at her with big, brown eyes and reached out to touch her through the bars.

'Hey there, little guy,' Jana cooed, reaching a hand through the cage to stroke his cheek. 'Don't worry, you're soon going to a wonderful new home.'

She glanced around the hospital ward at the other animals. There were so many of them. A sudden fear gripped her. Monty was one of the lucky ones. If the plan to reopen the zoo failed, she'd be responsible for putting many of them to sleep. It was a heartbreaking prospect.

Jana shook her head to clear away the grim imaginings. She tried to focus on more positive thoughts. It was Tuesday afternoon and Mark was coming over after work. They planned to head into town for a pub meal and go over spreadsheets and work schedules. Their project deadlines were on track, and thanks to Mark's stellar financial management, they hopefully weren't too far over budget either. With any luck, this evening's meeting would confirm the good news.

Still, she wasn't exactly looking forward to dinner with Mark. Tonight would be their first time together since that drunken almost-kiss in the Wombatarium. She'd agonised over whether he deserved an explanation for her sudden departure. Probably, but it was an explanation she didn't feel inclined to give.

Jana had a sudden urge to talk the situation over with Sash. She was meant to ring her sister tomorrow night for a general update on Odessa, but she couldn't wait that long. The problem was that Sash had no idea about the historical problem Jana had with Mark. Nobody did – except for Penny. Jana toyed with her phone and glanced at the time. Four o'clock in the afternoon. Sash was probably out and about on the property somewhere, and Odessa had notoriously poor phone reception away from the house.

Jana called the number anyway. A gush of relief hit her when her sister answered, but her voice sounded distant and far away.

'Hi, sis,' said Sash. 'What's up?'

'Not much.' Jana didn't know how to bring up the subject of Mark from a cold start. 'Just checking how everything's going.'

'Great,' said Sash. 'Womble's starting to come out of his pillowcase and totter around. You should see his ears – they're enormous! He looks like he might fly away like Dumbo the baby elephant. And Tracey is a godsend. I have no idea where Mark found her, but not only is she great with the animals, but she's also great in the kitchen. Her lasagna is to die for. She does it in the pizza oven out back and it has this lovely smoky flavour.'

Since Jana could barely boil an egg, this news provoked a twinge of jealousy. 'What – you mean she's living there?'

'I've given her your room. Don't worry. Your stuff is safely stored in the shed.'

Jana hadn't thought about the logistics of hiring a replacement for her role at Odessa. Of course it made sense for Tracey to live there. She imagined Sash, Luca and Tracey at sunset, laughing and joking around the fire, drinking beers and waiting for their meal to cook. A deep ache welled up inside her – an unexpected wave of homesickness.

Sash's voice was breaking up. 'Sorry, but Tracey and I are planting along the bank above Bahloo Billabong, and I've only got one bar . . .'

A loud, prolonged crackling signalled the end of their totally unsatisfactory conversation. Jana closed her eyes and wished she could somehow be spirited away to join Sash. Wished she could help with planting the tubestock they'd so painstakingly propagated: red gum, lignum, cumbungi and a dozen other species endemic to the Murraylands. She could almost smell the chocolatey fragrance of vanilla lilies, hear kookaburras chortling in the treetops and see sleek rakali skimming through the dark waters of the billabong.

A soft touch from Monty brought Jana out of her reverie. The monkey pulled at her hand, silently asking for more pats. She resumed her rhythmic stroking of his cheek.

'Sorry, boy. I have this wonderful zoo, all of you gorgeous animals, and here I am, daydreaming about somewhere else. What a fool I am.' Monty sighed his agreement.

Mark arrived just as the sun was setting. Jana watched through the kitchen window as he came down the path towards the house, broad shoulders silhouetted against the orange sky. Her stomach flipped over.

'Knock, knock,' Mark called as he pushed the door open. 'Evening, Hazel.' The old woman glanced up from shelling peas at the bench and frowned. Mark favoured Jana with a dazzling smile. 'You ready to head into town?'

Jana tried to keep her voice steady. 'Just let me go change.'

Against her better instincts, Jana went upstairs, leaving Mark alone with Hazel. Surely even those two couldn't get into an argument in the time it would take her to shower and change.

Jana washed away the sweat and grime of the day, then dried off and debated what to wear. Perversely, in spite of her reservations about Mark, Jana had a sudden urge to dress up. It had been so long since she'd worn anything but cotton shirts and trousers.

She slipped into a sleek black frock, one of the few dresses that she owned. It was in no way revealing, but it hugged her curves in all the right places. Jana barely recognised herself when she glanced in the mirror and almost changed again. But no – the effect was bold and sophisticated and as great a contrast to her normal appearance as possible. Wasn't that what she wanted? So she tugged a comb through her wet hair and found a pair of black leather sandals to match the dress. She toyed with the idea of searching through her toiletry bag for lipstick, then decided against it. She didn't want to give Mark too much of a shock.

Raised voices echoed up the staircase. Good grief. Mark and Hazel were arguing about football this time. Those two were incorrigible. When Jana entered the kitchen, the bickering came to an abrupt halt. Mark gazed at her in open admiration. Hazel *harrumphed* disapprovingly and left the room.

'Shall we?' Mark offered his arm.

Jana took it, almost shyly, and they headed for the door.

Mark was in awe as he walked with Jana to his car. She was always beautiful, even in her work clothes, but tonight – in that simple black dress – she was a vision.

He'd endured what had felt like an agonisingly long wait before getting this chance to see her again. He and Karly had spent the day at Overland Corner with his father and Gwen on Sunday, visiting his daughter's new dog. The puppy was just the tonic she'd needed, and Mark had agreed for them to stay the night and return to Rivertown first thing on Monday morning.

In consideration of Karly's upset over her mother's failed visit, Mark had arranged for her to attend Scarborough as a day student for a few days. This meant leaving work at three o'clock and joining a handful of other parents at school pick-up time. Howard Turner, his firm's senior partner, was not amused. 'I didn't employ you on a part-time basis,' he'd grumbled.

Mark suddenly had first-hand experience of how difficult employment must be for many women with children. Howard showed his displeasure by heaping extra work on Mark and calling it 'homework'. This led to evenings glued to his computer after putting Karly to bed, when all he really wanted to do was see Jana. But tonight, Karly was safely back at boarding school and Mark had the whole evening free. The possibilities were intriguing.

As they arrived at the Rivertown Tavern, a frisson of anticipation ran through him. He had to keep reminding himself that this was a business meeting, not a date. With Jana looking so stunning, it wasn't an easy task.

The restaurant, though it had seen better days, held plenty of charm. The walls were lined with black-and-white photographs of the town's heyday: paddle-steamers, dock workers, and carts laden high with sacks of wool and grain. It was unseasonably warm for so early in September. They sat in the beer garden overlooking the river, watching the moon's dimpled reflection in the water.

Mark ordered a steak, while Jana chose the salmon. They shared a bottle of wine and toasted their hard work and the exciting news that the Wildfell Park projections had turned out to be even better than expected. The zoo looked set to meet the opening deadline, all within budget.

It was a thrill to see Jana in a celebratory mood. She couldn't stop smiling, and so neither could he. Mark had rarely seen Jana smile. It lit her face with a special radiance, her brown eyes sparkling with warmth. Mark was utterly captivated. No matter how the evening turned out, it was enough to sit with this beautiful woman on a balmy night and bask in her glow.

They lingered in the warmth of the moment, and when the time came to pay the bill, they lingered still. Finally, they stood, and Mark contemplated taking Jana's hand in his as they walked out. After a few agonising seconds, he decided not to. He hadn't been so happy in a long time, and he couldn't bear the thought of possibly spoiling the moment.

When they arrived back at Wildfell Park, Mark raced around the car in time to open the door for Jana. Her body brushed against him and he could no longer resist. His fingers seemed to slip into hers of their own accord, and it felt so natural as her hand melted into his. Together they climbed the front porch steps.

Beneath the pale porch light, they turned to face each other. Jana's eyes bored into his and Mark felt a little hypnotised.

'Thanks so much for all you've done,' she said, her voice soft and heartfelt. She squeezed his fingers and gave him a peck on the cheek.

The air felt charged, and Mark's heart seemed to pound right out of his chest. He'd wanted to kiss her for so long, but he didn't want to rush things, especially since she'd run away last time. He could see hesitation in Jana's eyes, but also a willingness that gave him hope. Mark reached out to gently cup Jana's chin, his thumb brushing the smooth skin of her cheek. Her breath caught as she leaned into his touch.

'Jana?' whispered Mark, tenderly. Her fingers lightly grazed his arm, a silent reassurance. Mark's lips brushed hers in a feather-light kiss. Time stood still as he briefly tasted the sweetness of her mouth.

But as his lips let hers go, Mark couldn't help expressing his thoughts. 'Jana,' he said, his voice hoarse with desire. 'I wish I hadn't been such an idiot back at school – wish I'd realised then how incredible you are.'

Jana's eyes widened and she abruptly pulled away, a shadow crossing her face. For some reason, his words had touched a raw nerve. Mark was taken aback, his heart sinking at her sudden change in demeanour.

'What's wrong?'

She couldn't even look at him.

'Jana, I didn't mean to upset you . . .'

But she was already slipping through the front door, walking inside.

CHAPTER 27

The soft light of morning drifted through the open curtains as Jana woke, feeling drowsy and content. That was until she remembered how last night had ended. The dinner with Mark had gone amazingly well: the venue perfect, the meal perfect, the wine perfect. The company perfect. And, best of all, the zoo was on track to meet its deadline for reopening. She should be over the moon, and she was on nearly every front – except for one.

Thinking of Mark and their kiss left her a little flushed. After such a romantic evening, she'd been ready for it, ready to let down her guard and explore the connection that they clearly both felt. But then it had all gone sour. It was Mark's fault. Why couldn't he have kept his mouth shut? Didn't he know that any mention of high school was bound to spoil the mood?

Jana stretched, then rose and showered, reliving the previous night and trying to evaluate her feelings. She glanced out the window while she dressed, pleased to see the clear blue sky. It promised a perfect day, and she opened the window to let in the breeze, fragrant with tea-tree and river mint at this time of year. She breathed in a deep lungful of perfumed air.

A faint murmur of voices drifted through the window. Curious, Jana hastily dressed and went downstairs to investigate. Oh no! A crowd of animal rights protesters milled around in front of the house, chanting slogans and waving homemade banners. More were pouring in the driveway. How had they managed that? The front gate now required a code to open it.

Jana recognised the woman addressing the gathering and groaned – Annie West. So far, the Wildfell Park project had been flying under Annie's radar. Maybe they should have held off on making the zoo's new website live. It had achieved terrific reach and attracted a lot of community support. But now, apparently, it had also attracted the attention of the Animal Defenders.

Well, it had been bound to happen eventually. This could be the perfect opportunity to get Annie on side – to explain to her that Wildfell Park would be more than an old-fashioned zoo.

A frowning Bruce joined Jana on the verandah. 'How did that lot get in?'

'No idea,' she replied. 'Come on. We'd better talk to them.'

The pair approached the group. Annie was a tall, striking woman in her thirties with short red hair, a nose ring and steely blue eyes. She wore an Animal Justice Party T-shirt, canvas trousers and seemed to exude an air of authority – quite an intimidating presence.

Jana introduced herself. 'It's good to meet you, Annie. Yes, I know who you are, and I have a lot of respect for your work, especially your advocacy against live sheep exports. Would you like to come inside for a chat?'

Annie and a young man followed them inside. The mood in the kitchen was tense. Annie looked to Jana and Bruce in turn before speaking in a clear, firm voice. 'I'm here to convince you why this zoo shouldn't go ahead. It's abhorrent to keep animals in captivity, especially in zoos. They're notoriously cruel places that always do more harm than good, and Wildfell Park is no exception.' Jana stayed quiet and listened politely.

When Annie was finished, it was Jana's turn to make her case: 'This zoo will be more than a tourist attraction. Not only will it house a new educational centre, but it will also provide us with captive breeding opportunities for endangered species like the black-flanked rock-wallaby, the southern brown bandicoot and the swift parrot. Efforts are already underway at Wildfell Park for a conservation program for Tasmanian devils and southern hairy-nosed wombats.'

Annie only seemed to be half-listening. She raised an eyebrow, clearly unimpressed. 'The solution should be to protect habitats and prevent their endangerment in the first place.' She leaned back in her chair, arms folded across her chest.

'I agree zoos aren't a perfect answer,' said Jana. 'But we do what we can to ensure that the animals in our care are healthy and happy. We provide them with enrichment activities and ensure that their enclosures replicate their natural habitats as closely as possible.'

Annie looked unconvinced. 'I've heard that before and been disappointed. So often the intention doesn't match the reality. Have you considered the psychological impact of captivity on your animals?'

'We're aware of the ethical considerations, and our team of dedicated keepers are working tirelessly to ensure the animals, physical and psychological wellbeing. Let me show you around and you can see for yourself.'

Annie shook her head. 'I'm sorry, but I just can't support this project.' She stood up and grabbed her bag. 'Expect a spirited campaign of opposition.'

'You may as well give up now,' said Annie's young companion with a sneer. 'One way or another, we'll stop this zoo from reopening.' The pair marched back outside.

'One way or another,' said Bruce, scratching his head. 'Was that a threat?'

'I don't know,' Jana replied. 'But I do know that we've got a truckload of trouble on our hands.'

Hazel entered the kitchen. 'Who was that woman? And what's all that commotion outside? I was having a lovely sleep-in and it woke me up.' After Jana explained, Hazel said, with wild, indignant eyes, 'Why, that pack of unwashed hippies isn't fit to set foot in Wildfell Park. What would they know about animal welfare? I bet none of them have nursed a sick water-buffalo calf or raised an orphan monkey.'

'That's a fair bet,' agreed Bruce. He and Jana exchanged amused glances.

'Those idiots are a disgrace,' said Hazel. 'What do they think will happen to the animals if they close us down?' She began putting on her boots. 'I'm going out there to give them a piece of my mind.'

Bruce caught Jana's eye and shook his head.

'Hazel, I don't think that's a good idea,' said Jana, imagining Hazel and Annie in a punch-up on the lawn. 'We don't want to escalate things.'

'There's no reasoning with Hazel when her dander's up,' warned Bruce. 'Best take her shoes.'

'Don't you dare,' growled Hazel, as Bruce grabbed her boots and raised them over his head. As she danced around the mountain of a man, vainly grasping for her footwear, the chanting grew louder.

'Zoos are cruel! Zoos are cruel! Zoos are cruel!'

Bruce swore. 'What do we bloody well do about that lot? We can't just leave them there. The RSPCA inspector will be here this afternoon to examine the new monkey house.'

Jana sighed. 'We'd better call the police. I don't want to pick a fight with these people, but what choice do we have?' And after that she'd have to call Mark.

Mark arrived just as the police were moving the last of the protesters along. Jana filled him in on the morning's events.

'Annie's having a meeting in town tonight,' he said, frowning. 'There are posters all over the place. I'll go along to see if I can get some sense of what she's planning.'

'I'll come with you,' said Jana, instantly aware that she hadn't thought it through.

'You? You'll be recognised right away. Nobody knows me, though.'

A glance out the window revealed the local police sergeant climbing the front porch steps. 'Perhaps you can talk to him,' suggested Jana. 'See if he can spare us a patrol or two.

Meanwhile, I'll speak to the staff. This protest must have given them the jitters.'

'Will do,' said Mark. 'Then I'll need to get back to work.' His eyes held hers, drawing her in like a magnet. 'But I'll see you tonight after the meeting.'

'No need,' she said quickly. 'It will be late, and I want an early night. Call me in the morning.'

A fleeting look of puzzled disappointment crossed his features. Well, so what? Did he expect her to feel sorry for him? He'd never spared her an ounce of pity at Scarborough, and he still hadn't apologised or even acknowledged how he'd humiliated her back then. No – whether Mark liked it or not, she was calling the shots this time.

Mark arrived at the town hall that evening and stood stiffly in the corner of the room, trying to blend in while searching for a seat. The Animal Defenders had attracted quite an audience, and it didn't only consist of counterculture gen Zs as he'd expected. The curious crowd contained a fair number from all age groups.

Mark chose a chair close enough to get a good view of the stage, but far enough away that he wouldn't be too obvious. A tall, slim woman in a purple dress and purple Ariat cowboy boots stepped up to the mike. Was that Annie West? She had close-cropped red hair, a long, elegant neck and a commanding air, but she was younger than he'd imagined. More attractive too, in spite of the nose ring and tattoos, which weren't usually Mark's thing. He'd expected a forty-something harridan with a grey ponytail and wearing dungarees.

The microphone briefly hummed a high-pitched whine. 'Zoos are cruel,' Annie began. 'No matter how hard you try to dress them up another way, it's all lipstick on a pig.' Her bold voice echoed round the walls and seemed to fill the whole hall.

She spoke with confidence and a deep sense of belief. The woman up there on stage was advocating for his zoo to stay closed, yet Mark felt a grudging admiration for her. Annie West was a persuasive public speaker with an undeniable passion for her cause, and Mark had to admit that she knew how to turn a phrase. She punctuated her speech with anecdotes that were both heartwarming and heartbreaking: accounts of bears and monkeys and lions released from years of torment in zoos and how their once-miserable existence had been transformed.

He glanced around at the audience, noting how their faces softened with agreement as they listened. Annie was winning them over. When she finished, her words were met with enthusiastic applause. Mark's heart sank.

Annie took questions.

'I was quite disturbed by what I saw when I last visited,' said a stout middle-aged woman in a floral frock. 'The monkey exhibit was overcrowded, and some just sat in a corner and rocked endlessly.' There were murmurs of assent.

'The buildings and fences were dilapidated,' said someone else. 'The parrot aviary leaked, and I was always frightened that the lions would escape.'

'Me and the missus felt right sorry for that bear,' added a man in a hat. 'All alone for years. It must have done the poor bugger's head in.'

Mark didn't dare write these comments down for fear of drawing attention to himself, but he carefully committed each one to memory. Jana needed to know people's specific objections so she could address them. But as he listened to the attendees voice their concerns, he recognised the truth behind their words. On Hazel and Reg's watch, the monkeys had been kept in cramped cages, the lion enclosure was rundown and insecure, and the sun bear had lived a life of isolation with only a tyre swing for entertainment. Mark always knew that reopening the zoo would be difficult, but it seemed there was a lot more local opposition than he'd expected. Somehow, they had to convince the community that Wildfell Park had changed.

The meeting began to break up. As Mark turned to leave, he noticed a huddle of people speaking in hushed tones and glancing occasionally at the door. They seemed to be plotting something – something that didn't involve Annie. She was busy chatting to a young couple on the other side of the room. His curiosity got the better of him and he inched closer, hoping to listen in on their conversation.

'. . . that's the plan, then.'

Mark strained his ears harder, hoping to catch more of the conversation. But before he could hear anything further, the group headed for the door.

Mark followed them out into the chilly evening, wishing that he could go back to Wildfell Park and tell Jana what he'd learned. But it was late, and she'd made her feelings clear. He'd have to make do with phoning her in the morning.

CHAPTER 28

Jana ended the call, tossing her mobile onto the stainless-steel bench in the vet clinic examination room. Mark's account of last night's Animal Defenders meeting had left an unpleasant taste in her mouth. Clearly there was more community opposition to the zoo reopening than she'd thought. And the idea that a splinter group might be plotting something made her skin prickle.

At times like this she missed Sash. It would have been great to have her level-headed sister as a sounding board. It seemed like forever since they'd seen each other, and phone catch-ups just weren't the same. It didn't seem to matter to her sister, though. Sash behaved exactly as she would if Jana was in the room with her. She reported on the animals in care, the Odessa habitat projects and how things were going with Tracey and Luca.

But Jana found it harder to open up over the phone. Maybe it was because she knew that someone might be listening at the other end. Or maybe it was the sense of distance between them. But for whatever reason, the connection wasn't quite there. She'd do anything to have Sash standing beside her right now.

Jana shook her head, trying to dispel the nagging fear that something was amiss. She brushed a few strands of hair from her face. No point jumping at shadows. Time to get on with the main task of the day – health checks for the animals that were leaving for other zoos or wildlife parks.

Seven macaques were leaving next week for the Black Forest Safari Park north of Adelaide. Jana had seen photos of their new home. Called the Banana Cabana, it boasted large grassed areas with trees, thatched shelters and a playground, all surrounded by a moat. She'd like to have something similar at Wildfell Park one day. Four Barbary sheep, two young dingoes, some squirrels and a pelican were also going to Black Forest.

Jana had desexed the dozens of feral rabbits and guinea pigs, most of which were due to be collected by a local animal shelter for rehoming. Although Jana believed petting zoos deserved no place in a serious conservation facility, Karly had asked her to keep the older, tamer animals.

'Kids will want to pat something,' she'd insisted. 'If they can't pat a rabbit, they might try to pat something else. Didn't a monkey bite off the tip of Hazel's finger once?'

They both knew it had. The veteran rodents stayed.

Jana's most satisfying achievement was having found a new home for Cleo, one of their lionesses, at a New South Wales open-range zoo. She'd be leaving at the start of November. In addition to her comprehensive health check, Cleo required a long-term contraceptive implant. Jana had done her research on the best drug to use and decided on deslorelin inserts. They were generally out of favour among zookeepers because they worked too well. Deslorelin had been used safely and effectively on over a hundred lionesses around the world, but the problem was, it hadn't worn off. Only nine animals had shown reversals when the birth control was withdrawn. The implants, meant to last six months to a year, were still in effect three, four, even five years later.

This lack of reversal wouldn't be a problem in Cleo's case. It might even be an advantage, because such an inbred animal would never be used in a breeding program. So, now it was time for the daunting task of sedating the lioness and transporting her to the veterinary clinic. Johnno was their licensed operator for the tranquilliser gun – a type of air rifle using high-pressure carbon-dioxide gas cylinders to propel the sedative darts. He was also a crack shot, but Jana still wasn't looking forward to this. She checked the operating room one final time. Good – everything was ready. Then she took a deep breath and headed for the big cats' enclosure.

Jana didn't feel at ease with the big cats in the same way that Hazel and Karly did. No matter how much time Jana spent with them, she remained wary of their teeth and awestruck by their size. Maybe it was some primordial instinct at work, a throwback to a time when humans feared what lay beyond their campfire's glow. But for whatever reason, Jana could never shake the idea that people were never meant to be so close to these predators.

Yet here she was, preparing to enter the den of Cleo the cranky lioness, who was even crankier than usual. Cleo was hungry, having been fasted prior to the upcoming general anaesthetic, and she grumbled in deep, throaty growls. The other keepers gathered around. Jana wanted all hands on deck in case of trouble, but they would have come anyway. Any medical procedure on a lion was bound to draw a crowd.

Johnno arrived with the tranquilliser gun that Jana had calibrated and loaded earlier. Cleo greeted him with a bad-tempered roar. She seemed to recognise what was coming next. Johnno expertly targeted her rump, and within ten minutes Cleo was snoring peacefully. Johnno ventured into the enclosure and tugged Cleo's tail, testing the cat's level of sedation. Receiving no response, he gestured to the others that it was safe to come inside. Now they had to act fast. The keepers hurried into the den, rolled the unconscious Cleo onto a canvas tarp and transferred her to a trolley cage.

'Right,' said Johnno. 'Let's get this pussy cat to the vet clinic.'

Jana helped Johnno and Bruce roll Cleo onto the big stainless-steel table. Looking around, it was hard to believe this sparkling, modern surgical suite was all hers. Sophisticated monitoring equipment and powerful adjustable lighting. X-ray and ultrasound machines positioned nearby for easy access. A defibrillator and a well-stocked drugs cabinet. There was even an automated suction and waste-disposal system. What a privilege to work in such an excellent space.

Jana administered another sedative, waited a minute, then nodded to Maggie. 'Ready?'

As a qualified vet nurse, it was Maggie's job to inject an anaesthetic agent into Cleo's IV line and monitor her vitals: heart rate, blood pressure, oxygen concentration and core body temperature. They'd worked together before, and Jana had great confidence in Maggie's competence. The zoo was lucky to have her.

Next, Jana caught Johnno's eye, where he stood by the door with both a rifle and tranquilliser gun. She'd said the rifle wasn't necessary, but he'd shaken his head. 'It's standard procedure, just in case. We both know a dart won't work quickly enough in an emergency.' She hadn't argued.

Jana began the examination at Cleo's head, shining an ophthalmoscope in her eyes to check for problems such as cataracts or corneal ulcers. She checked the lioness's ears, nose, and the lymph nodes under her jaw to make sure they weren't swollen. She opened Cleo's mouth and peered around the oxygen tube to inspect her teeth. The lioness flinched in her sleep and a line from a fairy tale unexpectedly came to mind. *Grandma, what big teeth you have! All the better to eat you with!*

Jana had a stern word with herself. What on earth was she doing, frightening herself like that? She took her stethoscope and listened to Cleo's heart and lungs. She palpitated her abdomen for any sign of an enlarged liver or abnormal bladder. So far, the lioness was in tiptop shape. No matter what Mark thought about Hazel's old-fashioned zookeeping skills, this animal's good health was a credit to her.

Jana moved on to the limbs. She checked the enormous claws, flexing and extending the broad pads to ensure they had full range of movement. Cleo flinched again.

'How's she going, Maggie?' No answer. Jana looked up. Her assistant's expression was strained.

'Blood pressure and heart rate are both up.'

'Increase her anaesthesia.'

215

A pause. 'I just did,' said Maggie. 'It hasn't made a difference.'

'That can't be. Up it again.' Cleo blinked, and a chill ran up Jana's spine. 'I said up it again!'

Jana could hear panic rising in Maggie's voice. 'It's not working.'

Cleo's breathing was no longer steady. It had become fast and erratic.

'More oxygen,' called Jana.

A whisker on Cleo's muzzle twitched, then another, triggering a jolt of fear in Jana. Then her own heart rate skyrocketed as the lioness's eyes flicked open. Cleo stirred, and tossed her head, shaking the oxygen tube from her mouth. She sat up on the examination table, dragging out her cannula. Then she staggered to her feet and took a halting step.

Johnno raised the rifle and nestled the butt into his shoulder. Jana turned her head to look as Maggie ran for the door.

Jana took a deep, steadying breath. If she let this animal die, it would be the end of Wildfell Park. She'd come too far and worked too hard to let that happen.

'Don't shoot!' she ordered and stepped in front of Cleo.

'Jana, move,' said Johnno, his voice low and urgent.

Cleo swung her head, growled and fixed Jana with baleful yellow eyes. Jana was close enough to feel the lioness's warm breath on her cheek. Gritting her teeth, she slowly turned around to face Johnno. 'I'll move when you swap that rifle for a dart gun.'

'For fuck's sake, Jana! Don't you know better than to turn your back on a lion?'

'Swap the gun,' she said in a trembling voice. At any moment she expected to feel the agonising rake of claws and teeth. Part of her wanted to scream and run, but she remained rooted to the spot. 'Just do it.'

Johnno swore, but ever so slowly reached for the tranquilliser gun.

'Now drop the rifle and back out of the room. Don't worry about me,' Jana said, with one hundred per cent more confidence than she felt. 'Cleo's still groggy. Once you're outside, stay by the door, and I'll make a dash for it. Then you can dart her.'

Johnno's face was thunderous, but he did as she asked. What choice did he have, with her blocking his shot? For an instant, Jana thought this was madness, but the moment passed. It would take a few more seconds of courage to save the zoo. *Focus on the door*, she told herself, hoping her jelly legs wouldn't let her down.

'Run!' yelled Johnno.

Jana didn't need telling twice. She was out the door in a flash, her heart exploding in her chest with fear. Behind her she heard a bloodcurdling snarl. Johnno fired. Jana spun around to see Cleo leaping from the examination table as Johnno slammed the door shut. Just as she'd hoped, the lioness had been too uncoordinated for an effective attack. Or perhaps she'd never wanted to attack in the first place. Jana had been a stationary target while she'd talked Johnno down. There'd been every opportunity for Cleo to strike.

Jana remembered something that Hazel had said. *Cleo's a grumpy old girl – a bit like me. But neither one of us is dangerous.* A gush of gratitude towards the lioness left Jana weak and she wobbled alarmingly on her feet.

'I've got you.' Maggie's arms were around her, guiding her to a chair. The rest of the staff crowded around, some congratulating her, others expressing shock and dismay at her actions. But they were unanimous about one thing – their praise for her courage. Including Johnno.

'Well, I'll be damned,' he said with a scowl. 'You're the daftest person I've ever laid eyes on – and the bravest,' he added, grudgingly. 'What you did back there took nerves of steel.'

And it had. Jana had impressed even herself. She found her balance, got to her feet and peered through the glass window in the door. Cleo lay on the floor, yawning. Ten minutes later, she was snoring again. Pride swelled Jana's chest. That magnificent creature was alive because of her.

She turned back to the others. Their chattering stopped as she raised her hand. 'About this, ah . . . incident. I'm sure I don't need to impress upon anybody the need for confidentiality. If word gets out that we had an uncontained, un-sedated lion loose in the clinic, well – let's just say it wouldn't look good for our licence application, would it?' Her words were followed by murmurs of assent. 'Thank you,' said Jana. 'Thank you all from the bottom of my heart.'

But even as she spoke the words, a creeping suspicion was taking hold. This incident should not have happened. Maggie was an experienced vet nurse who didn't make basic mistakes. The level of anaesthetic she'd administered should have well and truly knocked Cleo out. The conclusion, although disturbing, seemed unavoidable: someone had sabotaged the medication.

CHAPTER 29

Mark hurried into the manor house and found Jana on the sitting-room couch, nursing a cup of tea. Amber hovered close by, offering Jana cushions and trying to persuade her to eat a biscuit. The girl's red eyes showed that she'd been crying.

'Jesus, Jana! What on earth were you thinking? You could have been killed.' He'd dropped everything and rushed to the zoo, alerted by a call from Johnno, and he was beside himself with worry and, yes – anger. How could she have put herself in such danger?

Jana regarded him calmly and sipped her tea. 'I wish Johnno hadn't told you. I wanted to do it in my own time.'

'Damn it, Jana. I had a right to know, and straight away.'

'Well, yes. I suppose so.' She started recounting the events of the morning, then paused and glanced at Amber. 'Stop fussing, Amber. I'm fine. Will you go and give Cleo a treat for me? Maggie has put aside a nice piece of liver for her. I think she deserves it, don't you?'

Amber seemed unwilling to leave.

'I'll look after your boss,' said Mark, reassuring her. 'You go ahead and check on Cleo.'

'Well, if you're sure? But don't you dare yell at her, Mark.' Amber's nostrils flared. 'Jana's courage saved Wildfell Park. You should have seen her.'

Mark flinched. He was rather glad that he hadn't. He didn't think his heart could have stood it.

Amber continued. 'What do you think would have happened if we'd had to shoot an out-of-control lion? The zoo would never have got its licence back.'

Mark wanted to say, *And what if Cleo had injured or killed Jana? How would our application have fared then?* But he bit his tongue. 'I won't yell at Jana, as you put it,' he said. 'I promise.'

Amber reluctantly left the room.

'Thank God she's gone,' said Jana, watching the door close.

'Amber cares about you,' said Mark, feeling his nerves slowly settle. 'We all do. You can hardly blame her for being concerned.'

'That's not what I mean.' Jana glanced around, as if she wanted to make doubly sure that they were alone. 'Take a seat.' Mark sat beside her on the couch and Jana pinned him with big, worried eyes. 'Cleo waking up during her examination was no accident. Someone tampered with her anaesthetic.'

Mark was dumbstruck. Had he heard her right? After a few moments silence, Jana repeated her extraordinary allegation.

'Surely not,' he said at last. 'There must be another explanation.'

Jana fished around in her pocket and pulled out an empty

plastic capsule in a ziplock bag. 'This ampoule contained the anaesthetic agent used to keep Cleo under once the initial sedative wore off. The surgical assistant, in this case Maggie, twists the top off the sealed ampoule before withdrawing the contents into a syringe and injecting it into the IV line.' She tossed the empty capsule into the air, caught it and handed it to Mark. 'See anything unusual?'

Mark took the clear plastic container and examined it, not sure what he was looking for.

Jana helped him out. 'It's on the bottom.'

Mark turned the little capsule over. 'What?' he said. 'I can't see anything.'

'Look more closely.' Jana leaned over and pointed to an asymmetrical raised dot in the centre of the base. 'Compare it to this one.'

She fished another ampoule out of her pocket. This one was unused – still sealed and filled with clear liquid. He checked the base. It was completely smooth. He looked at Jana blankly. What was she getting at?

'I'll tell you what I think happened.' She took the used capsule from his hand. 'Someone inserted a needle into the bottom of this ampoule and syringed out the contents. Then they replaced it with some other clear fluid and used a tiny drop from a hot glue gun to seal the hole.'

'Hang on a minute. That's pretty far-fetched.'

Jana shrugged. 'Maybe.' She made a fist around the used ampoule. 'I'm about to run this little beauty over to the Rivertown Medical Clinic. They have a pathology lab and a doctor who owes me a favour. I saved his dog from a snake bite. Anyway, he's agreed to test the residual contents of the ampoule for me. But until then, we must assume that a staff member has defected to the Animal Defenders and is out to sabotage the zoo. God knows who. I don't lock the clinic during the day, and the staff have keys anyway.'

'Good grief, Jana. If that's true, someone we trust was prepared to risk your life – and Maggie's.'

'Who's to say it wasn't Maggie?' said Jana, her voice barely more than a whisper. 'She was right there on the spot, and she's the only staff member with medical training. But the truth is, it could have been anyone.'

'No,' said Mark, vigorously shaking his head. 'I refuse to believe that Maggie is capable of such treachery. She was in as much danger as you were.'

'True,' said Jana. 'Anyway, I have to check on Cleo. Can you lock up the vet clinic and ask for everyone's keys? Nobody gets in unsupervised from now on.'

Mark nodded. His mind was racing with the implications of Jana's discovery. If someone had indeed tampered with Cleo's dose, then that person was capable of anything. He thought of the online threats that had been made. *Zoo directors don't deserve to breathe.* Mark rubbed his temples, feeling a headache coming on. He hadn't thought that Annie West would go so far. But maybe she hadn't. He remembered the clique of people with their heads together after the town meeting. Had one of the zoo staff joined a radical breakaway group? It was an unbearable, inconceivable notion, but he couldn't let personal feelings get in the way of the truth. If someone had betrayed the zoo – betrayed Jana – he intended to find out.

*

Lexie, Maggie and Amber were in the lunchroom of the vet clinic when Mark arrived. Cleo had been returned to her quarters. Medical checks and contraceptive implants would have to wait.

The women crowded around him, all talking at once, eager to relay the dramatic events of the morning. But Mark wasn't really listening. Their voices blurred, and a pall of suspicion dulled his hearing. Was one of these people a traitor who'd threatened Jana's life? And if so, which one?

'If you don't mind, I'd like you all to leave,' he said, abruptly.

That stopped them talking, for a few moments at least. Then the protests began.

'We can't,' said Lexie.

'We're only halfway through the examinations,' said Amber.

'Yes,' agreed Maggie. 'We may not be able to do the monkeys or dingoes by ourselves, but we can complete final check-ups on the rabbits, guinea pigs and squirrels if Jana doesn't feel up to it. There are still twenty-three to go, and they're due to be picked up tomorrow.'

'Didn't you hear me?' Mark raised his voice. 'I want you all to leave. Right now. And hand over your keys to the clinic.'

The protests stopped, replaced with incredulous stares. Mark didn't care. He just wanted them out of there. Until the true culprit was identified, he'd treat all the staff the same. Guilty until proven innocent. It was true that Maggie had been in danger today too, but that didn't automatically exonerate her. Maybe she'd designed it that way to allay suspicion.

Who knew what lengths an extremist might go to? His fear for Jana, and indeed for the whole Wildfell Park project, prevented him from feeling sympathy for anybody else.

'Why do you want our keys?' Maggie's eyes filled with confusion.

Mark made a conscious effort to calm himself. He'd already raised more conjecture among the staff than he'd meant to.

'Jana asked for them – just for now. She wants to examine all the equipment in the surgery and wants everything exactly the same as when Cleo woke up. Does that make sense?'

'Is Jana okay?' asked Lexie. When Mark nodded, she added, 'You could simply *ask* us to stay out of the clinic.'

'I could,' said Mark. 'But I guess Jana wants to be absolutely sure that nothing is touched.'

'Johnno and Bruce have keys too,' said Lexie. 'I don't know why you're singling us out.'

'I'm not.' Mark forced a smile, wanting to lighten the mood. 'I'm going to ask for their keys too, just until we get to the bottom of what happened.'

That seemed to satisfy the women. Lexie and Amber took out their key cards and handed them over. Maggie hesitated, her eyes glistening with tears. She opened her mouth to speak, but Mark pressed his lips together, shook his head and held out his hand. She gave him the card and trailed out after the others.

Two hours later, Mark followed Jana back into the house, and once again they took a seat on the sitting-room couch.

'I was right.' Jana handed him the lab analysis print-out

she'd just picked up at the medical centre in town. 'The empty ampoule used on Cleo contained saline solution. Barely a trace of anaesthetic agent was found.'

Mark appeared stunned, clearly trying to process the information. It didn't matter that they'd half-expected the result. It was still a punch in the guts. He put a hand on Jana's knee and met her troubled eyes. 'I don't know about you, but I need a drink.'

Soon they were both downing brandies sourced from the antique liquor cabinet in the corner of the room.

'Do you think Hazel will mind?' asked Mark.

'She won't know,' said Jana. 'I'll replace the bottle before she gets back from her trip to Adelaide.'

'Well then.' Mark poured them both another one. He swirled the golden liquid around in his glass before drinking it. 'I reckon it's time for the police.'

Jana didn't respond. Instead, she picked up her glass, considering his suggestion.

Mark wiped his mouth with the back of his hand. 'I said, I think it's time to—'

'No.'

'Okay . . . Why not?'

'Think about it. If the cops start interviewing people, the news will be all around town in a flash. The keepers will be upset already, thinking they're under suspicion – which they are, of course, but I'd rather leave the cops out of it. It might even spark resignations, which we absolutely cannot afford. We're short-staffed as it is.'

'True,' conceded Mark. 'But what's the alternative? I feel uncomfortable keeping this from the police.'

'I don't mean forever,' said Jana. 'We'll call them in once we discover who the saboteur is.'

'And exactly how will we do that?'

She gulped her brandy, feeling the smooth liquid gently burn her throat, and shot him a wry smile. 'That's the part I haven't worked out yet.'

Mark swirled the brandy in his glass again. 'It's a tough situation all right, but you put yourself in real danger today.' He reached over, placing a hand on her arm. 'I understand your passion for these animals, Jana, but please don't take any more risks,' he said. 'I . . . I don't know what I'd do if anything happened to you.'

There was no doubting the anxiety etched on his face or the sincerity of his words. Something warm stirred in Jana's chest as Mark's gaze stayed on her with such heartfelt concern. For now, the past had lost its grip. Their eyes locked, and the room seemed to shrink around them.

Jana moved nearer, her voice low. 'Mark, I understand why you're worried, but sometimes I have to trust my instincts. I couldn't let Cleo die.'

Mark's expression softened and he leaned in, his face just inches from hers. 'I know, Jana. You're brave and passionate, and that's one of the things I love most about you.'

Their lips met in a hesitant kiss. The kiss deepened, fuelled by the emotions of the day and the undeniable chemistry they shared. Jana saw the hunger in his eyes and a fierce wanting claimed her. She got up to lock the door, feeling wanton and reckless.

They kicked off their shoes and began undressing each other, Mark moving slowly, as if unveiling a costly gift. She peeled off his shirt, admiring his strong shoulders and lightly muscled torso. Her skin burned beneath his touch. Mark kissed the pulsing hollow of her throat. His lips trailed from her neck, over her full breasts and down to her stomach, provoking little gasps of delight from her. Then he wrapped her tight in his arms and kissed her like she'd never been kissed before.

Time stood still. She could have stayed like that forever, lost in a world of their own where nothing mattered except each other. But when she tugged at his belt, Mark put the brakes on. 'I'm desperate to make love to you,' he managed, his voice hoarse. 'But we don't have protection, and I've learned to be responsible the hard way.'

He stood up and began pacing the room, trying without much success to hide the large bulge in his pants.

'You're right,' she said, her voice low and husky. 'So go to the store and then meet me upstairs in my room.'

Mark didn't need telling twice, misbuttoning his shirt in his haste and hopping about trying to put his shoes on.

'Oh, and Mark?' she called as he opened the door. 'When you come back, don't speak. Don't say a word.'

CHAPTER 30

Mark stayed over. The soft light of morning drifted through the open curtains as Jana woke, feeling drowsy and satisfied. It had been a wild night, and Mark was every bit as good a lover as she'd hoped he'd be. Jana's brush with death made life seem all the sweeter, and she was determined to make the most of it. But she remembered to hold back her heart. This was lust, not love, and she would not forget it.

She yawned, half-believing that last night had been a dream and wondering what Hazel would think if she caught Mark emerging from the bathroom, where he'd gone for a shower. But there was no danger of that; Hazel was in Adelaide visiting relatives. Jana tried to evaluate her feelings. Did she want to sleep with Mark again? Definitely. Could she keep herself from becoming attached? Probably. She wasn't a schoolgirl in puppy love any more. As long as she recognised this for what it was – a healthy attraction between two consenting adults – she wouldn't get hurt. Sex with Mark was explosive and passionate – the perfect spring fling. But she must never take it seriously.

'Mark,' said Jana when he returned. She stopped to slip on a shirt. 'Can I ask you something?'

'Anything, honey. Your wish is my command.' He tried to pull her close, but she ducked away.

'Is it cool if we keep this casual?'

Mark tilted his head in apparent confusion. 'What do you mean?'

'You know – no strings. A friends-with-benefits kind of thing.'

He was visibly taken aback and blinked uncomprehendingly. 'Forgive me if I'm being dense, but could you be more specific?'

'How much more specific can I be? We hook up when we feel like it and don't let it interfere with our lives otherwise. Let's not complicate things by starting something serious.'

She'd managed to render him temporarily speechless. 'Okay,' he said at last. 'If you're sure that's what you want?' She nodded, firmly. 'Okay, friends with benefits it is.'

Jana gave a small, relieved sigh. 'I'm glad you understand.' She straightened the coverlet. 'So, you won't mind if I don't always ask you to stay over?'

Mark's smile seemed forced. 'Of course not.' He gently touched her hair. 'I just want you to be happy.'

Jana smiled back at him, her eyes twinkling. 'Then come back to bed.'

Later, as Jana basked in the afterglow of their lovemaking, her thoughts turned to the day ahead.

'I'm going to have another go at implanting Cleo today.

But don't worry, nobody will enter the clinic until I do. And I'm using anaesthetic that comes in tamper-proof glass ampoules.'

'That's reassuring.' Mark kissed her fingers. 'I've been thinking about when the water buffalo escaped. You said a big branch dropped over the fence.'

'That's right. From an old red gum.'

'Do me a favour.' He traced the curve of her cheek with his forefinger. 'After I leave for work, have a good look at that tree. Go by yourself.'

'Why?'

'Maybe the branch had some help to fall.'

Jana felt her stomach turn, feeling like a naive fool. She'd always assumed that the boundary breach had been acci-dental. Now it was time to question everything – all the little things that had gone wrong around the zoo that she'd put down to bad luck. The unlocked gate that had allowed the macaques to escape. The fridges breaking down, causing a week's supply of food to spoil. A feeding mix-up that had caused the dingoes to fall ill – grapes had somehow been added to their daily diet of meat, fruit and vegetables. The tartaric acid in grapes was toxic to canines, leading to stomach cramps and dehydration. Nobody could fathom how these mistakes had been made.

'We need to keep a very close eye on everyone around here, even the contractors,' said Mark. 'I'll talk to the security blokes and see if they can tighten their surveillance. Set up some cameras around the grounds, not just at the perimeter.'

'That's a good start,' said Jana, watching a moth fly into a spider web in a corner of the high ceiling.

'But we have to be careful,' said Mark. 'Taking everyone's

keys was one thing, but we don't want anyone panicking before we're sure of our facts.'

'Great,' said Jana, rolling her eyes. 'And how exactly is that supposed to happen?'

'Hang on,' said Mark, understandably confused. 'It was your idea not to call in the police. I assumed that you might have at least the ghost of a plan.'

'Well, you assumed wrong.' Jana couldn't look at him.

They both fell into a glum silence. The weight of their predicament hung heavy in the room.

Jana jumped out of bed and pulled on a robe. 'I'm going for a shower.'

'Wait.' Mark sat up. 'Why don't we plant an undercover agent among the staff?'

Jana swung around to face him. She rubbed her chin, deep in thought. 'It could work,' she said at last. 'We'd need someone who can blend in and gain the trust of the keepers. And they'd have to know a fair bit about animals, otherwise it will look phoney.'

Mark nodded. 'And it will need to be an outsider. Someone who doesn't have any connections to the zoo or the town.'

'It's a good plan,' said Jana. 'But where do we find someone willing to go undercover and work with animals? Not just anyone can do it, and we don't have much time.'

'What about hiring a private investigator?' said Mark. 'Give them all-area access. Have them report any suspicious behaviour.'

Jana shook her head. 'That wouldn't fool anyone. We've been extra careful to only hire experienced keepers. A rookie would stand out like a sore thumb.'

'Well, what about your sister, Sash? No one here has met her, have they?'

'No.'

'Perfect. And nobody will guess. There's not much of a family resemblance.'

That was true. Jana took after their father, with an olive complexion, shining jet hair and large dark eyes. But Sash resembled their mother, with fair hair and blue eyes.

'Your sister is an outsider in Rivertown,' continued Mark, clearly becoming more excited by the idea. 'She has all the experience we're looking for, and the best thing is that she's totally trustworthy. A private eye could potentially be bought, but not your sister. I've never met anybody more dedicated to animal welfare.'

'Really?' said Jana, in mock surprise.

'Apart from you, of course,' he added quickly.

'That's more like it. But Sash has her hands full at the wombat sanctuary as it is.'

'I'll hire someone to help Tracey and Luca – two people if necessary. We both know how excited Sash is about Odessa becoming part of the Aussie Ark project. She has as much of a stake in Wildfell Park succeeding as you do.'

Jana turned the idea over in her mind. Sash possessed all the credentials needed to pass as a highly qualified keeper. And the idea of having her sister work at the zoo gave Jana a thrill of excitement. Sash was somebody that she and Mark could safely confide in, and three heads were bound to be better than two. But the attraction wasn't simply because Sash was eminently suitable for the task.

For weeks now Jana had been longing for her sister,

longing to hug and laugh and talk with her. And yes, to tell her about Mark and their strange relationship. Jana had held herself tight for what seemed like forever, hiding her secret pain. Now something told her that it was time to start letting go. Time to be brave, and to finally tell Sash about what had happened all those years ago, and why their parents had been speeding through the dark to Overland Corner on that fateful night.

Jana's thoughts turned to yesterday morning in the clinic. Yes, she'd been in danger; yes, she'd been scared – but she hadn't hesitated to put herself on the line for Wildfell Park. Perhaps her passion to protect the zoo was the inspiration she needed to finally find her courage.

Mark was gazing at her, eyebrows raised, waiting for an answer. 'Well, what do you think?'

'What do I think?' Jana jumped back on the bed and kissed him, forgetting in that moment her vow to stay detached. 'I think it's a fantastic idea. I'm going to ring Sash right after I check that red gum by the river.'

'Sabotage?' said Sash. 'You're kidding.'

'I'm afraid not,' said Jana, checking that she'd locked the office door. This was a phone conversation that she did not want anybody walking in on. Jana explained the situation in detail.

'When did it begin?' asked Sash.

'Almost as soon as I got here. The water buffalo escaped into the river after a fallen branch took out the fence. If not for Mark chasing them back with a jet ski, a whole paddle-steamer full of people would have seen them and there'd have been no chance of getting Wildfell Park's licence renewed.'

'Mark?' Jana could hear the amusement in her sister's voice. 'He seems like a nice guy, but a buffalo wrangler?'

'Yes, I know. Anyway, nobody suspected it was anything but an accident. Until this morning when Mark suggested I check out the tree. That branch that fell over the fence had been sawn through.' Jana quickly outlined her surprising proposal for Sash.

'Slow down, Jana. I'm not sure what you're asking.'

'It's simple. I'm asking you to spy for me.'

Sash laughed out loud. 'What am I supposed to do about Odessa? We have a full complement of orphans, not to mention the wombat mange-control program. There's no way that Luca and Tracey can manage on their own.'

'Don't worry. Mark's going to hire an extra person.'

'Mark again?'

'Shut up. Anyway, it won't be for long. A super-sleuth like you will crack the case in no time.'

Sash chuckled. 'I must admit, it sounds intriguing.'

'You'll come then?'

'Yes, I'll come. On the condition that Mark arranges some more help for Luca asap.'

Jana squealed with excitement, feeling like a dizzy schoolgirl. How good it would be working with Sash again. The sick feeling in the pit of her belly was fading, replaced with a steely determination to solve the mystery of who was sabotaging the zoo and why.

The three of them – yes, Mark included – would make a formidable team. The saboteurs didn't stand a chance.

CHAPTER 31

Jana stood on the house verandah. A ring of curious faces surrounded her as she introduced her sister, complete with a new pseudonym, to the other keepers.

'Please welcome Tash Kennedy to the Wildfell Park staff. She's from interstate, so will be staying here at the manor for now.' A murmur of hellos. 'We're very fortunate to have her. Tash is a triple threat. Not only does she have a degree in zoology and practical experience working at Taronga and Werribee Zoo, but on top of that she's a tech-head and a mechanical whizz.'

Bruce raised his eyebrows, looking impressed. 'Young Tash here sounds too good to be true.' Sash broke into a broad grin.

'How are you with motors?' asked Johnno.

Jana almost blew her sister's cover by saying that Sash had been tinkering with motors since she was five years old. 'You'll find out soon enough, Johnno. Tash will spend a few days working with each staff member in turn to get a comprehensive overview of zoo operations. She'll start with you, Maggie, learning the ropes in the large-herbivore department. I believe you're due to begin scans on the Barbary sheep tomorrow.'

Maggie clapped her hands. 'That's right, and it will be wonderful to have a helper other than grumpy old Johnno.'

Johnno grunted his displeasure at the remark. 'You'd best watch out for their horns, Tash. That big ram got me a good one last time, right through the bars of the crush. And don't be fooled – the females are crankier than the males.'

'We're going to hear the pitter-patter of little hooves soon,' said Maggie, 'and we want to know how many we're expecting. Have you ever seen anything cuter than a Barbary lamb?'

'They are very cute,' agreed Jana.

'When will we get our key cards back for the vet clinic?' asked Bruce. 'We really must have ready access to the medical supplies.'

'That's right,' said Lexie, frowning at Jana. 'When I needed a dressing for the baby macaque's leg this morning, I couldn't get in. It's annoying to have to find you for every little thing.'

'I know,' said Jana in a consoling tone. 'It's very inconvenient. But Mark is embarking on a full upgrade to zoo security. Your old cards won't work any more. You'll be issued with new ones as soon as they're ready. In the meantime, I'll work full-time from the office in the vet clinic instead of from the house. It will remain open while I'm there, so you can collect supplies as needed.' This seemed to satisfy people. 'Well,' said Jana, sounding far more upbeat than she felt. 'If there are no more questions, I'd like to give Tash a final briefing and show her around the surgery.'

One by one, the staff filed off. Jana watched them go,

feeling torn. She hated lying to them – hated spying on them and mistrusting them. She desperately wished that she was wrong, and that none of the keepers had betrayed the zoo. But Jana was a scientist at heart. Cleo's anaesthetic dose had been tampered with. That was a fact – a shocking and disturbing fact, for sure, but a fact nonetheless.

She heaved a great sigh and Sash gave her a knowing look, sensing her ambivalence. 'Are you sure that you want me to do this?'

Jana smiled, ruefully. 'You know me too well.' She glanced around to make sure nobody was watching, then gave her sister a long, heartfelt hug. 'Come on. I'll give you that briefing.'

When they reached the clinic, Jana unlocked the door, then locked it again behind her. The building was well lit, with large windows letting in the morning light. It had the unique odour of veterinary hospitals everywhere – a pungent mixture of animals, cleaning products and antiseptic.

Jana proudly showed her sister the brand-new diagnostic apparatus and intensive care unit. The X-ray, ultrasound and ECG machines. Blood analysers, endoscopy equipment and incubators. She showed off the two surgical suites, the hospital wards and the well-stocked pharmacy.

'Very impressive,' said Sash when she'd finished looking around and the two of them were seated in the clinic's office.

'Do you think it will satisfy the licensing board?'

'You're joking, right? I reckon this place is better equipped than the Rivertown Hospital. You said Frieda Abraham paid for everything?'

'Everything,' repeated Jana. 'We only have nine weeks left before the inspection. So far, we're within the original budget – just. But if there are last-minute costs, Mark says we can count on her to cover them.'

At the mention of Mark, Sash cocked her head to the side and raised her brows.

Jana ignored her and continued. 'He's conducting background checks on the staff to identify any red flags that might suggest involvement in the sabotage.' She kept her voice low. 'Johnno likes to bet on the horses, but his gambling isn't out of control. Two of the contractors spent brief stints in prison for drug offences, but that was a long time ago. They've been clean for years, and anyway, neither of them had access to the pharmacy. Maggie's interesting, though. From her Instagram activity, it seems that she's sympathetic to a radical group called Extinction Rebellion. She might even be a member. We don't know.'

'I've heard of them,' said Sash. 'They use civil disobedience to draw attention to ecological causes. But their protests are always nonviolent. To be honest, I'm sympathetic to them as well.'

Jana turned her sister's words over in her mind. Extinction Rebellion might well align itself with Annie West's Animal Defenders. It was hard to believe that either organisation would stage a stunt that put animals at risk – or people, for that matter. Still, Maggie's connection to the group would have to be examined.

'Has Mark turned up anything else?' asked Sash.

'Apparently Lexie took out a large personal loan last year, and it's not clear what it was for. Maybe you can find out?'

'I'll do my best.'

Jana looked down at her hands, clasped together in her lap. They didn't feel like her hands. She felt the fabric of her jeans, the smooth groove of the seam, the threads crisscrossing it in a pattern. They didn't feel like her jeans. Nothing about herself felt familiar. She'd always prided herself on being an honest, forthright person. She'd viewed things as either true or false, right or wrong. But now she was masterminding a deceit on the people she cared about. On the face of it, that was wrong. And yet it could expose the zoo's enemies, so that was right. No wonder she was confused. Jana recalled her visit to Tasmania, when she had asked if it was true that devils only saw in black or white.

'Not in black and white, but in shades of grey,' Penny had explained. 'If only more people would do the same.' Now Jana understood what her friend had meant. She thought about her conflicted feelings for Mark. Life was a complicated business.

Sash tapped her shoulder. 'Hey, sis? Come back to earth. Is there anything in particular that I'm looking for?'

Jana shook her head to clear it. 'You might not know it until you see it. Just try to gain people's trust and keep your ear to the ground. Are there any unusual alliances or animosities between the keepers, for example? Does anyone spend more time than necessary in a particular place or behave strangely around the equipment? You can't be everywhere, so Mark is installing cameras in strategic locations around the zoo to capture any suspicious activity.'

'Don't worry.' Sash's eyes shone with amusement. 'I've seen enough Phryne Fisher episodes to know how to investigate a mystery. Although I guess I won't get to wear the fabulous frocks.'

Jana grinned. 'As if you'd want to. You haven't worn a dress since Mum made you wear that flowery thing to our cousin's wedding.'

'I was mortified. How old was I? Fourteen?'

'Fifteen,' said Jana. 'I didn't think you'd ever speak to Mum again.'

Sash laughed. 'Neither did I. But no more playing "Remember when". It will make it harder to pretend that I don't know you.'

'Right,' said Jana. 'Down to business then. You'll be working with Maggie today. She moved back with her mother, Jean, so she could stay on as a volunteer when Hazel was struggling to pay the staff. I feel terrible that she's under suspicion. You'd never find someone more loyal or dedicated to Wildfell Park.'

'I'll be the judge of that,' said Sash, matter-of-factly. 'And you shouldn't feel bad. Everybody's under suspicion.'

How grateful Jana was to have her straight-talking sister back by her side. 'I can't wait for the others to go home so we can have a proper heart-to-heart.'

Sash raised an eyebrow. 'We're not talking about the zoo, now, are we?'

'All in good time, little sis.' Jana stood and unlocked the door. 'All in good time.'

CHAPTER 32

The delicious aroma of beef-and-onion stew filled the kitchen, a rich, hearty scent that made Jana's mouth water. She was thrilled to finally come home to Sash after spending what had felt like an eternity watching Bruce dawdle around the workshop, packing up his tools and supplies as if he had all the time in the world. He'd insisted on staying back after everybody else had gone home in order to finish welding some new fence panels for the sun bear's paddock. Normally, Jana would have appreciated his stellar work ethic. Today, it had been simply annoying.

Sash looked up from tasting the broth. 'This was supposed to be for tomorrow night, but you took so long, I think it's ready now. There's no rice, though.'

'It smells wonderful and I'm starving.' Jana went to the walk-in pantry and brought out a loaf of crusty bread. 'I've missed your cooking. I didn't inherit the gene from Mum.'

'Rubbish,' laughed Sash. 'You're just too lazy. Make yourself useful and get me some serving bowls. Oh, and fetch the bottle of shiraz from my bag by the door.'

'Gladly.' They might need more than one bottle of wine between them tonight, thought Jana, considering the confession that she had planned. 'So, what was your first day like?'

'I had a ball,' said Sash. 'Though I wish we were able to use those secret surveillance devices that we talked about.' In addition to the main security cameras that were visible to all, Sash had wanted to set up a series of tiny, hidden cameras that could record audio and video. 'I would have felt like a movie spy – hiding bugs in pot plants and sunglasses. And it would make my job a lot easier.'

'It would have,' Jana agreed with a laugh. 'Pity that it's illegal to record somebody without their permission.'

'Yes,' said Sash, ruefully. 'So Mark said. But for devices that are supposed to be illegal, there sure are a heap available online. And from Australian sites too.' She took a black-and-silver pen from her pocket. 'I ordered this from one of them. They even offered free shipping.' She handed it to her sister. 'Tell me what it is.'

Jana turned it over in her hand. 'It's a ballpoint pen. Rather a nice one, too.'

'Wrong. It's a voice recorder.' Sash clicked the top button to extend the nib. 'Now, say something.'

'Okay. My sister fancies herself as James Bond.'

'That'll do.' Sash clicked the top button again. Then she fished a pair of earphones from her pocket and plugged them into the nib hole. 'Put these on.'

Jana dutifully did as she was asked. Sash clicked again. Jana's mouth fell open as she heard her words repeated, loud and clear. 'That's amazing!'

Sash beamed. 'Don't you just love technology?' She took

back the earphones and popped the pen into her top pocket. 'But since your goody-two-shoes boss says I can't use it, I guess I'll have to conduct my undercover operation the hard way. At least he's letting me fly Bumblebee.'

'Bumblebee?'

'My drone. I said it would be good in an emergency for locating lost zoo animals.'

Jana quailed at the prospect of more lost animals. 'Let's pray we never have to test that theory. I've had enough of chasing buffalo and monkeys around these grounds.'

'I can get a bird's-eye view of Wildfell Park whenever I want. Maggie's fascinated with Bumblebee, by the way. I'm teaching her to fly it.'

'What did you think about Maggie?'

'She's a sweetheart. Not only is she a knowledgeable, hardworking keeper, but she's the loveliest person as well. Although she's a bit too nice for her own good, if you ask me. Treats those ornery sheep like they're her best friends. When the ram reared up and tried to charge us with his horns, she said, "Isn't that sweet. He wants to play."'

Jana smiled. That was Maggie all over. 'Any concerns?'

'No,' said Sash. 'She seems absolutely devoted to Wildfell Park. She said more than once that working here is her dream job. But you're right about her having sympathy for Extinction Rebellion. I mentioned their latest protest. You know, where they picketed the Pacific Islands Conference in Canberra to raise awareness about rising sea levels. Dozens of them were arrested and she sees them as heroes.'

'What does she think of their opposition to zoos and aquariums?'

'I think that's the only reason why she hasn't joined them. She agrees with their focus on protecting wild animals in the habitats where they belong. I think we all do. But she still sees zoos as a crucial part of protecting threatened species.'

Jana felt a release of tension, a lightness, on hearing that. She desperately wanted Maggie to be innocent. 'Did she mention Annie West's Animal Defenders at all?'

'Only to say that she hopes they don't cause the zoo any more trouble. She blames them for letting the monkeys out. If she's aligned with that group, she's not admitting it.' Sash ladled generous amounts of stew into the bowls. 'But then she wouldn't, would she?'

Jana's initial relief at her sister's reassuring words faded. Nobody was above suspicion, and she couldn't let personal feelings stand in the way of discovering the truth. 'Karly could be a problem,' she said. 'She comes here at weekends, and she knows you. We've clued her up on the whole undercover thing and warned her to call you Tash. We all will from now on, even when no one else is around. It'll make it easier for Karly to remember. She thinks what you're doing is cool, by the way. But if she slips up, I think you should have a code phrase to remind her. Something you can slip into a conversation without drawing too much attention.'

'Okay. How about I stretch and say, "Oh, my aching back."'

'That'll do, I guess.'

Sash looked at the two table settings. 'So, no one else is joining us for dinner?'

Jana sat down and poured the wine. 'Hazel's away in Adelaide. You'll meet her next week. She's quite a character; you'll like her.'

'I imagine I will. She must be a remarkable woman to have run this zoo for all those years.' Sash cut herself a piece of sourdough and dipped it into the rich broth. 'And what about Mark?'

Jana tasted the stew and added salt and pepper from the grinders on the table. 'Mark's busy,' she said, without looking up.

'You know that's not what I meant.'

Okay, here it was. The perfect opportunity to open up about their odd relationship. Now that the moment was upon her, Jana felt a terrible urgency, as if she had to spit it out before she lost her nerve. She put down her spoon and took a swig of wine.

Sash studied her expression. 'You're sleeping with him, right?' A grin spread across her face. 'Well, good for you. He seems like a great guy – and he's smoking hot, to boot. It's about time you got over that weird hostility you had towards him.'

Jana ran her finger along the grain of the tabletop. 'You might not be so pleased after what I'm about to tell you.' Jana took a deep, steadying breath. She could do this. She'd had a practice run telling Penny down in Tasmania, and now it was time to confess closer to home. She was weary of concealing the truth.

Jana told Sash everything, rushing her words, barely believing that she was sharing the secret that she'd guarded so closely from her family for more than a decade. Jana told Sash of the years of relentless harassment that she'd endured from Harper, Karly's mother, at Scarborough College. Of her schoolgirl crush on Mark, and her joy when it seemed he returned her affections. Of their brief online affair, and the foolish lovesick messages that she'd sent him. Sash listened in silence, never once interrupting, except to encourage Jana occasionally when she stumbled over her words.

'But it was all a cruel joke. Mark sent me a text saying he'd made me fall in love with him for a bet. In order to win, he had to share all my personal messages on the Year Twelve Instagram account.' Jana felt the prick of tears, as the old feelings of shame and humiliation rushed back.

'Jesus, Jana,' said Sash, eyes brimming over with sympathy. 'So that's why you ran away from Scarborough on the eve of your final exams.'

'Yes, and that's why our parents were on that godforsaken highway in the path of a truck at two o'clock in the morning. Now can you understand why I reacted to Mark the way I did?'

Sash whistled softly. 'What an utter bastard! Yet now you're screwing him?'

'I can explain—'

'I think perhaps you'd better.'

'He's changed, Sash. At least I want to believe he has. He's a terrific father and wonderfully supportive of the zoo – and of me. I don't know what I'd do without him.'

'Maybe so, but after what he did to you and how it affected our family?' Sash shook her head. 'I can't believe you've been living with the weight of this for so long.' She got up and wrapped Jana in a long hug. 'I know people can change. And it happened a long time ago. You were both just kids.' She topped up her sister's wineglass. 'Still, it was a dog act. Did he follow through with his threat to publicly share your messages?'

Jana blinked hard. The question surprised her. 'Well, of course he did. That was the whole point of the charade.'

'But do you know for sure?'

'I didn't stick around to find out.'

'What did Mark say?'

'I haven't asked him.'

Sash gaped at her in disbelief. 'You must have talked with Mark about what happened. Otherwise you wouldn't have forgiven him.'

'Well, I haven't,' snapped Jana, feeling defensive.

'Now I'm confused,' said Sash. 'What haven't you done? Talked with him or forgiven him?'

Jana shrugged. 'I haven't done either. It's the weirdest thing. When Mark eventually recognised me – and that took him long enough. I'm obviously quite forgettable. Anyway, when he did recognise me, Mark offered an apology – of sorts. He apologised for hanging around with the wrong crowd at school, and for not stepping in to stop Harper from bullying me. But that was it. No mention of the bet or phoney online affair. Either he has amnesia or he's in serious denial.'

Sash shook her head. 'I don't understand. Without a genuine apology, how could you sleep with him?'

'By keeping it casual.' Jana poked out her chin a little and tried to sound firm. 'The thing I have with Mark is simple, no-strings-attached sex – nothing more. You don't think I'd give him a chance to hurt me again, do you?'

Sash stood up, went to the window and stared into the darkness for the longest time.

The uncomfortable silence yawned between them, and Jana felt compelled to fill it. 'I talked to a friend about how

Mark had hurt me in the past, and about how I had the hots for him all over again. Her advice was to go ahead and get him out of my system.'

Sash turned to face her sister. 'I take it this friend doesn't know you very well.'

'Well, not as well as you, obviously.'

'And it doesn't sound much like you're getting Mark out of your system to me.'

Jana swallowed hard.

Sash sat back down. 'This is madness.' She reached across the table for her sister's hand. 'You talk about this thing with Mark like it's a series of one-night stands.'

'That's essentially what it is. A fling.'

Sash's eyes drilled into hers.

'Well, perhaps *flings* would be a better description.'

Sash's brow furrowed into a frown. 'If you think that, sis, then you're fooling yourself. You work with this man, see him almost every day. By not being straight with him, you both lose. You have to hold on to your heart for dear life, and he never gets to be accountable for what he did back then. How can you ever forgive him for what he won't acknowledge?'

Jana shook off her sister's hand and pushed away the bowl of stew. Her appetite had fled.

'You do realise that you're cheating yourself out of a chance for a genuine relationship, right? Or maybe you enjoy punishing him, is that it?'

Jana squirmed in her seat. She didn't have answers to her sister's questions.

Sash's eyes narrowed. 'How does Mark feel about you?'

This one was easy. 'I think he's pretty into me.'

'That's what I thought. When he called to officially offer me this keeper job, he was full of praise for you. He mentioned the fantastic work you were doing in every second sentence.' Sash sat back down and drained her glass. 'I swear, this won't end well, sis. My advice is to confront Mark about what he did to you at school. Tell him how devastated you were and why you left that night. Tell him about our parents' accident and the long-lasting effect it's had on all our lives. Then either get a genuine apology or move on.'

CHAPTER 33

Mark had been struggling all morning to concentrate on the computer screen. There were far too many distractions whirling in his head. Ever since her sister had arrived to work undercover at the zoo last week, Jana had seemed nervous around him, as if he somehow made her uncomfortable. It was bad enough that she'd insisted on treating their relationship casually, as if it didn't matter. Now he wondered if she might soon end it altogether.

Apart from the hot sex, Jana had remained frustratingly cool with him since they'd become intimate. Friends with benefits, that's what she'd said. The notion should have been very appealing, especially for a busy single dad. All the perks of a sexual relationship without any of the melodrama. Just pure physical pleasure. So why did he feel like some lovesick, rejected schoolboy?

If this was the deal, it wasn't the one Mark wanted. He'd had his fill of one-night stands and non-committal relationships. In every case until now, he'd been the one to hold back his heart. It was confronting for the boot to be on the other foot. Here he was, falling headlong in love with this woman, and she wanted to keep things casual.

He wanted all of Jana. He wanted her to be his girl-friend – to have a permanent place in his and Karly's life. Mark bit his lip, knowing that he had to keep his emotions in check. Jana was obviously not ready for a serious relation-ship, and he didn't want to push her into something she wasn't comfortable with. For now, he would leave his doubts and insecurities to the side. He was in love with Jana and he'd do whatever it took to be with her. Although he had no idea how he'd be able to keep a lid on his feelings.

Sometimes he caught her studying him when she thought he wasn't looking. At other times she fixed him with intense eyes, like she wanted to say something to him. Once, after they'd discussed the options and costs for café flooring, Jana had put a hand on his arm. 'Mark, I need to—' She'd stopped mid-sentence, mouth hanging open for several seconds before saying, 'Never mind.'

Had she been about to break it off? The thought of losing her terrified him. Mark had never felt this way before. He'd always been the one to easily brush off relationships and move on to the next one without too much fuss. But with Jana it was different. He'd never felt so vulnerable and exposed. Losing her would mean losing part of himself.

Mark returned to his work, forcing himself to focus on the budget forecasts that Scott & Son Real Estate had asked for. The sooner he started, the sooner he'd finish. It was Friday, and he'd promised to pick his daughter up from school half an hour early. His father was driving up to Rivertown this afternoon with Karly's puppy, and the prospect of having Bandit for the weekend had put her in a far better mood than usual. There hadn't been one irate phone call from Scarborough about Karly's behaviour all week. On the contrary, he'd received an email praising her contribution to the school's horticulture program. Apparently, she'd planted more red-gum seedlings along the river than any other student.

Time slipped away and eventually he became engrossed in his task. Mark had always enjoyed working with numbers, and he found satisfaction in analysing the data before him, calculating figures and identifying spending patterns. He'd almost finished his fiscal projections when the phone rang, startling him. He felt an inexplicable chill. His grandmother would have said someone had walked over his grave. Superstitious nonsense, of course, but he couldn't shake the feeling that something negative lurked on the end of the line. Was it the school? What a shame if Karly had tarnished her good record so close to the end of the week. Or was it something worse? Maybe Jana couldn't bring herself to dump him in person, so she'd decided to do it via a phone call? *Quick*, he told himself in a sudden panic. *Answer the damned phone and find out.*

But it was neither Karly nor Jana. It was Harper.

'What do you want?' he asked in a sharp voice as his feeling of foreboding grew.

'That's a lovely way to greet the mother of your child.' Harper sounded genuinely peeved to have not received a warmer reception. Well, what did she expect, after promising to come last month and then letting Karly down so badly?

'If you're planning another trip to Rivertown, I'll need a decent amount of notice this time. And you'll have to find your own accommodation. You won't be able to stay with us.'

A long silence. 'Well, that's me told!' said Harper at last in an icy voice.

Maybe he should have been a bit more conciliatory. It wouldn't help anyone to make an enemy out of Harper.

'I rang to say that I'm getting married. His name's Arthur Anderson and he's Director of Wealth Management at the Pan Pacific Bank.'

Now it was Mark's turn to go quiet. Harper's news didn't surprise him – he'd expected her to marry years ago. But he did wonder how Karly would take it. 'Congratulations,' he managed. 'Have you told our daughter?'

'Arthur and I can't have children,' she said, seeming not to hear him. 'I had my tubes tied when I was eighteen. I didn't want to risk another pregnancy after the trauma of having Karly. A few months ago I tried to have the procedure reversed. Unfortunately, there were complications.' Her voice seemed to break with emotion. 'I should have sued the hospital.'

She sounded so angry that it wouldn't have surprised Mark if she'd threatened to sue him as well. He was super confused, though. Why was she telling him all this? *Just wait and listen,* he told himself. *She'll get to the point of her call eventually.*

'Arthur's older than me – twenty years older, to be exact. He has adult children from his first marriage, but he was hoping we could have our own family. He's the one who encouraged me to reverse my tubal ligation.'

Okay, but none of this explained why she'd called him. He wanted to say *Get to the point*, but he bit his tongue. For some reason, Harper was revealing incredibly personal information, and although she sounded cold and unemotional, it still must be hard for her. Harper had always disguised her vulnerabilities with an air of smug arrogance. Mark suspected it was due to the unequal treatment she'd received from her parents. They'd doted on her academically gifted older brother, Oliver, who'd graduated as dux of his year, while Harper had always struggled with her grades. Recently, Mark had pondered why Harper had taken such an instant dislike to Jana at Scarborough; it may well have been that the clever scholarship girl reminded Harper too much of her own failings.

At school Harper had sometimes got into trouble for wearing make-up or breaking curfew – largely because of Mark. When her parents called to berate her, she liked to annoy them by conducting the conversation over speaker-phone. Mark had often heard them call her *idiot* and *stupid girl* and other insults. Instead of crumbling under the weight of her parents' disappointment, Harper had always laughed it off as if it didn't hurt her. But it did hurt – he'd seen it some-times when her mask slipped. Perhaps Harper truly was upset about not being able to give Arthur children. She was good at hiding her pain. She'd had a lifetime of practice.

If her parents had been so harsh over minor school infringements, Mark hated to think what they must have said all those years ago when they learned of Harper's pregnancy. When Mark discovered that Karly was living with them, he'd worried they might undermine his daughter's confidence in the same way. But apparently they'd been better grandparents than parents. Karly said they were always kind. Their venom seemed to have been reserved for Harper alone.

Maybe it was time to take control of this conversation. 'Have you told Arthur about Karly?' Mark asked.

'Yes. I told him about my teen pregnancy, and he was very supportive.'

'Good. He sounds like a nice guy.'

'He is,' agreed Harper. 'The nicest man. I want him to be happy in our marriage.'

'Of course.' Mark heard a slight sound, a mere breath. He sensed it was a tiny sigh of relief.

'So, you understand why I need Karly back.'

Whoa. Mark was left speechless, his brain trying to comprehend what he'd just heard. Was she kidding? There was no way he'd agree to give up his daughter. Fury exploded inside him, replacing any compassion he'd felt for Harper. The woman had effectively abandoned Karly to go gallivanting around the world, leaving her elderly parents to raise the child, knowing how unsuitable they might have been. Then when they'd become ill, she'd given Karly to Mark, knowing that he barely had a relationship with the girl. Careless of whether he'd be a good father or not.

'Not straight away, mind,' continued Harper. 'She'll need to finish the school term and I'd like to bring Arthur down for a visit first.'

'It's not happening,' said Mark, trying to contain his anger.

'But Arthur wants to meet her. You can't expect Karly to move in with a complete stranger.'

'I'm not talking about Arthur's visit,' he said, marvelling at Harper's hypocrisy. Moving in with a stranger was exactly what she'd expected Karly to do when she dumped the child on his doorstep. 'What's not happening is Karly leaving Rivertown.'

'Don't be silly. I thought you'd be pleased. You're a player,

Mark, we both know that. A child must really cramp your style. And you can't offer Karly the kind of stability that I can.'

Mark could feel the blood rush to his head. Harper's condescension towards him was infuriating. He may have had his issues in the past, but since taking custody of Karly he'd been a responsible and caring father.

'Don't you dare talk to me like that,' he said, his voice low and menacing.

There was silence on the other end of the line, and Mark took a deep, steadying breath. He didn't want to lose his temper.

'I love Karly,' he said, his voice softer now. 'And I'm not about to simply hand her over because you suddenly decide you're ready to be a parent again.'

'I understand that you're upset, Mark, but this isn't about you. It's about what's best for Karly.'

'And what's best for Karly is staying in Rivertown, where she's building a life,' replied Mark, firmly.

'This isn't some passing whim, Mark. I'm getting married and Arthur wants a proper family. Karly needs to be a part of it.'

'Well, maybe you should have thought of that before you abandoned her,' spat Mark. 'You can't just waltz back into her life and expect everything to be okay.'

There was a tense silence on the other end of the line, and Mark wondered if he'd pushed things too far. He knew that Harper could be volatile and unpredictable, and he didn't want to provoke her into doing something rash.

'Mark, I'm sorry,' said Harper, her tone wheedling now. 'I didn't mean to sound callous or dismissive of your role in

Karly's life. I know you've done a lot for her these past few months, and I'm grateful for it. But that's all it's been – a few months. She's at boarding school during the week and I imagine that she's often with your parents on weekends. What sort of a life is she really building with you?'

The truth of her words struck him like a physical blow. 'I just don't want to disrupt Karly again,' Mark said warily. 'She's already been through so much.'

'And I don't want to cause her any more pain or confusion either,' said Harper. 'I just want to be a part of her life again. Is that really so unreasonable?'

Mark hesitated. He didn't want to give in to Harper's demands, but he also didn't want to deny Karly the chance to know her mother. Being angry wouldn't help anybody. Karly was twelve – old enough to make up her own mind. And as much as he hated to admit it, this had to be her decision.

A sickening realisation hit him. Now he was at risk of losing both Jana and his daughter.

CHAPTER 34

Jana watched from the window as Mark pulled up in front of the house in his sleek sports car. She inhaled sharply, her stomach filled with a mix of anticipation and dread. She'd never been one to dodge hard issues, and yet here she was, hesitating, her palms damp with sweat.

Sash's words of warning about Mark echoed loudly in her mind. It was becoming harder and harder to pretend that it was just sex between them. She could no longer deny their connection and that terrified her. Look what had happened the last time she let her heart run away with her. She was setting herself up to be hurt all over again.

Jana had wrestled with her sister's advice for days. Finally, she'd made up her mind. Sash was right. Mark had to face the truth about what he'd done all those years ago. So, Jana would confront Mark and make him admit it. There'd be no more living in denial for him. Then if he acknowledged how he'd wronged her and if he apologised sincerely enough, perhaps they could move forward together. If not, she would break it off and continue their relationship on a strictly professional basis. It would almost be a relief. She'd grown weary of the emotional push and pull.

But when Mark got out of the car, he had someone with him. With all that was going on at Wildfell Park, she'd forgotten that Karly was coming this afternoon. And what was that? Aww . . . Karly nursed a black-and-white puppy in her arms. How adorable! With Karly here, her heart-to-heart with Mark would have to wait. Jana was half happy and half sad about putting it off. Never had she felt so torn.

'This is Bandit,' said a beaming Karly as Jana met them downstairs. 'Do you want a cuddle?'

Jana took the wriggling pup. He snuggled into her arms, white-tipped tail wagging overtime. She held Bandit close to her face, smiling into his bright, amber eyes. 'Well, aren't you adorable?' His warm, pink tongue darted out to lick her nose and Karly giggled. The child had seemed much happier lately, even before the puppy. Bandit's arrival could only improve things further. It warmed Jana's heart whenever Karly smiled. She was truly fond of the girl.

Jana turned when she heard another car pull up. 'Hazel!' She hadn't realised how much she'd missed the old woman. Karly's eyes lit up on seeing her too.

'My goodness!' exclaimed Hazel, throwing up her hands and widening her eyes in mock surprise. 'We've never had a wolf cub at the zoo before.'

Karly pealed with laughter. 'Bandit's not a wolf,' she said, unceremoniously plucking the puppy from Jana and handing him to Hazel instead. Jana grinned. It seemed that Karly had missed Hazel as much as she had.

Next Bruce arrived with his daughter. 'Lisa was feeling a

bit crook, so I popped out to collect her from school. I tried ringing you earlier, but you know what phone reception is like around here. Do you mind if she stays for a while? I promised Tash we'd finish excavating the new devil dens today.'

Lisa spotted Bandit and rushed over. Karly proudly showed him off and the girls began talking.

'Lisa can rest up here at the house,' said Jana, noticing how friendly the two girls seemed. 'She and Karly can play with the puppy.'

Lisa overheard them. 'Yes, Dad. I'll stay here while you go dig your boring old holes.'

Bruce looked relieved. He waved goodbye to his daughter and strode off. The rest of them entered the house, Karly chattering away to Lisa and Hazel without pausing for breath. Jana half-expected the child to faint with excitement. It was wonderful to see her so animated.

But when she glanced at Mark, she got a shock. His demeanour was the exact opposite of Karly's. She couldn't miss the odd set of his jaw and the tension in his shoulders. She knew his body language so well. What was bothering him? True, he was no fan of Hazel and hadn't been looking forward to her return. Could that be it? But Mark wasn't side-eyeing the older woman or casting annoyed glances her way. He wasn't crossing his arms and making little eye rolls of displeasure. In fact, he wasn't reacting to Hazel at all. Mark was in a world of his own.

Jana pulled him aside while the others were gushing over Bandit in the kitchen. 'What's wrong?'

Mark ran his fingers through his hair and shuffled his feet. 'I don't think I'll be very good company. Karly seems happy enough showing Bandit off. Would you mind if she stays here and I pick her up a bit later?'

'I most certainly would,' said Jana. 'And so would your daughter. Karly doesn't see you all week, and then you plan to leave her with us? Don't give Hazel any more ammunition to use against you.'

Mark looked so miserable, with an unshaved face and shadows under his blue eyes. 'She thinks I'm a terrible father, doesn't she? Maybe she's right.'

Jana couldn't believe what she was hearing. Since when did Mark meekly accept judgement from Hazel? Where had his confidence gone? It was true that Hazel had been scathing about Mark's parenting skills, but it was only because of his decision to leave Karly in boarding school all week. Apart from that, she'd secretly admitted to Jana that Mark was doing a great job with his daughter. Not that he'd ever hear her say such nice things to his face. The two of them were like oil and water.

'What's got into you?' asked Jana, genuinely puzzled. 'It's like you left here as one person and returned as another. I've never seen you looking so defeated.' When Mark couldn't meet her eyes, Jana's puzzlement turned to worry. 'Is there something you're not telling me about Wildfell Park? Is there a problem with the zoo licensing board?'

Mark hurried to reassure her. 'No, nothing like that – well, not yet anyway. It might be a different story if we can't get to the bottom of this sabotage thing.' He glanced around to ensure the others weren't in earshot. 'Has Sash come up with anything?'

'Not yet,' said Jana. 'And don't change the subject. Tell me what's bothering you. I'll keep badgering until you do.' She tugged him into the sitting room, and then down onto the couch beside her. 'Now, spill,' she said, tucking her feet up under her.

Mark exhaled and scrubbed his hands over his face. 'It's about Harper. I know she's not your favourite person.'

'Keep going,' urged Jana. 'I'm a good listener.'

Mark trailed his fingers along the couch's smooth leather. 'Harper wants Karly back.'

Jana's heart dropped and a pang of anger hit her – jealousy, too.

Mark snorted a brief, bitter laugh. 'You look as shocked as I feel.'

'She wants custody?'

Mark nodded. 'She's getting hitched to some rich old man. He wants kids, but apparently Harper can't have them. She thinks that by taking Karly, she can offer this bloke a ready-made family.'

Jana shook her head in disbelief. 'I thought I could believe anything of Harper, but this? Using her own daughter as a bargaining chip in her marriage? She must be out of her mind.'

'Quite possibly.' Mark slumped down in his seat. 'But then I got to thinking. Karly has only been with me for six months. Before that I barely knew her. Harper says that I'm kidding myself if I think that Karly has developed a bond with me.'

Jana felt the hairs prickle on the back of her neck, like a mother dog raising her hackles, ready to protect a pup. 'Well, Harper's wrong. I've seen the special rapport that's grown between you and Karly. She adores you, and she knows that you'd do anything for her. That sort of trust in a parent is exactly what a child needs, especially one who's been pushed from pillar to post like Karly has.'

Mark pressed his lips into a thin line and gave her a sad, rueful smile. 'Karly knows that I'd do anything for her – except have her with me during the week. She asks me all the time.'

'But Scarborough doesn't usually take day students unless you're a staff member.'

'I know. Perhaps I should pull her out and send her to Rivertown High.'

'No,' said Jana, thinking quickly. 'At least not right now.'

Mark wrinkled his forehead in surprise. 'Hazel suggested it. I thought you'd agree with her.'

'I do agree with her, but it's time to act strategically,' said Jana. 'If Harper sues for custody, it will look much better for you if Karly is attending an elite school, especially her parents' alma mater.'

Mark's face drained of colour. 'Oh God. My daughter's tried so hard to be fair to both Harper and me. I couldn't bear it if we had to fight over her in court with lawyers assassinating our characters and making her feel like she has to choose one of us. That would break her heart.'

'But the alternative might mean giving Karly away. It's ultimately up to you, but I care about Karly, and I know what a bully Harper can be.'

Mark hung his head in what looked like genuine shame. 'I'm sorry I was a part of that.'

Here it was, the perfect segue into asking Mark to open up properly about what had happened between them back at school. But one look at his stricken face told her that this wasn't the time. *Way to go, Harper,* thought Jana. *More than a decade later and you're still stuffing up my life.*

'Honestly, do you think Harper would be a good full-time mother?' Jana put her hand on his in a comforting gesture.

'I've thought about this quite a bit, trying hard to be objective. But I can't find any qualities that lead me to believe she'd ever put Karly's needs ahead of her own.'

'Then you have your answer,' Jana said. 'What's the old saying? When someone shows you who they are, believe them. Trust what you know to be true, Mark.'

He let out a long breath. 'So, the alternatives are to hand Karly over without a fight. That's not happening. Or duke it out in court. This is the very definition of a lose–lose situation.'

'There is one more alternative,' said Jana. 'Change Harper's mind.'

CHAPTER 35

Mark was ironing Karly's school dress for Monday morning when his senior partner, Howard Turner, rang. He picked up the phone, puzzled. Why was Howard calling on a Sunday night?

'There's bad news, I'm afraid,' said Howard. 'Frieda Abraham is dead. She suffered a heart attack at home and died shortly afterwards in hospital.'

'Frieda? No!' Mark struggled to process Howard's words.

'It happened on Friday, but Mrs Abraham's death is being kept out of the press until tomorrow. You know, out of respect for the family,' said Howard. 'It's a jolt to everybody. She was only sixty-two and there'd been no indication that she was ill.'

The great woman – dead. Their generous benefactor who'd stepped in with a lifeline to save Wildfell Park. It didn't seem possible.

'Mrs Abraham's death has some unexpected consequences for the Wildfell Park project.'

'It's terrible news,' said Mark. 'But I can't see how it affects the zoo, at least in the short term. Frieda put the project's funds into a trust.'

'Yes, but she received some very poor legal advice. Not from us, I'm happy to say. The funds to complete Wildfell Park were put into a trust, that's true. But it was a charitable trust.'

Mark couldn't believe what he was hearing. 'Are you sure?'

'Quite sure. A concerned ex-colleague works for the firm that's administering her estate. He's not merely an ex-colleague – he's a friend, and he's also a fan of the zoo project. One who's been keeping track of your progress with great interest. He told me himself.'

'But Wildfell Park isn't a charity.'

'Exactly. So the trust will fail. Mrs Abraham's two sons have already signalled that they'll contest the provision. Of course, with Hazel Roberts' agreement we can apply for charitable status and almost certainly get it in the end. But the matter will still be tied up in probate for months.'

Mark was dumbstruck, struggling with the implications of Howard's news.

'What's your deadline for re-licensing Wildfell Park?' asked Howard.

'The first of December – about eight weeks.'

'And what costs are outstanding?'

Mark could barely bring himself to answer the question. Only a single progress payment had been made to the builders so far, at roughly the three-month mark. He mentally ran through what still needed to be paid for. Nearly all the expensive stuff: the café renovation, the new vet clinic, the monkey house, the reptile house and half-a-dozen other enclosures. Thank heavens he'd talked Jana out of the noctarium for now. The almost finished state-of-the-art devil compound had cost enough as it was. He'd argued with Jana that the compound shouldn't be built until they'd obtained their licence, but Jana was persuasive and had talked him into it. After all, with Frieda's backing they'd essentially had a limitless bucket of money.

Then there was the landscaping and building materials. Oh, and wages. Jana had been hanging out for two new, experienced zookeepers to arrive. They were due to start in two weeks. How on earth would they pay them now? For that matter, how would they pay the staff they already had, including the extra person they'd hired to help Luca and Tracey at Odessa while Sash was undercover at the zoo?

When Mark tallied it all up in his head, the outstanding costs topped three million dollars. He thought about trying to cover the sum himself. He was a wealthy man, but even he'd have trouble coming up with that much money in the space of a few weeks. He'd sunk a great deal into Paddlewheel, the luxury waterfront home he'd bought from Tony Alfonso for top dollar. Then he'd made a loss on the urgent sale of his Adelaide CBD apartment.

And he had Karly to think about. If they were unsuccessful in their re-licensing bid, he'd have poured all that money down the drain. Wildfell Park would become a retirement home or be sold to a developer. The brand-new vet clinic, along with the other renovations, would be bulldozed and he'd have lost his investment.

Howard groaned when Mark revealed the true extent of the damage. 'Why didn't you insist on seeing the estate-planning documents before you commenced work? I must say, Mark, I'm disappointed in you.'

Mark flinched. He knew exactly why he'd gone ahead

before viewing the trust deeds that would apply in the event of Frieda's death. There'd been a delay in drawing them up at her end. Ordinarily, he'd have shown caution and waited. But if he *had* waited, the zoo renovation would never have been completed in time. So he'd accepted the assurances of Frieda's lawyers that the zoo would be properly provided for. And why had he adopted such a reckless course of action? Because he was in love with Jana and hadn't wanted to disappoint her.

Mark did not offer Howard this particular explanation. 'There was a drafting delay at their end. I didn't follow it up. It's unforgivable.'

Howard snorted in disgust. 'Such negligence should lose you your job. And it would, had any of the expenses been incurred by our firm. As it stands, the contracts all name Wildfell Park as the party liable for costs. Hazel will be bankrupted and there'll be a lot of angry local contractors. Still, most of them will get their money when the place is sold.'

Mark searched his conscience. He couldn't allow Wildfell Park to be auctioned to the highest bidder. It would break Jana's heart – and his own.

'Howard, I'm sorry that I stuffed up, but the project is close to completion. It's such a shame to let all that work go to waste.'

'Indeed, but I can't see a way around it, can you?'

Mark delved deep for an answer – an answer that would solve the problem and amaze Howard with his cleverness at the same time. But he drew a blank.

Howard sighed. 'No, I didn't think so. But unless you can come up with a plan to refinance by the end of the week, I'm pulling the plug on this project.'

Mark put the phone down and closed his eyes. Images came to him of the animals of Wildfell Park. Sol the sun bear, who'd celebrated his eleventh birthday last weekend. Jana had videoed it all for the zoo's website. Sol's gifts had included a colourfully wrapped cardboard box – filled with fruity treats, fresh honeycomb and a carrot cake – and release into his spacious new habitat. The lush area contained roomy tree hollows for daytime naps, climbing frames, decaying logs full of termites that would be regularly replaced, and a fern-fringed rock pool. Sol loved it, and Mark had watched the bear explore his new digs with a sense of pride. Jana had excitedly announced that a female sun bear might soon become available to join Sol. A pang of pain hit him. How would he tell her that it would never happen?

And what of the magnificent big cats? Cleo was moving to an open-range zoo near Canberra, but the rest weren't suitable to be of interest to other zoos. If he let Wildfell Park fail, the lions and tigers would never experience their new enclosures, which were designed to incorporate natural features, such as hummocks, granite ledges for sunbaking, ponds and shady trees. Discreet viewing platforms and windows gave visitors the chance to observe without disturbing or stressing the animals. Everyone was looking forward to the day when the big cats could be released into their new habitat.

But now King and Nala would never tear at carcasses suspended from the broad limbs of an ancient oak. The tigers would never follow scent trails to find puzzle feeders filled with treats or swim in the deep reflective pool that was central to their new home. Genetic testing had shown them to be inbred – nearly impossible to rehome. It was a miracle they'd found a place that would take Cleo. How ironic that the sparkling vet clinic that had been built to heal, would instead serve to destroy; dozens of animals would meet their end there. How would he ever face Jana again? Or Karly, for that matter?

Mark felt the unfamiliar prick of tears behind his eyes. And he suddenly understood that he didn't just want to save Wildfell Park for Jana's sake. The zoo mattered to him too, more than he'd realised. He'd grown to love the animals and couldn't bear the thought of letting them down. No more than he could bear the thought of letting Jana or his daughter down. Somehow, someway, he would make the impossible possible.

CHAPTER 36

Mark sat beside Jana on the sitting-room couch. She hadn't seen him since Friday when he'd shared the news about Harper wanting Karly back. After that he'd taken his daughter to spend the weekend at Overland Corner with her grandparents.

Jana had been dying to know what was happening, but he hadn't come over – not so much as a phone call. She'd missed him far more than she should have. It was becoming harder and harder to keep her emotions at bay.

But here it was, Thursday morning, and he'd finally arrived. He looked tired and worn, but instead of bad news about Harper and Karly, he delivered an even more terrible blow. Jana froze. Frieda was dead. Time seemed to stand still, and Jana struggled to make sense of Mark's words as he spoke, slowly and deliberately explaining how her death affected the zoo.

'I didn't tell you earlier because I was hoping to find a solution to the problem – a problem that's all my fault,' he said. 'I should have waited to confirm the trust arrangements myself.'

'Hang on,' said Jana, trying to process what she'd heard.

'By the sound of things, we'd never have finished in time if you'd waited. Nobody could have predicted that Frieda Abraham would die.'

A deep groove furrowed his brow. 'She was a wonderful woman, and a generous one, sponsoring more than a dozen wildlife charities: the Koala Foundation, the RSPCA, the Conservation Foundation . . . You name it, she supported it. So often wealth belongs to the greedy bastards of this world.'

'Like her sons,' said Jana, scowling. 'Imagine contesting the will when they knew how much their mother loved animals? They must know that she intended the trust to stand. But we don't have to worry. Hazel won't mind Wildfell Park becoming a charity. In fact, we've already talked about it.'

Mark shook his head. 'It doesn't matter if Hazel agrees or not. Any dispute will tie up Frieda's estate in probate court for months.' His blue eyes glistened. 'We'll never get the funds released in time to get our new licence.'

Jana picked up on the emotion behind what he was saying, rather than the actual words. His commitment to the zoo rang through loud and clear. 'Well, we can't just give up. We'll have to get the money from somewhere else.' Jana raised a determined chin and put on a brave face. 'How much do we need? Maybe I can take out a loan.' She really had no idea how much the zoo owed. Mark had always handled the financial side of things. But she was pretty sure that it would be more than she'd be able to borrow.

Mark covered her hand with his. 'No need. I've put Paddlewheel on the market and priced it to sell. The agent already has a buyer who's agreed to a short settlement period.'

Jana's head spun and she couldn't believe what she was

hearing. That Mark would volunteer such a drastic solution, to sacrifice the house that she knew he adored and had only lived in for a few months. A gush of love and gratitude overcame her.

'Mark, I'm sorry. Where will you and Karly live?'

His smile was tinged with sadness. 'Don't worry about us. My daughter was never impressed by the luxury of Paddlewheel. Not the indoor pool, the home theatre, the games room – none of it. The truth is that she'd be just as happy living in a shed, as long as she had Bandit and was close to the zoo. I'll rent us a little place. Please believe that I'd do anything for Wildfell Park – and for you.'

The sincerity of his tone touched her deeply. Jana's heart seemed to stop as she looked into Mark's vivid blue eyes. She spotted something different there – a quality she'd never seen before. She couldn't describe it, but it made her feel warm and safe, like everything was going to be okay.

'Thank you, Mark.' She leaned in to give him a hug.

He wrapped his arms around her and briefly held her tight. Then he pulled away and held up a hand. 'We're not out of the woods yet. I have a mortgage on my house. Not a large one, but the sale won't cover all the zoo's debts. However, it will buy us some time and stop Howard pulling the pin on the project just yet. I'm selling my share portfolio and Dad has promised to lend us fifty thousand. I could probably get another few hundred grand by selling my car and the boat. I checked online. Second-hand sports cruisers are holding their value pretty—'

'Good grief. You'll need to do all that? Exactly how much do we have to raise?'

'Oh, and the jet ski. I know it's our official buffalo retrieval device, but it's probably worth ten thousand and every little bit helps.'

Jana frowned. 'Stop avoiding the question. Give me a rough dollar amount of what we're up for.' He wrung his hands and looked away. 'Mark, you're treating me like a child. Just spit it out.'

'I don't want you to become disheartened.'

'Mark,' she said with a small growl in her voice. 'Tell me.'

He threw up his hands. 'Okay, if you insist. We need to find over three million dollars.'

Jana's hand flew to her mouth in disbelief, and she could feel her heart beating out of her chest. Three million? It might as well have been three billion. Three million dollars was an impossible sum of money to find in eight weeks. She felt the crushing burden of the task ahead, but when she looked at Mark, she saw a fierce determination in his eyes.

'We'll figure it out,' he said, taking her hand and squeezing her fingers reassuringly. 'We're a great team.'

Jana couldn't help but feel a surge of admiration for him. She'd learned something wonderful about Mark today, some-thing important and unexpected. Maybe it didn't matter that he'd been a cruel and thoughtless teenager. Because he'd grown into the kind of man who didn't shy away from a chal-lenge and was willing to do whatever it took to save the zoo, even if it meant sacrificing all he had.

'We'll need a miracle,' she said, feeling the hopelessness of the situation creeping up on her again.

'Miracles happen, don't they?' Mark replied, his voice low and gentle.

A trembling smile formed on her lips. 'I don't know.'

'Then let me prove that they do.' Mark leaned over and kissed her softly on the lips, a kiss full of tenderness and promise. 'I mean it,' he said as he let her go. 'We'll find a way. You and me, together.'

Jana felt a shiver run down her spine at his words. Somehow, with Mark by her side, she felt like she could take on the world.

'Together,' she repeated, feeling the weight of his words. 'And the first thing to do is have you and Karly move in to Wildfell Manor.'

'I couldn't ask that of Hazel. There must be plenty of cheap rentals around.'

'Nope. Why do you think Amber moved in with Maggie and her mum? She's renting Jean's spare room. Amber viewed lots of places. Some of them were dumps, apparently, where you wouldn't want Karly to live, and she had to compete with a dozen other hopefuls. The cheapest house was three hundred and sixty dollars a week. You might not think that's a lot of money to save, but what did you say before? Every little bit helps?'

'I did, didn't I?' he said with a rueful grin,

'Yes, you did. And you'd pay a lot more than that to find something decent. Since the pandemic, work-from-home tree changers have caused regional house demand to skyrocket.'

Mark nodded. 'I guess that's why my house sold so quickly.'

Jana could tell he was wavering. 'Think how happy Karly would be to live at the zoo. It's every child's dream, and she could keep Bandit here. There are plenty of people around to care for a puppy during the week when she's at school.

Plus, you'd get to see me every day,' she teased, playfully nudging him.

Mark chuckled. 'That is a pretty great incentive.'

'I hoped you might think so.'

'All right, we'll move in, if Hazel will have us. But only until we raise enough money to save the zoo.'

'Deal. Now, we need to make a plan. What about a fund-raiser?' she suggested. 'We could hold an event and invite locals to contribute.'

Mark nodded. 'That's not a bad idea. We could reach out to some of the businesses in the area too. They might be interested in sponsoring the zoo and getting some positive publicity as a result.'

'Yes, and maybe a GoFundMe appeal?' Jana stood and began pacing the room. 'People can make pledges on our website. You'd be surprised how country folk will rally to help if they believe it's a worthwhile cause. Hazel is a well-loved institution in these parts, and I think the zoo has more community support than you know. We could give away free zoo passes and interactive educational sessions, stuff like that. Larger donations could earn behind-the-scenes encounters and lifetime memberships.' Jana paused. 'How much will you get for your house?' She had the grace to blush. 'Sorry to sound like a greedy bloodsucker, but I don't have anything to sell, except for my twenty-year-old Jeep.'

'It's fine, Jana. Once I've worked it out, I'll email you through an estimate of how much I can raise via the fire sale of my assets.'

'We'll need to keep track,' said Jana. 'Make up some sort of a spreadsheet.'

Mark looked at her sideways. 'I have a degree in law and accounting,' he said. 'I think I've got this.'

A surge of optimism caused her to leap into his arms. Mark caught her and held her tight. 'We'll save the zoo,' she said, feeling the truth of it in every fibre of her being.

'We will,' said Mark, his voice passionate and strong. 'We'll do whatever it takes.'

Jana laid her head on his shoulder. 'Thank you for being here,' she murmured, breathing in his scent.

'Always,' he whispered back, pressing a tender kiss to her hair.

They stayed like that for a few moments, wrapped up in each other. Then Mark lifted his head and looked at her with a small smile.

'So, do you want to help me pack up my house?'

Jana grinned. She was ready to take on this challenge with Mark by her side. It wasn't the time to dredge up the past, not when they were facing such a high-stakes threat. She should just forget about it, leave ancient history behind. But a small voice still nagged. Was she really ready to let it go?

CHAPTER 37

It was after dark when Mark lugged the final box of his belongings into the old ballroom at Wildfell Manor. The huge space had been closed up for years, but now they were using it for storage. He stowed the box in the corner under his stream-lined metal bed frame.

'Is that the last of it?' asked Jana.

'That's it.' Mark had hired a move-yourself van to bring his bulkier items over earlier. 'Normally I'd have got remov-alists to do all this,' he said, looking around the cobwebbed room, then stretching his arms over his head and interlacing his fingers. 'Those guys really earn their living. I'm buggered.'

'But think how much money you saved.' Jana resisted the urge to say something about learning how the other half lived.

'I'll use the existing furniture in the bedrooms,' he said. 'My modern stuff would look out of place anyway.'

'Not to mention saving us the task of carting bed frames, wardrobes and side tables up and down the stairs.'

Mark grinned. 'That too.' His hand on her shoulder was

warm and inviting. She could hardly believe that he'd be here every night from now on. Such a delicious thought.

'Come upstairs,' she said. 'You can pick which room you want for Karly.'

Mark chose the corner room for his daughter. It was a little smaller than the others but lighter and airier, with a dual aspect and better views. Bold parrot prints covered the fading blue wallpaper, and an elegant chaise longue sat beneath casement windows that were draped with dusty lace. Beside the mahogany four-poster bed sat a low oak dresser. An antique mirrored wardrobe stood against the back wall, next to a disused fireplace with a marble mantelpiece. A glass chandelier hung from the pressed-metal ceiling. The room must once have been very grand.

'How do you feel about swapping riverfront luxury for faded glory?' asked Jana.

'I'll get used to it.' Mark picked up a framed black-and-white photo from the dresser. It was of an attractive blonde woman, beaming and stroking a full-grown male lion.

'That's Hazel.'

Mark's brows lifted in surprise. 'She was quite a looker.'

'Yes. We sometimes forget that old people were once young.' Jana pulled up a chair and stood on it to take down the curtains. 'I'll wash these.' The worn floorboards creaked loudly at the movement. 'No sneaking out of bed at night for Karly,' she laughed. 'Everyone on this floor will hear her.'

Mark shifted his weight and the floor creaked again. 'I hope my room isn't the same.' He fixed her with intense e eyes. 'I might be doing a little sneaking out at night myself.'

A rush of warmth crept up Jana's cheeks and for a moment she lost her train of thought. She turned away to regain her composure. How on earth would she function with this man constantly nearby? 'Can you go downstairs and fetch one of your lovely woollen rugs?' she said. 'These bare floors are freezing when it's cold. You'll need one for your room too.'

He gave a small, disappointed sigh. 'If I must. Geometric designs and abstract shapes won't match the decor, though.' Glancing at the bedspread, he added, 'Grandma floral would be more the go.'

'Stop joking around,' said Jana. 'We still have a lot to do, and I'm supposed to be cooking dinner tonight.'

'Fish and chips for everyone then? My shout.'

Jana shot him a grateful smile. 'I've already dusted and vacuumed the rooms,' she said. 'So all you have to do is make the beds and put Karly's and your clothes away.' She picked up the curtains and headed for the door.

Their first dinner together in the dining room was an awkward affair. Since Mark had launched his brave bid to save the zoo, Hazel no longer criticised him like she used to. But neither could she find anything nice to say. Old habits died hard. Instead, she said nothing and ignored Mark entirely. He was equally reserved. Jana and Sash valiantly attempted to draw them into conversation, but it was hopeless. It wasn't long before Hazel retired to her room, along with her half-finished plate of fried scallops and chips.

After they'd eaten, Mark announced that he had some work to finish off before morning. 'I'll be in the upstairs office if anyone wants me.'

'I'll come too,' said Jana. 'I need to write a post for the website about the fundraiser. Do you mind clearing up here, Sash?'

'What did you just call me?' Sash stretched, groaned loudly and said, 'Oh, my aching back.'

'Are you okay?' Mark asked.

'*Tash* is fine,' said Jana, rolling her eyes at her sister. 'I'll explain later.'

A shining round moon loomed beyond the window as Jana finished typing the draft post for the website. 'Listen to this.'

Mark saved the spreadsheet file he was working on and turned to face her.

'"You are cordially invited to the Wildfell Park Open Day and Country Ball. All proceeds go to Save Our Zoo. The zoo was started fifty years ago by Hazel and Reg Roberts. Eighty-year-old Hazel continues to play an important part in caring for the animals."'

'Does she?' asked Mark.

'Well, she would if you'd let her,' said Jana. 'Hazel's dying to be involved with the lions and monkeys again, even if it's just feeding them and keeping them company. I swear that they miss her – Nala in particular. And since you're living here thanks to her generosity, I suggest that you graciously accept her help from now on.'

'Okay, okay. Point taken. Just as long as someone can adequately supervise her.'

Now let me finish. "Save Our Zoo aims to raise $500,000 ᴐ that Rivertown's iconic zoo can reopen. To launch this crowdfunding appeal, we're holding an Open Day, followed by a country ball and barbecue on 18 October. Guests will enjoy zoo tours and activities, followed by dinner and dancing on the grounds of the historic Wildfell Manor. Benny Miller and his Bluegrass Band will provide the music, there'll be a monster raffle and an auction of local celebrities. Tickets are $50 per double and $80 per family. This fun event is not to be missed!"'

'Celebrities? What celebrities?'

'Okay, scrap the celebrities,' said Jana, then continued reading aloud. '"The deadline for reopening the zoo is 1 December. Not only do we have staff to pay and more than one hundred animals to feed in the meantime, but we must also make final payments on our renovation program that is designed to bring the zoo into the twenty-first century. Donations will be held in trust. If we don't win our bid to reopen the zoo, they will be refunded in full. If you feel that you can help in any way, we will be extremely grateful."'

'Sounds great,' said Mark. 'Do you think fifty dollars per double is a bit cheap?'

'We don't want to price ourselves out, and we don't have many expenses. All the food and entertainment is being donated.'

'Okay, I'll leave that up to you. But I do think you should emphasise the conservation and educational aspects of the new zoo. And maybe try appealing to people who've visited in the past.'

Jana thought for a second and started typing. 'How's this?

"Wildfell Park is a place of beauty and wonder. It awakens a sense of childlike joy in all who visit. Join our zoo family and share in our passion for protecting the planet's wildlife and habitats.""

'Better,' he said. 'You've really captured the spirit of Wildfell Park. All this publicity is bound to attract Annie West's attention, though. Visitors might have to push past a crowd of protesters on the day.'

'If that happens, we'll deal with it,' said Jana, resolutely. 'Maybe I should meet up with her beforehand and try to head off trouble.'

'It couldn't hurt. But remember that her organisation, or maybe a splinter group, are prime suspects for sabotaging the zoo,' said Mark. 'By the way, I've received a good offer on the boat, and I'm negotiating the sale of the Audi to a bloke from Sydney. He seems keen.'

Jana went over and kissed his cheek. 'What will you drive, though? I suppose you can always borrow my Jeep. We can share it.'

'How old is that thing again?'

'I'll have to show you the trick with second gear,' she said. 'But it's tough and reliable. And it has character.'

'I'm sure it does,' said Mark with a grin. 'In that case, I accept your generous offer.'

'Good. Now, should I post this fundraiser invitation? We only have two weeks to build a buzz.'

'Let's do it,' said Mark.

Jana hit 'Publish' and leaned back in her chair. It was happening. They were making progress and were going to raise enough money to save the zoo. She still had reservations about her unresolved issues with Mark, but for now she would set them aside and focus on the task at hand.

As Jana returned to her desk, Mark's phone rang. He looked at the screen and hesitated before answering it. 'Hi, Harper,' he said, his voice guarded.

Jana watched him, curious about the conversation. She could hear a faint, muffled voice murmuring on the other end, but she couldn't make out any words. Mark's expression darkened and he rubbed his hand over his head.

'Do you want to take this call in private?' whispered Jana. 'Shall I leave?'

He gestured for her to stay, before turning his attention back to his phone. 'No, Harper, I haven't changed my mind. You and Arthur are welcome to come for a visit. In fact, I encourage it. Karly should meet your intended. But where our daughter lives will be her decision.'

Mark moved the mobile away from his ear as the other voice grew louder and shriller. Then he put the phone down. 'She hung up on me.'

Jana felt suddenly guilty. She'd been so wrapped up in her own problems that she hadn't been paying attention to the strain Mark was under. A disturbing thought struck her. 'Do you think she'll take you to court? Will it go that far?'

He shrugged, absently tossing his phone from one hand to another. 'I don't know.'

'How will you afford a custody battle when you've sunk everything you own into the zoo?'

Mark pinched the bridge of his nose and closed his eyes as if searching for an answer. Jana reached out to touch his face, felt the rough stubble beneath her cool fingers.

'All I can do is wait for Harper's next move,' he said, 'and pray that it doesn't come to that. But I was between a rock and a hard place. If I'd let the zoo fail without a fight, Karly would never have forgiven me. I couldn't break her heart like that. Anyway, we shouldn't dwell on something that might never happen.' He gave Jana an encouraging smile. 'We have a fundraiser to plan.'

He strode to the window, gazing out over the moonlit grounds. A spark of desire flared within her. It wasn't just the sight of his tall, erect frame and square shoulders that aroused her. She found Mark's resilience and commitment utterly compelling. He turned, and an answering spark flared in his own eyes. Seconds later he was beside her, pressing searing kisses onto her hungry mouth.

Her first wild impulse was to lock the door, strip off their clothes and give into passion like they'd done many times before. But this time something stopped her. The rules had changed. Her sister's words echoed in her ears. Jana *had* been treating her relationship with Mark like a series of one-night stands, determined to stay uninvolved. She *had* been holding on to her heart for dear life. But she'd lost her grip. Sex with Mark now would be a white-knuckle roller-coaster ride of emotions that she could not risk.

Jana pushed him away and bolted for the door.

CHAPTER 38

Since Karly had been spending her weekends at Wildfell Manor, Jana couldn't believe the joy that the girl had brought to the house. Karly revelled in the space, and the proximity to so many fascinating animals, including her puppy, Bandit, who now lived full-time at the zoo. She asked endless questions and was a willing helper, always pitching in when jobs needed doing. And she made an excellent adviser for Jana when setting up kid-friendly displays in the educational centre for the Open Day that was just around the corner.

'We'll have a petting zoo,' Jana had said. 'And posters of different South Australian ecosystems and the animals that live there. Maybe a "Can you identify this feather or this poo?" activity.'

Karly had looked decidedly unimpressed. 'You need something more exciting than that,' she said. 'Kids like dangerous things. How about live snake shows where they can hold a python? And Tash could do venom-milking demonstrations, explaining how the zoo can help save the lives of snakebite victims. And what about getting Hazel to fly her hawks?

She loves talking to people, and she could tell them all about the history of the zoo at the same time. And we could have a gold coin donation to guess how many squirrels are in the squirrel house for a prize. Even I don't know the answer to that. And why not set up one of those nature trails where children have to visit exhibits to answer questions on a card, and if they answer them all, they get a prize? And we could have a parade for the little kids, where they dress up as their favourite animals. And what about a spider display?'

'We don't keep spiders at the zoo,' said Jana, head spinning from all of Karly's suggestions.

'But we should,' said Karly, her enthusiasm level at ten-out-of-ten. 'I'll go find us some. I saw two redbacks with egg sacs in the woodpile behind the workshop. And Hazel said there are sometimes funnel-webs in the damp earth near the river. Does Tash know how to milk them as well as snakes? That would be sick.'

'Whoa.' Jana had held up her hand. 'You've come up with some amazing ideas. But I think we'll draw the line at deadly spiders.'

Hazel seemed twenty years younger when the child was around. She stood up straighter, moved more briskly and hummed tunes as she baked scones and homemade dog biscuits. Being a grandmother suited her. She beamed when Karly raced up and down the stairs with Bandit in tow, never chiding her for running in the house. The pair could do no wrong in her eyes, and the little collie had taken to sleeping in Hazel's room during the week when Karly was at school. Even Hazel's frostiness towards Mark was starting to thaw. And she loved being involved with the lions again. She visited them every day with their favourite treat – tubs of yoghurt. It was true what people said about age being only a number, Jana realised. It was passion, purpose and love that truly defined youth.

Sash also liked Karly. The girl loved tinkering alongside her in the workshop and learning how to fix things. Sash had even given her a small tool kit that Karly carefully cleaned each night and kept by her bed.

And Mark seemed much more relaxed now that he had a surrogate family to help care for his daughter. 'I finally get what "It takes a village to raise a child" means,' he'd said. 'Doubt I'll ever hear Karly complain about being bored again.'

Four days until the fundraiser, and Jana woke up that morning with a feeling of hope. Drawing back the curtains, she was greeted by a cloudless sky and sunshine warming her face. She checked the forecast on her phone. Great – the start of a spell of perfect weather to coincide with their big event. They'd planned the Open Day to happen during the school holidays, which would likely give them a boost in numbers.

The team's hard work had paid off and the zoo grounds were looking beautiful. Sol was enjoying exploring his new habitat, and at the weekend the sun bear would be able to walk right over the top of visitors via a sky bridge linking his old enclosure with the new rainforest area. Clancy and Dusty, the dingoes, were behaving themselves on their daily walks in readiness for public meet and greets. Lexie had rounded up an assortment of cute baby animals to show off: peacock chicks, twin Barbary lambs, an inquisitive little macaque and several wallaby joeys just emerging from their pouches. And much to Karly's delight, Womble would take centre stage to highlight the plight of the riverlands' unique southern hairy-nosed wombats. Luca was driving up from Odessa with him on Friday.

The café still wasn't fully functional, but it would be able to serve tea, coffee and cans of soft drinks. Three food vendors had agreed to set up their trucks by the outdoor seating area. They'd sell a limited menu of chips, dim sims, pies, donuts and ice cream, sharing half their proceeds with the zoo. To counter all that indulgent food, Mark had also invited along stall holders from the local farmers market, in return for a small donation each. Bruce had cleaned, tested and fitted new gas cylinders to the barbecues, and the local supermarket had donated meat and salads. Everything was going according to plan.

Sash's work, however, had not been going as well. She'd been undercover for three weeks now and seemed no closer to uncovering a saboteur among the staff. However, for someone who'd sometimes struggled to make friends, she'd found her social feet at Wildfell Park. Sash had become particularly close with Maggie and Amber, sometimes going with them to hear bands at the local pub and staying overnight at Jean's house.

'I can't imagine anybody on the staff wanting to hurt the zoo,' she'd told Jana. 'Everyone seems so dedicated.'

But the fact remained that someone on the inside had tampered with Cleo's anaesthetic. This unsettling reality was never far from Jana's mind. Still, there'd been no incidents for a few weeks now, so maybe the culprit – or culprits – had given up. Perhaps she'd get some clues when she met with Annie West later today.

Mark's distinctive knock came at the door. Jana grabbed her brush from the dressing table and ran it through her hair. Since he'd moved in almost two weeks ago, they hadn't made love once. She hadn't even kissed him again since that one time in the office, and her initial fantasies of spending each night wrapped in his arms had vanished into smoke. She'd lost her ability to stay detached and dared not risk it. Now the thought of being with him was as terrifying as jumping off a cliff. Instead, she made excuses, claiming weariness or headaches, when what she really wanted was to give herself to him body and soul. But she couldn't do that until he acknowledged the past. She'd been putting it off for too long. It was finally time for some answers.

'Come in,' said Jana, annoyed by the shakiness in her voice. She expected Mark to move in for a kiss – as he'd done each time they'd been alone so far – and she prepared herself to rebuff him. But to her surprise and, yes, disappointment, he seemed preoccupied and kept his distance. Had her recent rejections made him give up on her?

'Harper and her new bloke,' he said, glumly. 'They're coming to the fundraiser.'

'What?' So much for everything going to plan. Harper was Jana's least favourite person in the world. Her simple presence would put a downer on the day. Jana sat down on the edge of the bed, feeling deflated. The news had burst her bubble of optimism. She knew it was irrational, but she couldn't help a surge of anxiety that pricked at her nerves. Harper was a troublemaker. She'd find some way to ruin things.

'Does Karly know?'

'Not yet. Harper will call her later. I asked her not to

mention her custody bid, and she agreed that she'd wait and tell Karly in person at the weekend.'

'How do you think Karly will take the news?'

'Well, I hope she'll say, "No thanks, I'm staying with Dad." But I can't know for sure. Look how excited she was when her mum promised to visit, and how upset she was when Harper didn't show.' Mark looked thoroughly miserable. 'Karly might think that if she doesn't go, she'll never see her mother again.'

Jana gazed at his crestfallen face, debating whether to finally confront him about high school. He was already down in the dumps. Was it fair to make things worse? But then it never seemed to be the right time. Maybe there'd never *be* a right time. Maybe she had to take the bull by the horns and just go for it.

She took a bottomless breath and patted the place beside her on the bed, steeling herself. 'Sit. There's something important that I need to clear up with you.'

Mark sat beside Jana, taking her hand and interlacing their fingers. 'There's something I'd like to clear up with you too,' he said. 'I've been living here for weeks now, and you've been avoiding me.' His voice grew husky with emotion. 'What's wrong, Jana? Do you know what it's like lying awake each night, wanting you, missing you – knowing that you're so close?'

Oh, she knew all right. Each night was pure torture, knowing that Mark lay on the other side of her bedroom wall. Wondering if he was feeling it too. But she refused to risk her heart with this man when the past remained unresolved. Did he know what was coming? Surely he had an inkling of what she might be about to say.

'Mark,' she said. 'Is there something you want to tell me?'

She searched his face for a glimmer of understanding, some hint that he recognised the elephant in the room. Nothing. Had he really forgotten about their fake online affair? Or had he written it off as a mere childish indiscretion? If so, it did him no credit. Such cruelty should, at the very least, have left a loud echo of remorse. At most, he should have been full of apologies, eager to unburden himself and seek forgiveness.

'Yes, there is something I want to say.' He stole a swift kiss. 'I'm in love with you, Jana Malinski. Madly, head over heels in love.'

Jana was thrilled and dismayed all at once, but she refused to be derailed by his extraordinary declaration. She offered him a sad smile full of regret. This was going to be a difficult conversation. 'In that last year of school, after Harper left, you struck up an online romance with me. Remember?'

Mark looked clueless, so she went over everything – every agonising, distressing detail. Throughout the story he kept hold of her hand, although she was expecting any moment for him to let it go.

When Jana finished, Mark looked utterly dumbfounded. 'No wonder you were so cold when we met again,' he said. 'What an insensitive bastard you must have thought me.'

'Exactly,' she whispered, her voice breaking. 'Every laugh, every kiss, every shared moment – there's always been this shadow between us. And then when you finally did apologise, it was only for hanging around with Harper and her drop-kick mates. No mention of the fake relationship at all. I was flabbergasted.' She hesitated, but there was no stopping now.

'There are two options. You've either genuinely forgotten about it, or you've been too cowardly to bring it up.'

Mark's face had turned deathly pale. 'There is a third option.' He pinned her with wide, earnest eyes. 'I didn't do it in the first place.'

She'd played out this conversation in her mind so many times, trying Mark's possible responses on for size. Complete denial hadn't been one of them. A surge of irritation hit her. 'What, so you're saying that I've made up the whole thing? That I ran away from school on the day before our final exams on a whim? Causing my parents to be out on the road at two a.m. in the path of a truck?'

'Of course not. I'm devastated that someone did that to you, and I'm heartbroken about what happened to your family. But Jana, it wasn't me. I swear on everything I hold dear. Some other boy must have impersonated me. I would never, ever play with your feelings – or anybody's feelings – like that.'

Jana snatched her hand away from him. She searched his face for any hint of deceit but saw only a pain that mirrored her own, and a touching vulnerability that hadn't been there before. She tried to reconcile the Mark she knew with the ghost of her past heartbreak. The room seemed to close in, suffocating her. Could she have been wrong for all these years?

'Jana.' Her name sounded like a prayer on his lips. 'Please believe me. I didn't do it! And as far as I know, none of your private messages were ever shared at school.'

If that was true, it was a huge relief, but Jana had no way of knowing for sure. She'd left Scarborough and never looked back, closing all her personal social media accounts. Tears welled in his eyes. Should she believe him? His story seemed so unlikely – and yes, even self-serving. But what was the alternative? Losing this man she cared about, who might very well be innocent of any wrongdoing? It had all happened so long ago. There was no way to verify his story now.

Jana felt the weight of her past, the crushing burden of mistrust, and the tentative hope for a future free from pain. So, she took a leap of faith. 'Yes, I believe you.' It was the choice she had to make, but it still left a sour taste in her mouth. She'd hoped to put this behind her once and for all. But now a cloud would forever linger over the issue. It could never be one hundred per cent resolved.

CHAPTER 39

Jana was meeting Annie West at the Rivertown Country Club. It surprised her that a maverick like Annie would choose such a swanky place. She supposed that she'd have to pay, having called the meeting in the first place. That was a bummer, but if it meant she might convince Annie and her protesters to leave the zoo's fundraiser alone, it would be worth it.

She arrived at the restaurant with butterflies in her belly, the talk with Mark playing over and over in her mind. *Leave it*, she told herself. This meeting was far too important. She couldn't afford any distractions. The historic clubhouse was as traditional as they came, built of stone, with a slate roof and mullioned windows. The waiter led her to a table set in an outdoor patio area offering spectacular views across the Murray to the yellow limestone cliffs beyond. The beauty of the surroundings settled Jana's nerves. This was her heartland. Sun sparkling on the water in a thousand pieces of light. Fragrant air, aromatic with the scent of eucalyptus. The rich, melodic piping of a distant butcherbird.

By the time Annie West's imposing figure approached the table, Jana was feeling grounded and ready to argue her case. This was a high-stakes game, not just for the zoo animals themselves, but for the future of conservation in South Australia's riverlands. It was time Annie understood that.

Jana rose to greet her and shook her hand. The tall woman's firm handshake impressed her, as did the gorgeous quoll tattoo on her forearm. It must have been covered up the first time they met. Jana would never have forgotten something like that.

Annie noticed her looking. 'I'm obsessed with quolls and devils,' she said. 'Marsupial carnivores of all types actually, and not just the big ones.' She rotated her wrist to show the charming image of a dunnart nestled in the palm of her hand, looking exactly like it was sleeping there.

'We recently discovered dunnarts at Odessa, our property at Tanunda,' said Jana, dispensing with the polite small talk that she'd planned. 'They've shown up a few times on our trail cameras. I can't tell you how excited we were to see them.'

Annie's eyes lit up. 'How marvellous! Common? Fat-tailed?'

'Stripe-faced.'

'Really?' said Annie. 'Tanunda is way south of their known range. What sort of habitat did you find them in?'

'Rehabilitated grassland. I grew up at Odessa and had never seen one before. I guess because the place was covered with degraded pasture back then. But when we destocked and replanted native grasses and shrubs, it only took a year for the dunnarts to show up.'

Annie leaned forward, eyes bright with curiosity. 'Why did you destock?'

'We wanted to rewild the property and turn it into a wild-life sanctuary. My sister and I run a wombat rescue there.'

A waiter arrived and asked if they required drinks. They waved him away.

'That's marvellous,' said Annie. 'But won't you be too busy for that if the zoo reopens? You'll be its full-time director, right?'

'Well, yes, but Odessa will become an overflow sanctuary for Wildfell Park, suitable for soft releases for orphaned animals and such. Did you know that more than a quarter of all native species in the Murraylands are threatened? My dream is to build a predator-proof boundary fence around the perimeter and rewild the entire two thousand hectares.'

'Along the lines of Mallee Cliffs National Park,' mused Annie, resting her chin on her hand and giving Jana her undivided attention.

'That's right,' said Jana, her enthusiasm for the conversation running away with her. 'Imagine reintroducing bilbies and phascogales to the riverlands. Or western quolls? If the zoo gets its licence, Wildfell Park and Odessa will become part of the Aussie Ark program, housing insurance populations of healthy Tassie devils. I already have the approval of Dr Penny Abbott.'

'Penny Abbott from Binburra?' Annie raised her brows approvingly. 'She's doing some wonderful work.'

'You know of her?' Jana had almost forgotten the original aim of the meeting, so thrilled was she to have found a kindred spirit.

'Penny's a good friend of mine. I might be against zoos, but I'm all for conservancies like Binburra that aim to protect and rewild natural landscapes.'

'But that's exactly what I want to accomplish at Wildfell Park.' Jana's voice rang strong and full of purpose. 'The Ark program has plans to return devils to the wild in mainland Australia. If the zoo regains its licence, Odessa will become a release site.'

The waiter tried his luck again. 'Are you ladies ready to order?'

'No,' they sang in unison.

Annie poured them glasses of water from a jug on the table. 'I must say that what you've told me has made me rethink my opposition to your project.'

Jana's heart lifted. Who could have imagined their meeting going so well? She should have bitten the bullet and approached the woman months ago. 'So, what exactly does "rethink" mean?' asked Jana, wanting some clarification as to Annie's revised position.

'It means I'll take the time to investigate what you've told me. I'll talk to Penny Abbott, for starters. Rest assured that if your story checks out, my organisation won't cause you any more trouble.'

'And in the meantime?'

Annie gave her a knowing look. 'Ah, your Open Day. We *were* planning to visit you next Saturday. I wonder how many people would have run the gauntlet of three hundred chanting, banner-wielding protesters? But for now, I'll call off the hounds.'

Jana exhaled. 'You're welcome to visit the zoo whenever you want, to show our commitment to transparency. And perhaps you'll come to our Open Day?'

Annie inclined her head in a gesture of assent. Mark would

never believe what a success this lunch meeting had been. 'Of course, I can't promise that no protesters will turn up. Some of our more radical members might ignore my call to stand down. But I can't imagine there being more than a handful of them.'

'That's manageable.' Jana glanced at the young waiter hovering impatiently nearby. 'If we don't order soon,' she whispered, 'we may be thrown out.'

Annie let out a loud laugh and clicked her fingers. The waiter appeared by her side. 'We'll have the vegetarian menus now, Joel. And a bottle of French champagne.' She smiled at Jana. 'To celebrate our new understanding.'

Jana's mouth fell open. With her trainers, baggy men's jeans, short spiky hair and nose ring, Annie stood out among the conservatively dressed club patrons like a sore thumb. Jana was faintly surprised that she was even allowed in. Yet here she was, behaving like she owned the joint. Jana sneaked a look at the drinks menu. Crikey – that bottle of French wine would set her back an arm and a leg!

Annie noticed her consternation. 'Drinks are on me,' she announced, airily. 'Lunch too. I can recommend the pumpkin risotto. Now tell me more about your wombats.'

That evening, as Jana and Mark strolled along the zoo's river path, she told him about her extraordinary lunch. 'Annie's guaranteed that there'll be no protest by the Animal Defenders to disrupt our Open Day. As long as the information I gave Annie checks out – which it will – their campaign against the zoo is officially over. In fact, I think they might end up supporting us.'

'Great work,' said Mark. 'So I guess their campaign of sabotage is over too. Should we come clean with the staff about Tash?'

'I don't know,' replied Jana. 'After talking to Annie, I'm not convinced that the Animal Defenders were behind the sabotage in the first place. She seems so genuinely open and direct about what she believes in. I can't imagine her sneaking around to get what she wants, or putting animals and people at risk.'

'Who then?'

'Annie doesn't have full control of the Defenders. She said a few discontented members might still show up at the Open Day. Perhaps a radical splinter group is acting alone. Let's keep Tash undercover until we're sure.'

'Okay, but I sure feel a whole lot better knowing that Annie's on our side. How ready are we for Saturday?'

'There's still a fair bit to do. We have a few more donations to collect for the raffle and Bruce has to source some marquees in case the weather turns. We need to make sure that we have enough volunteers to help with the guided tours. And I still need to confirm the food trucks. Oh no – I forgot to book the portaloos.'

'Don't worry,' said Mark. 'It's done. What about the evening barbecue? Do we have plenty of food for everyone?'

Jana frowned. 'I'm not sure. We've ordered enough for the number of pre-sold tickets, but we haven't allowed for ticket sales at the gate on the day. And I didn't organise a vegetarian option.'

'Leave the catering to me,' said Mark. 'You concentrate on completing thorough safety and security checks on all the animal enclosures. We don't want any nasty surprises when we're under the spotlight.' He reached for her hand, and she let him take it. 'You do believe me, right? About what happened back at high school?'

'Yes,' she managed, although the truth was that she hadn't fully processed the day's events. Mark loved her – he'd said so. How should she react to that? Did she love him too? He'd denied that he was responsible for what had happened all those years ago – what she'd blamed on him for over a decade. And although she'd decided to believe him, it would take time to let go of the pain.

CHAPTER 40

A shrill alarm sounded, dragging Jana from the deepest of slumbers. Then she felt a firm hand on her shoulder.

Mark's voice penetrated the fog of sleep. 'Jana, wake up.' Another shake, rougher this time. And all the while the alarm assaulted her ears. She sat up, still groggy. What day was it? Perhaps she was dreaming. 'Get dressed. Somebody opened the enclosures overnight.'

That woke her quick smart and details began to fall into place. It was Friday morning, barely light, and the eve of their Open Day. Tomorrow they'd have hundreds of people swarming the grounds. She pulled on jeans over her pyjamas. 'And you're saying animals are loose? Which ones?'

He grabbed her coat off the hook on the wall and threw it to her. 'I think the lions are our main worry.'

'Fuck!' Jana dashed downstairs barefoot after Mark, pulling on her boots at the back door. 'Have you called the keepers?' She looked out to where trees and flowerbeds were emerging in the pale dawn light. 'Where's Sash?'

'Yes, and I don't know,' said Mark, his voice tight and

strained. 'She didn't have dinner with us, and I can't tell if her bed's been slept in. She never makes it. But I've sent her a message. Did you see her last night?'

'Well, no.' Jana glanced around as they strode outside, half-expecting to see a lion charge from the gloom. 'I thought she must have stayed over with Amber and Maggie at Jean's house.'

'Well, we'll soon find out. The keepers are all on their way in.'

Jana tried ringing Sash, but it went to voicemail.

Mark's face was suddenly fierce. 'Nobody goes searching for any animals until Johnno arrives to cover us with the rifle, understood?'

'There's Sol,' whispered Jana, pointing towards a stand of blue gums to their right. The sun bear was tearing a fallen log apart with his powerful claws, occasionally stopping to snuffle up tasty insect treats.

A 4WD screamed into the driveway. Johnno jumped out, looking grim. 'What happened?'

'A single alarm woke me at five o'clock,' said Mark. 'It was the only one working – Hazel's original, old-school, hard-wired variety. Someone had disabled the critical security systems by hacking into my computer. The cameras were down, and the animal enclosures automatically unlocked.'

'Like in *Jurassic Park*,' said Jana.

'Exactly. I did a check of the grounds before I woke you. Somebody has gone around physically opening gates as well. I think whoever it was must have been disturbed in the process, because many exhibits remain secure. The animals didn't realise that they could push out. Those damned squirrels are still safe, and the tigers stayed put, thank God, as did the large herbivores. But the monkeys are out again, along with Sol, the dingoes – and the lions.'

Panic rose in Jana's throat like bile, threatening to choke her. Several more cars drew up at the front of the house. The keepers were all there now – all of them except Sash. Jana quickly brought them up to speed.

Johnno noticed the bear, still working on the log about a hundred metres away. 'Bruce and I will go get the rifle and tranquilliser gun.'

'Maggie, you go with them,' said Jana. 'We'll need lots of sedative doses of varying strengths. We won't have time to trap the monkeys like we did last time.' She felt faint. They had such a tight timeline to fix this. The thought of hundreds of people flocking into the zoo for tomorrow's Open Day made her blood curdle.

'I'll go get some honeycomb to encourage Sol to stay around while Johnno darts him,' said Lexie.

A monkey chattered at them from the manor house roof. 'Better get some baskets of fruit too, with a triple serve of bananas,' said Jana. 'Put one in the monkey house. We might tempt some hungry escapees back with breakfast. And bring some meat for the dingoes.' They, at least, would be easy to catch. Jana and Lexie had been taking them for daily walks around the grounds in preparation for their ambassadorial role at tomorrow's fundraiser. They were used to coming to the keepers for treats.

'Amber, have you seen Sash?' Dammit. Her agitation and fear for her sister had made her forget to use her pseudonym. Hopefully Amber would think that she'd misheard.

'Not since yesterday.' Amber began to softly sob. Jana put a consoling hand on her arm and hoped that the girl could hold it together. They needed every member of the team on board.

'What time did you see her?' asked Jana, gently.

Amber gulped back tears. 'About five-thirty. She said she might go listen to a band last night.'

'What – by herself? That doesn't sound like Tash.'

'She's made a few new friends down at the pub,' said Amber. 'And she stayed with them overnight once when she'd had a few too many drinks. But I don't know who she planned to meet up with.'

'Why isn't she answering her phone?'

'It's still early,' suggested Amber.

That was true – six o'clock and barely light. 'Never mind,' said Jana, trying to calm her own fears as well. 'So long as she's not wandering around here with the lions on the loose.'

'Right,' said Mark. 'While we're waiting for the others to come back, does anybody know where those big cats might go? We still have an intact perimeter fence. Looks like the hacker couldn't breach our backup control with the outside security company. So the lions are somewhere within the grounds.'

That was a reassuring, if unsettling, thought. 'Does Hazel know?' asked Jana.

'She's still sleeping,' said Mark. 'Must have been wearing those ear plugs.'

'Let her sleep,' said Jana. 'She stays awake half the night listening to audiobooks and doesn't usually get up until ten. At least she's safely out of the way. Amber, go upstairs and post a note on the inside of Hazel's bedroom door explaining what's happened. Make it a whole sheet of paper with large writing so she can't miss it. Tell her to text me as soon as she wakes up and warn her not to go outside.'

Amber ran off just as the others returned with their supplies. They exchanged dismayed glances as a dingo raced across the lawn in pursuit of a panicked peacock.

'One thing at a time.' Johnno tossed the rifle to Bruce and, after consulting with Jana, loaded a large dart into the tranquilliser gun. 'Let's get that bear. Someone bring one of the vans around, along with a hammock to lift him.'

When the van arrived, they piled into it and headed towards the gum trees. Sol was having a lovely time and did not appreciate being disturbed. He was generally an amiable soul but could be aggressive when provoked. His strong jaws, large canines and raking claws made him potentially dangerous.

'Give me the honeycomb,' said Johnno, as he and Bruce alighted from the vehicle. 'The rest of you, stay here.' The men looked nervously around them. They were all imagining lions in the shadows.

Sol growled and swung his head, but continued ripping into the log, allowing Johnno to approach within twenty metres. Bruce covered him with the rifle. But when Johnno raised the dart gun and nestled the butt into his shoulder, Sol grew more defensive. Many of the zoo animals recognised that threatening posture.

He reared up on his hindlegs and barked a warning. Johnno threw the honeycomb with his free hand. Sol lumbered towards the prize, offering a clear shot of his fleshy upper shoulder. The dart hit its mark, delivering an intra-muscular mixed dose of ketamine and xylazine. Sol roared his displeasure and loped away.

The men jumped back into the van. 'Follow him!' Jana ordered. Mark, who was driving, took off after the bear, dodging trees and fallen logs until he reached the clearing beyond. The drugs began to take effect when Sol was in open parkland. Once he was finally down, Jana and the men approached, prodding him from behind to test his level of consciousness. Jana quickly checked Sol's vitals – temperature, heart rate and respiration.

'All good. Let's get him onto the stretcher.'

Sol only weighed seventy kilos, but his dead weight was awkward to move. They had to be careful not to let his head flop too much, or let his full weight crush his chest. When they'd replaced him in his habitat, Jana administered the reversal drug.

'Come on,' said Johnno.

'Wait a minute.' Jana called Amber. It went to voicemail. She texted her instead. *Come to Sol's enclosure. Someone needs to monitor him until he's fully recovered.*

Why didn't Amber answer? Jana swore out loud. 'And where the hell is Tash?' she said to nobody in particular. 'She knew how much there was to do today, even without having to recapture half the animals. We need all hands on deck, and Tash could have flown her surveillance drone to help us locate the escapees faster.'

'I know how to fly Bumblebee,' said Maggie. 'Tash showed me.'

'We can't wait around here,' urged Bruce.

Jana nodded as Sol stirred. Thank Christ for that. She called Amber and Sash one more time, but to no avail. 'Johnno, can you drop Maggie and me at the workshop? We'll see if we can get that drone in the air. Then go back into the park and find those lions. But be careful, everyone. Don't take any chances.'

Bumblebee was essentially a flying camera. 'It's working!' said Maggie as the drone lifted off and soared into the sky.

Jana checked the video screen in the workshop. By switching between four screens – north, south, east and west – she could get a three-hundred-and-sixty-degree snapshot of the view below. 'Can I connect this to my phone?'

'Give it to me.' Maggie pressed a few buttons. 'There.'

Jana checked the screen. 'Fly north,' she said. 'Let's check the paddocks.'

Maggie jiggled the joystick controller and the viewfinder swept towards the river.

'There's the van,' said Jana. 'Parked in the small-herbivore paddock.' The drone dipped lower. 'And there are the lions. Two of them, anyway. King and one of the lionesses.'

They exchanged excited glances. The drone flew lower still. 'Hang on. What's that?' Maggie's hand flew to her mouth.

Jana gasped in fright. A blood-soaked carcass lay at King's feet. He looked skywards and tossed his head.

'King's spotted the drone,' said Jana. 'Back off.'

Maggie jiggled the controller and Bumblebee swerved away.

'Land it somewhere. We'd better get out there.' Jana tried

calling her sister again. Where *was* Sash, and why wasn't she answering? Jana's stomach churned with apprehension. She had a very bad feeling about this.

CHAPTER 41

Mark edged the van closer over the rough ground, acutely aware that Bruce was on the roof, clinging to the roof rack with the rifle and trying to maintain his aim.

'We want to be within thirty metres,' said Johnno. 'That shouldn't be too hard. Neither King nor Cleo will want to abandon their kill.'

The two lions stood guard over the half-eaten carcass of the Barbary ram, who'd died defending his flock. His brave stance against the predators had allowed the ewes and lambs time to escape.

What was that sound? King looked up and Mark followed his gaze. A drone whirred overhead, then spun up and away. A clever way to spot the lions, if they hadn't already located them – well, two of them anyway. Nala was nowhere in sight.

'That'll do,' said Johnno, and Mark stopped the van. He leaned out the window. 'You all set, Bruce?' Then he tapped once on the metal divide behind him. 'You all right back there?'

A muffled response. Lexie was riding in the back and would only emerge when a double knock told her it was safe. Johnno aimed out the open window and fired a dart at King, hitting him square on the flank. The lion roared and charged the van, just as the window rolled up. He swatted in annoyance at the glass. Mark held his breath as King sprang towards the roof where Bruce was perched with his rifle. At any moment he expected to see either the lion felled by a bullet or Bruce torn from the roof. But the van's exterior was steep and slippery and King was starting to feel the effects of the expertly placed dart. He staggered a few metres away and Mark could breathe again.

Next Johnno successfully targeted Cleo. She must have been tired after her night of hunting and feasting, because after a few brief grunts, the lioness wandered over to her recumbent companion, lay down and went to sleep beside him.

'Nice shooting,' said Mark, knocking twice on the dividing wall to summon Lexie. He texted Jana, asking her to meet them at the lion house. Lexie cautiously emerged from the back of the van under Bruce's watchful eye, and the team waited for the lions to be solidly under.

They worked fast, rolling Cleo and King onto stretchers, hauling the animals into the van and setting off towards their dens. Jana and Maggie met them at the gate, full of questions. 'Did you get them both?' asked Jana as she opened the van doors.

'We did,' said Bruce. 'Still no sign of Nala, though. Keep that drone in the air. It's our best chance of finding her.'

Jana kneeled beside the lions and checked their vitals. 'They're okay.'

The team quickly moved them back into their sleeping chambers. Jana administered the reversal drugs and the lions groggily shook their heads, looking around in confusion and doubtlessly wondering where their breakfast had gone.

'It was me flying the drone,' said Maggie, proudly.

Johnno gave Jana a searching look.

'Tash still isn't here.' Jana could hear the fear in her own voice. 'I'm getting worried. And has anyone seen Amber? I sent her to the house an hour ago to warn Hazel. I assumed she was with you.'

'And I assumed that she was with you.' Mark tried Amber's phone, but she didn't answer. Now he was worried too. Amber and Sash both appeared to be missing. Not only was the team two helpers down when they needed all hands on deck, but he also feared for the women's safety. There was a lion on the loose, along with a dangerous saboteur – one who was prepared to risk people's lives to discredit the zoo.

'Maybe it's time to call the police,' suggested Jana, looking beaten.

'Once the licensing board learns of our stuff-up it will be the end of the zoo,' said Mark, echoing all their thoughts. He checked the time. 9.45 a.m. 'Let's give it a few more hours. The perimeter fence wasn't breached. Nala must be here somewhere.'

'It wasn't our stuff-up, though,' said Maggie. 'The security system was deliberately tampered with. How is that our fault?'

'It won't matter whose fault it is, not with a lion on the loose,' said Mark, uncomfortably aware that one of the keepers gathered here could be the culprit. 'But the decision to keep the authorities out of it has to be unanimous. Who agrees that we hold our nerve for now?'

Every hand shot up without hesitation – a resounding yes. When she saw the display of solidarity, Jana couldn't hide her tears. She stammered out her thanks. The group's overwhelming camaraderie and strong commitment to Wildfell Park moved Mark as well. He was proud to be part of something bigger than himself. And it was suddenly obvious. If anyone here wanted the zoo to fail, all they needed to do was vote no. Yet nobody had.

Mark pulled Jana aside. 'It's time we trusted these people. They need to know the truth.' Jana nodded her assent, and they returned to the group. Mark took a big breath. 'Jana and I have something to confess.' He told the team of their suspicions that the sabotage had been an inside job. He told them that Tash was actually Jana's sister, Sash, and had been working undercover to discover the identity of the traitor. 'We're sorry that we doubted you.'

There were a few moments silence as the news sank in. Bruce glanced about at the shell-shocked faces of his colleagues, then stepped forward. 'There's no denying that we're hurt that you suspected us. But I can understand your reasoning. Some of us have been thinking the same thing. We even doubted Tash.' There were general nods of agreement. 'The internal security system could have been hacked remotely, but somebody must have physically been here on the zoo grounds last night to open the enclosure gates. And if it wasn't Tash—'

'That leaves Amber,' said Jana, her voice shaky. 'I sent her into the house to warn Hazel ages ago.'

'I didn't see Amber at home last night,' said Maggie.

'When I arrived this morning and she was already here, I just assumed that she'd got up early.' She licked her lips nervously. 'What if she stayed on after work yesterday? If the cameras were down, nobody would have spotted her.'

'I'll have a look around the vet clinic.' Mark struggled to control his anger. 'Then I'll go check on Hazel. The rest of you – find Nala.' As he turned to leave the lion house, a curious dingo nosed in the door, tail wagging, attracted by the lingering smell of meat in the dens. 'And somebody catch that damned dingo!'

Mark found Hazel making toast in the kitchen and playing with Bandit, blissfully unaware that there was even a problem. 'Have you seen Tash or Amber?' he asked.

Hazel shot him a withering glance. 'Well, good morning to you too.' She took a second look. 'Whatever's wrong? You look like your best friend just died.'

'Sit down, Hazel, and I'll tell you.'

Hazel stirred her tea while Mark talked. He left nothing out. By the time he'd finished, all the colour had drained from her lined face and her tea had gone cold. 'This is a dark day for the zoo,' she declared. 'In fifty years, there hasn't been a serious escape from Wildfell Park. If I ever get my hands on the bastards responsible, they'll be sorry. They deserve to be hanged, drawn and quartered!'

It was the first time that Mark could remember agreeing with Hazel.

'And you say that Tash is Jana's sister? I don't know why you couldn't have told me.'

'We didn't tell anybody. It was strictly on a need-to-know basis.'

'This is my house,' said a frowning Hazel. 'And I have a right to be told what's going on.'

'Well, you know now,' said Mark. 'Have you seen either Sash or Amber?'

'Not Amber,' said Hazel after an infuriatingly long pause. 'But I saw Tash – I mean Sash – last night in the kitchen. Oh, it must have been about three o'clock in the morning. She couldn't sleep, you see. I get like that too. We shared a cuppa. She was drinking coffee and I told her that caffeine at that time of night—'

Mark interrupted. 'What happened next?'

Hazel glowered at him. 'She went for a walk. It didn't seem strange to me. Tash often wanders around at night. She likes to make friends with the nocturnal animals.'

'Did she say where she was walking to?' asked Mark.

'The vet clinic, I think. She wanted to check that it was securely locked.'

Mark turned the information over in his mind. Had Sash merely been doing a routine check, or had something alarmed her? 'Stay in the house with Bandit until we locate that lion.' He turned to leave.

'But I can help,' called Hazel. 'Nala trusts me.'

'It's too dangerous.' Mark didn't have time for this.

'Dangerous? Pfft, Nala wouldn't hurt a fly. Why, before all this health and safety nonsense, I used to walk her around the grounds on a leash like this puppy here.' Hazel slipped Bandit a triangle of Vegemite toast.

'Thank Christ for health and safety, then,' muttered Mark as he left. He called Jana. 'Any luck?'

315

'We have the dingoes, and most of the monkeys returned of their own accord for breakfast. I think there are three still on the run. But no sign of Nala – or Sash for that matter.'

'Is that drone in the air?'

'Yes, and it's saving us heaps of time. Ooh, it's just spotted a monkey on the café roof. But we'll have to manually check the treed areas. Have you found Amber?'

'She's probably long gone.'

'How's Hazel?'

'Upset and angry,' said Mark. 'But otherwise, fine. I told her to stay in the house. Listen, can you leave the staff to it for a bit and meet me at the clinic?'

CHAPTER 42

Jana sprinted down the path to meet Mark, crossing her fingers for good news. She noticed something odd upon entering the clinic. The door to the hospital ward stood open. She couldn't resist peeking inside, even though she could see Mark waiting for her in the dispensary.

'Oh, poor babies!' An owl with a splinted wing huddled on the floor in one corner. Three recently spayed squirrels chittered on top of a cupboard. Hadn't there been four? Then she noticed the carpet python that was being treated for a skin infection. It was curled up in the squirrels' cage with a suspicious bulge in its middle.

Mark came in to see what she was doing.

'Someone's been in the clinic.' A tumultuous mix of emotions washed over Jana as she surveyed the chaos: anger, anguish and helplessness. The safe haven she'd built for these creatures had been utterly violated – and so had she.

'That's why I called you.' He tried guiding her from the room.

'They let my patients out. Sebastian ate a squirrel.'

'I'm sorry,' he said. 'But I really have to show you something.'

Jana shut the door and followed Mark into the dispensary, where she got another shock. Half-open drawers. Toppled chairs. Medicine containers and syringes littered the room, and the drug cupboard stood open. Clear signs of a struggle.

'What happened here?' Jana inspected the floor more closely. 'Is that blood?' She blanched and a chill ran through her. What if it was Sash's blood? Was sweet, innocent-seeming Amber truly capable of hurting her sister?

Jana noticed something else on the floor. 'This pen.' She picked it up. 'Isn't this Sash's spy pen?' She clicked the top. Nothing happened. 'How do you switch it on?'

Mark took the pen and turned it over, clicking the top button. Then he double-clicked it and put the pen to his ear. 'I can hear something.' He examined it again. 'When I double-click the top button, the nib retracts. Can you find me some headphones?'

Jana ran to the office with Mark on her heels. She fished around in her desk drawer. 'Yes!' She handed a set of headphones to Mark.

'Let's pray they fit.' He plugged them into the pen.

'Can you hear?'

Mark gave her the thumbs up. It was torture, just standing there, waiting. Minutes ticked by. Suddenly he pulled the headphones off. 'Sash is in one of the vans.'

They ran to where the zoo vehicles were parked in a row behind the workshop. One van stood out, parked haphazardly a distance away from the others. The vet clinic's trolley cage stood nearby.

'Listen.' Jana could hear a faint rhythmic banging. They rushed to open the van doors. 'Sash!' Inside lay her sister – bound and gagged, with a cut on her head. She groaned when they untied her, and Jana hugged her in relief. 'What happened?'

Sash attempted to sit up, groggily warding off Mark's helping hand. 'It was Amber. I found her wrecking the clinic in the middle of the night. We struggled when I tried to stop her and she hit me with a chair, knocking me down. But not before I activated my spy pen.'

'A stroke of genius,' said Mark. 'That's how we knew where to find you. It recorded everything.'

Sash flinched as her fingers found the bloody gash on her forehead. 'When I tried to stand up, Amber jabbed me with a needle. She said she was sorry, but she'd have to lock me in a van until she could get away. I don't remember anything else until I woke up in the back. Lord knows how long I've been here. What time is it?'

Jana hugged her again. 'Thank God you were there to stop Amber. You're a hero, do you know that? If you hadn't interrupted her, who knows what that psycho might have done next? For all we know, she could have poisoned the food in the zoo kitchen or burned down the manor house. At the very least we'd have more escaped animals, including the tigers.'

'What do you mean?' Sash's face lost its last bit of colour. 'Are there animals loose?'

'Amber, or somebody working with her, hacked the zoo's

internal security systems,' said Mark. 'That took the CCTV out and automatically unlocked the enclosures.'

'Like in *Jurassic Park*,' said Sash.

'Yes, except at least we don't have giant dinosaurs constantly testing the gates,' said Jana. 'Most of our animals are happy with where they live and didn't even realise they could get out. So apparently Amber was moving around the zoo and physically opening the gates to make the escape routes more obvious. She must have decided to stop by and ransack the clinic along the way. That's when you confronted her.'

'Have you recaptured the escaped animals?'

Jana glanced at Mark. 'Mostly. All except three monkeys . . . and Nala.'

'Shit!' Sash tried to stand and collapsed back to the van floor with a moan.

Mark kneeled beside her. 'You need to rest. And we'd best get you to a doctor for a check-up. The police—' He stopped abruptly.

Jana knew exactly what he wanted to say, and why he didn't say it. They should call the police. Amber was dangerous and still at large. But so was Nala. If they could find the lioness first, disaster might still be averted.

'I do need a coffee, but I don't need a doctor,' insisted Sash. 'And I don't need a rest. I've just had hours of drug-induced sleep. Let's find Nala.'

Mark helped Sash to her feet, and this time she managed to stand. 'I'll let the team know that we've found you.' He checked his phone. 'Eleven o'clock.' He gave Jana a tight-lipped glance. Time was running out. 'You take Sash back to the house and check on Hazel. I'll join the others and keep looking. Nala must be somewhere here in the park. When the staff leave for the night, I signal the security company to do a hard lockdown of the perimeter. Nobody gets out until I send the company a code in the morning. I haven't done that today. Even we can't get out of Wildfell Park until I do.'

Jana was puzzled. 'Then how did the staff get in this morning?'

Mark helped Sash from the back of the van. 'Oh, people can come in all right if they know the front-gate passcode, but they can't get out again.'

'So that's it,' said Jana as the penny dropped. 'I was wondering why Amber didn't simply leave last night after attacking Sash. She couldn't get out of the gate. And that means that she's still here too.'

An hour later and still no sign of the fugitives. The keepers had split up to search, and Mark and Jana were doing a sweep of the poultry pens in case Nala had fancied herself a chicken breakfast. As they headed towards the dingo enclosure, Mark's phone rang – Scarborough College. What had Karly done now? In three and a half hours he'd need to pick her up from school. They'd captured the last three monkeys, but he couldn't bring his daughter home to the zoo with Nala and Amber on the loose. He'd have to bite the bullet before then and call the police. It was almost a relief knowing that one way or another, this torture would soon be over.

Mark picked up. 'Mrs Hall, hello. What can I do for you?'

'You can respect the school rules,' said the principal. 'You can't simply take Karly out of school whenever it suits you.

We had a swimming carnival today, which doesn't equate to a day off. We expect all our students to attend and cheer on their house.'

What on earth was the woman talking about? 'Don't worry. I'll be there at the normal time to collect my daughter. Unless the carnival will make her late,' he added hopefully. That would be handy. 'What time would you like me to come?'

A long pause. 'Mr Bell, Karly isn't here. She told her housemother that you intended to collect her this morning at nine-thirty. Mrs Stuart really should have informed me earlier, especially since Karly was quite teary before she left. A phone call from her mother had upset her apparently.'

'What?' The line crackled and dropped out. He glanced up to the thickening clouds and a sky growing darker by the minute. Reception was always worse with rain coming. Damn this crappy regional phone service. Mark tried calling back but couldn't connect. He tried to get his head around the news. Karly had run away. He froze on the spot, unable to decide what to do first. What had Harper said to distress their daughter so? A rising combination of anger and fear made it hard to fill his lungs.

He took a series of deliberate, slow breaths and gave himself a mental kick up the bum. Right now, it didn't matter what Harper had said. Right now, he had to find Karly, and to do that he needed to think like his daughter. Where would she go if she was upset? The answer was obvious. She'd come home to the zoo. Karly knew the front-gate passcode, and the security cameras were still down, so she could have entered unobserved. His heart stalled at the thought of Karly roaming the grounds, along with a lion and a violent criminal.

It was time to admit defeat. He'd go back to the house and use the landline to call the police. Tears pricked the back of his eyes and he let them fall. Months of work gone for nought. Nala wouldn't have run off if she knew that she'd lose her life when the zoo closed. Jana hadn't been able to find an alternative home for either her or King. The staff would lose their jobs. Hazel would lose her home, and there was every chance that Mark would lose Jana. He wasn't convinced that she fully believed him about what had happened back at school, that he had never been behind the fake relationship, and who could blame her? Under the circumstances he wouldn't be surprised if she pulled away. Grief at losing the zoo might well be the last straw.

And most importantly, of course, there was Karly. Once Harper learned of today's disastrous events, custody would be hers for the taking. Mark couldn't provide a safe environment for their daughter. Harper might not be the perfect parent, but at least with her Karly wouldn't be at risk of being eaten by a lion.

Jana glanced across and saw him crying, but he didn't care. All pride had left him. The old him – the smug, self-important man who'd always had tickets on himself – was no more. In his place stood a person humbled by the depth of his love for others: for Karly, for Jana and, yes, for the zoo animals that he'd let down so badly.

Jana enfolded him in the sweetest of hugs. 'What's happened?'

Mark wiped his eyes, cleared his throat and told her of Karly's disappearance. He didn't deserve the sympathy and understanding in her eyes.

'It's time,' she said, taking hold of his hand. 'We'll go to the house together and call the police.'

'I'm sorry,' he sobbed.

Jana shook her head, smiling through her own tears. 'It's all right, Mark. You tried your best; we all did. None of us could have predicted that this would happen. Come on. Let's find Karly.'

Jana tugged him towards the quad bike. Mark took his seat and Jana wrapped her arms around his waist. He cherished the feeling of her body against his, perhaps for the very last time.

CHAPTER 43

When they reached the house, Hazel was waiting for them on the verandah.

'Thank goodness you're safe,' said Jana, sprinting up the steps and embracing her. 'Karly's run away from school. She'll probably turn up here. Have you seen her?'

'No, but—'

Jana guided Hazel inside, with Mark hot on her heels. 'There's still no sign of Nala or Amber. I'm sorry, Hazel, but we're going to call the police.'

'Don't do that. I'm trying to—'

'No buts,' said Mark. 'I can't risk anything happening to my daughter.' He strode to the hall table and picked up the phone. 'I should have done this hours ago.'

'Oh, no you don't.' Hazel marched up to him, snatched the phone with surprising vigour, and stamped her foot. 'I'm trying to tell you that I've found Nala.'

'What?' Mark stared at her in disbelief. 'Where?'

'Right underneath our feet. She's in the old coal cellar. Reg and I used it for wine, and I fetched a bottle of sherry up last week. I must have left the door open. All Nala had to do was go down the stone steps near the base of that broken dragon statue in the garden. The entrance is partly overgrown by roses.'

Jana felt like she might faint with relief. 'How did you discover her?'

'There's no time for stories,' said Mark, while texting on his phone. 'We need those guns here, pronto.'

'Guns?' cried Hazel, her voice shrill with alarm.

'It's okay.' Jana put a soothing hand on her arm. 'We're talking about a tranquilliser gun.' No need to mention the rifle.

'Oh, my lord,' exclaimed Hazel, fanning herself with a handkerchief she found in her pocket. 'You almost gave me a heart attack.'

'Damn,' said Mark. 'The message didn't send.'

'It's this weather.' Jana's racing pulse began to calm. 'Should one of us go find the others?'

'They could be anywhere on the grounds,' said Mark. 'It will take forever.'

'I don't know what the hurry is,' said Hazel. 'Nala's quite happy in the cellar and the door is shut. I gave her a lamb leg from the freezer to keep her busy.'

'You went in there?' asked Mark, looking shocked.

'Well, why not? You forget, I raised that lion from a cub, bottle-fed her since she was two days old. When she got too big for my room, she used to sleep in that cellar. I slept with her too, at first. My camp bed is still set up along the back wall. Nala feels safe in there, like it's her own private den.'

Jana began to relax. With Nala located, maybe they could

hold off on the police for a while yet. She repeated her earlier question to Hazel while Mark vainly tried to contact the keepers. 'How did you discover where she was?'

'I was simply walking around outside the house searching for her. I heard a crashing noise downstairs and peered through the cellar window. You know that low narrow gap that you pass on the way to the vegetable garden? Well, there was Nala, staring back at me. She'd knocked over a case of wine. So, I took her the lamb roast and shut the door.'

'How long ago was that?' asked Mark, who'd temporarily given up on trying to call the others.

Hazel gave him a contemptuous glance. 'It was just after you *ordered* me to stay inside and said that I couldn't help, because it was too dangerous for a little old lady. Isn't it ironic that I was the one to find Nala?'

'And I'm extremely grateful that you did,' said Mark. 'Now, let's take a look through that window to confirm Nala really is safely locked in the cellar. Then we'll figure out our next move.'

The coal-cellar window was a small rectangular opening in the thick stone of the southernmost wall of the manor house. It was strategically positioned to provide ventilation below, while also allowing light to filter in.

Jana pulled her hat down tight against the rain and looked through the window, catching a glimpse of the dark, cavernous interior of the cellar, where stacks of coal were once neatly arranged. It took a few moments for her eyes to adjust. Yes! There was Nala, curled up in a corner. And something else as well. Jana's heart forgot to beat. Karly lay curled up beside Nala, arms wrapped around the lioness's neck in a tight hug.

'Karly,' Jana called quietly, trying to keep her emotions in check so as not to startle either the girl or the lion. 'Are you okay?'

'What the hell?' Mark pushed Jana away from the window and peered inside. 'Karly, sweetheart!' he yelled, his eyes wide and wild with fear. 'Don't worry, we're coming.'

Jana heard a snarl from below. 'Mark,' she whispered. 'Not so loud. You'll frighten Nala. We need to keep her calm.'

Hazel tapped Jana on the arm. 'Are you saying that Karly is with Nala?'

'How do we get down there?' urged Mark.

With agonising slowness, Hazel made her way to the adjacent flowerbed. She poked around with her walking stick. 'The entrance is a bit hard to find . . .'

Mark shoved past her and kicked about in the bushes. 'Here it is!' He hurried down the steps, almost slipping on the damp stone, followed by Jana. Hazel brought up the rear, using her walking stick for balance. They were confronted by a heavy wooden door with a round iron handle. Mark raised his fist to knock on the door.

'Softly,' warned Jana. 'Don't scare Nala.'

A few gentle knocks later, Mark called, 'Sweetheart, I'm going to open the door, okay?' He took hold of the handle. 'What the hell is Karly doing in there anyway?' he whispered. He was strung tight as a drum. Jana could almost hear his heart pounding out of his chest.

'Let me.' Hazel took hold of the doorhandle.

Mark and Jana exchanged worried glances, then stepped back. Somebody had to get Karly out of the cellar, and Nala trusted Hazel. She was their best bet.

Hazel needed to use two hands before the latch would budge. The door swung wide, and there, in a dark corner of the dusty cellar, were Nala and Karly. There was no doubting the lioness's fierce body language. She was crouched protectively over the girl as if guarding her own cub. Karly looked shockingly small and fragile beside the one-hundred-and-fifty-kilogram lioness.

'Karly, honey, are you all right?' managed Mark.

She regarded them with eyes red-rimmed from crying. 'Mum wants to take me away,' Karly sobbed. 'She wants to take me away from you, and Jana, and Hazel, and Nala . . .' With that, she dissolved into tears and buried her face in Nala's golden neck.

Mark moved slowly into the room. Nala let out a roar of warning and he froze.

'Don't.' Karly gently cuffed the lion's chin. 'You'll scare Dad.'

Nala purred and rubbed the girl's cheek with her own, much like an affectionate house cat.

'For goodness' sake,' said Hazel, pushing past Mark. 'Can't you see Nala doesn't mean to harm the child?' She marched boldly forward. 'Come on, Karly. You've caused quite a stir, but it's time for Nala to go home and for you to come up to the house.'

'I'm not going anywhere until Dad promises that I can stay here at the zoo with him.' She glared at her father defiantly. 'I won't go, Dad, and you can't make me.'

'Sweetheart,' he said in a low voice that cracked with emotion. 'I love you, honey, and I'll move heaven and earth to keep you here with me. I promise.'

Karly peered more closely at her father. 'Dad, have you been crying? You have!' As she attempted to reach him, Nala wrapped an enormous paw around her. Karly struggled but Nala held her tight. Mark gasped and jumped forward. The lioness, who'd been watching his every move, leaped to attention, snarling and thrashing her tail, menace showing in each line of her muscled body.

'Naughty girl!'

Jana's jaw dropped as Hazel tapped Nala firmly on the head with her walking stick. Nala flinched and let the girl go. In an instant Mark had gathered Karly in his arms and dashed outside with her.

Jana's heart burst with joy and relief. 'Come on, Hazel.'

'Wait one minute,' said the older woman. 'Nala needs her reward for being so good.' She emptied a packet of Bandit's liver treats onto the floor. Nala purred and started to lick them up. Jana bundled Hazel from the cellar and slammed the door behind them.

'You're safe,' murmured Mark, over and over, while holding Karly in a tight embrace. She began to squirm, but still he didn't release her.

'The poor child can't breathe,' said Hazel, disapprovingly. 'Let her go, or you'll get a taste of my walking stick too.'

Mark eased his grip, but Karly snuggled back contentedly into his arms. 'You can wallop me with that walking stick as hard and as often as you like, Hazel. You saved my daughter's life and I'm forever in your debt.'

'Fiddlesticks. Nala never meant to hurt her.' But Hazel's smile showed how pleased she was.

Mark carried Karly into the house and laid her down on the sitting-room couch. Bandit jumped up beside her and licked her dirty face. She was a mess, with cobwebs in her tangled hair, a scraped knee and a tear in her school dress.

'What happened at Scarborough?' he asked. 'And why were you in that cellar?'

'Mum rang,' said Karly, her voice barely a whisper. 'She's getting married.' Mark nodded. Karly sat up, kissed Bandit, then looked at her father accusingly. 'You knew? Did you know that she wants me to go live with her?' Karly could read in his face that he did. 'Why didn't you tell me?'

'Harper said that she'd talk to you in person this weekend. I wanted to be there when she told you. I didn't want you to find out when you were at school by yourself.'

'But that's exactly what happened.' Karly wiped away a few tears. 'After Mum rang, I tried calling you, but couldn't get through. So I lied to Mrs Stuart and I ran off when everyone was lining up for the swimming carnival. It was easy to get to the zoo without being seen – I just followed the river. There's a path the whole way. Then I got scared that you'd send me back to school, so I decided to hide. I remembered Hazel telling me about the cellar, and when I peeked through that funny little window, I saw Nala. She looked like she was hiding too, so I thought we could hide together.' Karly gulped hard, stifling a sob. 'That way we wouldn't be so lonely.'

'Weren't you scared that Nala would hurt you?'

Karly cuddled Bandit closer. She didn't appear to understand the question. 'She's a *tame* lion, Dad.' She said the words very slowly, as if he was five years old. 'And she's my friend.'

CHAPTER 44

By the time Sash and the rest of the team were filled in on what had happened, the zoo was taking on a celebratory air. Karly was eating her favourite treat – bottomless bowls of vanilla ice cream smothered in Milo, and Bandit was chewing a ham bone under the kitchen table.

Nala was safely back in her den with a whole haunch of mutton and a big bowl of milk. There'd been no tense scenes trying to sedate and transport her from the cellar. While Jana and Mark were in the house comforting Karly, Hazel had simply tempted Nala back to her quarters with tubs of yoghurt.

Jana had gone back down to the cellar and scrounged up some bottles of wine and sherry. She was offering drinks and Tim Tam biscuits all round, while Sash and Lexie made stacks of pancakes for a belated breakfast.

Needless to say, nobody had called the police. For now, it didn't seem to matter that Amber was still hiding somewhere on the zoo grounds. After all, she couldn't get out. The perimeter was still in hard lockdown – Mark hadn't sent the daily exit code. And they all needed a little breathing space before alerting the authorities. They also needed to get their stories straight. Once Amber was in custody, the escape of the animals would become public knowledge. Perhaps, if they put their heads together, they could think of a way to minimise the seriousness of what had happened and avoid putting Wildfell Park's re-licensing bid at risk.

Jana watched Mark, who was laughing and playing tug of war with Bandit. His appearance had changed since she'd met him – or re-met him – a few short months ago. His hair was longer and not combed to perfection. It was still styled, but not gelled or slicked back. The tousled look suited him. Back then he'd smelled of expensive cologne, and now he smelled of sweat and damp earth. His chin sported three days' worth of stubble and he'd muscled up. Helping out at the zoo every spare moment, digging and fencing and carting soil and stone, had given his body a definition that his city gym hadn't. Mark was most definitely not soft around the middle.

But the change was much more than physical. He was more patient and understanding, more open to new experiences and ideas. He smiled more easily, laughed more – cared more. He'd put everything on the line to save the zoo. In the depths of her heart, Jana realised that she did love Mark. She trusted and believed in him. And she wouldn't jeopardise what they currently had for the world.

Karly ran up to her, eyes shining with happiness. 'Guess what? Dad says he's thinking of sending me to Rivertown High next year. That's where Lisa goes. You know, Bruce's daughter? I'd actually have a friend!'

'That's great,' said Jana, thinking how desperately she herself had wanted a friend when she'd been at Scarborough College. 'Now where's your father gone? I need to talk to him.'

Jana found Mark tucking into pancakes in the kitchen. The sight of him with maple syrup dripping down his chin sent a warm rush through her. A glance at the wall clock told her it was almost one. They needed to figure out their next step.

Jana sat down at the table opposite him and dipped a finger into the puddle of syrup on his plate.

'Can I get you some pancakes?' asked Mark, watching her suck her sticky finger.

'Later. Right now, we need a plan.'

Mark wiped his chin with a paper napkin and drained his coffee cup. 'Once everyone's had their fill of refreshments and they're in a good mood, we'll call a meeting. If we can all agree to downplay what happened when we call the police—'

'There's no way to downplay the danger of lions on the loose,' said Jana, 'even if they're all back now and nobody knows that Karly was at risk. At the very least we'll have to hold a press conference. Reporters will have a field day. I can just imagine the headline in the *Rivertown Courier*. "Rampaging Lions Spark Panic at Local Zoo". The licensing board won't be happy, and neither will the locals. How many people will come to the Open Day tomorrow if they don't feel safe?'

'It was sabotage,' said Mark. 'And the animals were all recovered with no harm done.'

'It doesn't matter whose fault it was. You've said that your-self. The very fact that Amber could get in and disable our security system . . . Forgive me, but I'm playing devil's advocate here.'

Mark looked glum. 'You're doing rather too good a job of it.'

'Well, it could be argued that we were negligent to let that happen in the first place.'

Mark pushed away the plate of half-eaten pancakes. 'Damn Amber. If not for her, nobody would need to know that the lions were ever out. All the other keepers would gladly keep that secret. But as soon as the police arrest Amber, she'll spill the beans. I almost feel like opening the gates and letting her escape.'

'So do I,' admitted Jana. 'But I doubt Sash would want that, not after what Amber did to her.'

'You're wrong.' Jana turned in her chair to see Sash standing behind her. Sash continued. 'I could forgive Amber if it helped save the zoo. We were good friends, or I thought we were. I'd like to know what made her do all these terrible things, though.'

It puzzled them all. Everyone had liked Amber, and she'd seemed to have such a genuine love of animals. Her actions did not accord with the young woman they knew. What had possessed her to turn on the zoo?

'You knew Amber best, Sash,' said Mark. 'Was she a bit of a tech head?'

'Christ, no. She was the total opposite. Apparently, her father was very religious and didn't trust the modern world. They didn't even have a television growing up. I had to show her twice how to enter records into our database, and she couldn't format programs or use spreadsheets if her life depended on it. I've never met somebody under thirty who was such a technophobe.'

'So, Amber would have needed help hacking into the security system.'

'Definitely,' said Sash. 'Maybe someone from that animal rights group. They're still who you think is behind all this, right?'

Mark shrugged. 'I don't know. But I do know that I'd give an arm and a leg to have a heart-to-heart with Amber before the police do.'

Jana called the team meeting for three o'clock. Hazel was to be included. Mark felt so grateful to her for rescuing Karly that he'd promised she could be included in all decisions about the zoo from now on.

To Karly's utter delight, Luca had arrived with Womble and Care Bear. He was shocked to see the cut on his girlfriend's head and amused to hear her referred to as Tash. Everyone knew Sash's true identity by now, but the keepers mostly still called her Tash. 'I don't mind,' she said. 'I've never had a nickname before.'

'Right,' said Jana, addressing the small gathering on the verandah. 'I'm still hopeful that our fundraiser can go ahead tomorrow as planned. So after this meeting we'll have to work like the clappers, doing double the preparation in less than half the time we should have had.'

'You can count on us,' called Bruce, and there was a cheer from the others.

'But before then, we have to decide what to do about

Amber. She's still somewhere here at the zoo, and as Sash can personally testify, she's dangerous. Once we notify the police, they'll descend on this place in force, searching the grounds, taking statements – making it not only difficult to get our work done, but jeopardising the Open Day itself. And once they find her and interview her, they'll hold a press conference. The mass animal escape will become public knowledge. So, do we hold off a while longer, in order to get cracking on the final preparations for tomorrow? Or do I ring them now?'

'The police will ask a lot of questions if we wait,' said Johnno.

'But once they're here, won't this become a crime scene?' asked Lexie. 'And what if they don't find Amber today? The zoo will remain locked down and the fundraiser will be ruined.'

People's elation at recovering Nala was fast disappearing as the gravity of their situation hit home. A ring of trusting faces looked to Jana, as if she might have a magic wand that could fix things. The weight of their collective expectations left her tongue-tied. And as it became clear that she had no clever solution, their hopeful expressions dissolved into ones of despair.

'Everything we've done will be for nothing then,' said Maggie, gloomily. 'The zoo will close. Nala and King will be put down, along with the tigers and half of the monkeys. Rafiki's too old to rehome. Even Cheeta and her baby, Bubbles. They're both horribly inbred. They'll die too.'

'No, they won't,' said a voice coming from the back.

Everyone turned to see who it was. Jana stood on tiptoes to see over people's heads.

Amber Brown stepped forward.

CHAPTER 45

Amber's hair stuck out at all angles, framing her tear-stained face. Her eyes were hollow, like she'd been crying for hours. Her clothes were filthy, her shoulders slumped, and her arms were muddy and grazed. People moved aside to let her pass. As she reached Jana, she straightened her shoulders and stood tall. 'I know it's too late to apologise, but for what it's worth, I'm sorry.'

Mark and Luca moved to stand protectively between her and Jana.

'Amber!' gasped Jana. 'Was it truly you all along? The fridges breaking down? The drug tampering? Letting the animals loose today, and the water buffalo and macaques weeks ago?'

'I didn't cut the branch in the buffalo's paddock or hack Mark's computer. That was Tony's men. But I admit all the rest.'

'Tony?' asked Jana. 'Who's Tony?'

Amber ignored her question. 'Are the animals safely back?' Her voice sounded shaky and faint.

'Well, yes,' said Jana. 'Although why you should care beats me.'

Amber swallowed hard. 'I'll try to explain,' she said, louder now. 'Tony Alfonso paid me to sabotage the zoo so that he could buy Wildfell Park to build a new prestige housing estate.' A collective gasp came from those assembled. 'Big blocks and river frontages. He plans to drain the wetlands and develop a new tourist precinct as well.

'When I first moved out of home, I went to work for Tony as a junior office assistant. I discovered the online world – in particular, online gambling. I was obsessed. When my funds ran out, I used my mother's bank account and credit card, chasing my losses, certain that the next big win was just around the corner and I'd be able to pay it all back.' She briefly buried her face in her hands. You could have heard a pin drop. 'And now my teenage sister, Jessie, needs a medical procedure overseas and Mum has no money left because of me.'

'What sort of procedure can't be done here?' asked Mark, looking sceptical.

'Jessie's already had an operation to remove a malignant brain tumour. But it's grown onto the brain stem, and they can't get that part. She needs an expensive emergency procedure called proton therapy that's only offered in Germany or the US. There is a treatment centre set to open in Adelaide, but not soon enough to help my sister. You should see Jessie – she's so brave and good. She's forgiven me for gambling away Mum's money, even though it means that she might die.'

Marks's doubtful expression faded. It didn't sound like a fanciful story. Each word seemed wrenched from Amber's heart.

'Why didn't you tell us?' asked Jana. 'We might have been able to help.'

'Why would you have helped?' Amber sounded genuinely puzzled. 'Anyway, none of you have any money to spare either. You've put all you own into the zoo . . . and despite everything, I don't want you to lose it. Jessie would be horrified to learn of what I've done. We used to come to Wildfell Park when we were kids. She said the first thing she wanted to do when she got well was to visit the zoo again. She's so proud of me for helping to save it.' The shame in Amber's eyes was painful to see. 'It will break my sister's heart to learn that I was actually doing the opposite.'

Jana looked up at Mark, and then around at the small crowd of faces. To a person, she saw only understanding and compassion for the young woman. She tried to put herself in Amber's shoes – tried to imagine Sash facing death because of Jana's own selfishness and stupidity. Wouldn't she do almost anything to put it right? Maybe, but Amber had risked everybody else's life in the process, including the animals. Jana briefly shut her eyes, trying to shake off the theoretical moral dilemma she'd put herself in. What was done was done. There was no rescuing Amber from her own folly, however sympathetic Jana might be.

'I'll turn myself in,' said Amber. 'But I won't say that I released the animals. It will jeopardise the zoo's licensing bid to hear that there were lions on the loose.' She gazed around, bravely meeting people's eyes. 'Tony Alfonso didn't know the specifics of my plan. So that means the only ones who know what actually happened here today are standing in front of me, right?' A few nods. 'Good. Then nobody else ever has to know.'

Sash stepped forward, frowning and pointing to the gash on her head. 'You did this to me. We were supposed to be friends, and you did this to me.' Amber looked down; her bravery had apparently fled. Sash continued, 'And that bloody great needle you jabbed me with. How did you know it wouldn't kill me? What were you thinking?'

'The truth is, I wasn't thinking. I was in such a panic. But I did use one of the syringes pre-loaded for the monkeys,' said Amber, softly. 'I knew the dose was too small to hurt you.'

'Well, I suppose that's something,' sniffed Sash.

'And I am truly sorry.' Amber gazed around at the people gathered before her. 'You've been so kind to me, and I betrayed you all.'

There were sympathetic murmurs. Amber's humble and heartfelt apology seemed to have gone a long way to appeasing the keepers.

Mark held up his hand. 'I have a proposition for you all.'

Jana shot him a searching look and leaned in close. 'What are you up to?'

'You're about to find out,' he whispered, then raised his voice to address the group. 'We all agree that Amber has behaved in a treacherous fashion, at times putting our lives and the lives of the animals in danger.' Mutterings of assent could be heard. 'Can we also agree that her sister's plight, though in no way an excuse, is a credible explanation of what motivated Amber to behave in such a shameful way?'

Maggie and Lexie turned to each other and exchanged a few words before nodding agreement. Bruce and Johnno stood stone-faced, their expressions hard to read.

'But after some soul-searching, Amber has decided to give

the zoo a second chance.' Mark wet his lips. 'I propose we do the same for her.'

This was met by an expectant silence. Jana was as curious as anybody else about what Mark would say next.

'Amber's correct when she says that those of us gathered here are the only people who know that the lions and other wild animals were roaming loose for hours earlier today. It will certainly be to our advantage if she keeps that quiet, and I thank her for that offer.' He rubbed his chin thoughtfully and shifted his feet before continuing. 'But it will also be to our advantage if Amber doesn't turn herself in at all. No police investigation means no scandal. It gives the zoo its best chance of winning a new operating licence. And Amber's mother won't suffer the double trauma of having one daughter critically ill, and the other facing criminal charges.'

Amber looked as shocked as everybody else.

'But what about Alfonso?' asked Johnno. 'He's the real culprit here. Are we just going to let him off scot-free?'

Amber put up a tentative hand, like a frightened schoolkid. 'I have evidence against Tony. Emails, texts and bank records to show that he paid me to bring down the zoo.'

'But those will also incriminate you,' said Mark, 'and we're trying to keep you out of jail here. Do you have anything else on him?'

Amber nodded. 'He was so sure of success that he bribed local councillors to ensure they'd approve his plans to drain the wetlands and make room for a new causeway.'

This news caused quite a stir and Mark called for silence. 'How did you come by this information?'

'I broke down at work one day and Tony found me crying

at my desk.' Amber's voice quivered alarmingly, and Jana wondered if she'd be able to go on. 'He asked me what was wrong, so I told him about Jessie. Tony said he could help me if I helped him clinch the deal to acquire Wildfell Park. But I thought I should have some insurance in case he reneged on the agreement.' She hesitated. 'I've kept copies of email exchanges and money transfers between him and the corrupt councillors.'

'Clever girl,' said Mark.

'I can strip out any metadata connecting that third-party information to Amber,' said Sash. 'And then I'll go fishing. Tony and his crooks aren't the only ones expert at hacking into other people's computer systems. If there's more proof of skulduggery there, I'll find it. After that we can submit the evidence to police anonymously, which will spark a corruption investigation of their own.'

Hope flared in Amber's eyes. Well, that might be a bit of an exaggeration, but she did look less like a condemned prisoner on her way to execution.

'Sounds like a plan,' said Mark. 'Does that satisfy your concerns, Johnno? And what about the rest of you? Any more worries or questions?'

Nobody said a word.

'Then this is my proposition.' Mark cleared his throat. 'I propose that we take a vow of secrecy about today's unfortunate series of events, and the part that Amber played in them. All in favour, say "aye".'

The response was an overwhelming and unanimous yes. Amber crumpled into sobs and Sash put a supportive arm around her.

Next Hazel pushed to the front of the small group and stood beside Mark. She took hold of his hand, held it aloft and called for three cheers. Karly ran over and wrapped her arms around her father. Jana joined in the shouting and applause, her heart bursting with love for the man.

'Okay,' said Mark, his face suffused with pleasure and pride. 'Let's get this show back on the road. We have a zoo to save.'

CHAPTER 46

The next day dawned bright and clear – a perfect mid-spring day. Sunshine warmed Jana's face as she rushed about the grounds, carrying out a last-minute check of their preparations. Karly and Mark had adorned the front gate with balloons and a banner announcing the Wildfell Park Open Day. Jana stopped to admire their efforts, shuddering to think how close they'd come to cancelling.

The grounds were alive with birdsong: carolling magpies, laughing kookaburras and fluting butcherbirds. The rich liquid notes of a shrike-thrush sounded from a nearby treetop. Bees buzzed among the crimson bottlebrush and butterflies danced in the air. It seemed that all of nature was celebrating the day.

Jana continued her tour. The petting zoo was ready, enclosed by bales of straw, and requiring a gold coin donation for entry. Cute lambs, rabbits and guinea pigs played or slept on the grass within. The snake-handling tent looked enticingly dangerous, with a giant boa constrictor painted on the side, and sleepy Sebastian wound around a branch in a terrarium at the entrance. Chairs were set up for Hazel's hawk-flying demonstration that would happen after lunch.

Amber was washing the last dingo outside the educational centre. Clancy kept trying to climb out of the tub, and Amber seemed to be wetter than he was. Inside the centre, volunteers were setting up an interactive presentation on animal welfare and wildlife conservation.

After spending most of yesterday catching the escaped animals, some of their original plans had fallen by the wayside. They hadn't had time to set up the kids' mystery trail, which was just as well, because they hadn't had time to buy the prizes. And the face-painting table wouldn't be happening either. But they'd pulled together most of the main attractions, and who could be disappointed on such a sparkling day?

Food vans were arriving in the café precinct. One of the vendors gave Jana a cheerful wave and said, 'Nice day for it.'

Jana nodded and smiled, all the while imagining a snarling lion padding around the corner to confront the man. He wouldn't have been so cheerful then. 'Stop torturing yourself,' she said aloud, trying to calm her racing heart. How grateful she was that no outsiders knew of the chaos that had reigned at the zoo yesterday. The Wildfell Park team had always been close, but their vow of secrecy had formed them into a tight-knit family.

From the vantage point of the café, Jana noticed a late-model Range Rover approaching the zoo. She checked the time. Not even nine o'clock. The gates wouldn't open to visitors until eleven. Yet after a few moments' delay, someone buzzed the SUV through.

Then it hit her. Harper and her new man were coming

today. Jana watched the vehicle travel up the drive towards the manor. She should stay away. There was plenty still to do, and Mark and Karly deserved some privacy. But her feet, with a mind of their own, were already hurrying towards the house.

Mark waited anxiously in the kitchen. 'Karly,' he called. 'Your mum's here.'

Karly knew that her mother was coming that morning, and even though Harper was a bit early, Mark had still expected his daughter to be waiting with him. But instead, she was nowhere to be seen. What a contrast to last time, when Karly'd had conniptions the moment her mum was a minute late. And then Harper hadn't shown up at all. The memory of Karly's disappointment still pained him.

'Knock, knock?' Harper Clark pushed in the door wearing the sunniest of smiles, a figure-hugging, lace-trimmed red dress and a dove-grey pillbox hat adorned with a feathery fascinator. She'd complemented the ensemble with a pair of sky-high stiletto heels that seemed to defy gravity. Where did Harper think she was going today? The Melbourne Cup?

A shortish, middle-aged man with a silver comb-over followed Harper into the kitchen.

'Mark, darling,' gushed Harper. 'How are you?' She gave him a peck on the cheek and gestured to her companion. 'This is Arthur Anderson, my fiancé. Arthur, meet Mark, Karly's father.'

At first glance Arthur appeared nondescript enough, but when he met Mark's gaze with clever grey eyes, there was something about his expression that commanded a quiet respect. Arthur extended his hand and Mark returned his firm handshake. He'd been ready to dislike the man, but how would that help the situation? Like it or not, Arthur was going to be a part of Karly's life. It was important to keep an open mind.

Harper looked around the kitchen. 'Where's my daughter? I thought she'd be excited to see us?'

'Excuse me a moment.' Mark texted Jana. *Harper's here. Do you know where Karly is?*

Just then Jana opened the back door and ushered a clearly hesitant Karly into the kitchen. Harper beamed, bent at the knee and reached out with open arms. 'My darling girl.' Karly glanced to her father for support before stepping forward to be wrapped in Harper's smothering embrace.

'Should I go?' Jana asked him in a low voice.

Mark gave her a tight smile. 'Would you stay . . . please?' Jana nodded and moved behind the table. Mark's jaw tightened as he watched Harper's show of affection. If she could have stopped making everything about herself for a second, she might have noticed the apprehension etched on her daughter's face. Instead of a melodramatic reunion, what Karly needed was some quiet reassurance.

Bandit bounded in, a wiggling ball of black and white joy, and jumped up on Harper. She recoiled. 'Ow! Get that smelly dog off. Its nails are scratching me.'

'Bandit doesn't smell,' said Karly, indignantly. 'I gave him a bath this morning. He's my very own puppy and he's only trying to be friendly.' Karly briefly hugged Bandit before Mark bundled the dog out the door.

'That's better,' said Harper, rubbing her legs. 'Now, let

me take a good look at you.' She grasped Karly's shoulders and turned her this way and that. Karly stood stiffly under her mother's critical gaze. She was wearing jeans instead of a dress, and her golden hair was pulled back in a tight pony-tail. It seemed that Harper was struggling to find something complimentary to say. Mark wanted to scoop up his daughter and whisk her away.

'That's an adorable shirt,' Harper managed at last.

'Thanks,' said Karly in a small voice. 'Jana bought it for me.'

'Jana?' Harper seemed to notice her for the first time, standing quietly in the corner of the kitchen.

Karly smiled adoringly at Jana. 'She's Dad's girlfriend. He loves her, and I love her too.'

This finally got Harper's attention and her eyes narrowed. Jana sputtered and started to protest, but Mark interrupted her. 'That's right. You've met her before, actually, a long time ago.'

Harper studied Jana for a few moments, but no recognition showed in her eyes. 'I'm sorry, but I'm afraid I don't remember you.'

Jana's eyes flashed with anger. 'Well, I remember you,' she said, coldly. 'We were at school together. But you didn't call me Jana back then. You called me Stinky Malinski.'

'Mum,' said Karly, sounding horrified. 'You didn't?'

Harper seemed as shocked as Karly. Her eyes narrowed further. 'You're *that* Jana?'

An uncomfortable silence reigned in the room. Arthur was standing back, silently observing.

Harper managed a high, nervous laugh, but her eyes betrayed annoyance – and something else. Guilt? Things were clearly not going according to her plan. 'Well, we were just kids back then, weren't we. Silly kids.' She flashed a dazzling smile, but nobody returned it. 'May I speak to you privately, Jana?' She turned to Karly. 'This is Arthur,' she said. 'He'll be your new father.'

'Stepfather,' added Arthur.

'Yes, of course. Stepfather. That's what I meant.' Harper ran her tongue over ruby-red lips. 'Perhaps Karly and Arthur can get to know each other while Jana and I have a little talk – a chat between old school friends.'

Mark could see that Jana was about to arc up, so he put a steadying hand on her arm.

Harper tipped her chin towards the sitting room next door. 'Would you mind?'

'Okay,' agreed Jana, 'but I want Mark to come.'

'I was hoping . . .'

Mark held up his hand. 'Jana doesn't go without me.'

Harper opened her mouth to argue, but there was no doubting the conviction in his tone.

'We'll be all right out here for a bit,' said Arthur. 'Karly and I can have our own private chat.' He turned to the girl. 'You can introduce me to that fine pup of yours.' He opened the door to let a delighted Bandit back into the kitchen. 'And you can tell me how you feel about maybe coming to live with your mother and me.'

The genuine warmth of Arthur's smile seemed to put Karly at ease. 'It's okay, Dad. You go ahead. I'd like to talk to Arthur.'

That surprised Mark. Karly was rarely so forthcoming with strangers. But Jana needed him, and he'd make sure that

Harper kept the reunion short. He gave Karly a swift kiss. 'See you in a few minutes, sweetheart.'

Harper sat on the old armchair facing Jana and Mark, who sat side by side on the sitting-room couch. She was clearly finding this – whatever *this* was – difficult.

Harper coughed softly to clear her throat. 'Jana. Back at school I may not have been as kind to you as I should have been. It's no excuse, I suppose, but it was a difficult time for me. I guess you know the story?' She glared accusingly at Mark. 'He got me pregnant, and I had to leave Scarborough and all my friends. It's always the girl who suffers, isn't it?' Silence. 'You were still there at Scarborough, Jana, where I desperately wanted to be. Everyone knew you'd be dux of the school. My parents would have done anything for me to be such a brain. And you were there with Mark too – I knew he liked you, even though he never said.' Harper was rushing her words, as if trying to get them out before she changed her mind. 'I was jealous, I suppose. That's why I catfished you.'

'Catfished?' Jana looked nonplussed.

'I mean when I pretended to be Mark online, trying to put you off him and make you feel foolish. It was cruel and stupid, and I want you both to know that I'm sorry.' She glanced hopefully from Jana to Mark. 'Let's put all that childish high school stuff behind us, shall we? I don't want old resentments to stand in the way of being reunited with my daughter.'

Harper waited for a reaction but was rewarded only with blank stares. 'Well, that's it then. I feel better now we've cleared the air.' Harper stood up and walked back to the kitchen.

Mark followed, utterly outraged by her confession. He glanced behind him. Jana was still sitting on the couch, looking shell-shocked.

When they entered the kitchen, Hazel was making a cup of tea. Karly and Arthur were nowhere to be seen.

'Karly's taken Arthur to see the lions,' she explained. 'What a nice man – quite the charmer. Karly seems to like him as well. The two of them were talking a mile a minute.' Hazel turned her attention to Harper and frowned. 'I suppose you're Karly's mother.' She almost spat out the words. 'It's a disgrace the way you've treated that child.'

Harper, clearly taken aback by this attack from a complete stranger, looked to Mark for support. Under other circumstances he'd have been tempted to reproach Hazel for her bad manners. But today he agreed with her one hundred per cent.

Hazel poured herself a mug of tea and cast a brief, scornful glance in Harper's direction. 'If you need me, I'll be down at the mews getting Captain and Spirit ready for their flights.' And with that she hurried out the back door.

'Well,' said Harper, watching her go. 'What a rude old woman!'

Mark just stared, too angry for words.

Harper broke the awkward silence. 'It sounds like Karly and Arthur have hit it off. I thought they would. Arthur loves children.'

Still Mark didn't speak. He was wondering if he should go back to Jana or go after Karly.

'I'm dying for a coffee.' Harper glanced at the espresso machine.

'Make it yourself,' said Mark and he marched back to the sitting room.

CHAPTER 47

Jana was sitting exactly where he'd left her. She barely noticed him arrive. She was too busy re-evaluating the past. For all these years she'd been consumed with resentment, blaming Mark for the malicious trick that had broken her trust, broken her heart, and wreaked havoc on her life. It had humiliated her, derailed her career and changed her family's life forever. All indirectly maybe, but if it hadn't been for that damned fake online romance, Jana would never have run away from Scarborough on that fateful night.

And now she knew that Harper had been behind it all along. Harper had manipulated her emotions, toyed with her vulnerabilities and shattered her dreams. It was a painful revelation, and Jana was overcome by a sense of remorse for the years she'd spent blaming the wrong person.

Mark sat beside her and gently took her hand. 'It all makes sense. This explains why your private messages were never shared on the student social media accounts. As an ex-student, Harper wouldn't have had access.'

Regret shone in Mark's eyes. 'You could have safely stayed

and sat your exams. Your parents wouldn't have been hurt and you'd have qualified as a vet years earlier.'

Jana didn't know how to respond. The revelation that it was Harper who'd orchestrated the online romance had her reeling with shock and competing feelings. Relief to know that Mark was truly innocent. Remorse for having misjudged him so severely. Fury towards Harper. As these emotions swirled within her, Jana began to feel the weight of the bitterness she'd been carrying lift from her shoulders.

The decision to put it behind her and move forward was not immediate, but as she processed her feelings, a sense of clarity emerged. Clinging to anger would leave her trapped in the past. Jana made a conscious decision to let it go. It gave her a newfound sense of freedom and a desire to make amends with Mark, to explore what could be between them without the shadow of a decade-old lie.

'It's good to finally know the truth,' murmured Jana.

Mark's face darkened with anger. 'Harper has a lot to answer for.'

'She does,' said Jana, her voice growing stronger. 'But it's time to move on. I don't ever want Karly to find out what a cow her mother was back then.'

'And still is, I'll wager.'

'I don't know.' Jana managed a smile. 'People can change.'

Mark moved in closer, gazing at her with laser intensity.

'What?' Jana could see the wheels in his head turning.

'So . . . the whole friends-with-benefits business. That was to make sure I didn't hurt you again, right?'

'Of course.'

Mark shook his head in puzzlement. 'If you thought

I was such a low-life, why did you start anything with me at all?'

Jana's expression grew tender. 'Because you were driving me mad. I could barely think about anything or anyone else.' She leaned over and kissed him softly on the lips. 'I would have withered away if you hadn't taken me to bed.'

She'd been worried that Mark might blame her for not opening up to him sooner, but his broad grin said it all. 'You couldn't live without me, right?'

Jana was ready to protest his presumption, but why? What he'd said was true. She smiled and touched his face. 'I don't think I could ever imagine my life without you. The truth is . . . I'm in love.'

Mark let out a loud whoop and picked Jana up, laughing and twirling her around the room. Then he laid her on the couch and kissed her like there was no tomorrow.

Neither of them noticed Harper push in the door until she said, 'Get a room.'

Jana and Mark hurriedly sat up, smoothing down their hair and clothes. Jana checked the wall clock. 'I'd better be off. The gates open in half an hour.' She looked Harper square in the eyes. Jana studied her appearance with mild surprise. Harper looked, well . . . ordinary. Oh, she was pretty enough, with her flash clothes and flawless hair and make-up. But Harper wasn't the drop-dead gorgeous beauty that Jana remembered from school, and she no longer felt like an ugly duckling by comparison. 'But first I have something to say to you.' Her voice was calm, but the gravity of her words was unmistakable. 'Harper, I accept your apology, but I need you to understand the depth of the hurt you caused.' Jana's expression held a mix of sadness and resolve. 'What you did changed the course of my life in ways you can't imagine. But I'm choosing to move past this, not for you, but for Karly, for Mark and for myself.'

Jana glanced at Mark whose face flushed with pride. He took her hand in his.

'Karly means a lot to me,' continued Jana. 'I know she loves you, Harper, so I'll try to put this behind us. But please know, the pain you inflicted was real and deep. I hope you've truly learned from this.'

Jana's voice was strong and unwavering, yet devoid of bitterness, and for once Harper was rendered speechless.

Mark held Jana's hand until she slipped away. He looked at Harper in her ridiculous clothes with a sense of revulsion. How he longed to confront this woman about all the harm she'd caused. But Jana was right. Karly must never learn of the history between the three of them.

'You and her?' Harper looked after Jana and shook her head. 'Weird.'

'Not so weird,' Mark said through gritted teeth. 'You were correct when you said that I liked Jana back at school. I did. And now we're in love. I plan to marry her.'

'Marry Jana?' Harper burst out laughing. 'She's not really your type, is she? I heard you went more for blonde fashion models who owned racehorses and villas in Tuscany.'

Mark struggled to keep his temper. How on earth could his sweet, kind Karly have such a shallow, self-absorbed mother? He grabbed Harper's arm, marched her back to the kitchen and sat her down at the table. 'Now, tell me the real reason you suddenly want Karly. And don't give me that doting mother crap. You don't have a maternal bone in your body.'

Bandit burst in the door. 'Get down,' cried Harper as the pup put a paw in her lap. 'Mark, get it away. I'm allergic to dogs.'

'Allergic?' asked Karly, as she and Arthur came into the kitchen. 'But Bandit's mine. He goes where I go.'

'Well, I can't possibly have a puppy around, darling. When you come to live with us, you'll have to leave it here. I'm sure Daddy won't—'

'Karly won't be coming to live with us,' announced Arthur. 'She's staying with her father.'

Harper stared at him in astonishment. 'But I thought—'

'Mark,' said Arthur. 'Can I have a word?' He pointed to the sitting room. Mark couldn't get in there quickly enough. If Arthur had changed his mind about wanting custody, Mark was all ears.

Harper stood to follow them. A frowning Arthur turned and gestured for her to sit down again. 'Spend some time with your daughter, sweetheart. I want to talk to Mark man to man.'

Arthur settled himself on the couch, while Mark sat in an armchair opposite. 'I owe you an apology,' Arthur said. 'Harper told me that you took Karly under sufferance when her parents became ill, and the child was unhappy with the arrangement. She said it was a temporary measure, just until she could rearrange her work life to accommodate looking after her daughter full-time.'

Mark bit his tongue, determined to hear Arthur out.

'Harper also told me that you were an unsuitable parent – a workaholic and a womaniser.' Arthur took off his glasses and cleaned them with a tissue from the side table. 'Yet I can see that you're completely devoted to the success of this zoo. If that makes you a workaholic, then more power to you.'

Mark breathed a sigh of relief. It seemed that Arthur could see through Harper's spin.

'As for you being a womaniser?' Arthur raised his bushy eyebrows. 'I don't see it. Karly tells me that you're head over heels in love with Jana, the lovely zoo director. I can't say that I blame you. She's an impressive woman, and Karly's a big fan.'

Mark stayed quiet. So far he was winning.

'When I proposed to Harper, I can't deny that I wanted more children. I have two sons from an earlier marriage – wonderful boys, but they're grown and don't need me.' Arthur smiled, but there was a genuine sadness behind his eyes. 'I'd always wanted a little girl. And when Harper agreed to reverse her tubal ligation . . . but the procedure didn't succeed. I thought perhaps Karly could be the daughter that I'd never had.' Arthur stood up, went to the antique bar standing in the corner, and held a bottle of whisky aloft. 'May I?'

At Mark's nod, he poured them both a glass and sank back into his chair. 'No doubt you think me foolish, but I do love Harper. She's sassy, pretty as a picture and bursting with life. Harper makes me feel young again.' He swirled the whisky around in his glass. 'That's a rare gift for a man of my age. And she cares for me too, in her own way. She's never really had anyone to love her before, not properly, not even her family. But I'm not blind to her faults, Mark. Harper sees the world in terms of her own needs. She wanted to please me by giving me a child, so she offered up Karly as a sort of sacrificial lamb.

'You have a remarkable daughter, Mark. Not only did she take me on a fascinating and enlightening tour of this zoo of yours, but she made it clear that she's determined to stay here.' Arthur downed his drink in one gulp, and then stood to pour himself another. 'I'd still like to know Karly better, but in the context of holiday visits, and then only if she agrees. I hope that can happen. It would be good for Harper to spend time with her daughter. She does want to, Mark, even if she doesn't always show it.'

'I appreciate that,' said Mark, trying to keep his cool but feeling like he'd won the lottery.

'Good. Then we understand each other.' Arthur held his glass aloft and Mark did the same. 'Cheers.' They each took a large swig. 'You really should hire your daughter as a PR consultant. Karly made a formidable case for supporting Wildfell Park and the amazing conservation work that you plan to do here. I intend to make a substantial donation.' He drained his glass and smacked his lips together. 'You're a lucky man, Mark. With a worthy cause to champion, and Karly and Jana by your side? I'd give a lot to find that sort of satisfaction in my life.'

Harper opened the door, pouting. 'Truly, Arthur. I won't be ignored for one more minute.' She marched into the room. 'What on earth are you two talking about?'

Arthur slapped his thigh and gave a great belly laugh. 'You, of course, my dear.'

Harper frowned. 'I don't understand. Why won't Karly be coming to live with us? It just won't do, Arthur. My mother will be most upset, and I've already told all my friends.'

Mark gasped at her response. *And what about you?* he thought. *Will you be upset too?* He studied Harper's perfectly made-up face, looking for a crack in her mask. And then he saw it – the pain she was trying to bury with her offhand remarks. The disappointment hidden behind her eyes. He'd always known she wasn't the ice queen she pretended to be. Harper was Karly's mother, and despite everything she'd done, Mark would always care for her. Although they'd all be much happier if she'd allow herself to be vulnerable once in a while. It warmed him to know that Harper was with a man who understood her.

'I promised Karly that we'd help out with a demonstration in the Education Centre,' said Arthur. 'And as to why Karly won't be coming to live with us? I'll explain on the way.' He took Harper's arm and steered her towards the door. 'Now, my dear, how do you feel about snakes?'

CHAPTER 48

The Open Day was going swimmingly. It seemed that every man and his dog was there. A contingent of students from Scarborough College had even arrived, along with three sharp-eyed teachers riding shotgun. Crowd numbers were way up on what Jana had expected.

She and Sash finished their guided tour of the vet clinic with a visit to Womble in the nursery. The little wombat was asleep in his fleece-lined pouch but woke up long enough to drink a bottle of milk and allow the visitors to pat him. The joey was fat, healthy and gaining weight daily. Luca had done a wonderful job taking care of him while Sash was away. Jana remembered with a pang that her sister's work at Wildfell Park was done, and she'd soon be going home to Odessa. She'd miss her terribly.

Jana busied herself rinsing Womble's bottle at the sink while Sash fielded some final questions from the tour group. When she turned around, Annie West was standing there with a broad smile on her face. Amid all the drama, Jana had forgotten that she'd agreed to come.

'I'm impressed,' said Annie. 'I must admit that I was

sceptical about your ambitious conservation plans at first. Many people talk the talk, but few have the conviction to follow through. Yet after taking a thorough look around, your vision is crystal clear. I particularly like the education centre and the way the wombat and devil enclosures are designed. They're patterned on Binburra, I imagine?'

Jana nodded.

'Well, it's clear that Wildfell Park will be much more than an old-fashioned zoo meant to entertain the masses.'

Jana beamed with pleasure. 'Let me introduce my sister, Sash. She and her partner run our sister property, Odessa. Like I mentioned when we met, it will be used as a soft release site for all kinds of natives – including devils – once we get the go-ahead for a mainland release.'

Annie's eager smile matched her own. 'I've done my due diligence. Dr Penny Abbott confirmed that you're a prime candidate for joining the Aussie Ark project – as long as Wildfell Park regains its operating licence. So with that in mind, I'd like to present you with something on behalf of the Animal Defenders.'

A photographer appeared as if from nowhere. 'I'm with the *Rivertown Courier*,' he said. 'We'd like to get a few shots of this, please.'

Jana shot Annie a puzzled look. 'Mark asked the *Courier* to send someone along today, but the editor said he'd only be interested once the zoo officially opens. He said it would depress his readers to do a story on Wildfell Park only to have the zoo fold. How did you manage it?'

Annie shrugged. 'It helps when your family owns the newspaper.'

Jana stared at her, mouth agape.

'I might look like a feral without two cents to rub together, but my uncle is Randall Menzies.'

'*The* Randall Menzies?'

'One and the same. He's the major shareholder in SouthWest News, which in turn owns a portfolio of regional media, including print, radio, television and online news outlets. That's how I got my regular radio spot on Riverland FM. Uncle Randall and I are close, which is odd, because he's a mad capitalist and I'm what he calls a raging hippy. But somehow, we get on. I'm even changing his mind on some issues. From next month the *Courier* will be running a monthly environmental feature. How farmers can reduce carbon emissions, for example, or protect local waterways.'

Jana continued to stand open-mouthed. Today the surprises just kept coming.

'And then there's this, also compliments of my uncle. Turns out he likes zoos.' Annie ducked outside the clinic and returned with a metre-long novelty cheque – for two hundred and fifty thousand dollars. The photographer snapped away, Annie smiled for the camera and Jana stood by like a stunned mullet.

It was almost five o'clock when Jana finally caught up with Mark. He was with Lexie at the front gate selling raffle tickets to those who were arriving for the country ball and barbecue. Only a few people were leaving; it seemed that most were staying on for the evening's festivities.

Jana couldn't wait to give Mark the news. 'Take a gander

at this,' she said, trying to remain poker-faced as he looked at the photo on her phone.

'Two hundred and fifty grand?' he said, incredulously. 'From Annie West?'

'It turns out her family is loaded, and she's well and truly on our side now.'

Jana knew what the faraway look in Mark's eye meant. He was doing sums in his head.

'What do you think? Will we make our target?'

'We're getting damned close, baby.' He handed the raffle tickets to Lexie and drew Jana in for a passionate kiss. She felt a jolt of pleasure, and not just because of the kiss or Mark's optimistic prediction. He'd never called her 'baby' before. It was a small thing, but the term of endearment seemed to suggest that their romance had moved to another level.

'Are you hungry?' he asked when he let her go.

'Hungry for what?' she whispered, feeling breathless.

He winked at her. 'Dinner – for now. We've been on the go since first light. I don't know about you, but I'm bloody starving. Let's go check out those food vans and get coffees.'

At the thought of food, her belly rumbled loudly enough for him to hear.

'That settles it.' He took hold of her hand in a confident, proprietorial way that made her proud. 'Let's get a feed.'

On their way to the café, Jana heard something that she'd hoped to never hear again. Something that she'd recognise anywhere – the shrill, sarcastic voices of mean girls who'd found themselves a victim. She tugged Mark in the direction of the sound. Half-a-dozen girls were surrounding Karly and Bandit near the row of portaloos.

'That your dog?' asked one girl.

Karly nodded, looking wary.

'It's cute, which means you're lying. Nobody as ugly as you could own a cute dog like that.'

Bandit whined and squeezed between Karly's legs. She set her chin and tried to manoeuvre around the group, but they blocked her way.

'In fact, you're so ugly, I think you must be a monkey dressed up,' sneered the tall blonde girl, who seemed to be the ringleader.

'Shut up, Tegan.' Karly tried in vain to sidestep her tormentor.

'Someone should catch you and put you back in your cage.' They all laughed, and Karly looked dangerously close to tears.

Mark's jaw clenched. 'I'm putting a stop to this,' he whispered. 'Where are their bloody teachers? After I finish with them, those kids will be in detention for the rest of their lives.'

'No.' Jana put a hand on his arm. 'If you rescue her, it will only make it worse for her next time. I've got a better idea. You stay back.'

Jana approached the group. 'Ah, there you are, Karly. I've been looking all over.'

'Who are you?' asked Tegan, clearly annoyed to have her fun interrupted.

Jana gave the girl a sunny smile. 'I'm the director of this zoo, and I want to ask Karly's advice about something. It's Nala – she seems a bit down. You're the expert on that particular lioness. What might cheer her up, do you think?'

Karly's expression grew thoughtful. 'There are some tubs of yoghurt in the fridge. She loves them.' The girl's guileless answer showed she was completely unaware of what Jana was up to. Which was exactly the way that Jana wanted it.

'Okay, I'll try that.' Jana checked her phone. 'It's time to feed the other lions. Can you help me, Karly? I've got a million things on today.'

'Wow! You help feed the lions?' enthused one of the girls.

'I help look after all the animals,' said Karly, not big-noting herself, but simply stating a fact. 'The dingoes, the sun bear, the tigers . . .'

'Tigers?' asked another girl. 'Isn't it scary?'

Karly shook her head. 'Not to me.'

Jana smiled. 'Would your friends like to come and watch us feed the lions?'

'Yes, please,' came an excited chorus of voices as hands shot up. All except Tegan's, that was. Her nose was firmly out of joint. Bandit led the way as the group of girls headed for the big-cat house. Tegan trailed after them, looking deflated, while Karly fielded a string of eager questions.

'What do you feed the bear?'

'Do you get to play with the dingo pups?'

'Can you hear the lions roar at night?'

'Do the animals ever bite you?'

'Can you cuddle the baby wombats?'

Karly answered all the questions expertly and honestly, clearly happy at the changed dynamic. She seemed even happier when her friend Lisa found her and joined the group.

Mark caught up with them. 'I see what you did there.'

Jana let the girls go on ahead. 'Karly must learn to play to her strengths if she's going to deal with those bullies.'

'Agreed, but thankfully she's not going to have to for much longer. I'm withdrawing her from Scarborough College. Hazel was right all along. When the school term resumes, Karly will be attending Rivertown High.'

'Where Lisa goes?' Jana clutched his arm. 'Why, that's marvellous news! Have you told her?'

'Not yet. But first things first. I've called Bruce to supervise the lion feeding. Don't worry, I've clued him in so he knows to talk Karly up in front of those girls. But I'll be supervising a different feeding – yours and mine.'

Jana laughed and rubbed her stomach.

'Come on,' said Mark. 'I'll shout you a pie.'

As evening fell, the country ball got underway. The soft glow of sunset cast a magical aura over Wildfell Park. Jana had changed into a flowing sundress with comfortable sandals, and Karly wore a knee-length blue dress that Hazel had bought for her. It had a wide, white belt and the bottom of the skirt was decorated with silky ruffles. Karly loved it and couldn't stop twirling.

Tall candles adorned trestle tables, and fairy lights illuminated the pathways, casting a warm glow on the festivities. As dusk settled, the lively chatter of the crowd mingled with the sounds of a country bluegrass band that had taken the stage. Their music resounded through the park, prompting people to tap their feet and sway to the rhythm.

The raffle was a highlight of the evening, with a variety of prizes donated by local businesses and individuals. The anticipation grew as Mark called out the numbers, causing cheers and applause to erupt whenever a lucky winner claimed their prize.

As the night progressed, the tantalising aroma of barbecued delights filled the warm air. Grilled tofu and vegetables, corn on the cob, sizzling sausages and chicken skewers satisfied the hunger of guests. Plates were piled high and conversations flowed as friends, families and strangers connected over the shared enjoyment of good food and the ambience of the evening.

The band played on, and people got up to dance: couples, singles, children – nearly everyone joined in. Amber and Maggie did a country two-step. Mark even asked Hazel for a turn around the floor. When Harper refused to dance, citing a dislike of country music, Arthur took Annie for a spin instead. The pair began a bootscooting line that soon attracted dozens of others. Karly and Lisa bounced around together, occasionally falling over their own feet with laughter, while Sash and Luca slow-danced like there was nobody else in the world.

Mark and Jana moved in sync with the music, hearts beating in harmony, their connection electric. It was a night of pure joy for them both, daring to imagine a shared future – a future filled with love, adventure and endless possibilities. Marvelling at how far they'd come.

As the night drew to a close, Jana stood by the zoo's front gate with Mark and Hazel, shaking people's hands as they left and thanking them for their support. Karly and Lisa ran over.

'Go on,' said Lisa, nudging her friend in the ribs. 'Tell them.'

'Tell us what?' asked Mark.

'You two don't have to sleep in separate rooms just because I'm here,' Karly blurted out. 'I'm not a baby. I know about sex.'

'Do you just?' said Mark as the pair burst out giggling and ran off. 'Cheeky little devil.' He trailed his finger over Jana's bare shoulder. 'But I believe she has a point . . .'

CHAPTER 49

Two years later

The first rays of summer sunshine breached the horizon, painting the sky in glorious hues of pink and orange. Although it was barely dawn, the air carried a palpable heat, already hinting at the scorching day ahead. As the sun continued its ascent, the Murray River revealed itself to the north. Its muddy waters meandered through the land, bringing life wherever it went.

Jana admired the scene with a sense of pride. The magic of the Murraylands was unfolding before her eyes. Undulating plains of golden grasses, spinifex and native scrubland stretched to the horizon, a testament to the hard work of so many people who'd devoted themselves to restoring Odessa's ancient landscape.

To her left gleamed a predator-proof fence that surrounded a forty-hectare parcel of land – the first stage of a barrier that would protect Odessa in its entirety. Standing 1.8 metres tall, the sagging top of the cyclone fence made it look unfinished, but it had been designed that way. If a fox or cat tried to climb it, they'd find no purchase once they reached the floppy wire.

A fifty-centimetre skirt beneath the soil prevented them from digging underneath.

Annie West stood close by, next to an old river red gum. The sunrise was bright enough to cast odd shadows beneath its twisted limbs. She took a deep sustaining breath. 'I adore the smell of river mint . . .' But her words were drowned out by screeches and raucous calls as a flock of corellas landed on the branches above.

'It's old enough to be a hollow bearer,' said Jana, patting the tree appreciatively. 'No wonder the birds love it.'

Nestled within a copse of grey box and stringybark lay a small compound of dens, enclosures and connecting runs. Six carefully chosen Tasmanian devils, imported from Binburra, had called this place home for the last four months, to familiarise them with their new surroundings before being released. They were part of the Aussie Ark program, which provided insurance populations of devils for mainland zoos – healthy devils free of the dreaded facial tumour disease.

However, these six animals were special in another way as well. They would be the first devils to run free in South Australia for over three thousand years. Well, not free exactly, but free enough to foster their wild behaviours, learn to fend for themselves and hopefully breed.

The *Courier*'s reporter and photographer came over. 'When's it all happening? We want to be on the spot to capture the big moment.'

'This is a soft release,' explained Jana. 'There is no big moment. We just open the gate.'

The reporter screwed up her nose. 'Ugh, what's that pong?'

Mark and Luca were dragging a day-old road-killed kangaroo into the compound. The devils, sporting new radio collars, sat up on their haunches and sniffed the air. The ripe carcass smelled irresistible to them.

'Are we ready?' asked Annie, who'd been given the honour of releasing the animals.

Jana gave the signal and Annie swung the gate wide. The devils took no notice, distracted by the kangaroo, so it was a bit of an anticlimax, but a cheer still went up from those gathered there.

The photographer took some snaps and the reporter asked Jana to say a few words.

She cleared her throat, then delivered her prepared statement. '"Having partnered with the Frieda Abraham Foundation and South Australia's Animal Defenders, we're proud to announce the Wildfell Park Devil Comeback Program. We're laying the groundwork for a broad, nationwide effort to rewild Australia and help our devils regain their original niche." That's it. If you need something more, ask Annie.'

Jana looked around for Mark. He was washing his hands at a tap by the shipping container that was being used for on-site storage. 'Come on.' She tugged his arm. 'I want to show you something.'

They jumped in the Jeep and Jana drove a few minutes north of the release site. 'Look familiar?' she asked as she parked beside a gnarled old paperbark.

Mark studied the tree for a few moments, then gazed about at the landscape pitted with wombat warrens. 'This is where I met you two years ago. Well, re-met you. I dragged you feet first from a wombat hole.'

'Yes!' she said, delighted that he remembered. 'You were my hero.'

He raised his brows. 'You didn't treat me like much of a hero. As I recall, you couldn't wait to get rid of me. And you never thanked me for my service.' He held up his hand as she opened her mouth to speak. 'No, don't apologise. You can thank me now.' He looked at her expectantly, making her giggle. 'I'm waiting.'

Jana jabbed him playfully in the ribs. 'There. Will that do?'

Mark laughed and pulled her close, kissing her so thoroughly it made her toes curl. 'Now let's get back,' he said. 'I have a wager with Luca about which devil will venture out the gate first. A bit like betting on a yabby race.'

'You idiots.' Jana smiled and tossed him the keys. 'Here, you drive.'

It was hard to believe how much had changed in the past two years. The size of her belly for one thing. Jana was due to give birth to their first child in a few short weeks. Sash and Luca would be godparents.

Her father had even been well enough to attend Jana and Mark's wedding last year – with Mum pushing him in his wheelchair, of course. But even though he wasn't verbal, Jana was sure that when she'd said 'I do', she'd seen him smile.

Wildfell Park had survived all the challenges fate had thrown at it. It had finally received charitable status and Frieda Abraham's bequest had been upheld by the Supreme Court. The perpetual trust gave them an operating budget well into the future.

Amber was now a senior keeper, and the zoo couldn't have wished for a more devoted champion. Her friends and family had scraped together the money needed for her sister's treatment, and so far the prognosis looked good, although Amber was still paying off her gambling debts. And the karma bus had caught up with Tony Alfonso, who was facing a slew of corruption charges.

Hazel seemed to get younger each year and was teaching falconry to the other keepers. Karly was thriving at Rivertown High, making friends and getting good grades. And Mark had quit his accountancy job to devote himself full-time to Wildfell Park, working hands-on in the workshop as often as he did in the office. Jana couldn't imagine a more perfect life.

Mark's second-hand Jeep stalled as he crunched the gears. He swore softly beneath his breath as he tried to coax it forward. Jana suddenly wondered if he was as happy as she was.

'Do you ever miss your sports car and jet ski and holidays in France?' she asked.

He shot her a reassuring smile. 'A very wise person once told me that the less money I had, the better off I'd be.'

'Hazel *is* very wise,' said Jana with a grin.

'Then she said, "All you need is love" and hummed some corny tune. And do you know what? She was absolutely right.'

ACKNOWLEDGEMENTS

As I reflect on the journey that led to the creation of *The Rivertown Vet*, my heart is filled with immense gratitude. This book, like every story I've told, has been a collaborative endeavour, enriched and shaped by the support and guidance of many.

First and foremost, I extend my deepest thanks to Ali Watts at Penguin Random House Australia. Ali, your passion for storytelling and your unwavering belief in this project have been the guiding lights in this journey. Your encouragement and wisdom have not only made this book better but have also made me a better writer.

To my insightful editor, Shané Oosthuizen, and the entire Penguin Random House publishing team – your keen eyes and sharp minds have polished this story, helping to bring out its true essence. Your dedication to excellence is evident on every page, and I am profoundly grateful for your contributions.

I am endlessly thankful to my agent, Clare Forster at Curtis Brown. Clare, your support and advocacy have been pillars of strength for me. Your belief in my work, even in moments of doubt, has been a source of comfort and motivation.

To my writing friends and my dear family – your patience, understanding and invaluable advice have been my constant companions through the highs and lows of this creative process.

A special note of gratitude goes to the Aussie Ark Project. Your incredible conservation efforts, dedicated to preserving Australia's unique wildlife and ecosystems, have been a deep source of inspiration for *The Rivertown Vet*. Your commitment to creating sanctuaries, restoring natural environments and educating the public about the importance of conservation has been truly enlightening. Organisations like yours remind us of the delicate balance we share with nature and the critical role we play in preserving it for future generations.

Last but certainly not least, to my loyal readers – your enthusiasm, feedback and unwavering support have made this writing journey not only possible but also immensely fulfilling. Each story I write is a conversation with you, and your engagement with and love for my work continue to be the greatest rewards of my career.